THE GREEK KEY

by the same author

DEADLOCK
THE JANUS MAN
COVER STORY
TERMINAL
THE LEADER AND THE DAMNED
DOUBLE JEOPARDY
THE STOCKHOLM SYNDICATE
AVALANCHE EXPRESS
THE STONE LEOPARD
YEAR OF THE GOLDEN APE
TARGET FIVE
THE PALERMO AMBUSH
THE HEIGHTS OF ZERVOS
TRAMP IN ARMOUR

THE GREEK KEY

KEY

Colin Forbes

GUILD PUBLISHING
LONDON · NEW YORK · SYDNEY · TORONTO

This edition published 1989 by
Guild Publishing

by arrangement with William Collins Sons & Co. Ltd

Copyright © Colin Forbes 1989

CN 8953

Printed and bound in West Germany
by Mohndruck, Gütersloh

AUTHOR'S NOTE

This novel is based on facts told to me about a strange and grim murder committed over forty years ago. *That murder remains unsolved to this day*.

It happened in Cairo in 1944 – inside a weird triangular-shaped building near the banks of the River Nile. Not only the building was weird: it housed a mix of army, naval and air force personnel, and secret units whose missions were unknown to the other inhabitants.

The story moves to the present day and all the facts are provided for the reader to identify who was responsible – but I emphasize that the characters portrayed are creatures of the author's imagination and bear no relationship to any living person. Also, the island of Siros – as described – does not exist.

FOR JANE

CONTENTS

Prologue 11

Part One: The Moor of Death 29

Part Two: Devil's Valley 179

Part Three: The Greek Key 435

Epilogue 574

Prologue

Cairo, February 1944. Staff-Sergeant Higgins – 'Higgy' to his friends – had no warning this would be the last time he would ascend in the creaking lift climbing slowly to the fourth floor of the Antikhana Building.

At ten in the evening it was silent as a tomb within the walls of the three-sided building. The only sound was the ghostly creak of the old lift as it crawled upwards past deserted landings. Through the iron grille of the cage he could see the stone staircase which rose round the central lift shaft. It felt as though no one else was in the place – no one except the Sudanese receptionist behind his desk on the ground floor.

Not surprising if he was the first to get back, thought Higgy. The few military men who slept there occupied small bedrooms on the rooftop. And they rarely arrived back from drinking and eating in Cairo before eleven. Personally, he liked an early night . . .

He frowned as he slid the door of the cage shut when it had wobbled to a stop. They switched off the lights in the corridors running round the three sides of the building at seven. So where was the glow of light beyond the entrance to the corridor coming from?

He hesitated, listening. Normally he would head straight for one of the three spiral staircases at each corner of the building – the enclosed staircases which led to the rooftop. The light was gleaming from under the closed door at the end of the corridor. The Greek Unit's quarters.

He had no idea what Ionides, who had escaped from

11

German-occupied Greece, did. Something connected with propaganda, they said. He must have forgotten to turn off the light before leaving for his billet. Or he could just still be working.

Hitching up his khaki drill trousers, he walked quietly along the tiled passage. The first twinge of unease ruffled him when he thought he heard a noise from the room next to the last one. Also part of the Greek Unit's quarters, the two rooms were linked by an inner door. But no light glowed from under this second door. Who would be moving about in the dark?

He paused, grasped the handle, turned it slowly, pushed. The door wouldn't budge, was locked. He stiffened. He'd never known that door to be locked before when one of the Greek Unit was working.

Higgy walked a few paces further and stopped at the second door. Beyond, at the corridor's end, the black hole leading to the spiral staircase gaped. He took a grip on the handle of the door, turned it, entered. He froze.

At the last moment, it occurred to him it might be Ionides' colleague, Gavalas, who was working late. But it was Ionides all right. Except he wasn't all right.

Higgy had his share of battle-hardened courage. An ex-tank commander, he'd seen friends in the desert scorched to death in what they cynically called a 'brew-up'. Not the normal brew-up of tea – the fearsome sight of another tank, hit by a German shell, going up in flames. Locked inside their steel box, few escaped alive.

The office, with barred windows facing the native quarter across the street, looked as though a hurricane had struck it. Drawers were pulled out, contents scattered across the floor. Filing cabinets had been overturned. Crimson splashes smeared the white walls.

The black-haired young Ionides lay amid the carnage,

sprawled on the floor on top of a mess of papers. He was drenched with blood, his dark eyes stared sightless at the ceiling, his head had been almost severed from his neck, his face was slashed brutally, the weathered skin coated with more blood. Blood was everywhere – spattered across the desk where presumably he had been working. The splashes on the walls were more blood.

Higgy shivered. He closed the outer door. Six feet tall, well-built, twenty-eight years old, he stood motionless, gazing at the horror lying a few feet away. Then he remembered the noise he'd heard from the locked room. He stared at the communicating door. God! The maniac who had done this must be inside.

Panic gripped him. His first instinct was to haul open the outer door and run like hell for the roof up the spiral staircase. His throat felt parched. His hands trembled. The silence from the room beyond the communicating door was insidious, made him want to yell.

The silence went on: not a hint of a sound from behind that closed door. Higgy sucked in a deep breath. Had it been imagination, nerves tingling from the empty building? Had he, in fact, really heard anything? He glanced down and saw again the dreadful corpse which had recently been a living man. A black foot-long circular ruler of ebony lay on the floor. He picked it up, took a firmer hold of himself, walked towards the closed communicating door. Still no sound.

He was scared shitless. He was growing more convinced the next room was empty, but if the murderer was still there he wasn't going to let the bastard escape. Ionides was a nice chap, always liked a chat and a joke. Higgy held the ruler like a baton, reached for the door handle with his left hand.

If the killer was inside he was probably holding the knife used to inflict the terrible mutilations Ionides had suffered. The state of the office showed the Greek had fought for his life. No, Higgy thought, should the assassin still be here I'm damned if I'm letting the swine get away.

He opened the door a few inches. The room beyond was dark. He reached his left hand inside, found the light switch, turned it on. Light flooded the second office and he pushed the door wide open, flat against the wall. His right foot tangled with something. A screwed-up bundle, a whole mess of it, and all the sheets were stained a darkish red. Blood.

He took a step inside the office often used by Gavalas. He had heard a rumour that Gavalas had gone on leave. There were no signs of disturbance in this room as far as he was able to see. He gripped the ruler tightly and walked in.

He walked across the empty office which showed no evidence of the ghastly death struggle behind him. He must report this at once. In his dazed state he tried to open the door leading to the corridor without turning the key. *It opened.*

The significance of this hit him like a second shock wave. The door had been locked when he had tried to open it from the corridor. The confirmation that the assassin had been hiding inside the darkened room minutes – moments – after completing his hideous act was too much for Higgy.

He felt his bowels loosening. Throwing open the door, he ran for the nearest toilet, locked the door. Afterwards he was never sure how long he sat on the lavatory.

He went back down through the deserted building by the stone staircase. The lift cage was a potential death-trap. The Sudanese receptionist stifled a yawn as he appeared at the foot of the stairs, gazing at the black ruler Higgy was still holding, sat up straight and adjusted his red fez.

'Who has left the building since I came in here?' Higgy demanded.

14

'No one, sir. I would have seen them. They have to pass my desk . . .'

'I know that. Who came into the building?'

'No one, sir,' the Sudanese replied in perfect English again. 'You are the only person here at the moment.'

'Selim. You fell asleep,' Higgy accused.

'No, sir,' Selim protested. 'The night shift is my usual duty. I sleep in the day.'

'Then call the SIB. Now! Urgently.'

'SIB?'

'Special Investigation Branch, idiot.' Higgy regretted the insult the second he had spoken. 'Just call them,' he repeated. 'Someone has been killed. I'll talk to them when you get them on the line.'

He sat on the stone steps while the Sudanese used the telephone. He felt washed out, drained. To stop his hands trembling in front of Selim he gripped the ebony ruler like a vice. And while he waited he kept asking himself the question. How could anyone have got into the building unnoticed when the only way in was the two huge double doors beyond Selim's desk?

Second Lieutenant Samuel Partridge of the SIB sat beside his chief, Captain Orde Humble, who drove the jeep slowly as they came close to the dirty grey Antikhana Building. It was the morning after the late night call from Sergeant Higgins and it was going to be another glorious sunny day.

'Seems we were here only five minutes ago,' Partridge remarked as a horse-drawn gharry with an Arab driver pulled up at the entrance to the building.

'Precisely three hours,' growled Humble and parked the jeep by the kerb.

Partridge, a one-pipper, twenty years old, wished once again he'd kept his mouth shut. Humble was fifty-six, ex-Scotland Yard, long-faced and pessimistic. He never

15

missed a chance to put Partridge in his place. The lowest of the low – one-pippers. Not that it was Partridge's fault he had been posted to the SIB at his youthful age. You didn't create fallen arches under your feet. Hauled out of his regiment by a medical officer who had spotted this physical defect. 'Feet like that. You can't wear Army boots, my lad . . .'

An attractive fair-haired girl in her late twenties, wearing a wide-brimmed straw hat, a blue frock, high-heeled shoes, paid off the gharry driver and started up the wide steps leading to the huge closed double doors. Partridge felt the adrenalin start to pump as he studied her snow-white skin.

Humble leapt out of the jeep and intercepted her. She stared arrogantly at him, reaching for the doorbell. A wrinkled face stared back from under the peaked military cap, his eyes cynical, the thin mouth of a man who has learned over the years to choose his words.

'Don't press that bell. You're not going in there. Who are you, anyway?'

'Flying Officer Malloy's wife. His unit is based here. And may I enquire your authority to order me about? Incidentally, who is that young boy getting out of your jeep?'

With appraising interest she watched Partridge alighting from the vehicle. A gaggle of Arab street urchins appearing from nowhere surrounded the jeep.

'This is my authority. SIB.' Humble waved his ID card in her face. 'A particularly unpleasant murder took place inside this building yesterday.'

'Not really? Some wog got in, I suppose. I tried to phone my husband and the operator refused to put me through. Such damned sauce.'

'Acting under orders, madam. No communication is permitted for the present. I suggest you go straight back to your married quarters.' He put two fingers in his mouth

16

and whistled down a passing gharry. 'There's your transport home.'

'You've a bloody nerve. I shall complain . . .'

As she strolled back down the steps Partridge was handing a few piastres to the leading urchin. 'Watch this jeep until we get back. If it's OK you get the same again.'

It was a necessary precaution. They could have returned to find the wheels missing. He had heard every word of the conversation between Humble and Mrs Malloy. He passed her on the way up the steps. She gave him a direct look with half-closed eyes and was gone.

'Barmy outfit, this one,' Humble complained as he thumbed the bell. 'Allowing women like that to visit the place. Our first stop is Colonel Grogan. Right tartar from what I hear. Runs this pansy bunch of propagandists.'

'That attractive girl you were talking to . . .' Partridge began.

'Married to some RAF type. Flying Officer Malloy. And she had her eye on you. If you know what I mean.' Humble made a crude gesture with his fingers which Partridge found distasteful.

'I was going to say,' Partridge persisted as Humble pressed the bell again, 'it was odd. She never asked who had been murdered.'

'Who knows what goes through a woman's mind?'

The door was opened by a private in the SIB. 'They're still examining the murder room,' he informed Humble. 'Haven't found anything that helps much yet, sir,' he continued as he escorted them into the lift. 'The body was removed hours ago.'

'I know. You needn't come up with us. Colonel Grogan's on the third floor? We'll find him.'

'Anything from the pathologist yet?' Partridge enquired as the lift began its rheumatic ascent.

'He's been up all night working on the *corpus delicti*. All he'll say so far is that the weapon which carved up Ionides

17

could be a commando-type knife. *Could* be,' he snorted. 'I have yet to get a straight answer from any of those buggers.'

Colonel Grogan's door faced the lift beyond the entrance to the corridor running round the building. Humble knocked on the top panel, a voice rapped out, 'Come in, close the door, you're two minutes late.'

'Accounted for, sir, by the two minutes we had to wait outside to gain admittance to this place.'

'Sit down. This place, as you call it, is one of the most sensitive propaganda centres in Mid-East Command. And who am I talking to?'

Humble introduced himself and his companion, produced his identification, which Grogan glanced at and settled back in his chair. Humble had him weighed up at a glance. A regular soldier, contemptuous of all those 'in for the duration', which appeared to include his visitors.

Grogan, he estimated, would be in his late fifties. His thatch of white hair was trimmed close to his bony skull, his clean-shaven face was craggy, his expression bleak. He sat erect as a poker in his hard-backed chair.

'What do you want?' he demanded.

'Well, sir, we are investigating a particularly horrific murder which took place on these premises . . .'

'Get to the point. I haven't all day.'

'Up to this moment we have interviewed Sergeant Higgins who found the body. Nothing much he could tell us. But I understand that among the units you oversee . . .'

'Command!' Grogan snapped.

'As you say, sir. I understand there is a secret unit led by a Colonel Maurice Barrymore . . .'

'Half-colonel. Temporary appointment. Lieutenant-Colonel Barrymore you must be referring to.'

Oh, my God, Humble thought, no wonder they gave him a desk job a thousand miles behind the lines. A World

18

War One type. Up boys, and at 'em. Never mind the casualties – take that machine-gun post. He changed tactics.

'I need to interview this Lieutenant-Colonel Barrymore – and his men. I understand they've just returned from some training course. That they've only been back here in Cairo for two days . . .'

'Good luck to you.' Grogan stood up. 'They're waiting for you. Can't imagine why you're interested in them.'

'I don't have to explain my reasons. Sir.'

'Can't imagine why they call you Humble.' Grogan glared. 'Follow me.'

Stiff in his walk, he led the way down the corridor, back straight, the veteran of a thousand inspection parades. Turning along a fresh corridor, he stopped in front of a closed door, opened it and walked in. He made a dismissive gesture towards Humble and Partridge.

'SIB. Over to you.'

Without a glance at them, he walked out, closing the door. The three men waiting in the room stared at their visitors in silence. The windows – again barred – over-looked the front street where the jeep was parked, Partridge noted as Humble made introductions.

'Better sit down, I suppose,' the half-colonel behind a desk suggested. 'Although we can't give you long. We have things to do.'

'So have we, sir,' growled Humble. 'Like investigating a grim murder . . .'

Partridge, seated next to his chief, assessed the three men with interest. Lieutenant-Colonel Barrymore had spoken in a languid voice, was dark-haired with a trim moustache, thin-faced with an aquiline nose. Effortlessly, he carried an aura of authority and command.

The records showed he was only twenty-one years old but from his air of sophistication Partridge would have guessed he was in his thirties. He sat back in a swivel chair, turning a short swagger cane between strong fingers. He pointed with the cane to the two men seated in hard-back chairs on either side of the desk.

'Captain Robson. Company Sergeant Major Kearns. Members of my unit.'

'Which unit is that, Colonel?'

'Classified.' He used the tip of the cane to push a typed sheet of paper across the desk. 'That explains.'

Partridge studied the other two men while Humble scanned the letter. Robson was twenty-two, more heavily built than the lieutenant-colonel. Brown-haired, he also sported a moustache, straggly, and his whole manner was more relaxed. He sat with an arm stretched across the back of his chair and his expression was amiable. He reminded Partridge of a country doctor. Again, he looked older than his years.

Kearns was tall, thin, clean-shaven and hadn't moved a muscle since they entered the room. His brown eyes reminded Partridge of glass marbles. He sat very erect and his expression was bleak, his jaw clenched. All three men had skin tanned the colour of mahogany.

'I can still ask you some questions. I'm going to do just that. It's my job,' snapped Humble, pushing the letter back over the desk-top, the letter from GHQ signed by a general.

'Let's hurry it up, shall we?' Barrymore suggested in his silken tone. 'I'm beginning to get irked.'

'Unfortunately Ionides can no longer be irked. You have met him, of course? All of you? Seeing as you have your unit stationed in the same building?'

Humble's gaze swept over the three men. Nothing changed in Kearns' expression. Barrymore tapped his small white teeth with the tip of his cane. It was Captain Robson who replied.

'Personally speaking, no. I gather he was stuck away up on the next floor. As far as I know I've never set eyes on the chap. Horrible business. Any clues – as to who did it?'

'The investigation is continuing.' Humble turned to Kearns who was studying Partridge like a hangman measuring him for the drop. Only twenty years old. Must be the youngest CSM in the British Army.

'What about you?'

'The same as Captain Robson.' There was a snap in his voice. He'd be a bastard on the parade ground, Humble thought. It was the sheer immobility of Kearns which fascinated Humble. He looked at Barrymore.

'What about you, sir? I've heard there are special units which slip into Greece to help the Resistance there. And Ionides was Greek.'

'Rather an obvious observation. That last remark.' Barrymore made no attempt to conceal the sarcasm. 'No is the answer. And now, I think we've told you all we can. I'd prefer this interview to draw to a close. You've read that letter . . .'

'Which authorizes you not to answer any question affecting military security. No, I haven't quite finished, Colonel Barrymore. I understand the three of you returned to Cairo forty-eight hours ago. That means you were all in the city last night. Where were you between the hours of nine and eleven? Last night. And *that* has nothing to do with military security.'

'If you must know . . .' Barrymore sounded as though he were having trouble stifling a yawn. 'All three of us were getting some well-earned kip aboard a houseboat on the Nile. The location is top secret.'

'Any witnesses to confirm your story?'

Despite his tan, the hint of a flush of blood appeared on Barrymore's face. He stood up and Humble saw for the first time his khaki drill trousers were thrust into the tops of gleaming leather cavalry boots. Walking to the door, he opened it.

'I am not accustomed to being insulted in front of subordinates. May I suggest the interview is concluded? That you both leave now. If you please.'

Humble stood up, nodded to Partridge, and strode out of the room. The door closed behind them as they headed for the lift.

'Botched that one, didn't I?' observed Humble. 'Sprawled right into it. Gave him just the excuse he was looking for to chuck us out. What did you think of them?'

'Funny trio. I couldn't get it out of my mind there was a lot of tension under the surface.'

'Which there would be if they've just returned from some mission to the Greek islands. They're Special Operations Executive – and commandos to boot.'

'SOE? Then that explains . . .'

'It explains a lot,' Humble interjected as they ignored the lift and walked down the staircase. 'It explains why some flaming desk wallah of a general at Grey Pillars provides Barrymore with a letter giving total immunity from questioning. It explains why he could throw me out on my ear. And we can't check their alibi. That houseboat is where the SOE plan operations. It's called *Tara*. Don't know why – but it's off limits even to us.'

Partridge waited until they were settled inside the jeep before he asked his question. First he paid off the chief urchin of the gang guarding the vehicle. 'Not enough!' the urchin screeched. '*Imshi! Yallah!*' Partridge bawled. They ran off, shouting obscenities.

'Did you notice Captain Robson qualified his statement that he'd never met Ionides? *As far as I know I've never set eyes on the chap.*'

'You spotted that, too? You're learning. Gives him an out if we came up with a witness who saw them talking together. Any idea how the murder was done?' he asked as he started the vehicle moving.

'From our visit in the night it seems impossible. The only

way out is the front entrance – guarded by the Sudanese receptionist. Our people searched the place from top to bottom. No one there. All windows are barred. You *can* get out on to balconies from certain rooms on the upper floors. But you're thirty feet from the ground. Yet the killer had to be behind that locked door Higgins tried before he went into the next room.'

'And we found traces of blood in the bathroom. My bet is Higgins sat on that lavatory seat quite a long time. I can't say I blame him – but that was when the murderer was cleaning himself up before performing his vanishing trick.'

'Unless the Sudanese receptionist was bribed?'

'I talked with Selim. I've carried out enough interrogations in my time to know he wasn't lying. You know something, Partridge? I've a hunch we're not going to solve this one.'

'This is a bloody waste of time. You do know that?' Humble rapped out as he pulled the jeep into the kerb in front of the Antikhana Building. It was dark, the street was deserted.

Partridge checked his watch. 'Ten o'clock. The exact time Higgins arrived back on the night of the murder. I want to walk right round the outside first. Then go inside – just like Higgins did.'

'You're on your own, laddie. I'll wait here. And watch it at the back. The native quarter . . .'

Partridge jumped down on to the pavement and began walking slowly away from the entrance steps. Although it was dark there was plenty of light from the street lamps. He looked up as he walked, stared at the projecting balconies with their iron grilles.

It was very quiet. The only sound the smack of his shoes on stone. No one about. Probably it had been like this on the night of the murder. He turned the first corner of the building and the side street was a canyon of gloom. He unbuttoned his holster flap, felt the butt of his Service revolver. Butterflies in the stomach. The silence became oppressive, sinister.

He turned the next corner, walking more slowly, trying to make no sound. Across the narrow street to his right loomed the ramshackle tenements of the native quarter. Black as pitch now. He looked up again. The roof of the building was a blurred silhouette against a distant background of star-studded sky. He heard a scuffling sound and his hands were moist. A half-starved cat scuttled across the street.

Completing the circuit, he saw Humble leaning over the wheel, the red glow of a cigarette near his mouth. He mounted the steps, pressed the bell. An SIB sentry opened the right-hand door, Partridge showed his pass, went inside, nodded to the Sudanese behind the desk.

'No one in the building?' he asked the sentry.

'Yes, there is, sir. Colonel Barrymore is still in his office. Professor Guy Seton-Charles is also working late. And Sergeant Higgins is sitting on the staircase.'

'Why?'

'Better, maybe, sir, you ask him that yourself.'

The heavily built ex-tank commander was seated out of sight on the sixth step. Hunched forward, hands tightly clasped, he looked embarrassed and stood up as Partridge appeared.

'Sorry, sir. It's just that I can't go up there alone. I'm waiting for Clanger Wilson, my room-mate.'

'Let's go up together. I'm on the way to the roof myself.' Partridge hastened to put the burly sergeant at his ease. 'Why Clanger?'

'It's his nickname. Nothing malicious. He's always knocking things over. Bit like a bull in a china shop. Everyone likes him. Just a bit of fun. Calling him Clanger.'

24

'I think you're sensible to wait for company,' Partridge assured him as they climbed the staircase together. 'Think I'd have done the same thing myself in your place. After all, we still have to catch the blighter. Does Colonel Barrymore work this late often?'

'He's still here?' Higgins sounded surprised. 'Never known that to happen before. Not that any of us have a clue what that lot do. We call them the Hush-Hush Boys.'

'Let's look in on him before we go on the roof.'

Partridge opened the door to the office where a light shone from beneath it without knocking. Barrymore was bending over a file behind his desk. He looked up, closed the file quickly and laid a hand flat on it.

'I saw the light,' Partridge explained quickly.

'What the devil do you mean invading my quarters without so much as a warning knock?'

'I've just explained that. I saw the light and thought maybe someone had forgotten to turn it off. And I smell smoke. Is that mineral water, sir?'

A metal wastepaper basket stood by the side of the desk with smoke drifting up from inside. Partridge had pointed to a large glass jug on the desk next to a tumbler. 'Yes. Your powers of detection are extraordinary.' Barrymore noticed Higgins standing in the corridor. He jumped up, strode towards him. 'What are you doing? Snooping around at this hour?'

Barrymore's back was turned when Partridge picked up the jug, doused the papers burning inside the basket. Stooping, he retrieved an intact remnant with a few visible words. *Report on Siros raid.* He turned to face the door. 'Higgins is with me. We were just making our way to the roof.'

'Then kindly make your way.'

As Partridge, cap under his arm, walked back into the corridor Barrymore slammed the door behind him. Going back to the file, he emptied more sheets into the basket and set light to them.

Partridge was walking alongside Higgins towards the corner of the building when a door opened. A man of slim build wearing a pale civilian suit emerged from an office and locked the door. 'Who is this?' Partridge whispered.

'Professor Guy Seton-Charles. Boffin type.'

Twenty-three years old, Partridge recalled from his study of records at GHQ. Rejected for military service on grounds of poor eyesight. The thin-faced man walked towards them hugging a green file under his arm. Everything was thin. Hands, his long studious face. He wore rimless glasses.

'A word with you, sir.' Partridge produced his identity card. 'SIB. We haven't got around to interviewing you yet. What is your precise job here?'

'Difficult to be precise about anything. All problems have shades of meaning. I am concerned with propaganda to the mainland.'

'Mainland?'

'Greece. The authorities are getting it all wrong, of course. The left-wing ELAS *àndartes* are the real guerrillas fighting the Germans. The Republican EDES lot are hopeless. But can I convince people here? Even if ELAS are Communist?'

He spoke in a pedantic petulant tone and was obviously launched into a lecture. Partridge stopped him.

'Propaganda? Greece? Then you must have worked with Ionides.'

'Never, my dear chap. No idea why those two – Gavalas and Ionides – were here. Making jobs for themselves, I suspect . . .'

'We must go,' Partridge interjected. 'We'll talk later.' He headed for the end of the corridor. 'Funny type.'

'We've given him a nickname. Cuckoo.' Higgins chuckled.

'I'll lead the way,' Partridge suggested tactfully and began to climb the stone spiral staircase. It was very narrow, curving sharply, and there was no lighting. He felt his way up the wall with one hand, emerging suddenly on to the rooftop.

It was flat, enclosed by a waist-high wall with an iron rail on top. Higgins led the way, heading for one of a row of cabin-like structures erected on the rooftop. Taking out a key, he opened the door, switched on the light and showed Partridge his sleeping quarters. Alongside either wall leading from the door to a window at the far end was a camp bed neatly made up with Army blankets. Higgins indicated the one to his right.

'That's where Clanger sleeps. Luckily we arrived at the unit early enough to grab a cabin. Better than being billeted in Kasr-el-Nil Barracks across the road. No privacy in that madhouse. I'll show you round. Not a great deal to see. Except the Pyramids.'

Partridge made for the side of the roof at the back. Behind him he heard Higgins relocking the cabin door. His macabre experience had shaken the ex-tank commander to the core. Partridge placed a hand on the iron rail perched half a foot above the wall-top, gripped it, tested its strength and peered over. The dark canyon facing the squalid tenements of the native quarter was like an abyss. It was very quiet as Higgins joined him and made his remark.

'I heard you hadn't been out here long, sir. Going into the native quarter is forbidden. For a very good reason. Lord knows how many squaddies have staggered in there dead drunk. They never come out. The body is found days later by Military Police patrols. Throat slit. Wallet gone.'

'So it would take a brave man to go in even stone cold sober?'

'Sober – and armed – he'd probably be all right. Let's look at something more savoury.'

They walked across to the wall overlooking the front

entrance. Below, Humble was smoking behind the wheel of his jeep. Higgins pointed south. 'There they are.'

In the far distance, by the light of a waxing moon, Partridge saw the dark silhouettes of the Pyramids of Giza. He pulled at his shirt. He was sweating but the temperature seemed to have dropped suddenly.

'My Gawd! Look at that. Here she comes,' Higgins commented.

What seemed like a black cloud was blotting out the moon, the Pyramids below. Partridge had the impression smoke from a huge forest fire was sweeping into the city. It was a sight which stayed with him for the rest of his life.

'*Khamsin*. Sandstorm. Ever seen one?' asked Higgins. 'You've a treat in store. Inside ten minutes that cloud will blot out Cairo like a London pea-souper. Better get back to your jeep – you'll be lucky to make it back to GHQ . . .'

Humble had the engine running when Partridge ran down the steps of the building. He glared and moved the gears as Partridge jumped aboard.

'I was about to leave without you. *Khamsin* coming.'

'How did you know?' Partridge asked as the jeep rocketed down the deserted streets, exceeding the speed limit.

'That breeze that's flapping your shirt, you stupid bugger. What kept you?'

'I think I know now how the murderer escaped without being seen.'

'Great! And you know who the murderer is?'

'No. No idea . . .'

'Great again! I think my hunch was right. We'll not be solving this one.'

And Humble was right. Up to a point. The case might never have been solved but for a man who hadn't even been born as they raced through the streets. A man called Tweed. Over forty years later.

PART ONE

The Moor of Death

1

May 1987. It was another rainy day in London. Tweed stood by his first-floor office window gazing across Park Crescent to Regent's Park. Seated behind her desk, his assistant and confidante, Monica, watched the Deputy Director of the Secret Intelligence Service.

'A penny for your thoughts,' she said. 'You're not here – you have that faraway look.'

'Harry Masterson,' he replied. 'Why has he chosen Greece for his holiday? Dammit, he's Sector Chief for South-East Europe. You'd think he'd want to get as far from that part of the world as possible.'

'He does speak fluent Greek – among his other languages.'

'And you saw him in Bond Street the day before he was due to start his leave. With an attractive girl you think was Greek.'

'So, it's simple. Harry is divorced, has lots of girlfriends. This time it's a Greek. Maybe she wanted to go there, felt homesick.'

'I'm not convinced.' Tweed, a compact, clean-shaven man in his forties who wore glasses, sat behind his desk, began cleaning the glasses with a handkerchief. Monica frowned. He often performed that action when he was disturbed. 'Harry can't take a proper holiday,' Tweed continued. 'He once told me he's bored in three days without a problem to get his teeth into. He's been out there for three weeks.'

'And not a word from him, you mean?'

'But there has been a word – if you can call this a word. I got in early this morning. This came in the post.'

Unlocking a drawer, he took out a package shaped like a cigar box. The wrappings were still intact although the package had been opened. Monica stood up, came round and stood by the side of her chief. The address was written in Masterson's clear bold hand. Marked 'Personal'. The stamps were Greek. Tweed lifted off the top packing where he had carefully slit along the edges. Inside was a cigar box.

'From Harry Masterson. I don't like it,' Tweed said grimly. 'It looks like pieces of evidence he's collected about an investigation he's working on. And sent to me in case something happens to him.'

'Aren't you over-reacting? What's inside the box?'

'See for yourself.' Tweed flipped back the lid. 'That girl you saw him with in Bond Street before he left for Athens. Is this her?'

He rummaged among a collection of papers, photographs and a small notebook. Selecting one of the photographs, he placed it on the desk.

'Yes, that's her,' Monica said, studying the picture. 'I'm sure of it. She looks slimmer in a white dress. Good figure. She was wearing a coat when I saw her. I wonder where it was taken? Looks like somewhere in Greece.'

'Look on the back. Zea. Wherever that might be. Notice anything odd about the picture?'

'There are a lot of expensive-looking pleasure craft moored behind her. And beyond, the buildings are stepped up a hill. What's odd?'

'I'm damned sure the girl didn't know her picture was being taken by Harry. She's looking at some book. I think he took it surreptitiously. That's suggestive in itself. I don't think he trusted her . . .'

'Don't use the past tense . . .'

'Come in,' Tweed called out as someone rapped on the

door. A slim, fair-haired man in his early thirties with an air of self-assurance entered. 'Marler, your timing is perfect as always,' Tweed commented. 'You know Greece fairly well.' He handed him the photo. 'Harry Masterson took this picture somewhere in Greece. Any idea of the location?'

Marler examined the print, turned it over, smiled drily. 'It all links up if it's Harry, doesn't it? An attractive female, a small port, very exclusive, millionaires' yachts. Nothing but the best for our high-life Harry. This is the port of Zea. It's along the coast road from the main Piraeus harbour.'

'Why so exclusive?' Tweed asked. 'Apart from the floating palaces? Drug traffickers can afford those boats these days – if they're at the top.'

'Because just behind Zea is the Royal Yacht Club. Nowadays it is officially the Yacht Club since Greece became a republic.' He picked up a magnifying glass from Monica's desk. 'Bet you a fiver some of these still have the initials RYC on their sterns. Are you on?'

'No. I'm fed up with losing money to you.'

'And you would have lost.' Marler was peering through the magnifier. 'Two of the yachts berthed do have those initials. A bit of rather nice snobbery,' he commented in his upper-crust voice. He laid down the glass. 'What's this all in aid of, if I may be so bold?'

'I'm worried stiff about Harry.'

'For what good reasons?'

Marler, dressed in an immaculate pale linen suit, blue-striped shirt, matching blue tie and handmade shoes skilfully weighted in the toecaps – 'useful for kicking your opponent in the balls' – sat down in Tweed's armchair. He lit one of his rare king-size cigarettes. Crossing his legs, the epitome of relaxation, he fixed his blue, ice-cold eyes on Tweed.

'Reason One, why choose part of his working sector for his holiday? Oh yes, I know he likes the sun, but the

33

Caribbean would have served. Reason Two, he always sends a rude postcard. No card. Reason Three, instead he sends this cigar box with stuff which looks to me like clues about an investigation he's conducting. Reason Four, Harry gets bored easily – so if someone has approached him with a problem which intrigues him he'd jump at the chance of occupying himself with it.'

'That the cigar box? May I see?'

'Over to you. See what you make of the contents. I've only had time to skip through them. I find the sending of that sinister.'

'Any note, letter, with it?'

'No. Monica saw him in Bond Street with that girl whose photo you're looking at.'

'When was that?' Marler asked.

'Three weeks ago. The day before he flew to Athens, I assume.'

'You *assume*?' Marler raised an eyebrow. 'These photos are a mix. Some obviously in Greece, some in this country. Don't know where.'

'I do,' said Tweed. 'That one of the outside of The Royal Oak Inn. I recognize it. Winsford. A village on Exmoor. So why do we have Somerset and Greece? Doesn't make sense.'

'Unless he hasn't spent his whole three weeks in Greece. The day he was seen by Monica he could have taken off for Exmoor. Gone on to Greece later. Suggests something the Greek filly told him led him to Somerset. Something he found there led him to Greece. A regular bloodhound, our Harry. Picks up a scent and won't let go.'

'The timing,' Monica agreed, 'suggests it could have been something the Greek girl told him sent him haring off to Somerset.'

'I wonder what,' muttered Tweed, sifting through the non-Greek pictures. 'This looks like Watchet, a tiny port on the Bristol Channel. One of the front, another of the

34

harbour. I remember that line of lampposts along the front with the small hill at the eastern edge of the harbour. Dunster High Street, not a doubt. The front entrance to the Luttrell Arms, leading hotel in Dunster. Another of a Tudor-style mansion behind a stone wall. Familiar. Near the Doone Valley if I remember right.'

Marler had emptied the cigar box and was fiddling with the base of its interior. He raised a thin sheet of wood pressed down on the base, extracted a folded sheet of paper.

'Seen this?' he enquired. 'The scene widens. Take a shufti.'

Tweed studied the opened sheet. Harry's distinctive writing. *MOD. Brigadier Willie Davies.* Ministry of Defence. Harry had visited the place, presumably before he flew to Greece, maybe even before he'd driven down to Somerset. There were two more words written on the sheet of paper. *Somerset Levels.*

Tweed felt a prickling of the hairs at the back of his neck, an unreasoned sense of foreboding. He became aware that Marler and Monica were watching him.

'Something's wrong,' said Monica.

'I hope not.' He passed the sheet to her. 'I don't think we've told you yet, Marler, that Brigadier Davies is our most friendly contact at the Ministry of Defence. He's also a member of the same club as Harry. They were close.'

'Chums, you mean?' Marler enquired. 'As well as a professional relationship? This business is getting a bit weird. So many strands. And what the deuce is – are – the Somerset Levels?'

'One of the most benighted and lonely spots in England. The area between Taunton and Glastonbury where they dig peat. In the time of Charles the First the sea used to flood in. Now they have constructed waterways – they look like canals. It is like a bleak marshland. I don't understand any of this – too many strands, as you said.'

35

He stood up and walked over to the window. It had stopped raining. Now they had May sunshine. The pavements were drying out, leaving damp patches. He stood with his hands clasped behind his back. He was, Monica knew, on the verge of taking a decision.

'I want Harry recalled from Greece immediately. Isn't his deputy for Greece, Patterson, at the British Embassy?'

'Yes,' said Monica promptly. 'Harry appointed him a couple of months ago. Patterson speaks Greek and has travelled widely in the archipelago. You're assuming Harry contacted him after he reached Athens.'

'Which he probably didn't,' Marler commented. 'Running his own investigation unofficially, he'd play it close to the chest. Why the MOD? Or again was it something the Greek girl told him? Incidentally, Monica, what made you so sure she *was* Greek?'

'When he stopped me he said something in a foreign language. She looked annoyed. Then Harry said, "The Greeks always have a word for it." Looking back, I almost think he was sending me a signal.'

'Fair do's,' Marler agreed. 'She is Greek.'

'And now,' Tweed said impatiently as he returned to his swivel chair, 'I want that call made to Athens recalling Harry. A direct order. He's to return instantly, the moment they locate him.'

Monica was reaching for her phone when it began to ring as a raven-haired girl with good bone structure came into the office. Marler jumped up, grinned, offered Paula Grey, Tweed's assistant, his chair. He spread his hands, adopted a theatrical pose.

'Lothario offers you his comfortable seat. How is it you look more ravishing every time I see you?'

'Flannel,' rapped back Paula. 'You think I haven't heard all about your women?'

She was crossing her legs when she stiffened. She was looking at Monica who had been talking on the phone. In a broken voice Monica nodded to Tweed to lift his receiver.

'Athens on the line . . . Larry Patterson for you.'

Tweed grabbed up his receiver. It became very silent and still in the office. They watched Tweed whose expression had become poker-faced. In a quiet controlled voice he asked several terse questions, said, 'Yes, of course,' five times, thanked Patterson for calling and replaced the receiver. Leaning across his desk, he clasped his hands, gazed at them and spoke in a monotone.

'There is no easy way to break this type of news. Harry Masterson is dead. He was found today at the base of some cliff called Cape Sounion. I gather it is some distance southeast of Athens. The cliff is very sheer and is three hundred feet high. They will be flying the body home.'

'Oh dear God, no! Not Harry . . .'

It was Monica who burst out like a stricken animal. Her eyes filled with tears. Paula jumped up, put an arm round her and helped her to her feet and out of the room. The silence was oppressive after the click of the closing door.

'Apparently, according to Patterson, he must have slithered over the edge early in the morning,' Tweed continued. 'About nine o'clock a coastguard launch patrolling the area on the lookout for drug smugglers spotted the body on some rocks at the edge of the sea.'

'Balls!' said Marler, his tone harsh. 'Which is what Harry would have said if they'd found me there. I know the area.'

'I'm listening,' said Tweed in the same monotone, twiddling a pencil between his fingers.

'Cape Sounion is about a two-hour drive along the coast road from Athens. It's the southernmost tip of Greece at that point. Perched on the summit of the Cape is the Temple of Poseidon. It's a lonely spot when the tourists aren't there. Beyond the temple the ground is covered with stubby grass which slopes gently towards the brink. You can easily see when you're coming to the end of everything.'

'So?' pressed Tweed.

'Harry had all his marbles – more than most of us. The idea that he slipped over the edge is fatuous.'

'So?' Tweed repeated.

'Harry was murdered. Absolutely no doubt about it. And I would like to know what the hell we are going to do about it.'

2

Action this day. A favourite maxim of Tweed's, borrowed from Winston Churchill.

Tweed had called for the afternoon what he termed a 'war conference'. Inside what Howard, Tweed's chief, insisted on calling the 'boardroom', six people were gathered round a large oblong table.

Like antagonists, Howard was seated at one end of the table, facing Tweed, who occupied the other end. Also present were Paula Grey, sitting on Tweed's right, notebook at the ready. Marler sat next to Bob Newman, foreign correspondent and close confidant of Tweed. Pete Nield, experienced agent, sat opposite Marler and Newman. Already the atmosphere reeked with tension and disagreement.

'Aren't we jumping to a lot of conclusions rather early in the game regarding this dreadful tragedy?' suggested Howard in his slow pontificating voice.

'It's not a game,' Tweed snapped. 'And Masterson's death does not sound like an accident.'

'Hold hard a jiffy . . .' Howard, six feet tall, plump-faced and perfectly tailored in a Chester Barrie navy blue suit, shot his cuffs to expose the gold links.

Oh God, thought Tweed, why did he have to turn up unexpectedly and attend this meeting? He stared hard at Howard as he spoke.

'Well, let's get on with it.'

'I was going to make the point that Patterson is already in place in Athens. He could take a look-see, send us a report. Oh, nothing personal, of course, but why is Mr Newman honouring us with his presence?'

'Because I asked him to. Because he knows Greece. Because he speaks Greek fluently and is flying out there with Marler.'

'Not necessary,' Marler interjected in his clipped tone. 'You know I work on my own . . .'

There was a heavy silence. Tweed kept the silence going while he deliberately arranged the pile of photos in front of him. Newman, in his early forties, well-built, clean-shaven, with thick sandy hair and a strong face, sat watching Tweed with a droll expression.

'I have to say,' Howard continued eventually, 'that I really don't see how Newman, able though he might be, fits in with such an assignment.'

Tweed launched his attack. 'He's fully vetted, as you well know. Patterson has only been in Athens for a short time. Let's get a few opinions.' He addressed Newman. 'Bob, you knew Harry Masterson. Can you see him stumbling off the edge of a cliff?'

'He was sharp as a fox. But I would like to collect a few more facts in Greece. Facts are what I go by.'

'Marler?' Tweed asked.

'So unlikely the idea is ridiculous.'

'Paula?'

'I heard he once left a party half-smashed and walked down the middle of Walton Street balancing a bottle of champagne on his head. The bottle stayed there. Sure-footed as the proverbial goat. Not a chance.'

'Pete?'

39

'Never in a million years.'

'Are you convinced?' Tweed asked Howard. 'If it was murder and we don't act fast the Prime Minister will call us to account.'

'I don't like blackmail,' Howard replied stiffly.

'Who does? You haven't answered the question.'

'Well,' Howard began, his manner breezy, 'first he's a fox, then he's a goat . . .'

'I don't find that the least bit amusing,' Tweed snapped.

'In that case, what do you propose?' Howard's well-fed face was flushed with annoyance. 'And I still maintain Marler could go on his own. Newman is surplus to requirements – I do realize he's rendered valuable service in the past . . .'

'Very generous of you,' Tweed interjected. The trouble was Howard realized Newman was wealthier than he would ever be. The foreign correspondent had made a fortune from his best-selling book, *Kruger: The Computer That Failed*. Tweed spoke decisively.

'Marler and Newman will travel to Greece together. Masterson went alone – and see what happened to him.' He glanced at Paula but she was already recording his instructions.

'Marler's deputy, Harris, can take over the German sector in his absence. Agreed, Marler?' He went on as Marler nodded. 'The investigation covers two very different areas. Greece. Dealt with. Newman reports back to me over Patterson's scrambler phone at the Athens Embassy.'

'Why not Marler?' Howard bleated.

Tweed, in full cry, ignored the interruption. 'I shall drive with Paula to Exmoor and check that area. Pete Nield will come with us in a separate car. He will appear not to know us. He will come armed.'

'Why?' demanded Howard.

'Because I don't know what we're walking into. One man has already been murdered.'

40

'That has yet to be proved,' Howard objected.

'Everyone I asked believes that. I have an open mind but I'm taking no chances. We start tomorrow – before the scent goes cold. The contents of this cigar box Harry posted me will be checked by our experts in the Engine Room in the basement. I want someone to visit Harry's country cottage in Sussex. What was it called?'

'Clematis Cottage, near Apfield,' said Paula, continuing her writing.

'I will contact Jim Corcoran of Airport Security at Heathrow. He'll check the passenger manifests of all flights to Greece over the past three weeks.' Tweed looked briefly at Howard who had lapsed into silence. 'If we can find which flight Masterson used we may find the name of that Greek girl Monica saw him with in Bond Street.' He turned to Paula. 'How is Monica?'

'Harry Butler took her home. He'll pull her round. Should he go down to check Clematis Cottage?'

'Good idea. And tell him to look at a power cruiser moored at a landing stage a few hundred yards south of the cottage. He turns off to the right along the first track.'

'Is that the lot?' Howard enquired with a hint of sarcasm.

'No. We need photos of Harry Masterson run off by the Engine Room urgently this evening. Newman and Marler will need them when they're tracking his movements in Greece. And I want careful blow-ups of the photo of the Greek girl at Zea. Some for Newman and Marler, some for me to take to Somerset.'

'I think I'm going.' Howard stood up. 'I do have other work calling for my attention. I can't rubber-stamp all this in a memo . . .'

'So you'll have a little extra time for that other work calling for your attention.' Tweed smiled. 'Thank you for your cooperation and attendance.'

Howard withdrew, closing the door behind him as

41

though it were made of glass. Round the table there was a sense of relief.

'I have held back two intriguing points,' Tweed told them. 'Harry made a reference to a friend at court at the Ministry of Defence. I hope to visit him before you leave tonight. I can't imagine why Harry went there.'

'And the other point?' asked Marler.

'Endstation.' Tweed looked round the table. 'Like a clue to a crossword puzzle. Mean anything? Suggest anything? The word is written – in Harry's writing – on the back of a British postcard. Just that one word. *Endstation*.'

'Sounds like Cockfosters, the last station on the Piccadilly Underground,' Paula suggested.

'Which doesn't link up with Exmoor – or Greece.'

'The fact that he wrote it on a *British* postcard points to a connection with Somerset,' Newman remarked. 'Harry liked little tricks like that. And he may well have had in mind that cigar box could have been intercepted.'

'So?' enquired Nield.

'He'd write any clue in code. Some puzzle he'd hope Tweed could unravel.'

'Puzzle is the word for what he sent me,' Tweed commented. 'Paula, book tickets for Marler and Newman to fly to Athens tomorrow . . .'

'I've already made a note to do just that . . .'

'But no one moves anywhere, leaves London, until I've seen Brigadier Willie Davies. We need to know why Harry went to the Ministry of Defence.'

Escorted by a male receptionist, Tweed walked down the endless corridor past doors carrying the names of military officers. He clutched in his hand the pass he would have to surrender before being let out of the MOD.

Brigadier Davies, a tall red-faced man with lapel tabs of the same colour, rose from behind his desk as Tweed entered and the door closed behind him. They shook hands.

'Long time no see,' Davies remarked in his crisp staccato voice. 'Take a pew. Long time,' he repeated, sitting down again, 'then we have a queue from your outfit.'

'Harry Masterson, you mean?'

'The great man himself.' Davies tugged at his ginger moustache, ran a hand over thinning hair of the same colour. 'But since you authorized the interview you'll know all about it. Always good for a laugh, Harry. Say anything outrageous.'

'You said I authorized the interview?'

'Course you did.' Davies pushed a sheet of paper with typing across the desk. Tweed glanced at it. A printed heading. General and Cumbria Assurance Company – the cover name for the SIS at Park Crescent. The letter was brief.

Dear Willie – If you could give Harry your cooperation re this one I'd be greatly indebted. At the bottom was Tweed's signature. Forged. Typical of Harry, Tweed thought nostalgically. Break every rule in the book to get what he was after.

'A lot's been happening. My memory must be going.' He phrased the next words carefully. 'The trouble is he took off on a plane without leaving me a report. Just caught his flight after leaving you, I gather. Could you bring me up to date? What he asked, what you told him?'

'Weird case. Going back over forty years.' Davies stood up, extracted a bunch of keys from his pocket and unlocked a green steel cabinet. 'Took me a while to locate the file for Harry.' He grinned as he pulled out a blue file with a red tab attached and handed it to Tweed. 'Still classified.'

Tweed left the file unopened on the desk. The typed inscription on the front in faded letters carried a brief message. *Commando raid on Siros Island, Greece, February, 1944.*

'If you'd bear with me, Willie, I went off abroad as soon as I'd provided the authorization,' he lied glibly. 'It would help if you could tell me what Harry asked you. I'm not sure exactly how much he knew about this business.'

'Oh, he had his facts all lined up.' Davies clasped his hands behind his long neck. 'I'd offer you coffee but why poison a friend? Harry said he first needed details of that four-man commando raid on Siros in February 1944. I expect you know Siros is a large island in the Cyclades, a strategic stepping-stone to Piraeus, the port of Athens. Couriers passed through Siros from Cairo on their way to the mainland to contact the Greek Resistance. Actually, the Resistance was active on the island. German-occupied, of course. And the HQ of the German commander of the Cyclades group. A General Hugo Geiger. All this came from Harry before he looked at that file. And a bit more. I wondered how he'd come about the information.'

'Tell me about the bit more.'

'A four-man commando team made the raid. From Special Operations Executive. Commanded by a Lieutenant-Colonel Barrymore. Had with him a Captain Robson, a CSM called Kearns, and the Greek.'

'The Greek?'

'You didn't know about him? Chap called Andreas Gavalas. He had got out in a motorized caïque, reached Cairo months before. The idea was he knew Siros well. The Resistance lot, by the way, were the Republican crowd EDES. As opposed to ELAS, the Commie faction. Barrymore was taking a fortune in diamonds to hand over to a courier from Athens. Last time Cairo financed them. Turned their cooperation completely to ELAS shortly afterwards. Word was ELAS were doing the real fighting out there against Jerry, even though they were Communists.'

'And that was the extent of Harry's knowledge?'

'No. Weird business. He knew about the tragedy. After

44

they landed on Siros successfully the diamonds were handed to Gavalas to pass on to his Greek contact. The commando team was returning to the beach down a gully and found Gavalas lying dead with a knife stuck in his back.' Davies' expression became grim. 'It was a commando knife.'

'You can't mean that one of . . .'

'The three commandos? No. Barrymore immediately gathered his team together and asked to see their weapons. All of them, including himself, had their knives.'

'Weird, as you say. Why didn't the killer remove the knife?'

'Well, that's something I can understand. Apparently it had been driven into Gavalas with great force. Ever tried to pull out a knife from a dead body? It can take some doing – if it's rammed in deep. Barrymore tried to pull it out and couldn't manage it. So they scarpered pretty damn quick.'

'And Harry explained all this before seeing the file?'

'I think he wanted me to realize he wasn't on a fishing expedition, that he knew a great deal about the murder on Siros.'

'And was it eventually brought home to the killer?'

'Not as far as I know.' Davies made a sweeping gesture with his hand. 'Look at the range of suspects. The EDES section which knew Gavalas was coming. The Germans occupying the island. They patrolled constantly, I gather.'

'And the diamonds had been handed over before the Barrymore team left Gavalas the first time – alive?'

'No, they hadn't.' Davies pursed his lips.

'So the first thing Barrymore would do when he realized Gavalas was dead would be to check for the diamonds.'

'Which he did. They'd vanished.'

'What was a fortune in diamonds worth then? Any data?'

'One hundred thousand pounds. God knows what they'd be worth now. That covers what Harry told me before I searched for the file and he sat in that same chair reading

45

it. His next request was what startled me. Tell you about it when you've scanned the file.' Davies smiled cynically. 'You can't, of course, borrow that file, photograph it, or make a single note. It's the regulations.'

'I know.' Tweed glanced up and caught the cynical smile. He understood. Davies knew Tweed's reputation for a photographic memory. He only had to read a long document once and he had total recall. Every word would be imprinted on his brain.

Five minutes later Tweed pushed the file back across the desk. He sat with hands clasped as he asked the question.

'And what was the request Harry made that startled you?'

'He asked me if I could give him the present whereabouts of Barrymore, Robson and Kearns – if they'd survived. I don't think I can take this any further, Tweed. It involves another department. Better ask Harry when you see him again.'

'Not possible, Willie.' Tweed paused. 'Harry is dead.'

Davies stiffened, his face froze. He opened a drawer, took out an ash tray, a pack of cigarettes and lit one. He dropped the pack back inside the drawer.

'Rarely smoke these days. You tricked me, Tweed. Not like you . . .'

'I thought you might close down on me. It's just possible he was murdered. I've thrown away the rule book. I'm going to find out how he died come hell or high water. You'd do the same thing if our roles were reversed.'

'You're right there,' Davies admitted. 'May I ask where and how?'

'In Greece. He's supposed to have stumbled off a three-hundred-feet cliff a good way south-east of Athens . . .'

'Bloody rubbish. Never!' Davies stubbed out the cigarette, drummed his thick fingers on the desk-top. 'Not

Harry. And you won't stop until you've found out what happened.'

'No, I won't.'

Davies stood up, went back to the cabinet, unlocked it, took out a thin blue file and laid it before Tweed. He sat down, lips tightly compressed before he spoke.

'You can look at that appendix to the other file. Same regulations apply . . . Hell, I don't have to tell you. When Harry asked for that information I didn't think I could oblige. I checked with this other department which keeps certain records. You see, Barrymore and Kearns stayed in the Army for a few years after the war. The girl who checks records like that is a tigress. Never gives up. I gave her all three names – Robson and Kearns as well as Barrymore. She located Barrymore easily. Then she obtained a copy of the phone directory of the same area. Came up with all three addresses. Better look in that file.'

A single sheet of paper. Tweed stared, unable to believe it. All the addresses were in Somerset. 'The last two are from the directory,' Davies explained.

'After all these years, they all live in the Exmoor area.'

'Odd, isn't it? Odd, too, that Harry died in Greece – not a hundred miles from the island of Siros from what you've told me.'

Tweed closed the second file, stood up slowly, his mind whirling. He thanked Willie, said they must have a drink soon. At the door he turned before he opened it.

'When I came in you said something about a queue from my outfit.'

Davies was standing close to him, hands thrust in his trouser pockets. He stood thinking for a moment.

'I wasn't too accurate there. You used to be with Scotland Yard. I made a subconscious connection.'

'What are you talking about?'

'A few days after Harry visited me someone else arrived – an ex-Chief Inspector from the Yard called Partridge.'

47

'Sam Partridge of Homicide? Now retired. I know him.'

'Might as well tell you the lot. Partridge carries no status here, of course. But he's a persuasive sort of chap. And coming so soon after Harry. Well . . . Long and short of it is he also wanted the present whereabouts of Barrymore, Robson and Kearns. I ended up giving him the addresses.'

'May I ask what was his interest?'

'He's still investigating a murder which took place over forty years ago. Never solved. Can't sit at home and cultivate a vegetable patch now he's retired. Very vigorous type.'

'The murder of Gavalas on Siros?'

'No. This is going to shake you. It did me. After Harry. Which is why I coughed up those addresses, I suppose. I'm sure there can't be a connection.'

'A connection between who?'

'The killing of Gavalas on Siros and the murder of some other Greek at the HQ of certain secret units in Cairo. Ionides I think he called him.'

3

'Jim Corcoran came through from Heathrow Airport Security,' Paula reported as Tweed walked into his office. 'We've got the data you need. Corcoran checked the computers. Harry flew out to Athens via Zurich on Swissair Flight 805. Ten days ago.'

'Which gave him about another ten days to poke about on Exmoor before he left. And I know now why he went there.'

'The news is even better. Harry booked two seats aboard the flight in advance. Guess the name of the passenger who sat in the seat next to him.'

'Not in the mood for guessing games. And I've got a mass of my own data to dictate to you . . .'

'A Christina Gavalas sat next to him.'

'My God, it's beginning to link up.'

'How?'

'Exactly how I've no idea. Ready for dictation? File One.'

Tweed stood quite still, eyes half-closed, while he recalled the contents of the Siros file. Paula took it down in her shorthand book, scrawled a fresh heading for File Two, recorded the three addresses Tweed reeled off.

'Two copies only,' he warned. 'One for Newman and Marler. The other for us.'

'Consider it done. Newman and Marler can collect the tickets from Heathrow if they're leaving tomorrow.'

'They are doing just that. I had a word with them on my way in. Let them have the first copy of the Siros file earliest.'

He was sitting behind his desk when the door opened and Monica walked in. She waved reassuring hands as Paula jumped up. 'I'm all right. Better back in the front line than moping at home.' She went to her desk. 'Can I help?'

'Yes,' said Tweed. 'Call the Yard. Superintendent Jack Richardson. Give him my best wishes. I need the home address of Chief Inspector Sam Partridge of Homicide, now retired.'

'Before you phone,' he said as Monica sat behind her desk, 'I want you to react quickly to this question. One possibly important clue from Harry's cigar box. One single word. Ready? *Endstation*.'

'The name of some operation. Codename.'

'Doesn't add up,' Paula intervened. 'It could have been

49

the codename for the raid on Siros. But there's no reference to any codename in the file. Also, Harry wrote it on a *British* postcard. That points to Somerset.'

She turned to Monica. 'Isn't all this pretty painful for you? You knew Harry well. Is it a good idea to come back yet?'

'Anything I can do to track down the swine who killed him. I want to be a part of this. I'll call the Yard.' She reached for the phone.

Tweed was heading for the door. 'Something else to pass on to Newman and Marler. Someone else is taking an interest in the Siros file. Partridge. What's the betting he's in Greece at this moment?'

'Do you think it's a good idea Newman going to Athens with Marler?' Paula asked after Tweed had left the room. 'They seem to fight like cat and dog. Square up to each other on every issue. Bob is early forties, Marler barely thirty.'

'And there, my dear, you have put your finger on it,' Monica assured her. 'They do scrap, I agree. But whereas Marler is quick off the mark, independent-minded – just the way Bob used to be until recently – Bob has become harder, tougher, wary. They could make an ideal combination once they're out there on their own. I think Tweed is banking on that.'

'What changed Bob? Made him a hard man? After all he was an international foreign correspondent. Still is, if a story interests him.'

'Ah, that was his experience behind the lines in East Germany when he went underground with a resistance group. A bitter, grim time, but he came through. Now, I'd better get on . . .'

When Tweed walked briskly back into the room Monica was putting down the phone. She waited until he had sat behind his desk, scribbled a note on his tasks pad.

'Did you know when you were at Scotland Yard they

had a nickname for you? Quicksilver Tweed, they called you, according to Superintendent Richardson . . .'

'A long time ago.' Tweed made a dismissive gesture. 'What about Partridge?'

'I have his phone number at Cheam. Thought I'd call him when you got back.'

'Yes, I'd like to talk to him personally.'

Monica dialled a number. She had a brief conversation with someone, then put her hand over the mouthpiece.

'Partridge isn't there. It's Mrs Partridge . . .'

'I don't know whether you'll remember me,' Tweed began, using his own phone, 'my name is Tweed . . .'

'I know you, it must be years . . .' She had a cultured voice. 'Sam worked with you at the Yard. We met once at a party. I recognize your voice . . .'

'Sorry to bother you, but I need to speak with Sam urgently.'

'He's not here, Mr Tweed. And I've no idea where he is . . .'

Tweed frowned, detected a note of anxiety in her voice now.

'Something wrong, Mrs Partridge? Why don't you know where he is?'

'You know how Sam is. He can't retire gracefully. Too active, restless. He's investigating some old murder case. I am worried. Before he left he said something he's never said to me before.'

'What was that?'

'He warned me never to open the door to strangers. Especially if they looked to be foreigners. He even had a spyglass fitted in the front door before he dashed off.'

'Dashed off where, if I may ask?'

'I've no idea as I said earlier. He packed his own bag. He's taken enough clothes to last him several weeks.'

'What sort of clothes?'

'Some of his old Army khaki drill suits. Plus a lot of

normal clothes – the kind of things he wears in this country.'

Tweed paused, wondering how to word it. 'Mrs Partridge, don't be alarmed by my call. It's something I'm working on connected with my insurance job as claims investigator. Wives are pretty clever where their husbands are concerned. They often spot a clue as to what they're up to. Have you any suspicions as to where he might have gone?'

'You're not thinking of another woman?'

Oh Christ, Tweed thought, are all marriages like this? Always the wives not a hundred per cent certain about their menfolk? Mrs Partridge went on talking.

'Sam's not like that. I'd know if it was anything untoward.'

'I phrased that badly. As you say, Sam is like the Rock of Gibraltar. It's his *destination* I'm interested in. I do need to contact him urgently.'

'Oh, I see what you mean. Sorry, Mr Tweed, I simply haven't a clue as to where he might be.'

'Here or abroad?' Tweed persisted, hating himself.

'I just don't know. He took off two weeks ago and I haven't had a word from him since. Mind you, he warned me that might happen. I just wish I could help . . .'

'That's quite all right. I'm sure you'll hear from Sam soon. By the way, I'd follow his advice. No opening the door to strangers, especially foreigners. I've no idea why he said that – but Sam usually knows what he's talking about. He'll explain it all when he gets back. Take care.'

He put down the phone and stared into the distance. Paula was typing the Siros file out, slim fingers skimming the keys.

'What was all that about?' asked Monica. 'And who is this Partridge character? Where does he fit in?'

'He called on Brigadier Davies after Harry had been there. Wanted the addresses of the three commandos who made up the team which raided Siros. You'll understand

52

that bit when Paula gives you the file for a quick look before it goes to Newman and Marler. Where does Partridge fit in? I wish I knew. It's a peculiar business. Partridge told Davies he was investigating the murder of a Greek called Ionides over forty years ago in Cairo.'

'My God!' Paula paused briefly. 'That makes two murders. And both of them Greeks.'

'And Partridge warned his wife against opening the door to any foreigners. Greeks? Partridge has disappeared off the face of the earth, went off on some trip a fortnight ago. Destination unknown. I've got an awful feeling of presentiment. Harry walked into something too big even for him to handle.'

'But you'll find out what it is,' Monica told him.

'We'll try. Paula and I drive to Somerset tomorrow. You hold the fort. I'll keep in touch – for any messages from Newman.' He clenched his fist on the desk. 'One of us has to come up with something.'

4

'Ten minutes before we land,' said Newman and peered down out of the window of the Swissair DC9 as the plane banked and swung eastwards.

'And we've got damn all to go on,' Marler observed.

From thirty thousand feet Newman stared down as they left the sapphire blue of the Adriatic Sea behind and flew over a landscape of bleak mountains studded with *maquis* – scrub. Savage gulches cleft the terrain between the mountain ridges. A wilderness of rock. They were over Greece.

The air was incredibly clear, the sun shining brilliantly.

He felt he could reach down and touch the summits of the highest peaks. He looked at Marler sitting next to him, arms crossed, his face expressionless.

'If I were flying in to follow up a story I'd feel I had more than I normally had. We have to locate Christina Gavalas – the girl Harry flew to Athens with. We have copies of his photo to show round the hotels to find where he stayed. We've got Andreas Gavalas who went with the commando group forty odd years ago to check. We have the island of Siros to visit. We have Nick the Greek . . .'

'Who?'

'A driver who makes his living taking tourists from the Hotel Grande Bretagne on trips in his Mercedes. Nick is an old friend of mine. Very reliable, tough. He knows a lot about what goes on in this country.'

'You make it sound like a piece of cake. Anything else?'

'We have Cape Sounion to visit. I want to look at that cliff where Harry supposedly stumbled over the edge. And we have Chief Inspector Peter Sarris of Homicide in Athens. I once did him a favour – so he owes me one.'

'You know something, Newman?'

'You're going to tell me anyway.'

'I think we've got bugger all. And we should have brought someone to do the legwork.'

'If necessary, I'll do that while you prop up the bar at the Grande Bretagne,' Newman said quietly.

'I think Tweed is rushing it. I like a good basis of solid research.'

'He's moving fast before Howard writes Harry's death off as an accident.'

'I suppose it could have been just that.'

'You're forgetting the cigar box he sent. He knew he was walking a tightrope,' Newman said tersely. 'That he might not be coming back.'

'Trouble is I hardly knew Harry,' Marler reflected, still

keeping his voice low. The seats in front of them were unoccupied.

'But I did. And we're starting to descend. End of conversation.'

'Endstation,' Marler responded sardonically.

The big heat hit them like a heavy door as they descended the mobile staircase. Newman looked quickly round. Those bare hills loomed in close to the airport. The light was a glare. Mid-afternoon. Marler made a gesture as they walked towards the airport bus with the other passengers.

'Hardly Heathrow.'

'That has its advantages.'

But Marler had a point, he thought, as they boarded the waiting bus which would take them to the arrivals building which was smaller than any garage at London Airport. They passed the entry checks without any fuss and within minutes climbed inside a yellow taxi.

'Hotel Grande Bretagne,' Newman told the driver in English, 'and we're in a hurry.'

Marler glanced at Newman as they moved off. The driver had not understood the second instruction. That much was clear from his throwaway gesture. Marler marked up a notch in his companion's favour. Newman was concealing the fact that he spoke Greek fluently.

The Grande Bretagne is a solid-looking edifice standing on a corner of Constitution Square – Syntagma as the Greeks call it. The hotel looks as though it has stood there for generations, which it has. Inside they crossed the marble floor to reception.

'We have reservations,' Newman began. 'But first I would like a word with the chief receptionist.'

'You are talking to him, sir,' the man behind the counter informed him in perfect English.

Newman took an envelope from his breast pocket,

extracted a photo of Harry Masterson, laid it on the counter.

'I'm trying to find my stepbrother, Harry Masterson. I understood he stayed here. He may have left by now.'

The receptionist stared at the photo with a blank expression. Then he seemed to seek the right words.

'This, I regret to say, looks very like a man who fell off Cape Sounion to his death recently. There were pictures in the papers. I could be wrong, but they did give the name you mentioned.'

'Can't be the same man,' Newman protested. 'He did stay here?'

'Oh, no sir. I would have remembered. In view of . . .'

'Partridge,' said Marler. 'Does that name ring a bell?'

'Yes, it does, sir.' The receptionist transferred his attention to Marler. 'When I was serving my apprenticeship I went to Britain to learn the language. I was at the Gleneagles Hotel in Scotland. Plenty of partridge shooting up there. Which is probably why I noted this guest's name.'

'May I ask when he was here? Old chum,' Marler said smoothly.

'Let me check.' They waited. A small man wearing the dark suit of a hotel employee was lingering close to the counter – his eyes on the photo of Masterson. Newman stared at him and he wandered away. The receptionist came back.

'I was right. Mr Samuel Partridge?'

'That's him,' said Marler. 'Nice man. Told me he'd probably stay here. Best hotel in Athens.'

'Thank you, sir. Mr Partridge stayed one week. He arrived two weeks ago and then left. For the airport, I seem to remember.' He looked back at Newman. 'But Mr Masterson, no. He did not stay with us. If you would like to register?'

'Certainly.' Newman spoke as he began filling in the form. 'That small man who was standing near the counter. Who is he?'

'Oh, one of our temporary employees.' The receptionist made a resigned gesture. 'During the summer season we have to take on temporary staff. Unfortunate, between the two of us. They do not always understand the standards we set here.' He smiled with a certain satisfaction. 'Giorgos will not be with us after September . . .'

After opening his case in his own room, Marler walked along the corridor to Newman's. The foreign correspondent was standing with his hands on his hips, staring out of the window at the view of the distant Parthenon perched on the Acropolis.

'One up to me, I think,' Marler said pointedly as he sat in an armchair. 'Finding that Chief Inspector Partridge has trotted out here to have a look-see.'

'I'll give you that one.' Newman sounded absorbed. 'And Nick the Greek will be here shortly. I got lucky. I had his card in my wallet, the one with his home number he gave me when I was last out here.'

'What's the betting Partridge is now strolling round the island of Siros? You seem somewhat preoccupied.'

'Didn't you spot it?' Newman asked.

'Spot what?'

'One up to me. The receptionist recognized the picture I showed him of Harry because he said he'd seen it in the papers. What I want to know is how did they get that picture? He only became newsworthy when he was a smashed-up corpse at the foot of Cape Sounion.'

Giorgos slipped out of the side entrance of the Grande Bretagne, walking through the restaurant. There was no doorman on duty at this exit.

He hurried round to the far side of Syntagma Square where a row of phone boxes stood. Going inside a booth, he dialled a number and waited, tapping thin fingers on the coin box. If he was away too long that sod of a chief receptionist was going to notice his absence from duty. He spoke in Greek when a deep-throated voice answered.

'Giorgos here. I thought you should know two Englishmen have just arrived at the hotel. They are asking questions about Masterson. They have a photograph of him.'

'Another Englishman was there snooping around only two weeks ago. That man Partridge. This is getting dangerous. You have the names of these two new men?'

'No. But I can get them from the records. But only after the chief receptionist has gone off duty.'

'Get them,' the voice rasped.

'It may be late afternoon . . .'

'Get them,' the voice repeated in Greek. 'Call me the moment you have the information. And anything else about these two you can find out. We may have to take drastic action.'

Giorgos was sweating as he hurried towards the restaurant entrance door. And not only with the heat – it was in the high eighties. He was worried the chief receptionist might have sent someone looking for him to carry out some task.

He slowed down as he walked across the entrance and through the doorway leading into the main hall. A tall heavily built man in his forties, clad in a clean white short-sleeved shirt and spotless denims, was approaching the counter from the main entrance. He heard quite clearly what the new arrival said in Greek.

'A Mr Newman is expecting me. He arrived during the past hour or so. Could you tell him I am here?'

'Will do, Nick. It's getting hot early this year. He's in Room . . .'

Giorgos missed hearing the room number but made a mental note of two facts. If this was one of the men he'd phoned about then he already had a name. Newman. He fiddled with a plant in a large holder, moving it a few

58

inches. The receptionist put down the phone, said something impossible to hear, and Nick headed for the staircase.

Strolling after him, Giorgos mounted the luxuriously carpeted steps. He had earlier followed the two men after noting the floor they were making for over the lift bank, running up the staircase. He had been just in time to see Newman being shown into his room. Too far along the corridor to be sure which room. And he hadn't dared to follow Marler.

The Greek called Nick turned along a corridor, stopped at a door and knocked. The door opened and Giorgos clearly heard the voice of the man who had shown the photograph to reception welcoming him in English. He retreated back down the staircase, working out an excuse to ask the question.

'I think I know that man who just arrived, a friend of one of my cousins.' The chief receptionist stared at him. 'He did my cousin a good turn, if it's the same man.'

'What would the likes of you have to do with Nick? He drives a Mercedes. Rather out of your class. Don't waste my time. See that pile of luggage over there? Be ready to carry it to the cab when it arrives to take our guests to the airport . . .'

Marler stared straight into Nick's dark eyes as they shook hands. Firm grip. Hair, streaked with grey, cut short and trim. A strong face. A firm jaw. A hint of humour at the corners of the mouth. Marler was good at weighing up a man quickly. Formidable was the word which came to mind.

'Bob will do the talking,' he said and sat down.

'Take a seat,' suggested Newman. 'We're here about Harry Masterson who was killed down at Cape Sounion.'

'So, you think he was killed?' Nick sat down, crossed his powerful legs. 'The papers said it was an accident.'

'One thing while I remember, Nick. Officially I don't

59

speak or understand any Greek on this trip. You think it was an accident?'

'I said the papers did. They think he was drunk. I saw him drunk myself.' Nick smiled drily. 'I drove a friend to the Hilton one evening, carried her bag in for her. Beyond the entrance hall is a large seating area at several levels. A crowd was gathered, watching something. Masterson had perched himself on a rail no wider than my hand, was walking along it like a tightrope walker, a champagne bottle clutched in each hand. A fifteen-feet drop below him. He walked the full length of the rail, then jumped back on to the floor next to the rail on his left. Enough people saw his performance to recall it when the news came through from Cape Sounion a few days later.'

'And he was drunk?' Newman pressed, hardly able to believe it.

'No.' Nick smiled drily again.

'But you said he was.'

'I know enough about drink – and drunks – to recognize the real thing, and when someone is acting being drunk. Masterson was acting. Don't ask me why.'

'He was staying at the Hilton?'

'No idea.'

'And you think his death was an accident?'

'No. I watched his act at the Hilton closely. He was nimble as a goat. A big man but quick on his feet, reflexes as fast as mine. That type doesn't go stumbling over a cliff.'

Newman opened a briefcase, took out a cardboard-backed envelope, extracted three photos of Masterson. He held them while he asked the question.

'I need to know where he stayed. Do you know two men you can trust – really trust?'

'To do what, Mr Newman?'

'Take these photos round hotels in Athens and find out where he stayed. He might have used another name.'

'Yes. They use his name? No? Of course some will

60

recognize him from the pictures in the papers.' Nick was looking at a print Newman had handed him. 'I could do some of the checking myself – divide up the search. It would be quicker.'

'One thing puzzles me.' Newman handed three prints to Nick. 'I really need to find out how his picture got into the press. Doesn't make sense. No one was interested until he became very dead.'

'Yes they were.' Nick clapped his hands together. 'I've just remembered. It happened when Masterson performed his crazy walk with the champagne bottles at the Hilton.'

'What did?'

'They have a creep of a photographer who works the hotel restaurant at night. He was hanging around in the lobby while Masterson did his walk. And he had his camera equipment with him.'

'So what happened?'

'It could have caused a disaster, but Masterson had strong nerves. This stupid photographer took a picture of him with a flashbulb. Masterson wobbled, then recovered his balance and went on. There was a gasp from the people watching.'

'Stupid, as you say.'

'But that is probably where the newspapers got the picture from,' Nick continued. 'All these photographers are after extra income. He took the picture when Masterson was grinning at the crowd – and the picture in the papers was like that. Mind you,' he added grimly, 'that was the only picture he was allowed to take.'

'Somebody stopped him?'

'Yes. Several people protested. The receptionist rushed over and gave the photographer hell. Anything else I can do to help?'

'Drive us to the port of Zea, then on to Cape Sounion.'

'You have the time?' Nick asked. 'Two hours there and back. And it would be best to wait a couple of hours. The traffic.'

'A couple of hours from now then. You still have the Merc?'

'A new one. Parked outside. I'd better go check the meter.'

'Two more things, Nick. Does the name Ionides mean anything?'

'Hardly. It's a common name. I know two. Both shop-keepers. And the other thing?'

'Christina Gavalas,' Marler interjected. 'Does that name mean anything to you?'

'You are joking?' Nick was amused. Marler's expression remained blank. 'You both know Greece. Surely you have heard of Petros Gavalas?'

'You mean the legendary Resistance leader during World War Two?' Newman asked. 'I didn't make the connection.'

'Christina is his granddaughter. She hates him. The Gavalas family is a strange story. Maybe I wait until we drive to Zea and tell you then. If she is concerned in any of this you have big trouble on your hands, my friends.'

5

Leaving the room, closing the door, Nick glanced along the corridor to his right, away from the exit. A small man wearing the black clothes of one of the hotel staff stood making a fuss about closing a window.

Nick looked away quickly, made his way downstairs and out of the hotel to where his Mercedes was parked in the blazing sun. He used a finger to loosen his collar. The heat seemed even worse. Dry and like a burning glass as the sun shone out of a sky as blue as the Mediterranean.

He was polishing the bodywork, which already gleamed like glass, when the small man in black jacket and trousers strolled out of the restaurant exit and round the corner. He was smoking a cigarette as he stood admiring the Mercedes.

'That is a real car. You are taking one of the customers for a drive?'

'Who knows when business will turn up?' Nick stopped polishing and stood facing the little man, the same man who had sneaked up behind him when he first arrived and asked reception to inform Newman he had arrived. Dark eyes too close together between a thin ferret of a nose. A smear of a black moustache above full lecherous lips.

'What is your name – and why aren't you on duty inside the hotel?' Nick demanded.

'I am Giorgos. I am entitled to an afternoon break. You think it is a pleasure working in this heat?'

'Get yourself another job if you are not happy. They pay you, don't they? Now, move away from my car. I am busy even if you can fritter away the day.'

Nick turned his back on the little man, polishing the car as he watched Giorgos walking back up the hill towards the restaurant entrance. In the wing mirror he saw Giorgos pause at the corner, take out a notebook from his pocket and scribble in it before he disappeared. He had recorded the registration number of the Mercedes.

To conceal his action half an hour later, Giorgos waited behind a corner before joining a crowd of pedestrians walking over a street crossing. Nick was still working on his car.

Giorgos made his way along the top side of the square facing the pink-washed building which had once been the

63

Royal Palace. Now it was the Parliament since Greece had become a republic.

In the centre of Constitution Square is a park filled with a variety of trees and shrubs. Tall railings fence off the park from the pavement beyond. Walking rapidly in the opposite direction from the one he had previously taken, Giorgos slipped inside a phone booth. Again he dialled the same number. Again he had to wait for it to be answered.

He glanced at his watch. His off-duty period was almost over. At least the chief receptionist had gone home, the bullying bastard. The same heavy-timbred voice came on the line.

'Giorgos here. More news. I discovered the names of those two men. Newman and Marler . . .' He spelt them out. 'I think they will be going somewhere in a Mercedes with a Greek driver. The registration number of the car is . . .'

'Any sign of them leaving immediately?' the voice enquired.

'No. The driver is still cleaning the Mercedes. But they may leave at any time. A silver-coloured Mercedes.'

'I can have a car following them in ten minutes.'

'Let us hope they are in time. Oh, there is one more thing.'

'Yes?'

'This is hard work for me. Maybe a little dangerous. More money would be welcome.' Giorgos swallowed, then stiffened. 'Another twenty thousand drachmae would be welcome – if I am to continue this work.'

'Be at your place in the Plaka at nine this evening.' The connection was cut before Giorgos could say 'thank you'.

He was surprised at how easy it had been.

88°F. 31°C. They were driving down Syngrou Avenue, sitting in the back of Nick's silver Mercedes. It was early evening and the scalding sun shone out of the azure sky as clear as a sea without ships. Nick used a handkerchief to wipe sweat off the back of his hand, his forehead.

'Syngrou is the longest avenue in Athens,' he remarked. 'As you can see, it's mainly car showrooms. BMW, the lot.'

Newman glanced back again through the rear window. Marler, wearing the lightweight linen suit he'd changed into, was careful not to look back.

'Some problem?'

'I think we may be followed,' Nick replied.

'The black Mercedes with amber-tinted windows?' Newman suggested.

'That's the joker. We'll know more when we fork for Piraeus. Someone may have been on the lookout for you coming into the city.'

Ruler-straight, Syngrou Avenue, lined with dusty poplar trees, stretched away forever into the distance. Nick maintained the same speed, kept glancing briefly in his rear-view mirror.

'What facts have you to back up that statement?' Marler demanded.

'The fact that one of the temporary staff at Grande Bretagne took an interest in your arrival. Followed us up the stairs when we used the elevator. He was peering round the corner when Mr Newman was shown into his room. The fact that later when I left the room he was hanging around in the corridor, pretending to fool with a window. The fact that he came and tried to get information out of me when I was cleaning the car ready for this trip. The fact that he made a note of my car's registration number. Which may explain that big black Mercedes keeping the same speed and distance behind us now.'

'Any idea who this character might be?' asked Newman.

'Name is Giorgos. Don't know his second name. He's a small creep with a small dark moustache.' Nick made a quick stroke above his upper lip. 'Dark hair. Now, let us see what that black Mercedes does. Here we take the right fork to Piraeus. Left for Cape Sounion.'

He swung the wheel and grinned. 'Still with us. If he stays with us to Zea we shall know.'

'How far from Syntagma to Piraeus?' asked Marler.

'Ten, twelve kilometres. We are entering Piraeus now . . .'

The buildings lining the street were lower than in Athens. Nick pointed out derelict sites between them, the legacy of the wartime bombing of Piraeus. They crossed the main city square with the imposing town hall on their right built like an ancient Greek temple. Then they were swinging round the curve of the waterfront of the main harbour.

They passed large car ferries with their doors open, exposing yawning caverns. Nick slowed down. He gestured towards the vessels.

'The big ferries. They go to Crete and Corfu and Rhodes. The small one is soon sailing for Siros.'

Newman jerked his head. The name of the vessel was clearly marked on its compact stern. *Ulysses*. The last cars and trucks were edging their way up the ramp, forming three rows.

'How long to Siros?' he asked.

'Two hours.'

Marler was staring at the wall of buildings to the left facing the waterfront. Four-storey blocks, they carried names of various shipping lines, most of which he recognized. Watching him in his rear-view mirror, Nick grinned again and gesticulated.

'The headquarters of so many shipping empires. Others have registered in Panama. Some of those big men have yachts which come in to Zea. Petros Gavalas has a small yacht there – what these people would call a rowboat. And still our friends are with us.'

'That black Mercedes?' Newman enquired, careful not to look back.

'Yes. And we have made too many turns for it to be a coincidence. Let us see what he does when we turn down to Zea.'

They had left behind the big shipping company buildings. Now they were driving along a narrow street which twisted and turned, following the indentations of the coastline. On the landward side were small old apartment blocks. Freshly painted, they had pots and tubs holding decorative shrubs standing on their balconies.

'It would cost you a fortune to live at Zea,' Nick said. 'Only the very rich have an apartment here . . .'

Staring ahead beyond the windscreen Newman saw a signpost to the right as Nick slowed to a crawl. *Zeas Port*. He turned down a sloping track leading to the sea and along a platform below a high stone wall. The small harbour was crammed with ships moored hull to hull – and each worth hundreds of millions of drachmae. The million-dollar class.

Nick drove along the jetty which curved round the exclusive harbour, protecting it from the sea. Executing a three-point turn, he pointed the car the way they had come. He was parked by the stern of a small yacht, *Venus III*. Jumping out, he opened the rear door.

'This is Gavalas' yacht,' he remarked. 'A very small fish.'

'How could he afford even this?' Newman asked.

'He buys cheap. During the oil crisis he buys it for one tenth of its value from a man who needs cash. Petros is cunning.'

'What happened to the black Mercedes?' Marler enquired, standing by Newman on the jetty.

'It stopped by one of the apartments on the hill, one man got out, carrying a violin case. Then it drove off.'

'Odd that,' Marler observed and lit a cigarette.

'Please?' Nick was puzzled. 'I do not understand.'

'The car follows us from Syntagma. He has no way of

knowing where we are going. We arrive here and they drop off one man at an apartment. Some coincidence.'

Newman was running up a flight of steps to a narrow ledge beneath the wall which was now waist-high. The view out over the harbour hit him. The emerald sea, very calm, sparkled with dazzling reflections from the sun. On the far side and further out a fleet of freighters waited, stationary, bows pointed towards the harbour, smoke drifting lazily from their stacks.

'For Christ's sake come down,' Marler called out.

Newman turned, leant his arms on the wall. It was so hot he could barely stand the heat. He stood looking down at the assembled craft. From one of the photographs taken by Masterson this was where he had stood when he took them. On the jetty just about the point where Marler waited.

He recognized the huddle of old apartment blocks, the hills rising behind, bare, mushroom-coloured, flecked with scrub. There had to be something here which would give a clue as to why Masterson had come to Zea. He walked down the steps and spoke to Nick, who was polishing the bonnet of the car.

'There's a whole queue of big ships, mostly freighters, waiting to come in.'

'The cargo docks on the other side,' Nick explained. 'They will be waiting for the signal from Marine Control to berth.'

Newman frowned as he saw Marler staring up at the bridge of the *Venus III*. He followed his gaze and sucked in his breath. Standing by the side of the bridge was a girl with a mane of black glossy hair, centre-parted. She had good bone structure and wore a polka-dot white dress with a thin belt hugging her slim waist. She held her right hand over her thick eyebrows, shielding herself against the sun. It was the girl in the photo Masterson had taken unawares.

Marler stared back with a dry smile. Then he raised his own hand and gave her a mocking little wave. Her mouth twitched. She waved back, then vanished. Nick also stood staring at where she had appeared, the cloth poised above the bonnet.

'Christina Gavalas,' he said in a low voice. 'That is very strange.'

'I want to have a word with her,' Newman said grimly.

A gangplank linked the vessel's stern with the jetty. Newman approached it, followed by Marler at a more leisurely pace. His movements were always slow and deliberate. Except in an emergency.

Newman reached the gangplank when three seamen came round the corner of the deck. They wore white sleeveless sweat shirts, blue pants. In their late twenties they were heavily built and two carried marlinspikes. One of them shouted at Newman in Greek, brandishing his marlinspike.

'What did he say?' Newman asked Nick, although he'd understood every word.

Nick laid a warning hand on Newman's arm. 'He says you are not allowed aboard. This is private property.'

'Tell him to get stuffed. I only wanted to invite the girl to join me for a drink.'

'I think we had better leave,' Nick warned again. He called out in Greek. 'We are just leaving. My passengers were admiring your beautiful boat.'

The Greek waved his marlinspike and the three crewmen walked out of sight. Marler was staring beyond the boats up at the apartment buildings above the small harbour. He saw the sun reflect off something, like one flash of a semaphore.

'Get into the car quick!' he ordered Newman. 'No bloody argument.' He pulled open the rear door and dived inside as Newman joined him. 'Nick,' Marler continued, 'move us out of here fast.'

Nick reacted instantly. For a large man he moved with surprising agility. He was behind the wheel when the shriek of several ships' sirens blasted over the wall. As the noise continued Nick started the engine. There was a heavy *thud*. At the same moment they heard a crackle of glass splintering behind them. The bullet passed between the heads of Marler and Newman, passed on through the open window of the front passenger seat beside Nick.

6

Nick accelerated along the narrow platform, braked, turned up the track leading to the main road. He glanced in the rear-view mirror. Newman and Marler both had their heads turned. The rear window had crazed, had a small hole in it.

'He fired from the top of one of those apartment buildings,' Marler remarked.

'We go up there, yes?' Nick enquired. 'We find the bastard before he can get away?'

'No!' replied Newman. 'Turn left. Head back for the town hall square. Find us somewhere we can talk. And somewhere you can hide the car.'

'I know a bar. Close to it is a bombed site. They will not find the car if I park there.'

'Do it,' said Newman. He turned to Marler. 'Is that why you tried to get me down off the wall?'

'Of course, my dear chap.' Marler was as calm as though he'd experienced an everyday happening. He adjusted the display handkerchief in his breast pocket. 'You normally catch on quicker. You had an absorbed look when you ran up those steps. Stood on that ledge like a target in a shooting gallery. Is it the heat, by any chance?'

His tone was mocking. He reached into his pocket and perched a pair of horn-rimmed glasses on his nose. 'They have seen me once. I don't think they'll recognize me so easily next time.'

'Those glasses make you look exactly like Michael Caine.'

'Flattery will get you nowhere. The lenses are plain glass.'

'You were expecting that shot?'

'Something like it. The black Mercedes follows us. Nick reports they drop one man carrying a violin case, then drive off. A violin case! Not much imagination there. Did they strike you as musical characters? A violin case,' he repeated. 'Just the thing for carrying a dismantled Armalite rifle. You are only alive because he had to assemble his weapon before he used it. I saw the sun flashing off his telescopic sight – which is when I told you to dive into the car. He was a better shot than I'd hoped. Very smart, too.'

'Why do you say that?' Nick asked.

'He had a bit of luck and used it. Those ships' sirens starting up muffled the sound of the shot.'

'They made one huge mistake though,' Newman said.

'Which was?' Marler enquired.

'Firing that shot, of course. Now we *know* someone murdered Harry Masterson.'

The bar was small, located up a side street, was furnished with plastic-topped tables, a plastic-topped counter. Only the floor had a hint of luxury. It was laid from wall to wall with solid marble. Nick had ordered *ouzo* for everyone. Newman asked for a large bottle of mineral water.

'We can't afford to risk dehydration,' he remarked, wiping the back of his neck with a silk handkerchief. 'First things first. That bullet-hole in the rear window of your car could be embarrassing for all of us. Can anything be done about it?'

'You don't want to report the attack to the police?' Nick asked, his broad tanned arms resting on the table-top.

'They could complicate life at this stage. Unless you insist?'

'I have many friends.' Nick drank half his glass of *ouzo*. 'I know a garage mechanic who will fix that overnight. A new window. No questions asked. OK?'

'OK,' agreed Newman. 'I pay the bill, of course. Next – when Christina Gavalas appeared on the deck of *Venus III* you said, "That is very strange." Why?'

Nick paused, refilled their glasses from the jug of *ouzo*. 'It is a bit . . . complex. Is that the word?'

'Tell me, then I'll know.'

'Petros is eighty years old, a ferocious tyrant. Pray you do not meet him. Born in 1907, he married when he was seventeen. His first wife produced two sons – Andreas and Stephen. Twins, but not identical. Andreas and Stephen also married when very young – only eighteen. It was the war in their cases, I suppose. That was in 1943 or 1944. After Andreas was killed on Siros his wife gave birth to Christina – Petros' granddaughter. Do you understand so far?'

'Perfectly,' said Newman. 'Go on.'

'At that time Petros fought with the Communists – the ELAS party. Andreas hated them. He escaped to Cairo, joined the anti-Communist party, EDES. Petros was furious. Called him a traitor. But blood is thicker than water. Petros had a grudging admiration for Andreas. When Andreas was killed in the Siros raid he swore to hunt down his killer. Then came the second tragedy.'

'Which was?'

'The other twin, Stephen, also hated his father and fled to Cairo to join the EDES forces. Then he, too, was

72

murdered. Later *his* wife gave birth also to twins, Dimitrios and Constantine. Again, non-identical. But the strain had run out. They are peasants working on Petros' farm in Devil's Valley.'

'A whole lot of hatred,' Marler observed.

'It gets worse. After the end of the Civil War in Greece between EDES and ELAS – which nearly wrecked my country – in 1950 Petros married again when his first wife died. His second wife produced a son, Anton. Maybe because Petros was then forty-two and his new wife was twenty-eight Anton turned out to be very clever. You see the scope for bitterness in that family?'

'How did Christina react?' Marler asked.

'A magnificent woman now, she is torn between two moods. Greek loyalty to the family – and her detesting Petros who treated her badly. As I told you, it is complex. But that is why I thought it strange to see her on *Venus III*. Petros only keeps the boat so he can watch those millionaires – wait for another to become in desperate need of money. Then maybe he picks up yet another bargain. He owns farms. One near Cape Sounion.'

'So he is rich?' Newman pressed. 'What kind of farms?'

'The one in Devil's Valley is in a remote part of the interior of the peninsula between Athens and Sounion. A dangerous area to explore. He grows figs and olives. His headquarters is an old farmhouse in wild country – reached by a track off the main highway to Sounion. There are even rumours he has a working silver mine. That I don't know about – whether it is working.'

'Let me get this clear,' intervened Marler. 'Petros was a one-time Communist. His son, Andreas, was killed on Siros. OK so far?'

'OK,' Nick agreed.

'And,' Newman suggested, 'this fierce old Petros is a Communist although he's rich?'

'Not any more from what I hear. Petros was sickened of

politics by the Civil War. It lasted from 1946 to 1949. A lot of blood was spilt. At the end of it Petros said all politicians could burn in hell. He devoted himself to farming, making money, but he has never forgotten the murder of his sons.'

'How and where was Stephen killed?' Newman asked.

'The rumour is it happened in a street brawl in a native quarter in Alexandria. There are other versions.'

'And Christina wavers between supporting Petros and hating him?'

'So it is told in Athens.'

Marler grunted. 'The only fact that comes out of all this is that Petros – and Christina – could still feel bitter about Andreas' death on Siros. After all, Andreas was her father.'

'That is what I have heard,' Nick agreed. 'And now maybe we should drive back to Athens so I can have the window repaired.' He finished off his *ouzo*, glanced at Newman. 'We forget about Cape Sounion – after what happened at Zea? For today?'

'Back to Athens. Another day we could visit this Petros? I'd like to ask him some questions.'

Nick grinned. 'You have brought some good weapons with you?'

'No. Nothing.'

'You go in Devil's Valley, you go armed. All Petros' men have guns. I said it before. A very dangerous place. You want to come out alive. Back to Athens . . .'

Newman saw the diesel train perched up on an embankment as it headed into Piraeus. He caught glimpses of it between buildings as they left the harbour behind.

'That's the Metro line, is it, Nick?'

'Yes. It starts at the other side of the city. The last stop this way is Piraeus.'

Newman looked at Marler. 'Endstation?'

'Who knows?' Marler adjusted his horn-rimmed glasses, perched his head back and closed his eyes.

Newman stared out of the window as a motorcyclist drew level. The rider, wearing a crash helmet and tinted goggles, turned and stared straight into the car for a few seconds. Then the machine was gone, zooming ahead of them, weaving in and out along the traffic.

'If you don't mind,' Nick suggested as they turned on to Syngrou Avenue, 'I will drop you close to Syntagma Square. That window is conspicuous. I want to get the car inside the garage before a policeman sees it. Then I have another job. I wish to have a word with Giorgos. He will tell me who it is he is working for – who followed us in that black Mercedes.'

'He may not feel like telling you,' Marler suggested.

'I have my own methods of persuasion. I will get his home address from reception. Oh, while I was waiting to take you to Piraeus I contacted my two helpers. Each has a photograph of Masterson. They must have checked with twenty hotels by now. Soon we will know where Mr Masterson stayed. May I drop you here? Only a five-minute walk to Grande Bretagne.'

'That's fine.' Newman had taken out his wallet. 'Time I paid you – for the trip, the repair to the window, and fees for your helpers.'

'Later.' Nick jumped out of the car, opened the rear door. 'You are well organized. Changing your traveller's cheques so quickly.'

He was referring to the regulations which only allow any tourist to bring in three thousand drachmae. Newman had changed cheques for a large sum at the hotel. As they stood on the pavement, the heat still hammering them, he laid a hand on Nick's arm.

'We would like to be there when you question this Giorgos. I have a few questions to put to him myself.'

75

'Late in the evening would be best. He will be relaxed and not expecting a hard time. I call for you at ten o'clock? If I find the time is wrong, I call your room?'

'Ten o'clock. See you then.'

They strolled along the street as Nick drove away. A park stretched away beyond iron railings to their right. Kiosks selling newspapers stood by the railings. People were queuing to buy plastic bottles of mineral water.

A motorcyclist cruised past. Newman frowned, watched the rider sliding in between the slow-moving traffic. The machine disappeared, heading for Syntagma Square.

Arriving at the main entrance to the Grande Bretagne, Newman handed Marler his room key. 'Wait upstairs in my room. I'll be right with you . . .'

Newman followed Marler inside, paused, waited for a brief time, then pushed open the door and peered out into the square. Full of traffic. He scanned the area rapidly. He found what he was looking for further down the hill.

The motorcyclist had parked the machine by a meter, still sat astride it. The same motorcyclist with the orange-coloured crash helmet and tinted glasses who had passed them in Piraeus. Who had later skilfully guided the machine between cars when they were walking.

The rider removed the crash helmet, perched it between the handlebars. She reached up with both hands and draped her waterfall of black glossy hair over her shoulders. Christina Gavalas had arrived. Things were warming up, and not only the temperature. Newman closed the door, went up to his room.

Ten o'clock. On the dot. Nick led the way to his parked car. It had a new rear window. Newman and Marler had dined in the oak-panelled restaurant. It was still daylight as they sat in the back and the Mercedes took off down the hill which was almost traffic-free.

'He lives in the Plaka, this Giorgos,' Nick informed them. 'That is the old quarter of Athens. It spreads out at the foot of the Acropolis, climbs part of the way up the hill.'

'I know,' said Newman. 'Any news about where Masterson stayed?'

'No. It is strange. My helpers have checked all the main hotels. No luck. He must have stayed somewhere. Would he choose some cheap place?'

'Not our Harry,' Newman said positively. 'He liked a bit of luxury. Live high was his motto. Maybe the hotels don't like giving out information about their guests?'

'My helpers are clever. They take round an expensive wristwatch. Say they found it with a credit card in his name. They want to give it back. And they don't read the papers, so they don't know he's dead. They get a reply. No, he didn't stay with us.'

Dusk was falling. The sun had slid down behind the Acropolis. Nick had entered a maze of narrow, twisting streets. There was little space to spare if he met a vehicle coming the other way. Through the open window Newman heard the mournful strains of the *bouzouki* from the open doors of small restaurants and cafés. Sometimes it was Western pop music. Every second door seemed to lead to an eating place. The pavements were crowded with sightseers and customers.

Nick drove into a small square with a muddle of buildings on three sides. The fourth side was open to a large level area littered with stones. The Parthenon Temple, perched on the Acropolis, was an ancient silhouette against the darkening sky.

'Monastiraki Square,' Nick announced. 'We park here and walk back to Giorgos' place. That way we surprise him. And parking is difficult.'

'Damn near impossible,' commented Marler.

Nick led them a short distance along a narrow street,

77

then he turned up a wide paved alley sloping like a ramp, lined with more eating places, more *bouzouki*. Newman and Marler strolled behind him and suddenly he stopped, held up a hand.

'Something is going on. Look at the crowd. We must be careful.'

'Where does he live?' Newman asked.

'Down that alley to the right. You see that car?'

The police vehicle was empty, parked half on the worn stone pavement. The crowd filled the street, was stationary, was staring down the alley Nick had indicated. They joined the crowd. Newman drew back, mounted the two steps at the entrance to a restaurant to see over the heads. He sucked in his breath.

A macabre sight. Beneath an old metal wall lantern attached to the side of the alley stood a large wine barrel. From the top projected two legs, bent at the knees. The legs were clad in black trousers, which had concertinaed, exposing tanned skin.

'What is it?' Marler asked, perching beside Newman.

'Look for yourself . . .'

Uniformed police swirled in the narrow confines of the alley. Several formed a cordon, holding back the crowd. Two stood on either side of the barrel. As Newman and Marler watched they took hold of the legs, slowly hauled up the rest of the body. Black hair dangled from the upended head.

Nick came close to Newman, whispered, 'I'll get in there. I know a couple of those police. Back in a minute . . .'

As he shouldered his way through the crowd the two policemen laid the body on the stone cobbles carefully, face up. Nick spoke to one of the police in the cordon, was let through, walked up the alley, which was a flight of steps, stopping beside the barrel.

'Looked a trifle queasy,' Marler remarked, and lit a cigarette. 'Did you notice?'

'The body's hair? Lank and dripping. Some liquid dripped off the shoulders when they hauled it out.'

'And since it is a wine barrel one might assume that's what it contains. Wine.'

After a few minutes Nick shook hands with both policemen and pushed his way back through the crowd. He used a handkerchief to wipe sweat off his head as he stood close to them.

'It's Giorgos. He didn't die too easily. They reckon he was grabbed, upended and lowered into that barrel. It is more than half full of wine. They drowned him in it. Held him with his legs kicking, I suppose. Held him upside down until he stopped struggling. Drowned. Then left him like that – legs crooked over the barrel's rim. Someone decided to make an example of him. To keep your mouth shut.'

'They certainly made their point,' Marler observed coolly.

'Let's get out of here,' said Newman.

He felt sick as they made their way back to the car. The shops were still open, shops selling a load of junk as far as Newman could see. Wicker baskets, leather bags, sponges. The shops were crammed between the tavernas. The *bouzouki* music had become louder, reminded Newman of a funeral march. The crowds were denser. Suddenly the Plaka had become a nightmare.

'Back to the hotel, Nick,' he said as they sank into the car. 'Back to civilization and peace.'

Peace was the last thing they found when they returned to the Grande Bretagne.

7

Marler and Nick stood in the corridor while Newman unlocked his door and walked into the room. They followed and Newman stood stock still, his expression grim.

Two men in civilian clothes were searching the room, checking inside drawers, examining the wardrobe. A third man, also in civilian clothes, sat smoking a cigarette. Hawk-nosed, in his thirties, dark-haired, thin and long-legged, his old friend, Chief Inspector Peter Sarris of Homicide, regarded him with no particular expression. He made no attempt to get up, to shake hands. Bad sign.

'May I ask what the hell is going on?' Newman demanded.

'You will all sit down in separate chairs. Not on the couch. No one will speak unless I ask him a question. This is a murder investigation. What is going on?' he continued in the same level tone. 'Surely it is obvious, Bob? We are searching your room. Before you ask, I have a warrant.'

'Best do as His Lordship says,' Newman told his companions.

'No need for sarcasm,' Sarris continued in perfect English.

'I'd have thought there was every need. You expect me to like this? And tell those goons of yours I expect them to replace everything exactly as they find it.'

'Be careful to leave everything neat – the way you find it,' Sarris said in Greek to the two searchers, then switched back to English.

'Only you are permitted to speak, Bob. Where have you just returned from?'

'You know the answer to that question. The Plaka.'

'And how would I know that?' enquired Sarris.

'Because the Volvo police car parked near the alley where Giorgos' body was found had a radio. One of the policemen was staring at me. I'm sure he recognized me. My picture has been in enough newspapers in the past. And my guess is Giorgos had something on him which showed he worked for the Grande Bretagne. One of the uniformed police radioed in to headquarters, reported to you . . .'

'That's enough,' Sarris said quickly. 'I know you are a top foreign correspondent, but you'd have made a good detective.'

'. . . and this is Marler, my assistant, learning his trade . . .' Newman was talking rapidly before he could be stopped. 'My driver Nick I have used on previous visits . . .'

'I said shut up . . .'

'. . . and this afternoon we used him to take us on a peaceful tour round Piraeus and the port of Zea . . .'

'*I said shut up!*' Sarris, livid, was on his feet. He gave the instructions rapidly in Greek to the searchers. 'One of you take the Englishman there to his room. This Greek, Nick, is to be taken immediately to a police car and held at headquarters.' As his men moved, he stood over Newman. 'I have one more word out of you and you will find yourself inside a police cell.'

'On what charge?' Newman enquired amiably.

'Suspicion of accessory to a murder . . .'

'Which one? Harry Masterson's?'

Newman shot out the words as Marler and Nick were bundled out of the room. In time for both to hear what he said. Sarris waited until the door closed and then offered Newman a cigarette, took one himself and sagged back into the same chair.

'Did you have to do that?'

'Do what? I thought you wanted information.'

'You're a bastard.' Sarris spoke in a resigned tone. 'But a clever bastard. When you've finished your cigarette you will have to come to police headquarters.'

'Why waste time? Let's get on with it . . .'

Outside the hotel Sarris was in time to stop Nick being taken away in a police car. 'Where is your own vehicle?' he asked.

'Parked down the hill. The silver Mercedes . . .'

'You will drive it to police headquarters. One of my men will accompany you.'

Sarris drove Newman by himself in an unmarked police car. He began chatting amiably as soon as they drew away from the kerb.

'I have to do this, I'm afraid, Bob. How long is it since you were last here?'

'Two, three years. I'm not sure,' Newman replied vaguely.

'I can see you are going to be difficult to interrogate. Maybe one of your companions will be more forthcoming. You will all be interrogated separately . . .'

'Bully for you . . .'

'A little cooperation would help all round.'

'Not after you searched my room without waiting for me.'

'We have a new police headquarters. Very modern. All the latest equipment.'

'Bully for you . . .'

'It's on Alexandras Avenue. Built about a year ago.'

'You make it sound like the bloody Hilton.'

'There are some similarities. Although not with the Athens Hilton. One of the places your hired snoopers visited when asking where Harry Masterson stayed.'

'Keep talking . . .'

Sarris gave up. Skilfully he drove through the night. Headlights appeared, flashed past them. They were on Alexandras now. Close to the football stadium on the opposite side a small colossus of a building faced with white marble loomed. A very modern rectangular block twelve storeys high it soared up towards the night sky above a vast entrance hall. No premium on space for government buildings in Athens, Newman thought as he followed Sarris inside.

To the left was a reception counter. A uniformed policeman hastily donned his peaked cap. Sarris led Newman to an inner lobby with a bank of four lifts on the right-hand side. His office on the eighth floor overlooked Alexandras. Sarris used an intercom to order coffee.

'Now,' he said, facing the seated Newman across his desk, 'may we start at the beginning?'

'We arrived in Athens . . .'

4 a.m. Sarris in his crumpled shirt-sleeves was showing signs of strain. The ash tray was crammed with his cigarette stubs. Only one of them belonged to Newman.

'So,' Sarris summed up, 'it comes to this. You came here to investigate the accidental death of Harry Masterson, sensing a story. Marler came to learn the ropes, despite his being described on his passport as an insurance executive?'

'I told you. He's fed up with that job. He wants a more adventurous life.'

'The murdered man, Giorgos, took an interest as soon as you arrived at the Grande Bretagne. He saw the photograph you showed the receptionist. Later, he tried to get information from your driver, Nick. You thought he could be a lead. So Nick found out where he lived from reception. You went there with your two companions to question him. You were too late?'

'End of story.'

'Bob, you really should have been a barrister. You so neatly make all the facts fit what I know . . .'

'Presumably because they do fit.' Newman drank more coffee. His fifth cup. 'Haven't we just about covered everything – except for what happened to Harry Masterson? An accident, you said.'

'I gave you the official explanation at the moment. He was murdered.'

Newman, cup raised, stared at the Greek. For the first time since the interrogation had begun he was taken aback.

'You change your mind quickly, Peter.'

Sarris stood up, wearily stretched himself, then leaned over the desk, spread both hands flat and stared straight back. His tone changed, became grim, almost spitting out the words.

'You think I have lost my touch? Homicide is my profession, my business. I'm supposed to be able to recognize murder when I see it. You think I park my backside here all day? Let me tell you something. I've visited Cape Sounion. No one with the savvy Masterson had staggers round above that cliff and walks over it. And I met Masterson by chance.'

'When? Where?'

'That night at the Hilton when he pretended to be high as a kite, did his death-defying walk along the rail beyond the entrance hall. I was attending a party. When I walked into the Hilton Masterson was just beginning that charade. I watched him. I tackled him afterwards, asked him what the hell he thought he was doing. Drunk? He was more sober than I am now after all that coffee. I talked with him for maybe ten minutes. He was able, tough, alert and street-wise. And he had the women in the palm of his hand.'

'Women? Any particular woman that night?'

84

'Christina Gavalas couldn't get enough of him. More coffee? You look shaken . . .'

A few minutes later. Sarris stood by the window, had opened the blinds. The first light, the false dawn, was casting a glow over the dead city. The peak of Mount Lycabettus was a massive silhouette in the distance.

'Why?' Newman asked. 'Why the official line that it was an accident?'

'The tourist industry is sacred to Greece, the billions of foreign currency it brings in, a commodity we're a little short of . . .'

'Oh Christ! Not the *Jaws* syndrome again?'

'*Jaws*?'

'The film about a shark off a resort island in America. The mayor didn't want to know about any sharks. Again, it might have frightened the tourists away.'

'Ah, yes, I remember. I see what you mean. Yes, there is a similarity. Murder – especially of an Englishman – would be bad publicity. The British come here like lemmings.'

'So you buried the case?' Newman said bitterly.

'You will apologize for that insult.' Sarris left the window, stormed back to his desk and sat upright in his chair. 'The case is not closed for me. No mealy-mouthed politician gives orders here . . .'

'You have your apology. Unreservedly.'

'It is early in the morning.' Sarris made a resigned gesture. 'We are both fully stretched. But maybe now you understand why I hauled you in? Informers – more than one – had told me men were going round the hotels showing Masterson's photo, asking where he had stayed. I had one in that chair, accused him of being an accessory to murder. He told me Nick was his employer. I phone the Grande Bretagne. They tell me you are the one who hired Nick.

Then I get another call from my men in the Plaka, investigating a particularly brutal murder – and he tells me he has recognized you. Now, do you think I do my job?'

'OK, Peter. You move fast. I'll give you that. Ever heard of Petros Gavalas?'

'Why?'

'I did my homework back in London before I came out. You're not the only one who does his job properly.'

'And you found the wolf has his lair north of Cape Sounion – where Masterson was killed?' Sarris had walked over to a filing cabinet. Unlocking it, he sifted through several files, extracted a glossy print from one, laid it on the desk before Newman. 'Petros.'

Newman stared at the print. He had rarely seen a picture which made such impact. A head-and-shoulders photo, the subject gazing away from the camera. An aged, ageless man. Like a prophet from the Old Testament. A great crooked beak of a nose, the eyes large and glowing under thick eyebrows, the face long, terminating in a heavy jaw. A bushy moustache above a thin wide mouth, the lips clamped tight.

'He didn't know his picture was being taken?'

'No,' Sarris admitted. 'We used a telephoto lens from inside an unmarked police van.'

'So he has a track record?'

'No, he hasn't.' Sarris pulled his shirt away from under his left armpit. Despite the open windows beyond the blinds, and a fan whirling overhead, the room was like an oven. The big heat was building up.

'Then why do you have his picture?'

'We think he could be trouble. One day. He has many hectares on his big farm in the wilderness. He rules it like a private kingdom – fief? Is that the word? I thought so. Armed men on horses patrol this kingdom to keep out intruders. They say they carry guns for shooting vermin – birds which feed on the figs. He hates what he calls the

English. Holds them responsible for the death of his son, Andreas, on Siros. An explosive situation.'

'And his granddaughter, Christina, was with Masterson?'

'That night at the Hilton? Yes. I don't know why. Maybe she just fancied him. She is a very beautiful woman. And now, perhaps you should go home with the others.'

Sarris took the photo, put it back in its file, relocked the cabinet. He poured more coffee from a fresh pot brought in by a girl.

'If you believe Masterson was murdered isn't there something you can do about it?'

'What?' Sarris spread his hands. 'I have no evidence. No one saw him at Sounion. The pathologist isn't much help.'

'But what did he say?'

'What I said. He has no evidence. When the coastguard cutter took his body off the rocks at the base of the Cape it was a wreck of smashed bone – smashed almost to a pulp the pathologist told me – showed me. Not a pretty sight. He only had one conclusion. The way the body hit the rocks the stomach was intact – plus its contents. No trace of alcohol. Only mineral water.'

'Time for me to push off.' Newman stood up. 'The others are coming with me?'

'Yes.' Sarris smiled drily. 'Their stories fit what you've told me. You can all go home. Maybe you and Marler should really go home – back to London?'

'You're deporting us?' enquired Newman as he opened the door.

'Wish I could.' Sarris grinned, slapped Newman on the shoulder. 'Take care of yourself. Greece could be bad for your health . . .'

Nick drove his Mercedes along Alexandras as streaks of the real dawn painted the sky with vivid slashes of red and

87

gold. Above a band of black receding night was a curve of pure cerulean, intense as a blue flame, warning that another scorching day was coming.

'Take us somewhere very quiet and lonely, Nick,' said Newman. 'Somewhere we can talk without interruption.'

'Lycabettus,' Nick responded. 'Very high, very lonely – at this hour . . .'

He swung off Alexandras. Soon they were climbing steeply up a road spiralling round the lower slopes of Mount Lycabettus. They drove higher and higher. And as they climbed, below them Athens receded, the view expanded. Newman gazed out of the window. Already the panorama was awe-inspiring. They went on climbing, Nick turning the wheel all the time, negotiating the large car round diabolical hairpin bends, blowing his horn in case a vehicle was coming down. They met no one by the time he stopped at the edge of a precipitous curve.

'End of the road,' Nick said, alighting quickly to open the door, but Newman beat him to it, stepping out and taking a deep breath of fresh clear air. Marler stood on one side, Nick on the other.

'How did you get on, Nick – with their questions?' Newman asked.

'I told the truth.' Nick grinned. 'Some of it. I told them you hired me when you were last here. That explained how you knew me. I told them I drove you to Piraeus to show you the sea, that we looked at the boats at Zea and then drove back. Thank God I had the rear window repaired. It would have been difficult to explain the bullet-hole.'

'I thought of that. Go on.'

'I told them you gave me pictures of Masterson to find out where he'd stayed. That reference you made to him just before we left your room tipped me off I could talk about that. I told them Giorgos was taking too close an interest in our activities, that you wanted to ask him why. So I obtained his address in the Plaka from one of the

88

assistant receptionists – by saying I owed him some money. When we got there we found he was dead. I kept it simple.'

'Which linked up beautifully with what I told Sarris. How did you cope, Marler?'

'I coped. Much the same story Nick told. Kept it simple. I only answered what I was asked. No elaborations. I must say I didn't care too much for your description of me as your assistant.'

'You'll get used to it.' He stared down. 'God, what a view.'

The huge eye of the sun was already glaring down on Athens. A city of white buildings crammed cheek by jowl, spreading out towards the horizon, merging with Piraeus, once a separate port. From that height the immensity of the capital showed dramatically.

In the far distance Newman could pick out a shoehorn-shaped bowl which was the new stadium they had passed on their way into Piraeus. Beyond, the Mediterranean was already a shimmer of hazy blue. It was the sheer *density* of the city of three million inhabitants which astounded Newman.

'Where the devil is the Acropolis?' Marler asked.

'I show you . . .'

Nick ran back to the car, returned with binoculars, focused them. He pointed below into the middle of the endless congestion. 'There. Perched up with the Parthenon on top.'

'Incredible.' Marler gazed at the ancient temple through the glasses as Nick went on talking.

'Most people who first come to Athens think the highest point is the Acropolis. But Mount Lycabettus towers like an old volcano far above anything else. And we are not at the top.'

Newman looked up to where Nick pointed. The mountain soared up further. Perched on its summit was a church with a brown-coloured dome.

'The Church of St George,' Nick explained. 'You can reach it by the funicular at the top of Kolonaki.'

'Kolonaki? I remember that from when I was here before. District for the people with big money?' Marler remarked, handing back the glasses.

'Christina Gavalas has an apartment in Kolonaki,' said Nick.

'The key is somewhere down there,' Newman reflected, gazing down at the vast sprawl. 'The key to who killed Masterson.'

Nick drove them back down another equally hair-raising spiral road into the city. The streets were still quiet. Outside a few shops women were spraying water on the pavements with hosepipes. As soon as their backs were turned the water shrank into damp patches, then evaporated.

'Another hot day coming up,' Nick commented. 'So we all sweat again. Grande Bretagne?'

'You can sweat,' Newman said. 'I'm going to sleep.'

They approached Syntagma Square along Sofias Avenue, a street which Newman remembered ran straight from the Hilton to the square. They would visit the Hilton later.

Nick was stopped by red lights at the entrance to Syntagma and Newman leaned forward, staring through the windscreen. Nick nodded.

'It is the same car . . .'

'With the same registration number . . .'

The black Mercedes with amber-tinted windows was parked across the street from the main entrance to the Grande Bretagne. Behind the tinted glass Newman could see two men sitting in front, two more in the rear seats. Nick parked at the foot of the steps leading up to the hotel. Newman got out slowly, stood upright, stared at the car.

One of the front windows lowered slowly, moved by

90

automatic control. A head leaned forward, looking direct across the street at Newman. He stood quite still, hands in his jacket pockets.

In real life he looked even more like an Old Testament prophet than in the photo Sarris had showed him. Aged and ageless. The curved beak of the cruel nose. The eyes intense beneath the bushy brows, the craggy forehead. Their eyes clashed over the width of the street. Newman sensed a look of pure hatred, venomous. The window closed slowly, shutting out the gaze of Petros Gavalas. The black Mercedes slid away from the kerb and was gone.

8

Petros Gavalas sat beside the driver, his grandson, in silence as the Mercedes headed down Syngrou Avenue. A very big man, he had pushed his seat back to its fullest extent to give comfortable leg room – so far back that the henchman sitting behind him had cramped knees. As they approached the point where the avenue forked, he spoke in his gravelly voice.

'Dimitrios, take the turn-off to Piraeus.'

'I thought we were returning to the farm . . .'

'Later. I have phone calls to make from the apartment at Zea. You are a fool,' he continued. 'I told you to shoot the driver of their car – to discourage Greeks from helping the English. You missed.'

'But we did not miss with Giorgos,' Dimitrios replied as he turned down the right fork. He chuckled unpleasantly. 'That one had his fill of wine forever.'

'People should not ask for more money than has been agreed. And he was a Greek. He should have known better. He knows now.'

'We are going to kill those two Englishmen?' Dimitrios asked.

'Not yet, cretin.' Petros shifted his bulk: the heat was making him irritable. 'I have already given orders. They will be followed night and day. Let us first see what they are up to. They had better not come near the farm. And they would be most unwise to start asking questions about Andreas. I trust for their sakes they do not go anywhere near Siros.'

'Does it matter? If they do go to Siros?'

It was the wrong thing to say. Petros hit Dimitrios on the arm. He almost swerved off the road. Petros swore at him, turned to glare at his grandson.

'Any English who goes near Siros could be involved in the great betrayal over forty years ago on Siros. Someone will pay for that. With his life . . .'

Marler ran a bath as soon as he entered his room. He stripped off, donned a robe, waited for the bath to fill. He ached in every limb. They'd sat him in a hard-backed chair for the interrogation. Standard procedure . . .

The gentle tapping on the outer locked door startled him. All his mental alarm bells began ringing. He picked up the ebony-backed hairbrush he always packed, held it in his right hand. He opened the door suddenly, leaning against the side wall.

A woman stood in the opening, a woman with a mane of dark glossy hair, a woman in her early forties, a woman clad in tight denims emphasizing her long slim legs and a white blouse unbuttoned at the neck, which exposed the upper half of her full firm breasts. Christina Gavalas.

'Aren't you going to invite me in, Mr Marler?' she

enquired with a slow smile. 'People may talk if they see us standing here together.'

'All right, come in. If you must.'

'Such a warm welcome,' she commented as he closed and locked the door. 'I thought it was time we talked.' She eyed the bed. 'I am a little tired. I don't mind where we talk.'

'That makes two of us.'

Marler stood with his hands on his hips, his mind racing as she unlooped her shoulder bag, dropped it on the dressing table. She reached for the hairbrush he was holding. 'May I? I look a mess.'

She stood in front of the mirror, brushing her hair vigorously, watching him in the mirror. Putting the brush down, she turned, put her arms round his shoulders, clasped her hands behind his neck and kissed him on the mouth, pressing her strong body into his.

'To what do I owe this honour?' Marler enquired as she pulled her head away from his, still grasping his neck. He watched her greenish eyes, his expression bleak and showing no excitement. She arched her thick eyebrows, half-closed her eyes, presenting to him her open front. Marler remained still, without reacting. Let her make the running. Her right hand slid inside his robe, felt his naked chest, moved down.

'I took a fancy to you when I saw you at Zea. I thought that you'd taken a fancy to me. You did wave.'

Her English was perfect. Her technique for rousing a man was good. The roving hand took its time. She gave him her slow smile again. Then she removed the hand, used it to take off her earrings, tossing them on to the dressing table.

'We won't be needing those, will we?'

'If you say so.'

'The cool calm Englishman. I love them . . .'

Standing away from him, still facing him, she undid her

blouse, threw it on the floor. She wore nothing underneath it. She watched for the effect she was creating as she undid her denims, slid them down her legs, threw them on top of the blouse. She kicked off her flat-heeled shoes, shoes fit for running in, for moving around with the least possible noise, Marler noted. He raised both hands, palms towards her, rested them on her bare shoulders and threw her back on the bed. Dropping his robe, he followed her, lying on top of her as she giggled and wriggled.

'My name is Christina,' she said ten minutes later as they lay side by side.

'Christina What?'

Marler lit a cigarette he didn't really want, stared at the ceiling as she pressed against him, the black mane spread over the pillow.

'Does it matter? Tell me something about the man I have just made love with.'

'I am training to be a newspaper reporter. I was in insurance before. Bored the hell out of me.'

'And what story are you working on at the moment?' She snuggled closer, her hand splayed on his flat hard stomach.

'This and that.' He leaned on his elbow, stared down at her and his expression was grim. 'I like to know who I've played with. Christina What?' he repeated.

'Does it matter?' She pouted.

He jumped off the bed, told her to stand up. Puzzled, she got to her feet. She faced him, then gave the same slow smile.

'What is your relationship with Petros?' he demanded. 'Did he send you?'

'Petros? If I am going to be cross-questioned I can get that at police headquarters like you . . .'

She stooped to reach for her clothes. Marler grasped her

94

by her strong pointed chin, stood her erect. 'I answered your question, now you answer mine.'

'I am going . . .'

Marler raised his right hand and hit her hard across the side of her face with the flat of his hand. She reeled under the blow, fell back on the bed. Her eyes blazed. He saw now they were black with greenish flecks. She leapt to her feet. Before she could speak he hit her again on the other side of her face, the blow harder. She now had two red weals. She leapt up again, came for him with clawed hands. She had become a raging wildcat. He grasped both wrists before the fingers tore his face, forced them downwards. She aimed a knee at his groin. He turned sideways, took the thrust on his thigh, dropped both hands suddenly, then hit her with real force. She sagged on to the bed, glaring up at him.

'What is your relationship with Petros Gavalas? You're going to answer before you leave. I didn't invite you here . . .'

'Why don't you go and . . . yourself?'

She no longer spoke her perfect English. She had lapsed into Greek and he realized she was watching him closely. One tough cookie, this girl. She had taken quite a beating but still she was probing.

'I beg your pardon?'

'Nothing,' she replied in English.

She started to get up and he used one hand to push her down on the bed again, digging his fingers into her shoulder. Both their bodies were gleaming with sweat from what they had done together, from the later struggle. The heat was building up in the room and Marler felt parched.

'Can I have a drink?' she asked.

'No. What is your relationship with Petros Gavalas?' he said again.

'I am his granddaughter . . .'

'I know that. It isn't what I meant. And you know that. Did he send you here to extract information from me – by using any method?'

'He wouldn't do that! No Greek would do that to his own kith and kin . . .'

'So you came yourself? Why? Because you love Englishmen? I recall you said that.'

'I hate Englishmen,' she hissed, pulling her hair back from her face. 'I want to get dressed . . .'

'You couldn't wait to get your clothes off when you arrived. If you hate Englishmen why did you take up with Harry Masterson when he arrived?'

'Who?' She drew back as Marler broke loose. Grabbing her by her long hair, he twisted it, pulling her down on the bed as he sat on her stomach, his mouth tight, pinning her down. He jerked her hair and she opened her mouth to scream. His hand clamped flat over her lips, exerting so much pressure she couldn't use her teeth to bite him. Her dark eyes were full of hate.

'Harry Masterson,' he repeated. 'Stop lying. You were seen with him at the Hilton. Other places, too. Now, I'm going to remove my hand. Yell – try to – and I'll knock you out.'

He jumped up suddenly, walked to his jacket, took a cigarette from his pack and lit it. The unexpected change of tactics threw her off balance. She stood up warily, slowly reached for her denims, slid inside them, wriggled herself into them, watching him. Straightening up, she adjusted the slacks, still naked above the waist. She spoke quietly as she made the threat.

'I'm going to accuse you of rape. The Greek police don't like foreign men who rape Greek girls.'

'There's the phone. Call Chief Inspector Sarris. I'm sure he'd enjoy a session with us. That he'll be interested to hear how you gave the signal for a marksman down at Zea to try and kill me. The bullet missed me by inches.'

'What are you talking about? There was no shot. I would have heard it . . .'

Marler was certain that for the first time she was telling the truth. He kept the surprise out of his expression. She reached for her blouse and held it dangling from one hand.

'You might just have managed it,' Marler speculated.

'Managed what?'

'Driven Harry Masterson so crazy over you that he fell for it. When you lured him down to Cape Sounion so he could be killed.'

'No! No! That was something I didn't do. What do you think I am?'

'That's easy to answer.' He pulled his wallet from his jacket. Taking out a sheaf of five-hundred-drachma notes, he looked at her. 'How much? What's your fee? For . . .' He gestured to the bed.

'*You swine! You lousy bastard!*'

'And I have diplomas to prove you're right,' Marler assured her.

She crammed her feet into her shoes, slipped on her blouse, hastily adjusted it. She glanced in the mirror. Her hair was a wild tangle. Marler handed her the brush he had picked up before opening the door earlier. As she used it, brushing her mane vigorously, she again stared at him in the mirror as he donned his bathrobe. This time she had a puzzled expression. His deliberate changes of mood were confusing her. He disappeared into the bathroom, returned holding a glass of water.

'You said you were thirsty. Next time I ask questions please give me answers, then we'll get on fine together.'

She drank the water in two long gulps, handed him the glass. 'I've never met a man like you before. Harry wasn't . . .' She stopped speaking.

'"Harry wasn't like you",' Marler completed for her. 'Tell me – before you go – why did you take up with him?'

97

'He was asking dangerous questions.'

'Such as?'

'About the Greek Key.'

'What's that?'

'Just pray to God you never find out. See you around, Marler.'

'It sounds as though you gave her a rough time. Just like you're giving me one,' Newman grumbled. 'I was fast asleep when you hammered on my door.'

'Thought you'd want to know the latest developments,' Marler replied, unrepentant. 'That you'd rely on your assistant to keep you informed.'

Heavy-eyed, his hair tousled, Newman tied the cord of his dressing gown more tightly, drank some of the coffee Marler had ordered from room service. He pursed his lips as he replayed in his mind Marler's account of his adventure with Christina.

'You have been enjoying yourself,' he said eventually.

'All in the line of duty . . .'

'Don't say that to Tweed. Significant that remark she let slip – "if I am going to be cross-questioned I can get that at police headquarters like you . . ." *Like you.* She knew we had been taken there by Sarris. No motorcyclist with an orange crash helmet followed us that I saw.'

'I thought I caught sight of that black Mercedes when I was taken in the police car,' Marler remarked.

'Did you now?' Newman drank more coffee. 'Then that would prove she *is* working under Petros' orders, that he told her about our visit. Which means she was lying – about acting under Petros' instructions.'

'Oh, she's a lovely little liar. Makes it a way of life.'

'Except on two points, you said. She didn't hear a rifle shot at Zea – which is possible with those ships' sirens blaring. And she wasn't the one who led Masterson down to Cape Sounion. This business is full of twists. And what the blazes is the Greek Key?'

'Maybe it turns the lock to the whole mystery.'

'If we could ever find that key. I'm going back to bed.'

'And our next move is?'

'Keep Nick and his helpers looking for where Masterson stayed. We might start making enquiries about the Greek Key. Someone must know what it is. In short, keep stirring the pot until something rises to the surface. And maybe take a look at Cape Sounion. While we're there we could try to locate old Petros' headquarters in the mountains.'

'Think I've already stirred one pot. It's called Christina Gavalas. I left her not liking us a lot. Which was the object of the exercise.'

'Exercise is the word for what you did.'

'Did you tell Newman everything about Giorgos, Chief?' asked his assistant, Kalos.

'What do you mean, everything?' Sarris demanded.

He stifled a yawn as he gazed down at the traffic jamming up Alexandras. Nine in the morning. It would get worse. He flexed aching hands. He wasn't up to these all-night sessions.

'The knife rammed into his back under the shoulder blade.'

'No, I didn't. We keep that quiet. I kept Newman away from the pathologist. That knife bothers me. Doesn't make sense.'

'The fact that he was drowned in the wine barrel first, then the knife was stuck in later? The lack of blood proves that.'

'Precisely. And it *is* an old British commando knife. The war museum has a specimen. I compared them. The knife in Giorgos is an exact replica. Macabre. Some kind of symbolic gesture?'

'Or something to put us off the real identity of the killer?'

'Could be. I just hope Newman doesn't go poking round in Devil's Valley. Petros Gavalas controls that area like some medieval baron.'

'And what about the number of accidents that have taken place in that area? Hikers and mountaineers who never come back?'

'I've never been able to pin anything on the old villain – but I'm certain his men tossed them over precipices. No one penetrates his territory and survives. He's the old school. Comes from Macedonia. They play rough up there. Yes, I do hope Newman gives that one a miss . . .'

2 p.m. 90°F. 32°C. Newman was freshly shaved, showered, his brain was alert, he had eaten a large lunch in the hotel dining room with Marler and they had returned to his room with Nick who had arrived promptly.

'We're going into action,' Newman rapped out. 'We'll stir the pot, as Marler put it earlier. Not to make it simmer – I want it boiling over.'

'The weather is boiling over already,' Nick remarked as he mopped his forehead.

'We'll drive down towards Cape Sounion,' Newman went on. 'My bet is we'll be followed. That will confirm we are getting somewhere. We'll enquire at the main hotels in the coastal resorts to see if we can find where Masterson holed up. We'll ask openly about the Greek Key . . .'

'What is that?' asked Nick. 'Sounds like a night club . . .'

'That is what we want to find out. And Christina will be in a rage after what happened. She may make a wrong move. Let's get to the car.' He picked up a large plastic bottle of mineral water and they left the room.

Nick ran ahead while Newman and Marler walked down the empty corridor. Newman never used elevators if they

100

could be avoided, if a staircase were available: elevators could become traps.

'You know, Marler, I think we're missing something. Maybe something under our noses.'

'Why the doubts?'

'This mystery is full of twists, unexplained contradictions. Why was Christina aboard that yacht, *Venus III*, *if* she is supposed to hate its owner, her grandfather, Petros? Who is paying for that expensive apartment she has in Kolonaki? We must visit her there.' He corrected himself. '*I* must visit her. She may tell me more than she told you.'

'I whetted your appetite,' Marler said cynically.

'What did Masterson find out that decided someone he had to be murdered? What was the link between him and Christina? Don't forget – they first met in London. Why did Masterson visit the Ministry of Defence to ask about that commando raid on Siros over forty years ago?'

'My head begins to spin . . .'

'I wish we had one man here who is a master when it comes to a manhunt, to untangling a complex web.'

'You mean . . .'

'Tweed. I miss Tweed . . .'

9

A sea of grey unbroken cloud pressed down like a smothering blanket: not a hint of blue anywhere. A fine drizzle like a sea mist covered the desolate landscape, settled on the windscreen of the Mercedes 280E Tweed had borrowed from Newman. He drove slowly along the narrow country road elevated above the grim marshland on either side. Not a soul in sight. At two in the afternoon they had the dreary world to themselves.

'Are we going the right way?' Paula asked as she studied the ordnance survey map. 'I'm lost.' She glanced out of the window, settled in the front passenger seat beside Tweed.

'We're right in the middle of the Somerset Levels, the area Masterson noted down on a scrap of paper in the cigar box he sent from Athens,' Tweed remarked. 'This is where the sea used to flood in centuries ago. Now they cut peat. I want to get the atmosphere of this place.'

He stopped the car, but kept the engine running as he stared around at the bleakness. Paula, dressed in a windcheater and a blouse and pleated skirt, shivered.

'I find this place creepy. Look, there's some kind of a building over there under those willows.'

'One of the farms – the peat-cutting farms.'

Below the road there stretched a ditch full of stagnant water. Paula lowered her window and wrinkled her nose as an odour of decay drifted inside the car. She opened the door, stepped out to take a closer look.

The ditch was coated with an acidic green slime across its surface. Patches of black water showed here and there. In the distance stood the ramshackle building Tweed had called a farm. Its roof slanted at a crooked angle. Smoke curled up from a squat chimney. Another smell assailed her nostrils and again she crinkled them in disgust.

'That's the smell of peat. You can see this side of that farm where they're cutting it. And someone is coming . . .'

Tweed's grip on the wheel tightened as he stopped speaking. Paula turned again to look towards the collection of hovels he had called a farm. Two men were advancing towards them, one walking behind the other along a grassy path leading to where she stood.

Both wore stained old pea-jackets, grubby caps and

muddy corduroy trousers stuffed into the tops of rubber boots. Each carried over his shoulder a long-handled implement. One was some kind of vicious-shaped hoe, the other a long spade more like an iron scoop. Both walked with steady intent, wide shoulders hunched, primitive faces staring at the intruders.

'Get in the car quick!' Tweed snapped.

He had the car moving as she slammed the heavy door and then increased speed. Paula let out her breath, a sigh of relief. Tweed started the windscreen wipers going.

'I didn't like the look of them at all,' Paula said.

'A couple of ugly customers,' Tweed agreed. 'The peat diggers are an enclosed community shut off from the outside world. I know this area well. Went to school at Blundell's near Tiverton. Hated every minute of it – like being in prison. During my spare time I used to cycle for miles – including round here. Pedalled like mad down this miserable road. Even then it frightened me.'

'Why cycle here then?'

'Kid stuff. Got a thrill out of scaring myself. You know something . . .' He glanced across the dank marshlands. 'This would be a good place to hide a body.'

'I'm glad you kept the engine running. There seem to be a lot of willows growing in this wilderness.'

'The other industry here. See those clumps growing by that ditch running away from the road? They're called withies. Shoots from pollarded willows. The osier-workers cut them and make wicker baskets to sell. Chairs, too. They can keep busy all the year round. When they've used up the withies and are waiting for next year's crop they dig up the peat. Goes way back over a couple of centuries. The Victorians were very keen on wickerwork.'

'And where are we?' She was studying the map again. 'I do hate to be lost.'

'Sign of a good navigator. Westonzoyland is probably

the nearest point of civilization. We left the A372 and drove north. We're heading for the A39. We turn left on to that, head for Bridgwater and then west to Dunster via Watchet.'

'Got it. What was in that large package which arrived from Harry this morning with the Athens postmark?'

'Look in the glove compartment. Another mess of clues. And after glancing at them I haven't one. A clue. See what you make of it.'

She sifted the contents of the reinforced envelope with the address again written in Harry Masterson's distinctive hand. Pulling out something as Tweed switched on the headlights to warn any oncoming vehicle, she examined it and then unfastened a clip, wrapped it round her wrist, closed the clip.

'It's a girl's bracelet. Why would he send that?' she wondered.

'No idea.'

'It's quite beautiful. You've seen the symbol the pendant has been designed as in imitation jewellery?'

'No. I told you I only had time to glance at the contents before we started out from Park Crescent.'

'It's the Greek key.'

Through a hole in the lowering clouds a shaft of sunlight like a searchlight moved across the great sweeping brown ridges in the distance. Tweed nodded towards them as they travelled along a hedge-lined road, approaching a small town.

'Up beyond there is Exmoor. A lonely place for the trio who long ago raided that island of Siros. And why should they all settle in the same area?'

'Let's ask them . . .'

'I intend to. We're close to Dunster now.'

They passed a signpost on their right pointing down a

104

narrow road. *Watchet*. Tweed grunted and Paula looked at him.

'You had a thought.'

'Watchet. I checked it in guide books before we left. My memory was right. It's the only port between here and Land's End. A real port, I mean. In a small way of business. It exports scrap metal and wastepaper to Scandinavia. And, guess where.'

'We turn left soon according to the map. Can't guess.'

'I know where we turn. I remember the road. From Watchet there is the occasional ship plying between the Bristol Channel and Portugal. Turn here . . .'

At The Luttrell Arms Tweed waited until they were settled in their separate rooms before strolling down the staircase to tackle the manager. Each room had its name on the door. Tweed had *Avill*, a large and comfortable room with a door leading to a garden at the back. The manager, a tall, pleasant man clad in black, looked up from behind the reception counter as Tweed placed a photograph on the woodwork.

'Can you do me a favour, please,' Tweed began. 'Has this man stayed here recently?'

The manager stared at the print of Harry Masterson without a change of expression. He looked up at Tweed.

'It is, I am sure you will understand, company policy not to give out information about other guests. If someone came and asked the same question about yourself . . .'

'Special Branch.'

Tweed laid the card forged in the Engine Room basement at Park Crescent alongside the photo. The manager stared at it with curiosity. He had a quiet deliberate voice, the kind of voice used to pacifying impossible guests.

'I have heard about your organization. This is the first time I have met one of you.'

105

'So I would appreciate it if you would answer my questions in confidence. A question of national security.'

'Oh dear.' The manager paused. Tweed replaced the card in his pocket in case anyone came past them. The place seemed deserted. 'I do recognize him,' the manager said eventually. 'He stayed here about three weeks ago . . .'

'For how long?'

Keep them talking – once you've opened their mouths.

'Five days, Mr Tweed.'

'In what name?'

'Harry Masterson. A jolly man. Well-dressed. A joker – made me laugh.'

'And this person?'

Tweed removed Masterson's photograph, replaced it with the blow-up of the picture of Christina Gavalas which had arrived in the cigar box. He watched the manager intently.

'No question of scandal involved, I hope?' ventured the manager.

'I did say in confidence.'

'Of course. Yes, she came with him. They had separate rooms,' he added quickly. 'As a matter of fact, Mr Masterson had the Garden Room, *Avill*, the one you have, the best in the house.'

'And the girl?'

'The same room as your Miss Grey. *Gallox*.'

'Registered in what name?'

'Christina Bland. She wore a wedding ring. You see why I was concerned about a little scandal. Foreign, I thought.'

'Don't be concerned. What did they do while they were here? I realize that's a difficult question – but everyone has to pass this reception area when they come downstairs. Did they spend a lot of time out?'

'A striking couple.' The manager eyed Tweed as though to confirm he was the genuine article. 'Yes, they did go out most of the time. They would have breakfast – I help with that when staff is off duty – and ask for a packed lunch each day. Then we wouldn't see them until long after dinner. We close that front door at eleven and late-nighters have to ring the bell for admittance. Twice I let them in at midnight. I thought maybe they had friends round Exmoor they visited. That's a pure guess. You will keep this between us?'

'You have my word.' Tweed paused, smiled. 'You will keep entirely to yourself the nature of my job?'

'Good Lord, yes, Mr Tweed. The privacy of the guests must be sacred.' He looked embarrassed. 'Yours is, of course, a special case.'

Tweed picked up the second photograph. He put it inside his pocket, turned away, then turned back as though a thought had suddenly struck him.

'In connection with the same investigation, would you happen to know any of these three men? A Lieutenant-Colonel Barrymore, a Captain Robson, a man called Kearns? I do have their addresses. Barrymore, for one, lives at Quarme Manor, Oare.'

The manager took his time fastening up the middle button of his black jacket. Giving himself time to think, Tweed guessed. So I've given him something to think about.

'Again in complete confidence, I assure you.'

'This is a strange business you're investigating, if I may say so.'

'Very strange, very serious, very urgent.'

'Well . . . The three of them are friends. Every Saturday night they dine here. Always the same quiet table at the far end of the dining room. A kind of ritual, I gather.'

'They were here last Saturday? Two nights ago?' Tweed asked quickly.

'Well, no. The colonel is very formal. Always phones himself to book the table in advance. They've missed

107

for three weeks. Probably on holiday. Only my guess, I emphasize.'

'Thank you.' Tweed paused. He looked the manager straight in the eye. 'When you wake tomorrow morning you'll possibly worry about what you've told me. Don't. Worry, I mean. It is Monday. If I am still here next Saturday I shall make a point of dining elsewhere. Then if they come back you won't have me in the room. We do consider people's feelings.'

'So it seems. I thought, if you won't resent it, that your outfit were more aggressive.'

'On the contrary, we find we get the best results by being exceptionally discreet. And the local police shouldn't know I am here. Then we can't have any gossip about my being in the area.' Tweed leaned forward. 'We keep it just between the two of us. So, sleep well.'

'Thank you, sir. And if it's not out of place, I hope you enjoy your stay here. I'm not worrying.'

Tweed went back upstairs and knocked on the door of the room named *Gallox*. 'Who is it?' Paula called out.

'It's me,' said Tweed. She called out again for him to come in.

'Just look at this,' she began as he entered. 'Isn't it marvellous?'

She was sitting on the edge of a huge four-poster bed with a large canopy. It gave the large room a medieval atmosphere. Five feet six tall, the mattress was so high her feet dangled above the floor.

'You should have plenty of room in that,' Tweed observed and sat in an armchair. 'I have just talked with the manager. A tricky conversation. I had to show him my Special Branch card before he'd tell me a thing.'

'I like him. There's something Dickensian about his appearance.'

'And he's a man of great integrity . . .' Tweed told her about their conversation. She listened, watching him, and he knew every word was being imprinted on her memory.

'That's queer,' she commented. 'We thought it peculiar that those three men should end up living in the same part of the country. After all these years they obviously keep in close touch. Why?'

'They could have stayed friends,' Tweed pointed out. 'They were together during the Second World War. Occasionally it does happen. But I think there's more than that to it – the trouble is I can't imagine what.'

'So where do we start?'

'We drive over by the coast road to Quarme Manor. I checked it on the map. Oare is down some side turning. That is after we've had a cream tea at the best place in this village.'

'Why? The manager said they were all away somewhere.'

'I want to see whether Barrymore – for starters – really is away. And if so, where he's gone – if possible . . .'

'This is one hell of a road,' Paula said with feeling.

'Porlock Hill. One of the most diabolical in Britain.'

Tweed was driving up a gradient like the side of a mountain. Added to the incredibly steep angle, the road twisted and turned round blind bends. Added to that, a grey mist was coming in off the moor, coils of sinister grey vapour creeping down the road.

Tweed drove with undipped headlights to warn any oncoming traffic, ready to dip them at the first sign of lights from the opposite direction. Like Tweed, Paula was tilted back in her seat as though inside an aircraft taking off. They passed a road turning off to their right and Tweed nodded towards it.

'That's the toll road, as they call it. That's fun too – it goes down like a water chute slide with a sheer drop on one side towards the sea.'

They had bypassed Minehead before they started the ascent and Paula patted her stomach. 'At least I'm full. That cream tea was fantastic. I'll get fat as a pig. And we're going to miss that turn-off to Oare,' she warned.

They had reached the top of the hill and drove along the level. No other traffic in either direction. The mist was thickening, making it as dark as night. The headlights picked up an inn sign. Culbone Inn.

'I'll check here for that turn-off,' said Tweed, swinging off the main road on to a wide drive.

He returned after a few minutes, climbed back behind the wheel. 'They say it's the next turn-off. A mile or so ahead. Easy to miss. And the road to Oare is very narrow.'

'Sounds great. Just what we need – for a car this size. How big is Oare?'

'Hardly a hamlet. Very spread out, as I remember. Two manor houses. Oare Manor and Quarme Manor, the stately home of Colonel Barrymore.'

'What exactly are we trying to do?' Paula was sat forward, braced against the seat belt, trying to spot the turn-off. At this height the mist was thinning. A chilly sea breeze blew in through her window. She pressed the button to close it.

'It's damn cold. Can I put on the heater?'

'As high as you like.'

Paula glanced at Tweed as she switched on the heater. He seemed impervious to extremes of both cold and heat. He wore a new hacking jacket, a pair of grey flannels, and a deerstalker hat which should have looked slightly ridiculous. But it suited him, gave him a commanding air. He read her thoughts.

'Dressed to merge into the landscape. Wear a London business suit out here and I'd stick out like a sore thumb . . .'

'Stop! You turn off here . . .'

He'd just checked the rear-view mirror, something he

110

did every ten seconds. He swung the wheel and they began to drop downhill. The country lane was so narrow the Mercedes just slid past the grass verges on either side. Beyond them a bank rose, topped with dense hedges. It didn't help visibility as the lane spiralled down steeply, a series of sharp bends. But the mist had evaporated and now they moved through a weird half-light as they dropped and dropped. At the bottom they drove across a gushing ford, reached an intersection. Paula desperately searched the map as Tweed swung right.

'Close to Oare,' he said. 'I remember that ford. From what the publican back at Culbone told me we should soon reach Quarme Manor. On the right somewhere.' The Mercedes was crawling as they navigated the winding lane. Above them in the distance Paula saw great sweeps of the moor, like tidal waves frozen in mid-flight.

'You asked me a few minutes ago what we are trying to do,' Tweed continued. 'We are trying to discover why Harry Masterson came here, what he discovered which led him to fly to Athens. In other words, what is the link between Exmoor and Greece? And who murdered Harry . . .'

He peered through the windscreen, still keeping the Mercedes at crawling pace. 'We have arrived. There is Quarme Manor.'

Paula was alone inside the car. Tweed had driven it into one of the lay-bys carved out of the side of the lane at intervals to allow one vehicle to pass another. He had instructed her to keep all the doors locked while he was away.

'Where are you going?' she had asked.

'To explore round Quarme Manor first, then call to see if anyone is at home . . .'

She sat with the heavy long torch in her lap he always

carried when driving. It was still daylight and she could see up on to the moor. She had turned off the heater, opened one window a few inches. Suddenly she stiffened, leaned forward.

She was looking at a ridge behind and overlooking Quarme Manor. It was uncannily silent. The wind had dropped. And despite the fact there was a dense copse of trees huddled round the manor house she hadn't heard the cheep of a single bird.

The horseman was perched on the ridge, silhouetted against the pale grey sky. Even motionless in the saddle, she saw he was a tall man. He held something with a long barrel in front of him, held it across the horse and parallel to the ground. A rifle.

Where the devil was Tweed? She watched the horseman, standing so still he might have been a bronze statue. Could it be Lieutenant-Colonel Barrymore waiting and watching over his property? Then the horseman moved, although his steed remained still.

He raised the rifle to his shoulder. He settled the stock in position and tilted the rifle angle downwards. He was aiming at something – someone – moving inside or just outside the grounds. Oh, my God . . .! Tweed was the target.

She raised the lever which unlocked the door, jumped out into the lane, still grasping the torch. Raising it with both hands like a revolver, she aimed the torch straight at the horseman, pressed on the light. The beam cut through the grey light. She knew it would never reach the horseman but she flashed it on and off time and again.

The horseman shifted in his saddle. The rifle swung in an arc, was now aimed at the car. She ducked down behind the Mercedes, waited for the crack of the shot. Nothing . . . She raised her head, ready to duck again quickly. There was nothing to see. The ridge outline was bare. The horseman had vanished. She had distracted him.

112

Shaking, she climbed back into the car behind the wheel, closed the door quietly, pressed down the lock.

Leaving the car, Tweed had walked quickly down the deserted lane. Coming closer, he saw Quarme Manor was a large Elizabethan pile built of grey stone with a wing extending forward from either end. The distinctive chimneys festooned the tiled roof. A high stone wall surrounding the place soon hid the house. He came to the entrance. Tall iron grille gates. A name plate. *Quarme Manor*.

No sign of lights. There should be lights if anyone was inside. The two-storeyed mansion was shrouded in gloom – made darker by the copse of trees sheering up inside the wall. Tweed peered through the closed grille gates up the curving drive beyond. A particularly fine example of the Elizabethan period, the mansion stood four square and seemed to grow out of the moor. All the mullion-paned windows with their pointed arches were in darkness.

He walked on along the curving lane, following the line of the wall. The silence was so intense he could almost *hear* it. His rubber-soled handmade shoes made no sound. He came to where the wall turned at a right angle away from the lane, climbing the steep slope towards a ridge behind the manor. A narrow footpath followed the line of the wall. He began climbing.

He had to keep his head down. The path was treacherous with slippery stones concealed beneath brown swathes of last year's dead bracken. He felt damp on his face, squelchy mush underfoot. He paused to stare at a second dense copse of trees – this one outside the wall and beyond the path. Out of the corner of his eye he caught movement. He looked up at the sabre-like cut of the ridge crest. Nothing. He could have sworn something moved.

113

Reaching the point where the wall turned again, running parallel to the front wall alongside the lane, he explored further until he found an opening. The gap was closed off with a single wide grille gate which was padlocked. He bent down.

By the gate the ground was cleared and in the moist earth were clear traces of hoof-marks. A back entrance to Quarme Manor which would take the owner straight on to the moor. And recently someone had ridden a horse here. He peered between the grille bars.

A gravel path led round a spacious lawn with ornamental shrubs arranged here and there. The lawn was cut, the topiary well-trimmed. Such attention cost money. He returned the way he had come.

The left-hand grille gate leading off from the lane opened at a push. His feet crunched as he walked up the drive. Inside the large porch he found an old-fashioned chain-pull bell. He tugged at it, heard it ring inside. A light was switched on, illuminating a diamond-shaped window behind an iron grille in the solid studded door. The lantern suspended over the porch came on. The small window opened. Tweed had a glimpse of a woman's bony face before the window slammed shut. The door was opened half a foot, a chain in place.

'What be it?' the old woman demanded.

'I wish to see Colonel Barrymore . . .'

'He b'aint be available.'

'You mean he is away somewhere?'

'He b'aint be available.'

She repeated the words as though she had been taught to say them by rote. She was tall, late sixties, her grey hair brushed close to the skull, her expression hostile. She was closing the door when Tweed spoke more firmly.

'The colonel will want to see me. When do you expect him to be back?'

'Name?'

'I shall have to tell him you were uncooperative. And he won't like that . . .'

'Phone for appointment . . .'

She was closing the door when they both heard the sound of a car approaching. It stopped outside. A shadowy figure opened both gates after jumping lightly out of the car. Before the headlights blinded him Tweed saw it was a crimson Daimler. Swinging round the short curve, it pulled up for a moment. A face behind the wheel stared out, then the car continued on round the side of the house. To the garage, he assumed.

'This is Colonel Barrymore?' Tweed asked the woman who still stood by the door.

'Better ask him, 'adn't you? Doesn't welcome strangers, you know.'

'It's becoming somewhat apparent,' Tweed remarked drily.

He turned as he heard the crunch of boots on gravel approaching from the side of the mansion. A tall, slim, elegant man in his mid-sixties appeared and stood, studying Tweed with an expression of disdain. Thick black hair was brushed over his high forehead and beneath his aquiline nose he sported a thin dark moustache.

He wore a sheepskin against the night chill and cavalry twill trousers shoved inside riding boots gleaming like glass. How the devil does he drive in those? Tweed wondered. The voice was crisp, offhand, as though addressing a junior subaltern.

'Who are you? If you are selling something you can take your immediate departure. And is that your Mercedes parked in the way down the lane?'

'Which question first?' Tweed asked mildly. 'And my car is in a lay-by. Plenty of room for you to get past even in your Daimler. That's what lay-bys are for . . .'

'I asked that stupid girl to move it and she refused . . .'

'She's not stupid and she's quite right to ignore

115

intimidation.' Tweed produced his card. 'Before you say another word you'd better know who I am. And while we're talking identification, who are you?'

'Colonel Barrymore.'

He moved under the lantern to examine the card, then looked up. 'It's all right, Mrs Atyeo, I'll sort this out myself.' He waited until she had disappeared, then stared at Tweed, handing back the card. 'Special Branch? A bit off the beaten track, aren't you?'

'So is Siros.'

Barrymore stiffened, stood even more erect. He jerked his head. 'Better come inside, I suppose. Just wait in my study until I'm ready to see you.'

By the light of the lantern Tweed saw Barrymore's skin was a tanned mahogany. He stood pulling slowly at one of the kid gloves he was wearing, taking hold of each finger and sliding it slowly half-way off. Even the slightest of the colonel's movements was slow and calculated.

'I'll go and fetch my assistant first,' Tweed said. 'She'll be taking notes . . .'

He was walking away before Barrymore could react. He felt he had left Paula alone in the car quite long enough. She greeted him with relief, told him quickly about the horseman on the ridge.

'That was very bright of you,' he said gratefully. 'To think of shining the torch. Oddly enough, Colonel Barrymore wears riding boots.'

'The man who stopped his Daimler alongside me and rudely told me to push off?'

'The very same gentleman. Surely there was plenty of room for him to pass?'

'Oodles. What do you think of His Lordship?'

'You said it. Let's get back to the manor. We have a right tartar to deal with. Something odd about him. Cold-blooded is the word, I suspect . . .'

116

10

'Go in there. No notes will be taken. I will join you when I can.'

Barrymore turned his back on them and disappeared through a doorway. They were standing in a stone-flagged hall. At the back a huge staircase mounted to the first floor, turning on a landing. Grim-faced, Mrs Atyeo stood holding open a heavy panelled door.

'In 'ere is where 'e wants you.'

'Always wears his riding boots, does he?' Tweed enquired as he walked towards the doorway.

'Part of 'is uniform, 'ain't it? 'E is The Colonel.'

'In capital letters, it appears.'

Tweed entered followed by Paula holding her notebook, the bracelet she had taken out of Masterson's last envelope still dangling from her wrist. Mrs Atyeo's expression changed, became ashen. She was staring at the bracelet and shrank back against the wall to let Paula pass, closing the door behind them.

'Tartar is the word,' Paula commented. 'And for some reason Mrs Atyeo nearly had a fit when she saw this bracelet.'

'I wonder why. Keep wearing it. Sit over there, notebook poised. It puts you offside from the chair behind that desk, may put the colonel off balance.'

The study was also a library. Three of the walls were lined with books. The door into the room was cut out of a bookcase wall and lined with green baize on the inside. The fourth wall was occupied by tall mullion-paned windows which overlooked the garden and the distant moor.

'Not very comfortable,' Paula remarked, staring at the tall hard-backed chair behind the desk, the spartan wood-blocks forming the floor, the lack of any soft furnishings and the desk which was a large block of oak. She shifted in her chair, trying to find a less awkward position. Tweed was looking at the books.

'What a man reads can tell you a lot about him. Military history of the Second World War, the campaigns of Wellington, a lot of travel books. None on Greece . . .'

'Prying, are we?'

The soft voice came from the direction of the well-oiled door which had opened silently. Tweed turned slowly and faced the colonel. He wore a dark silk shirt, a regimental tie, his cavalry twill trousers and the riding boots.

Tweed sat down in front of the desk, made no reply as Barrymore crept round the far side and sat upright in his chair, crossing his legs. The man moved like a cat. That was it, Tweed decided: cat-like in his movements and gestures.

'Well?' He waited for Tweed to respond but his visitor sat studying him. He glanced round at Paula. 'I said no notes.'

'And I said Special Branch,' Tweed snapped. 'A statement has to be taken of this conversation. If you object, we can always drive straight to London and conduct the interrogation formally. You know our powers.'

'Get on with it then.'

Barrymore opened a drawer. Taking out a ruler he held it between both hands. As they talked he bent the ruler slowly, then let it revert to its original shape. Substitute for an officer's stick.

'You've got yourself a good suntan, Colonel,' Paula intervened before Tweed began.

'Just back from the Caribbean.' He swivelled his gaze,

118

looking at her shapely crossed legs, her well-formed breasts outlined by her N. Peal cashmere sweater. Her windcheater was draped over the back of her chair. He took his time studying her. 'There are some lovely islands out there,' he went on. 'Not the package-deal spots. Islands with hotels like select clubs. Emphasis on privacy. The last bastions of a civilized holiday. Native servants to attend to your every wish. All the guests vetted. Word of mouth the only *entrée*. None of your wog nonsense like Marbella. You'd like it. I didn't catch your name.'

'Paula Grey.' She clamped her mouth tightly.

'Siros,' Tweed said suddenly. 'During the war you led a raid on the island.'

'Did I?'

'The Ministry of Defence files say you did.'

'Oh, you've been permitted to poke round the MOD?'

'No doors are closed to us. Especially when the murder of a Government employee is involved . . .'

'Which murder?'

The ruler was bent like a bow, close to snapping point. The colonel released the tension, straightened it. His eyes were dark under hooded lids. No trace of expression crossed his tanned face as he watched Tweed.

'The murder of Harry Masterson. You've met him? He was in this area – with a Greek girl.'

'He called here.' Barrymore paused. 'He asked a lot of damn-fool questions. Who was this Greek girl?'

'We're straying. You led the raid on Siros. Tell me what happened – what went wrong? And who came with you?'

'Someone knew we were coming. Cairo was a hotbed of gossip. We were carrying a fortune in diamonds to hand over to the Greek Resistance. To help finance them. Two first-rate men came with me. Captain Oliver Robson and CSM Stuart Kearns. Plus one Greek who knew the island. Andreas Gavalas. His job to hand over the baubles. Someone grabbed them off him. Mission aborted.'

'Haven't you left something out?'

'Probably. Over forty years ago? Is there much more?' He glanced at his watch. 'I've had a long journey. A bath would be welcome.'

He stifled a yawn, hand over mouth. Long slender fingers, more like those of a beautiful woman. Paula was writing shorthand in her book, recording every word. She looked up. Tweed was again waiting. She glanced at a side table near her elbow. A copy of *The Times* lay on it, folded open at the personal advertisements section.

'Andreas Gavalas was murdered,' Tweed said eventually.

'Top secret. They couldn't have let you read that file?'

'That was the most significant incident of the raid. Tell me about it.'

'Unpleasant. One of my few flops. The four-man party got separated. There was an alarm. Someone – forget who – said a German patrol had been spotted. We dived for cover. False alarm. When we found Gavalas he had a knife in his back – the diamonds were gone. We beat a hasty retreat – back to the beach for rendezvous with the motor launch. Then back to Mersa Matruh by night. That's a wog port on the African coast – inside the Gyppo border.'

'I know where Mersa Matruh is. What kind of knife?'

Barrymore slammed down the ruler. 'If you read the file you know. This isn't quiz time. A commando knife – as well you are aware. Embarrassing. I checked both Robson's and Kearns' equipment. Both had their knives. Showed them my own. Any more? I hope not.'

'One final question. Could you please – in a few words – give me your estimate of the characters of Captain Robson and CSM Kearns?'

It was the last question Barrymore had expected. Paula saw the puzzlement in his saturnine face. The colonel steepled his hands, a concentrated look in his dark eyes. Like a man reliving some experience of long ago.

'Robson was seconded from the Medical Corps. Steady as a rock in a tight corner. Cautious. Always looked where he was placing the next footstep. Never panicked. Dour.'

'And Kearns?'

'Courage came to him second nature. Fast on his feet, in his thinking. Could be impulsive. Didn't matter. Had a sixth sense for danger. In an emergency very audacious. Time you went.'

Tweed stood up, showed no sign of resenting the abrupt dismissal. Like the ending of a military inspection. Paula slipped her notebook inside her shoulder bag, walked after Tweed to the door without a glance at Barrymore.

Opening the door, Tweed stood aside and let her walk into the bleak hall. He glanced back. Barrymore sat behind his desk like a statue, hands still steepled, a glazed expression on his long-jawed face. Suddenly he seemed aware they were leaving. He stood up, remained behind the desk, bowed formally, said not another word as Tweed closed the door.

'You'll be leavin' now.'

Mrs Atyeo was waiting in the hall. She unclasped the hands which had rested on her thin waist, went to the front door, drew back bolts, peered through the diamond-shaped window, unleashed the heavy chain, opened it and waited as they filed past her into the night.

They paused under the lantern on the porch as the door was shut behind them. They could hear the bolts sliding back into position, the chain being fixed, a lock turned. The lantern went out, plunging them into darkness. Night had fallen.

Tweed looped Paula's arm through his and they made their way slowly down the drive. He waited until they were inside the car before he sighed and asked the question.

'What was your impression of Barrymore?'

'Nasty piece of work. Like a satyr. Did you notice how he was looking at me? Undressing me with his lecherous

121

eyes. I felt I was naked. Thinks a lot of himself. I can imagine him riding a horse inspecting his troops, riding very slowly along the line with an expression of cynical contempt. And he moves oddly – like a cat. Took those gloves off with a feline grace . . .' She paused and shivered. 'I'm glad you're back with me in the car.'

'You didn't think I'd leave you on your own in a lonely place like this, did you?'

Tweed was watching his wing mirror. Paula froze suddenly and then jerked her head round. A slim hatless man was walking alongside the car from behind them. He leant on the window ledge. She let out her breath, lowered the window. Pete Nield grinned, pulled at his small dark moustache with his index finger.

'How goes the battle?' he enquired.

'Where on earth did you spring from?' she asked.

'Pete has followed us in my Cortina all the way from London. I told you he was coming. He's been parked a short distance behind you ever since I left you.'

'In this road?'

'No,' Nield told her. 'I parked the car beyond a gate leading to a field. Then I sat in a hedge close behind you. I was ready to intervene when that character in the Daimler pulled up by you if he'd tried anything on.'

'But what about in Dunster?'

'Parked the car at the other end of the village. I still have to register at The Luttrell Arms – but I warned them over the phone I'd be late. They won't realize we're together. At the hotel, I mean.'

'You haven't told me what you spotted about the colonel,' Tweed remarked. 'Only that you dislike him. Irrelevant. Pete, get in the back of the car and listen. Now I want both of you to grasp this. Ready, Pete?'

'Jolly comfortable back here. Nice to see how the other half lives.'

'Masterson came down to Exmoor with the Greek girl,

Christina. All three men involved in a raid over forty years ago on Siros, a German-occupied Greek island, are living on Exmoor. Harry Masterson, I'm sure, knew that. From Christina . . .'

'Assumption,' interjected Paula.

'Listen! Our main task is to interrogate all three men. And *every* word said by these men is important. One of them may let something slip. There was something very peculiar about that raid on Siros. Now, Paula, you were there when Barrymore gave his version.'

'Well, he was very suntanned,' she said slowly. 'So he could have just come back from Greece . . .'

'Now we're getting warmer. You see, Pete, this Colonel Barrymore has a terse way of speaking. Typical Army officer. But when Paula remarked on his suntan he became positively loquacious – explaining at some length how he'd been to the Caribbean. No specific mention of locales. It was the only time he really opened up.'

'You mean he was lying?' Pete asked.

'Paula, when we get back to London, will type out the transcript of each of the three men's statements – including their description of what happened on Siros. You can read them, decide for yourself.'

'You also asked his opinion of the other two men,' Paula recalled. 'I couldn't see the point.'

'In the end the whole thing may hang on the *psychology* of these three men. Would one of them be capable of murder? And did you notice,' he asked Paula, 'that when I mentioned a murder, Barrymore said, "Which murder?" It sounded to me as though he was thinking of more than *one* murder. Who else could he be thinking of besides Andreas Gavalas who accompanied them on the Siros raid?'

'Harry Masterson?' suggested Nield.

'Or possibly a third murder over forty years ago – mentioned briefly to me at the Ministry of Defence. Back to

123

your car, Pete. We must tackle our next member of the trio.'

'Who is that?' asked Paula as Pete left the Mercedes.

'Captain Oliver Robson. He lives the other side of Oare. I was given directions at that pub at Culbone. Robson calls there for a pint occasionally . . .'

11

After the gloomy Quarme Manor the modern L-shaped bungalow perched on the hillside in the dark looked to be out of another world. Which, Tweed reflected as he stopped the car, in fact it was. A wild leap from the fifteenth century into the twentieth.

The residence was a blaze of lights, standing at the top of a tarred drive above the lane. A wide stone-paved terrace ran the full width of the frontage. Ornamental lanterns were placed at intervals along a stone wall below the terrace, shedding light over the long slope of rough-cut grass to the hedge by the lane. The white-painted gate was open.

Tweed studied the large bungalow carefully. Curtains were drawn back but it was impossible to see inside the picture windows from below. Searchlight beams flooded the night from each corner, illuminating all approaches. He drove in through the entrance slowly, glancing to left and right.

'They'll know we're coming,' he commented.

'They'll hear the car, you mean?' Paula asked.

'No. In each of the gateposts there are photo-electric cells. As we drove through that invitingly open gateway we broke a beam. It will have set off an alarm inside the bungalow.'

'I suppose it's wise to take precautions – living in such an isolated position on the edge of the moor.'

'Including spy cameras projecting from under the eaves? Every possible kind of security measure has been installed. I begin to see something Colonel Barrymore and Captain Robson have in common. When I trudged round Quarme Manor before going up to the front entrance I noticed the high walls were topped with barbed wire. And a straight wire ran beneath it. Electrified, I'm sure. Remember all the security precautions on the front door? Both places are like fortresses.'

'That's what the owners have in common?'

'No. Both of them are scared stiff of dangerous intruders. To an almost pathological extent it appears . . .'

He stopped speaking. He had parked the car at the top of the drive. The front door opened. Framed in the dark opening – the lights inside had been switched off – stood the silhouette of a man. Holding a pump-action shotgun. Aimed at the Mercedes point blank.

'I'll sort him out,' said Tweed.

'God! What a welcome,' whispered Paula. 'Worse than Quarme Manor . . .'

'Good evening.' Tweed had lowered his window. 'We are looking for Captain Robson. It says Endpoint on the name plate.'

'Who are you? What do you want?'

A trace of Scots accent. The voice clear, level in tone, controlled.

'Special Branch. My name is Tweed. We have just called on Colonel Barrymore . . .'

Tweed made it sound as though Barrymore had led them to Endpoint. He waited for a reaction, said no more. Silence is a potent weapon.

'You'd better come in then.' The shotgun was lowered,

still held ready for action as they alighted from the car and walked across the terrace. 'You have some identification?'

'Just about to show you. I'm taking my card out of my pocket . . .'

'It is very lonely out here. There have been two attempts to break in to my home. I'm Robson.'

As he looked at the card, shotgun tucked under his arm, Tweed studied Robson. Medium height, heavily built, but all of it muscle and bone, he was about the same age as Barrymore. And like the colonel his skin was deeply suntanned. The top of his rounded head was covered with an untidy thatch of brown hair and he had a straggly moustache of the same colour. Clad in shirt-sleeves rolled up to the elbows, his shirt was open-necked, but his well-worn grey slacks had a razor-edged crease.

'Better come in, I suppose.' He handed back the card. 'Special Branch? Sure you've got the right man? Let's go and make ourselves comfortable in the sitting room.'

'Oh, this is my assistant, Paula Grey,' Tweed introduced.

'Welcome.'

Robson hardly gave her a glance as he closed the door and walked across a hall towards an open door. A brown-haired woman of about the same age appeared wearing an apron over her dress.

'Who is it, Oliver?'

Tweed detected a note of anxiety in her voice. White-faced, she had an air of bustle. Robson gestured towards her.

'My sister, May. Looks after me. Keeps the place going. Be lost without her. It's all right, May. Barrymore sent them along. We'll chat in the sitting room.'

The moment she entered the hall the warmth hit Paula. Two old-fashioned radiators stood against the painted walls. The sitting room was long and large with a Wilton carpet wall to wall. Cosy-looking armchairs and couches were spread about and a log fire crackled beneath a huge burnished copper hood.

'Do take a pew, anywhere you like. This is my work room, too.'

He sat in an old swivel chair behind a desk with a scruffed top. A tumbler of something which looked like whisky stood next to a pile of newspapers. Robson stood up as they sat down.

'I'm forgetting my manners. What would you like to drink? I can do Scotch, white wine if you prefer . . .'

Paula had sat down close to him near the end of the desk. He stared suddenly as she adjusted the bracelet round her wrist. His right hand jerked, knocking over the tumbler. Liquid ran over the edge of the desk.

'Sorry. Damn careless of me . . .' He opened a drawer, took out a cloth and began mopping up the mess. 'Just back off holiday. Half here, half somewhere else.'

'I guessed that from your suntan,' Tweed remarked. 'You'd hardly have acquired that in this country. Go far?'

'Sailing off Morocco. Agadir and Casablanca. By myself. May can't stand the sea. Stayed back to guard the fort. Drinks?'

Both Tweed and Paula, notebook perched on her lap, asked for wine. Robson poured two glasses of Montrachet. Returning behind his desk, he produced a tobacco pouch and a pipe.

'Fire away.'

'I'm checking details of a murder which took place over forty years ago,' Tweed began. 'During your stint of duty in the Middle East.'

'A long time ago, as you say – that grim business when we made that raid on Siros. Barrymore was in command, but you know that – just coming from his place. Why has it become important now?'

'Because someone else investigating it has just been murdered. Ever met Harry Masterson?'

Robson's thumb, tamping tobacco in the bowl, remained poised for a second or two. Paula saw the pause. *Cautious* was a word Barrymore had used, describing Robson.

'Yes, he visited me. Jolly sort of cove. Life and soul of the party type. Asked some rum questions. What on earth is going on? "Just been murdered," you said.'

'That is what I am trying to find out. Could you tell me in your own words what did happen on Siros?'

'Who else's words would I use?' Robson smiled drily.

'And if you don't mind, Miss Grey will record your statement – for the record.'

'Of course not. Certainly she may. Special Branch. You have a system, I suppose. One thing I am entitled to, I assume. A copy of the statement. Siros.' He settled himself at ease in his chair, lit his pipe, watching Tweed from beneath his upswept eyebrows, his light blue eyes thoughtful. What a contrast to Barrymore, Paula thought: he's the soul of relaxation. And his house reflects his informal personality.

'Siros,' Robson repeated, puffed at the pipe, 'the main island in the Cyclades group. Shaped like a boomerang, a huge one. Steep cliffs along the southern coast – rising up to Mount Ida. Same name as the tallest mountain on Crete. No idea why. Siros was the headquarters of General Hugo Geiger, who commanded the German troops occupying the Cyclades . . .'

'Is Geiger still alive?' Tweed interjected.

'No idea. Bit long in the tooth by now if he is. Like our little group. Now . . . The Greek Resistance had made its own HQ on Siros. They thought hiding under the Germans' noses was a smart tactic. We were carrying a fortune in diamonds to hand over to the Resistance . . .'

'Who is "we"?'

'The colonel, of course. Myself. You wouldn't think I was a commando in those days. I'm a doctor. The Resistance lot were short of medical help. Plus CSM

Kearns, stout fellow. Lastly, the Greek, Gavalas. He was to be the contact with his own people. He'd escaped to Cairo. He was the one who carried the diamonds. To cut a long story short, we landed from the motor launch at night on the southern shore, made our way up a difficult defile cut in the mountainside – where the Germans would least expect a landing. It was wild terrain. Someone – can't remember who – sounded the alarm. German patrol. Every man for himself in that situation. We scattered, later re-assembled at an agreed rendezvous – and Gavalas was missing.'

'He'd handed over those diamonds?'

'No one knew. Unlikely. That rendezvous was several miles away on the *northern* slopes of Mount Ida. We were still to the south. We started searching for Gavalas. It was pretty dramatic – horrific. Barrymore found him. Dead. A knife sticking out from under his left shoulder blade. And the diamonds had gone. We headed back for the rendezvous with the motor launch due to take us off. Nothing else to do.'

'And the knife?' Tweed prodded gently.

'That made it more horrific. A commando knife. The colonel checked us. We all still had our own knives – including the colonel. Later we wondered whether the knife had been taken off one of the two earlier teams which had perished while raiding Siros.'

'Who by?'

'Could have been one of the Greek Resistance. Even a German soldier. Someone must have had quite a collection. There were six commandos who died on Siros.'

'And the value of those diamonds?' Tweed asked.

'A hundred thousand pounds. Wartime value.' Robson tamped his pipe, glanced at Paula writing in shorthand.

'One more question before we go, if I may. Could you please give me your assessment of the characters and temperaments of Barrymore and Kearns?'

'We make a good team. Kearns has a place on the way to Simonsbath, a stone's throw from here. The colonel is decisive, ice-cold in an emergency. The most controlled man I've ever known. Remarkable. Always ready for any danger, however outlandish. Never lets up his guard.'

'And Kearns?'

'A natural CSM. Very young in those days. Weren't we all? Your legendary man of action. But an excellent planner as well. The two don't usually go together. Could always see three moves ahead in the game. Still can. I think that sums them up. More wine?'

'Thank you, but I think we've taken up enough of your time.' Tweed stood up. 'Could I possibly visit your loo?'

'Of course. Remiss of me not to show you when you arrived.'

When he strolled back into the room Paula had slid her notebook inside her shoulder bag and was standing close to the picture window. Pete Nield would be out there watching and she was trying to signal to him they were leaving. Robson padded across and joined her by the window.

'I'm a lifelong bachelor,' he remarked, fiddling with his dead pipe. 'Not from choice. Once I was madly in love with a débutante. Can you imagine that?'

'Yes, I can. What happened, if I may ask?'

'Why not? It was all a long time ago. I thought my feelings for her were reciprocated. She left me standing at the church. Sounds like an old joke, but it happened. A telegram arrived. *Sorry, Oliver. It won't work. Very sorry. Diana.* And Diana was a Greek goddess in mythology. Went off and married a baronet. Rather put me off women. Present company excluded.'

'It must have been an awful blow.'

'It was a bit. She was a *silly* girl.' He made the comment with such vehemence Paula glanced at him. The eyes were like stones, the mouth twisted in an expression of bitter

130

irony. 'Her baronet hadn't a penny. Had to take a job . . .'

'Thank you for being so helpful,' said Tweed as he returned and stood on the other side of Robson. He tapped the long thin picture window. 'Good view by day, I imagine.'

'Yes, it is. A lookout point over the moor. As to helping you, my pleasure. I'll show you out.'

'You keep your home beautifully warm,' said Paula. It was the first remark which came into her head and she sensed Robson was embarrassed by his display of emotion.

'It has to be oil-fired central heating out here. Tricky during the oil crisis. We practically lived in this room. The log fire . . .'

In the hall the pump-action shotgun was perched in an umbrella stand, the twin barrels pointing at the ceiling. Ready to hand for the next caller, Tweed noted.

The door closed behind them and they climbed into the car. Before starting the engine Tweed looked back at the bungalow, at the security cameras. The viewing screen must be in a room he hadn't seen. 'Something odd about this place,' he said as he reached to turn on the ignition and then leant back. 'Look at the roof, the far end of the long stem on the bungalow. We couldn't see it when we arrived because of the dark and the glare of those searchlights.'

Paula stared through the windscreen. Projecting above the roof of the bungalow rose a wide circular column which reminded her of a lighthouse. Even more so because at the top was a circular rail and behind it the column was made of glass. She expected at any moment to see a slowly revolving light.

'The moon came up while we were inside,' Tweed pointed out. 'Which is why we can see it clearly now. It's like a watch tower. Mind you, when I went to the loo his sister, May, took me the full length of the bungalow behind the sitting room to the main bathroom. On the walls are

131

fishing nets with those glass balls suspended they use to keep nets afloat close to the surface. And fishing rods crossed like swords. Very much a man of the sea, Captain Robson.'

'There's someone inside the lighthouse. I can see his shadow against the moonlight.'

'Time to go.'

'Why did you liken it to a watch tower?' she asked while he drove down the drive and turned back the way they had come along the lane.

'I passed the base of the circular column on the way to the bathroom. It had a curved door, closed. Inside there must be a spiral staircase. Watch tower? Because I think Robson uses it to keep a close eye on the approaches to his home. The ridge along the moor continues from Quarme Manor, runs above Endpoint.'

'They both gave me the impression they're waiting for something dangerous to arrive – Barrymore with that wall and an electrified wire you saw. Now Robson – again with all that expensive security. The kind of thing you expect to see protecting a Beverly Hills mansion.'

'As though they were expecting Nemesis,' said Tweed.

12

Tweed, who had studied the map of Exmoor, drove back the way they had come and then turned on to a country lane leading away from Quarme Manor. Paula watched his expression as the headlight beams followed the twists of the hedge-lined road. The darkness seemed eerie, the moor closing in on all sides.

'Pete is still following us if that's what you're wondering,' she remarked. 'I saw his lights a moment ago behind us.'

'I was wondering about the name of Robson's bungalow. Endpoint.'

'Rather obvious. The lane comes to a full stop below where his bungalow is perched.'

'I noticed that. Something else came back to me. One of those notes Harry Masterson sent back from Athens – wrapped up as a clue only I would understand, he thought. *Endstation*. Close to Endpoint, wouldn't you say?'

'My God! It never occurred to me. Was Harry pointing a finger at Robson?'

'Who knows? It's early days yet.'

'It's getting late nights. Where are we off to now?'

'To pay a call on the third member of the party which raided Siros all those years ago. CSM Kearns. If we can ever find his place in the dark. I've marked where I think it is on that map. Navigate, girl.'

'Maybe he won't welcome a surprise visit at this hour . . .'

'So, maybe we catch him off guard. It's odd the way the three of them live so close together.'

'Perhaps they've remained close friends even after all these years.'

'And you don't sound any more convinced than I am . . .'

It was a difficult drive even when the moon rose, casting a weird light over the landscape. The light became weirder as a mist began creeping down from high up the moor. Behind the phosphorescent glow Paula could still see the ridge crests sweeping across Exmoor like giant waves.

They met no other traffic. They passed no villages. For miles on their way towards Simonsbath they saw not even one isolated dwelling. They were alone in the desolate wilderness as Tweed descended a long curving road, lights undimmed to warn any vehicle approaching from the opposite direction.

'What on earth is that?' Paula asked suddenly.

Lights suddenly appeared further down the slope, lights close together on their right-hand side. Tweed frowned, slowed to a crawl. They were still several miles from Simonsbath from his memory of the map. Woods now lined either side, and the lights gleamed between the tree trunks, flashing on and off as the trunks momentarily obscured them. He stopped the car and stared through the windscreen.

'It's a small estate of modern bungalows. They're crammed pretty close together. Must have been built during the past ten or fifteen years.'

'And I think we may have pulled up just outside CSM Kearns' house,' Paula commented.

To their left inside a gap in the trees stood an old stone two-storey house perched higher up the slope. Surrounded by a high stone wall, there were two six-feet-high solid wooden gates. Tweed reached for his flashlight in the glove compartment, asked Paula to lower her window, switched on the light. A large metal plate carried the name. *Woodside House*. 'This is his place,' he agreed.

He continued to move the light over the solid wooden gates. On the roadside was a grille covering each slab of wood. Reaching over to the rear seat, he grasped a heavy wooden walking stick he had purchased in Dunster. He was never sure afterwards what had made him do this.

'Let's investigate,' he said, switched off the engine and extracted the ignition key.

He locked the car before walking round it to join Paula who stood staring at the gates. Carrying the stick in his right hand, the light in his left, he swivelled the beam to the side of the right-hand gate and saw a bell-push. He pressed firmly with his thumb and they waited.

In the distance beyond the wall there was the sound of

a door being opened, a door which creaked loudly in the heavy silence of the mist-bound night. Footsteps approached with a brisk tread across what sounded like a cobbled yard. Suddenly a ferocious snarl murdered the night, followed by barking.

'My God, what's that?' Paula asked.

'Guard dog.'

'Sounds as though it's short of food – and thinks we'd make a good dinner.'

'Who is it?'

A cultured voice. Terse. Commanding. Talking at them through a small window flap opened in the right-hand gate.

'My name is Tweed. Are you Mr Kearns?'

'Yes. What do you want?'

'Special Branch. I want a talk with you. Now.'

'You have identification?'

'Of course. Wait a minute.' The unseen animal was growling, its claws pawing at the inside of the gate. It couldn't wait to get out. Paula shivered. Tweed produced his card, held it up to the spyhole, shone his torch on it.

'Stand quite still when I open the gate. Move and you'll be torn to pieces.'

'Charming,' Paula mumbled under her breath.

The flap slammed shut. A sound of bolts being withdrawn, the turn of a key and the right-hand gate swung inward. They were still faced with the heavy iron grille. Tactfully, Tweed switched off his light. Also, he wanted to regain his night vision. He felt Paula tense beside him.

The tall figure of a man stood inserting a key into the grille with his left hand. His right gripped a chain holding a huge dog. The creature became excited again, baying and snarling, lunging forward.

'Quiet, Wolf,' the crisp voice commanded. 'Come in. He's harmless . . .'

'You could have fooled me,' Tweed rapped back.

135

'And who is this girl? Not also Special Branch? She can wait in the car.'

'She can come in with me, for God's sake. She's not waiting by herself out here in the middle of nowhere. And she is Special Branch. My assistant, Paula Grey . . .'

As his exchange took place Kearns was closing the grille and the gate, relocking everything. Tweed wandered up the slope paved with stone flags towards the house. Over a hundred years old if it was a day. Paula kept pace, anxious to distance herself from Wolf, which she had now identified as an Alsatian.

'Wait here,' Tweed said as they reached the steps up to the front door. 'Back in a moment.'

He walked swiftly in his rubber-soled shoes round the left side of the stone hulk. At the entrance to a wide passage a horse had recently relieved itself on the stones. Rounding the corner, he was confronted with a stable door, the upper flap open. A horse's head regarded him, poked itself further over the flap and whinnied softly. Tweed held out a hand, stroked its neck. Its smooth hair was wet. It had been ridden hard. And not long ago.

'Leave him alone. What are you poking round here for?'

Kearns' voice was harsh, demanding. He moved as quietly as Tweed. Turning, Tweed smiled apologetically, made a dismissive gesture.

'I'm fond of horses,' he lied. 'That's a very fine animal . . .'

'Come back to the proper entrance.' The Alsatian, snarling like a mad dog, lunged for Tweed, who instinctively raised his walking stick. Held by an expanding lead, it almost reached Tweed and Kearns hauled him back. 'Prowl round here and Wolf will have your guts for garters.' Kearns made the statement in a calm tone.

Tweed followed Kearns at a distance. He switched on the flashlight as though picking his way. To the side of the paved area rough uncut grass and weeds cluttered the earth up to the base of the wall. His beam reflected off something metallic. Pausing, he prodded carefully with the stick. There was a grinding clash of metal. Two sabre-like blades, saw-toothed, sliced across the lower end of his stick. Kearns swung round.

'What the hell do you think you're playing at?'

'You tell me.'

'You just released a trap. We keep chickens and we're plagued with vermin – foxes and such like off the moor. That could have amputated your leg.'

'Let's go inside then. As you suggested . . .'

Inside, a bleak square hall was dimly lit with a forty-watt bulb. The woodblock floor was highly polished, doors led off the hall and a wide oak staircase climbed to a landing before turning to the next flight. From a door at the rear a blonde woman in her thirties appeared smoking a cigarette in an ivory holder.

She had a good figure, wore a powder-blue blouse with a high neck and a classic pleated cream skirt. She watched Tweed with a speculative eye, ignoring Paula. Kearns' mouth tightened.

'My wife, Jill. We have gatecrashers.'

'Would you like some refreshment?' she enquired, still eyeing Tweed. 'Coffee? Maybe something to drink . . .'

Her voice was soft, husky, but Kearns answered for her.

'Not necessary. They won't be staying long. Better come into the mess,' he told Tweed.

'He means the dining room,' Jill explained. She stroked her shoulder-length hair with one hand.

'In here,' Kearns went on. 'Sit down. Both of you.'

The rectangular-shaped dining room was oak-panelled, had an oak dining table and was illuminated by another forty-watt bulb inside an old-fashioned shade suspended high above the table. An atmosphere of spartan gloom pervaded the room. Tweed and Paula sat on chairs at the table while Kearns took up a standing position.

137

'First, I'd like to see your identification again,' he demanded.

Tweed handed him the card and studied their host while he examined the document. Kearns was over six feet tall, a lean and rangy man with a clean-shaven face and strong bone structure. He stood very erect in front of the fireplace which was laid with logs but unlit. Paula suppressed a shiver. It was chilly.

Kearns was in his sixties but he had worn well. His hair was still dark, his complexion was deeply tanned. He carried himself with an air of complete self-assurance and his eyes were like two brown marbles. Never off parade, Tweed thought drily.

He was clad in a pair of dark slacks, sharply creased, and a navy blue polo-necked cashmere sweater. There were traces of dried mud on his dark brown shoes, the only flaw in his otherwise impeccable appearance. He dropped the card on to the table so Tweed had to reach forward to retrieve it.

'Get to the point,' Kearns said.

'I'm investigating an unsolved murder which took place over forty years ago in the Middle East.'

'Oh, that macabre Ionides killing in Cairo. Can't help you. Why bring that up now?'

'Because it may be linked with the recent murder of one of our people. In Greece. At Cape Sounion. Know it?'

'No.'

Kearns stood with his feet slightly apart, hands clasped behind his erect back. He glanced at Paula who was taking notes in her book on the table. She had kept her expression blank during Kearns' reply. This was the first reference to Ionides.

'There are two of you,' Kearns decided. 'Bad tactics to be outnumbered. I also need a witness . . .' He walked quickly to the closed door, opened it, called out. 'Jill, come

138

and join us. Just sit and listen with that remarkable memory of yours. Sit there.' He made brief introductions.

As he returned to his position in front of the fireplace Jill Kearns, still smoking, carrying a porcelain ash tray, sat at the head of the table. She studied Paula, who stared straight back. Hackles rising, Tweed noted.

'Don't see how a recent murder could be linked with the Ionides business,' Kearns resumed.

'Tell me about Ionides. You used the word "macabre".'

'Not much to tell. We had just returned from a mission . . .'

'We?'

'Three-man commando raid on a Greek island. Antikhana – name of the building in Cairo where Ionides was slaughtered one night – was our official HQ. No one in the place knew what we were really employed for. Propaganda was supposed to be our job. Not even the CO of the building – Colonel Grogan – had a clue about us.'

'Tell me more about Ionides.'

'Some Greek who *was* working on propaganda – printing leaflets to send to the Resistance crowd. Two nights after we got back Ionides was apparently working late, alone in the building – a habit of his. Late one evening someone cut him to pieces. Blood all over the walls. He must have fought for his life – the room was a wreck. Ionides was slashed everywhere. Head pretty near severed from the body. Some maniac must have got in – and out. The Special Investigation Branch – equivalent of your crowd in the Army – never did solve it.'

'Did you ever meet a Harry Masterson?'

'Bluffed his way in here. Bit of a buffoon. Sent him packing.'

'You look very suntanned,' Tweed remarked, switching the topic without warning.

'I should do. Just back from windsurfing in Spain.'

'Your wife kept out of the sun from her appearance . . .'

139

'Didn't come with me. She hates the heat, loves the cold. Is this part of the interrogation? I haven't all night.'

'I have. And we're talking about murder. Maybe three murders. Where had you come back from just before the Ionides killing?'

'I told you. A three-man raid on a Greek island. Siros . . .'

'And the names of the other two men?' Tweed interjected quickly.

'The CO, Colonel Barrymore. A Captain Robson, medical officer.'

'And after all these years the three of you all live in the same area. Exmoor. I find that very curious – even strange.'

'Nothing to it. Barrymore and I stayed on in the Army after the war. Same unit. Robson got his demob soon after hostilities ended. Set up in practice as a doctor here. We kept in touch. When Barrymore and I left the Army we weren't sure where to settle. Robson offered to find us property round here. He knew the ropes. Barrymore and I told him what we could afford. Is that all?'

'Not quite. A Greek came with you on the Siros raid.'

'Oh, Gavalas.' Kearns shifted his stance, showed signs of growing boredom, even impatience. 'He was supposed to put us in touch with the Resistance group we landed to meet. Knew them, so he said. I had my doubts. There was a moment when we thought Jerry was near us in force. We scattered. When we met up Gavalas was missing. We found him in a gulch. Obviously he'd hidden there. He was dead. Knifed in the back. Commando knife, too. The colonel sorted that out. Checked that Robson and I had our knives. Showed us his own. Stickler for detail, the colonel. Not that we thought any of us had touched the Greek. Why should we?'

'For a hundred thousand pounds of diamonds that went missing.'

'Obviously taken by the assassin. Siros was crawling with odd characters. Fortunes of war.'

'Misfortunes in this case,' Tweed pointed out. 'For Gavalas. You ride much, Mr Kearns?'

'All of us do. One reason for living on Exmoor. And now . . .'

'Who is "all"?' enquired Paula.

Kearns turned his head as though he'd forgotten her presence and wasn't too pleased about her intervention. He stared at her coldly.

'The colonel and Dr Robson. As I was about to say before you interrupted, is that all?' He stared now at Tweed, looked pointedly at his watch.

'One more question. What odd characters? You just said Siros was crawling with them.'

'Republican Greeks, left-wing Greeks, Royalist Greeks, monks from the monastery. And the German occupation troops. Now . . .' He marched round the table to the door, opened it and went into the hall.

Jill Kearns, who had lit a fresh cigarette, leant across the table to Tweed. 'Are you staying somewhere near?' she whispered.

'Luttrell Arms, Dunster. You can get me there if something's bothering you,' Tweed replied in a low tone. He raised his voice. 'I think we may soon outstay our welcome, Paula.'

In the hall Kearns stood by the open front door. Somewhere close at hand Paula heard Wolf snuffling, growling, scratching at a door. Kearns had handed the dog's chain to Jill when they entered the place.

'Goodbye,' said Kearns stiffly.

'Just before we go,' Tweed persisted amiably, 'please give me your impressions of Colonel Barrymore and Captain Robson.'

Kearns' thin mouth tightened. 'The colonel is a first-rate commander. Can smell trouble a mile off.' He gazed straight at Tweed for a moment. 'Knows at once how to deal with it. No hesitation. Captain Robson was not a regular. More inclined to circle round trouble. Very determined in an emergency.'

'And that estate of new houses just down the road. Seems out of place.'

'Why? Occupied by businessmen, I gather. Probably commute to Taunton or Bristol. Like the country life. How would I know? I'll let you out now . . .'

Tweed and Paula prepared to follow him down the slope. Just before he stepped out Tweed glanced back. Jill Kearns stood watching him, holding her cigarette holder. She nodded at him.

'Goodnight,' said Tweed. 'Sorry to disturb you at this hour.'

'Any disturbance is welcome out in this Godforsaken wilderness.'

Kearns had both the wooden gate and the grille open when they reached him. He stood aside, said not another word as they walked out. The grille slammed shut behind them, followed by the main gate. Standing on the grass verge Tweed heard brisk footsteps retreating back towards the house.

'Well!' Paula blew breath between her teeth. 'That was really something. Imagine living with him.'

They climbed back into the car which was chilly inside. Tweed switched on the heater and tapped his fingers on the wheel before starting the engine. He was gazing at the glow of the estate lights in the mist.

'What was your impression?' Tweed asked as he fired the engine.

'A born CSM. Should still be in the Army, bawling contemptuous commands to his troops. Very self-contained. Could settle anywhere. A bloody iceberg.'

'And his attractive wife, Jill?'

'A manhunter. After more trophies to add to her collection.'

'That's pretty catty. Not your usual style . . .'

'I saw the way she watched you while you grilled Kearns.'

'She's a good few years younger than him – and it must get very lonely in that hideous old pile.'

'She's getting to you already.' Paula glanced at Tweed as he let the car cruise downhill. 'You devil, you're teasing me. I agree it can't be much fun married to the perfect CSM.'

'I thought he did that rather well – put on a clever performance. Just stopped short of caricature.'

'Tweed, what are you driving at?'

'Mr Kearns is a great deal more devious than you give him credit for. He was presenting a mask to us.'

'Talking about masks, I wonder about that peculiar little colony of bungalows,' she observed. 'They don't look real. Let's take a closer look. You know, they all look simply too good to be true to me.'

He slowed down even more as they passed the entrance to the estate and Paula counted six bungalows, three on each side of the cul-de-sac. All the dwellings had curtains drawn, lights on behind them. All had the usual status symbols of the upwardly mobile young and ambitious executives. Coach lanterns flanking each porch; more lanterns at the entrance gates to the drives; urn-shaped pots with evergreen shrubs like small exclamation marks.

'Like something out of the Ideal Homes Exhibition they hold at the annual Olympia exhibition in London,' Paula remarked. 'As I said before, they don't look real.'

'And Kearns, who lives on their doorsteps, doesn't seem to know a thing about them. Hard to swallow.'

'Makes sense to me. You said it yourself. He's a self-contained type . . .'

'I also said he was a good actor. What's the matter?'

They had left the bungalow estate behind, the road was now level, winding across the moor, open to it on either side. No hedges. In the moonlight on both sides smooth dark slopes swept up to high ridges silhouetted against the night sky. Paula had stiffened, was staring up to her left.

'There's that ghostly horseman again!'

'Where?' Tweed reduced speed to peer up the slope where transparent veils of pale mist rolled slowly over the moor, assuming strange shapes. Tweed was sceptical. One patch of mist looked like a centaur, then dissolved. 'I don't see any horseman . . .'

'Up there on that dip in the ridge, for God's sake. And he's got his rifle again. He's aiming it . . .'

Everything happened at once. A Cortina came up behind them and overtook, slowing as it pulled in ahead of the Mercedes. 'Pete is still with us,' Tweed remarked. 'I still can't see . . .'

He broke off in mid-sentence. Paula was not given to seeing phantoms as he'd imagined. Perched in a fold between two ridge crests a man on a horse stood still as a statue, rifle raised. Tweed rammed his foot down on the accelerator, turning out to pass the Cortina which had stopped. There was a sharp *crack!* At the same time the sound of splintering glass. Paula jerked her head round.

'Both rear side windows are crazed . . .'

'Bullet,' Tweed said tersely.

He pulled up at a point where two copses of trees shielded the road on either side, forming a shield. In the rear-view mirror he saw Pete Nield crouched behind the parked Cortina, both hands raised, aiming up the slope. The hard detonation of three shots fired in rapid succession echoed through the night. Nield stood up, climbed back behind the wheel, drove forward and stopped alongside the Mercedes. Tweed lowered his window full depth.

'He tried to kill you this time,' Nield remarked. 'How the hell did he make it all the way down here from the Doone Valley?'

'Did you get him?' Tweed asked calmly. Beside him Paula gripped both hands tightly to stop shuddering.

'No. The range of fire was too far for a handgun. Frightened him off before he could try again. Saw him vanish over a cleft in the hills. You didn't answer my question. How could he make it here from the Doone Valley?'

'He'd have to know the country well, have ridden over Exmoor a lot.' Tweed splayed his hands on the wheel. Paula was amazed by his reaction: he was cool as a cucumber. She was still shaking. 'Also there's a moon up,' Tweed went on. 'An experienced rider could have come across country direct while we drove in a half circle slowly.'

'So it could have been either Barrymore or Robson?' Paula suggested. 'Kearns told us they all rode . . .'

'Or even Kearns himself. Time to get back for a late dinner to Dunster.' He glanced at her as he released the hand-brake. 'Don't forget – Kearns is closest and the horse I saw in his table was still saddled up. But the attempt on my life proves that we came to the right place.'

13

The horseman appeared in the middle of the road as they came close to Dunster along a quiet hedge-lined country lane.

He sat motionless on his horse, one hand held up, the other holding the reins. Tweed saw him clearly in his headlights. He turned them from dipped to undipped and the twin glare showed up the waiting man starkly. He lowered his raised hand to shield his eyes.

Pete Nield's Cortina, close behind the Mercedes now,

overtook Tweed's car. Nield drove with one hand on the wheel, his other slipping the .38 Smith & Wesson from his hip holster. Stopping the Cortina, he jumped out of the seat, lifted both hands, gripping the gun, aiming point-blank.

'Don't shoot!'

Tweed had stopped his own vehicle, dived out and ran forward. He stood beside Nield, studying the horseman who remained as still as a bronze statue. Tweed blinked, wondering if his eyes were playing him tricks. Then he spoke briefly to Nield before walking forward.

'You won't need the gun. Incredible. I know who this is . . .'

Standing by the flank of the horse, he extended a hand upwards. The horseman reached down to shake the hand. Both men stared at each other. The horseman was stockily built, in his sixties, sported a brown moustache which matched his thick hair.

'Chief Inspector Sam Partridge,' Tweed said.

'Ex-Chief Inspector. Now retired. You gave me quite a chase over the moors. Where are you staying?'

'Luttrell Arms, Dunster . . .'

'Like me. It's the only decent hostelry for miles. I'll join you there for dinner, if I may. And they know me simply as Mr Partridge. It's only about a mile now. Why don't you drive on and I'll follow?'

'We'll wait for you in the bar,' replied Tweed and went back to his car, waving to Nield to take the wheel of his own vehicle.

'What was all that about?' Paula asked as the horseman turned and began trotting towards Dunster. 'And who is that man? He tried to kill you.'

'There was more than one horseman out on the moor today.' Tweed sat behind the wheel, watching Partridge's retreating figure.

'More than one?'

146

'The man who tried to kill me and that chap. Ex-Chief Inspector Sam Partridge of Homicide. I knew him at the Yard when I served my stint before joining the Service.'

'I don't understand this too well.'

'Neither do I. The long arm of coincidence is stretching itself to breaking point. There has to be some logic in this business somewhere. Partridge called at the Ministry of Defence after Harry Masterson – talked with Brigadier Willie Davies, the chap I went to see.'

'I still don't see . . .'

'When Partridge called at the MOD he told Davies he was still investigating a murder committed over forty years ago. In Cairo. A man called Ionides.'

'In Cairo? But Gavalas was murdered on the island of Siros.'

'Exactly. Odd, isn't it? Two different murders nearly half a century ago. I'm looking into one, Partridge is investigating another. He's staying at The Luttrell Arms.' He switched on the ignition. 'We're meeting Partridge when we get back to the hotel. Should be an interesting conversation, wouldn't you say?'

They sat at a quiet corner table at the far end of the dining room at The Luttrell Arms. Tweed had requested somewhere they could talk on their own. The manager in his dark jacket and trousers had escorted them and whispered to Tweed after pulling out Paula's chair.

'This is the table those three local gentlemen sit at when they meet here every Saturday night.'

'Which three gentlemen?' Paula asked when the manager had gone.

'Barrymore, Robson, Kearns . . .'

Tweed looked across the table at Partridge who sat opposite to him. Paula sat next to Tweed and faced Nield, sitting alongside Partridge. She studied the ex-Scotland

147

Yard man. Beneath his thatch of thick brown hair his face was weatherbeaten, had the ruddy glow of a man who spends a lot of time out of doors. His grey eyes had a steady gaze, his nose was short, almost pugnacious, but his manner and way of talking were gentle. The pursed lips and the strong jaw gave him an obstinate look. Not a man who gives up easily, she decided.

'The three men who are my suspects,' Partridge commented.

'Suspected of what?' Tweed enquired, glancing up from the menu. He noticed Partridge hesitate, glance at Paula and Nield. 'My companions are both fully trustworthy,' he assured him.

'Of the murder of a Greek called Ionides back in 1944 in Cairo.'

'That's a long time ago,' Paula remarked.

'I was hardly out of my teens in those days. For some reason I never understood they attached me to the SIB – Special Investigation Branch,' he explained to Paula. 'Military equivalent to Scotland Yard. I had a fool for a superior – a Captain Humble. Funny name for him – he was anything but humble. Knew it all, so he thought. Knew damn-all from what I could see. He'd been with the police in Manchester before joining the Army . . .'

He paused as the waitress came to take their orders. Paula was studying him again. He wore a hacking jacket, old grey slacks, and by his side on the banquette rested a much-worn check cap. A perfect outfit for merging into the Exmoor landscape. Tweed sipped water and then encouraged Partridge to continue before he could ask what Tweed was doing on Exmoor.

'Tell me a bit more about the murder of this Greek. Ionides, I think you called him.'

'Which wasn't his real name. I'll come to that later.' Partridge rested his elbows on the table and began to talk animatedly. Almost like a man possessed, Tweed noted.

148

'It was a horrific murder. Took place late one evening after dark in a weird building called the Antikhana. Near the Nile and backing on to a native quarter. Ionides had escaped from German-occupied Greece and was officially working on propaganda fed back into his country. A British sergeant who was billeted on the roof found the body. Blood all over the walls, the furniture, the floor. He had been cut to pieces with a knife. Head almost severed from the body.' Partridge looked at Paula. 'Sorry, don't want to spoil your meal.'

'I have a strong stomach. Do go on.'

'Humble was in charge of the case. Came up with nothing. No one in the building at the time of the murder, apparently. Only one entrance – and a Sudanese receptionist guarded that. Main entrance doors kept locked at night after six. Murder took place somewhere between eight and ten according to the pathologist. So theoretically the murder couldn't have been committed.'

'The windows?' Tweed suggested. 'The murderer could have got out by one of them?'

'Impossible. Bars on all the windows. Security was tight. The case has remained unsolved to this day.'

'So what are you doing prowling round Exmoor?'

Partridge waited while drinks and starters were served. He rapped on the table with his left-hand knuckles, a quiet tattoo. He ignored his soup, started talking again as soon as they were alone again.

'It's a bit complex. Three commandos were based officially inside that building. Two days before the second murder they'd returned from an abortive raid on an island called Siros.'

'Just a moment, Sam,' Tweed interjected, 'you're losing me. You said "the *second* murder" and "*abortive* raid . . ." What was the first murder?'

'The two questions are linked. The raid was abortive because attached to the three-man commando unit was a

Greek called Gavalas carrying a fortune in diamonds to hand over to the Resistance on Siros. They were desperately short of funds. On Siros Gavalas was murdered – knifed in the back. The diamonds he was carrying had gone. So, the mission was abortive. Two days later the three commandos were back in Cairo – *before* the murder of Ionides. You see where I'm leading?'

'Never like to assume anything, Sam. You must remember that from our days at the Yard.'

'Humble made a routine investigation of the murder of Ionides and then dropped the case. Something else came up. I was fascinated by the whole thing. The sheer brutality of the killing at the Antikhana. I kept on digging in my spare time. Ever since I've been convinced one of the three commandos was the killer of both men. On Siros, Gavalas. In Cairo, Ionides. The three men were Barrymore, Robson and Kearns.'

Tweed drank the rest of his soup while he thought. Nield, who was keeping quiet, had devoured his shrimp cocktail. Partridge was sipping his soup. Paula watched him as she went on eating her pâté. There were only three other couples eating late dinner.

'Sam,' Tweed began, 'you've spent your life as a detective. So far I haven't heard you produce a shred of evidence to back up this bizarre theory.'

'I told you I went on digging. I bluffed my way into Grey Pillars – as they called GHQ. I checked certain confidential records through a contact there. I found that Stephen Ionides – remember I said earlier it wasn't his correct name – was, in fact, Stephen Gavalas. Brother of Andreas Gavalas.'

14

Three people sat in what was known as the Garden Room – Tweed's bedroom with the door at the far end leading into the hotel's garden. It was elevated one storey above street level and at ten in the evening the curtain was closed over the locked door.

Paula sat in an armchair, her legs crossed, balancing a cup of coffee on her knee. On a couch Nield relaxed, nursing a glass of cognac. Only Tweed sat upright in a hard-backed chair. It helped his concentration.

'I think I'll pop off to bed, get an early night after all that riding,' Partridge had said as they left the dining room.

'So apparently there were two horsemen riding the moor while we were driving round,' Nield observed. 'Partridge was one, and the other is Mr X.'

'I was pretty mad when Partridge said he was the horseman behind Quarme Manor,' Paula reflected. 'Pointing that rifle at you – even if it was unloaded.'

'He used the telescopic sight to find out who I was,' Tweed reminded her. 'Must have had the shock of his life when he saw it was me.'

'But the other horseman near Kearns' place tried to kill you,' Nield pointed out. 'It's Mr X we want to track down.'

'That story about the Gavalas family still carrying on a vendetta worries me,' Tweed said. 'And I don't like the sound of the grandfather, Petros, who – according to Partridge – rules the family with a rod of iron. Sounds like a real ruffian.'

151

'Would anyone still carry on a vendetta after all these years?' Paula objected.

'The Greeks have a strong family sense. And an equally strong sense of family honour,' Tweed told her. 'According to Partridge two sons of old Petros were murdered. He could still be looking for the killers – or killer. Newman and Marler, who know Greece well, could fill us in on that angle best. Maybe when they return they'll have news.'

'But there is still no news from Athens?' Paula enquired.

'Nothing. I called Monica at Park Crescent while you were tarting yourself up in your room.'

'Tarting?' Paula grinned mischievously. 'Well at least he does notice when I freshen myself up.' Her expression turned serious. 'None of what we've learned gives us any data on poor Harry Masterson . . .'

She broke off as someone knocked tentatively on the door. Nield was on his feet in seconds, gun in hand. 'I'll check that.'

Tweed was also on his feet. 'Crouch behind the bed,' he ordered Paula. Switching off the main light, leaving the room dimly illuminated by table lamps, he moved his chair against the wall and sat down again. Nield approached the door silent as a cat. He stood against the wall to one side, grasped the key in the lock, turned it with great care, took hold of the handle with his left hand, threw it open.

A startled Partridge, still dressed, stood in the doorway. He glanced to his left as Nield slid the gun out of sight. Tweed asked him to come in and Nield closed and relocked the door.

'Very wise,' Partridge commented. 'And sorry to bother you at this hour. But I found things whirling round in my mind, facts I hadn't told you. A man called Harry Masterson was murdered while I was paying a visit to Greece . . .'

'What about this Harry Masterson?' Tweed asked after room service had delivered coffee. It was going to be a long night.

'I couldn't find out anything about his background – but I did discover he was squiring Christina Gavalas – that is Petros' granddaughter. Apparently they flew to Athens together. So I began to poke around.'

'Why? If you didn't know this Masterson?'

'Because where he went over the cliff – at a place called Cape Sounion – is close to the entrance to what the locals call Devil's Valley. That's where Petros Gavalas has his farm and his headquarters. It's hidden away in the hills near an abandoned silver mine.'

'Rather a flimsy connection,' Tweed probed.

'You think so? Masterson was with Christina Gavalas – and Cape Sounion was the location of his murder.'

'How do you know Masterson was murdered? Evidence, Sam – have you evidence? Something about the state of the body?'

'No. Just found by a coastguard cutter on the lookout for drug traffickers as it rounded Cape Sounion. Masterson's body was lying on some rocks. He'd plunged down two or three hundred feet.'

'I'm still waiting to hear some evidence,' Tweed insisted.

'Some years ago at a crime seminar in Athens I met a Captain Sarris of Athens Homicide. I visited him on this latest trip. He told me in confidence they couldn't prove anything, but Sarris was convinced it was murder.'

'Why?'

'He'd observed Masterson somewhere. Said he simply wasn't the sort of man to stumble over the edge of a cliff. Do you mind if I light my pipe? After all, you'll be sleeping here . . .'

'Light up! You think better when you're smoking, Sam. I can open the door to the garden later. Anything else?'

'Yes. There's a Greek called Anton riding around on Exmoor – Anton Gavalas, son of Petros. By his second wife. There was a rumour he slipped ashore off a boat from Portugal at Watchet.'

153

Tweed leaned forward. 'How do you know about this Anton?'

'Sarris told me just before I left to fly home. They keep an eye on the Gavalas family. I visited the harbourmaster down at Watchet. He told me ships do arrive from Portugal delivering cork. They take back wastepaper for recycling – there's a paper mill at Watchet. Then I ran into a roadblock.'

'What kind of a roadblock?'

'The harbourmaster. Got pretty indignant when I suggested maybe someone had slipped ashore without his knowledge. Pointed out his office overlooks the harbour.'

'You still think he came ashore illegally?'

'I phoned Jim Corcoran, Security Chief at London Airport. He checked all the passenger manifests – I'd hinted it might have something to do with drugs. No Anton Gavalas showed up. Maybe he flew in via somewhere like Manchester. Doubtful.'

'How could you know it was Anton?' Tweed pressed.

'Sarris showed me several photos of him.' Partridge looked surprised. 'Thought you'd be ahead of me there.'

'You remember how I used to be.' Tweed waved a dismissive hand. 'A stickler for precise facts. You've seen Anton, then? Here?'

'Riding across Exmoor. Doone Valley area. Using a monocular glass to study Barrymore's place, Quarme Manor. Then on to Dr Robson's bungalow. Same routine there. Later across country to Kearns' place. He knows where those three live.'

'And you know where this Anton is based?'

'No, dammit. And not for want of trying.'

'I'd like his description – unless you have one of those photos.'

'Sarris wouldn't release any.' He closed his eyes, sucked at his pipe. 'Late thirties. Hair black as sin. Small

154

moustache, same colour. Nose of a hawk – like Petros. About five feet six. Nasty piece of work would be my guess. First-rate horseman.'

'And how do you know that?' Tweed went on.

'Followed him. Saw him riding by chance when I was on the moor. Kept well out of sight but one day he caught me. A cunning type. I rode round a big crag and there he was – waiting for me. Asked in a sneering way why I was following him. He speaks perfect English. Sarris told me he'd spent time at a riding school while in Germany. Somewhere in Bavaria. Close to the main railway line between Munich and Lindau on Lake Konstanz – facing Switzerland.'

'What on earth would this Anton be doing prowling round Exmoor?'

'Obviously sent by Petros to locate the three men who took part in that commando raid on Siros. Petros is still seeking vengeance on the man who killed his sons, Stephen and Andreas, all those years ago.'

'And you're doing the same thing, in a way. Still trying to identify the murderer. It's folly, Sam . . .'

'It gives me an interest in my retirement.'

'But it must be costing you a fortune,' Tweed protested. 'Can you afford all this?'

Partridge grinned, sucked noisily at his pipe. 'If I just had my pension, no. That keeps myself and my wife comfortable. We're modest in our life style. You see, an uncle of mine left me a large legacy. Came out of the blue. That finances my hunt. I never could forget that unsolved murder at Antikhana. Haunted me, you might say . . .'

He stopped speaking. Paula had recrossed her legs. She reached down to stroke an itch above her ankle. The bracelet which had remained concealed under the cuff of her cream pleated blouse slid down her wrist. She glanced up. Partridge was gazing fixedly at her wrist, his expression frozen. He

155

realized she was watching him and smiled, looked away.

'I'd forget the whole business, Sam,' Tweed advised.

'I really came to your room to give you this.' Partridge produced a sealed manila envelope from his breast pocket, handed it to Tweed. 'In case I don't wake up one morning that's for you. Inside is the address and key of a safety deposit box. Nearly opposite Harrods in London. Not to be opened while I'm still alive and kicking. Agreed?'

'If you insist . . .'

'I do.' He checked his pipe, which had gone out again, tucked it in a pocket and stood up. 'This time I really am off to bed. Sorry to intrude. But it's been good talking with you – like the old days at the Yard.'

'Just before you go, Sam.' Tweed held up the envelope. 'Give me some idea of what I'd find if I ever visited that safety deposit.' Partridge hesitated, Tweed pressed. 'We worked together once – with Homicide. I'm entitled to an answer.'

'I've been building up a dossier on those three men. All the details are in a notebook inside the safety deposit. I'd like to leave it there.'

'Fair enough . . .'

Pete Nield had been fingering his dark moustache, studying the ex-detective. Now he spoke, his index finger pointed to stress what he said.

'Mr Partridge. On the ridge behind Quarme Manor you said you had used the telescopic sight on your rifle to look at Tweed – which is how you identified him. You also said your rifle was unloaded. Then you told us about following this Anton Gavalas over the moor. Was the Greek armed?'

Partridge turned to face Nield and frowned. 'Yes. He carried a rifle in a scabbard. I saw it clearly through my telescopic sight . . .'

'And your rifle was loaded then – because you felt the Greek was dangerous?'

'As a matter of fact, yes . . .'

156

'Are you still telling me that the rifle you aimed at Tweed was unloaded – knowing you might bump into that Greek again riding the moor?'

'I had the safety catch on.' Partridge paused. 'But you are right. It was loaded. I just thought it embarrassing to let Tweed know . . .'

'It's all right, Sam,' Tweed intervened. 'It's been a long day for you. Better get off to bed now. See you in the morning.'

'Goodnight everyone.'

On this note Partridge left the room. Nield followed him and locked the door. Returning to his chair he sat down and poured fresh coffee which he handed round.

'He's a nice man,' Paula remarked. 'I think he's under great stress.'

'He's also a liar,' Nield told her quietly. 'He lied about his rifle being unloaded when he aimed it at Tweed. Who knows what might have happened if you hadn't flashed your torch, distracted him?'

'Surely you can't suspect Partridge?' Paula said with a note of disbelief.

Nield grinned at her. 'I suspect everyone. Guilty until proven innocent. That's why Tweed employs me. And don't forget by his own admission he was in Cairo when Ionides – Stephen Gavalas – was slashed to pieces.'

'If he was involved he'd never have admitted that,' she objected.

'He's clever enough to know Tweed would find out sooner or later. Maybe he's under stress because *we* have arrived on the scene.'

'I will say that was smart of you to dig out the fact his rifle was loaded.'

'Simple logic. He could have carried night glasses if he just wanted to see what was going on. But no, he has a rifle.'

Paula turned to look at Tweed who had listened to this exchange in silence. He sat with his head rested against the

157

wall, eyes half-closed, miles away. She leaned forward, patted his hand. His eyes snapped fully open.

'A penny for your thoughts. A pound if you push me. And you look worried.'

'I am. About Sam. He's a man with an obsession. The most dangerous state of mind for a detective – or a spy. Fogs the judgement. That's not all.'

'So, tell me . . .'

'All this business about a Greek vendetta. I don't like that one little bit. That old hawk, Petros – he could have brainwashed his whole family into thinking they have one mission in life. To locate and revenge themselves on the man who did kill Andreas and Stephen – *if* it was the same man. And if Sam is right, Petros has harnessed the second generation to his obsession. Hence the arrival of Anton on Exmoor. I sense the kind of man Petros is. He reeks of ferocity and blood.'

'You don't normally use such melodramatic language,' Paula remarked.

'This isn't a normal situation. Not by a long shot. Literally. Someone did take a pot shot at me in the Mercedes a few hours ago. If we're not careful there could be more killings . . .'

'Which reminds me,' Nield suggested. 'In the morning I'll take the Merc to a garage in Minehead, get those windows replaced. I'll tell the mechanic it must have been a wild shot by someone out for sport on the moor.'

'There's a couple of other things, Tweed,' Paula continued. 'I wonder if you noticed Partridge's expression when my bracelet slipped from under my cuff? He stared at the Greek key symbol like a man transfixed.'

'Probably looking at your legs,' Nield joked. 'Enough to transfix any full-blooded male . . .'

'Oh, shut up! The other thing was when we met those three men. Barrymore, Kearns and Robson – all with dark suntans.'

'I did notice,' Tweed agreed. 'And they went to some length to explain where they'd been. Even Barrymore, who wasn't exactly voluble. Interesting that all three said they'd been away to places difficult to check – Morocco and the Caribbean . . .'

'Which, as I said earlier, means one of them could have just returned from Greece where Harry Masterson died.'

'Exactly. And the timing of their absence coincides with when Masterson was killed. Pure speculation, of course.'

'But odd that they should all be away at the same time,' she persisted.

'Now you're reaching,' Nield intervened. 'The month of May – the time when people who are free to go on holiday do. They avoid the crowds.'

'And that's not all,' said Tweed.

'It's enough for me tonight.' Paula stifled a yawn. 'But do tell me what else there is.'

'When we can I want to check Sam's story about Anton Gavalas.'

'How on earth are we going to do that?' she asked, standing up and clearing the coffee cups, arranging them neatly on a tray.

'When we can we visit Watchet. *I* ask the harbourmaster. Was there a ship which berthed from Portugal? *I* carry more clout than Sam, who is now retired. Did he see a man answering the description of Anton coming ashore?'

'Sleep well.' Paula bent down, kissed him on the cheek. 'Forget everything.'

'I'll try.' Tweed smiled grimly. 'I'm expecting developments. Maybe rather unpleasant ones.'

15

The following morning Paula was walking down the old oak staircase when Nield caught up with her. Both had breakfasted with Tweed. Paula had gone to her room to fetch her outdoor clothes, leaving Tweed to linger over his coffee in the dining room.

'I'm off to Minehead to fix the Mercedes,' Nield told her. 'You look thoughtful.'

'It's Tweed. He's worried. He enquired for Partridge before we had breakfast. The manager told him Partridge had early breakfast and had gone off to the stables. He's going to ride over Exmoor again. Tweed wishes he'd leave it alone – or cooperate with us.'

'Independent chap, our Mr Partridge. And, like Tweed said, he's obsessed with a forty-year-old murder. You can't reason with an obsession.'

'I suppose you're right . . .'

She half-opened the door to the dining room, then stopped, paused, and closed it again quietly. Checking the belt of her raincoat, she glanced up at Nield from under her thick eyebrows.

'She doesn't waste much time. I thought she was a manhunter.'

'Who?'

'You'll never guess who's sitting at Tweed's table. Jill, Kearns' ravishing blonde wife. She asked Tweed where he was staying just before we left Woodside House.'

'Tweed will handle her, maybe extract some information.'

'You could be right.' She hesitated. 'Do you mind if I come with you to Minehead, Pete? I can leave a note for Tweed.'

'I'd welcome the company . . .'

Tweed had been sitting quietly, sipping his coffee, sorting out in his mind what he had learned, when Jill Kearns walked into the dining room. Slipping off her suede gloves and her camelhair coat, she'd perched in the chair opposite him.

'I hope I'm not too early for you. Stuart – my husband – went off riding on the moor so it seemed an ideal opportunity to pop over and see you.'

She wore a tight-fitting powder-blue sweater which showed off her well-rounded breasts and had a polo-necked collar. Using both elegant hands she threw her shoulder-length hair over her shoulders, inserted a cigarette in the ivory holder, pausing before she lit it.

'Do you mind? My smoking while you breakfast?'

'Not at all. I'm only drinking coffee.'

'And there's no one else about, so it's an ideal chance for us to get to know each other better.'

'As you say . . .'

Tweed smiled to encourage her. She had excellent bone structure, a well-shaped nose, a full-lipped mouth painted with bright red lipstick. Her eyes were a startling blue beneath blonde arched eyebrows. She radiated animation and he guessed her age at something over thirty. About half Kearns' age. And very sexy.

'Let me tell you something about myself,' she began in the soft, husky voice he remembered well from the previous evening. 'My father was a squadron leader with the RAF in the Mid-East during the war. Stayed on afterwards as an adviser to the Egyptian Government. I was actually born in Cairo.' She cocked her head on one side,

161

staring straight at him. 'Is this all a frightful bore? It must
be . . .'

'On the contrary, I'm always interested in the background of a beautiful woman.' She inclined her head,
smiled impishly as she acknowledged the compliment.
'Please go on.'

'My mother was Clementine Hamilton. Born in
Dublin . . .'

'That name rings a bell.' He waited.

'My brother, David Hamilton, is a Member of Parliament. I was born late. My mother was forty.'

'Was? You mean . . .'

'Both my mother and father are dead. A car crash. They
were in a pile-up on the M25 . . .' She hurried on as Tweed
began to say something. 'It's all right. It was quite a few
years ago. Then I married Stuart – or he married me
might be more accurate. His first wife died in a swimming
accident. You'll have noticed the difference in age between
my husband and myself. I found the younger men callow,
quite boring. I didn't know Stuart at all well. He's very
handsome – but looks aren't everything.'

'I suppose not,' Tweed commented cautiously.

She reached across the table with her right hand and
placed it over his. Her hand was warm, the fingers supple
as they entwined Tweed's.

'I need an ally, a confidant, someone I can trust . . .'

'I'm afraid I might not fit the role,' he began.

'Someone right outside this tight social circle on Exmoor.
Wait,' she urged as he opened his mouth. 'Please, let me
finish. I am becoming frightened. Something is wrong.
Help me. Please.'

She released his hand but her eyes held his. Blue? More
like *lapis lazuli*. For a moment Tweed was aware of himself
standing mentally away from the table, observing his own
reactions. The woman was getting to him, exercising all
her charm, exerting an almost hypnotic effect.

162

He drank more coffee, gazed at the base of the inside of the cup. His brain began to tick over again. He chose his words carefully.

'What are you frightened of?'

'The atmosphere. As though something awful is about to happen.' She stubbed her cigarette, fitted a fresh one into the holder, lit it with a gold Dunhill lighter. Tweed reached across to the next table, put a clean cup and saucer in front of her, poured coffee from the pot. She said, 'No, thank you,' when he offered cream and drank half the cup of steaming black coffee. 'Thank you, Tweed. I needed that.' He sensed they were already on intimate terms as he asked the question.

'I'm afraid I don't understand yet – what atmosphere?'

'The moor, for one thing. Being shut up in Woodside at night – cut off from the world by high walls. Like being in prison. My only companion, Wolf, my dog.'

'And for another thing, Mrs Kearns?'

'Jill. Please call me Jill. Then there are Stuart's strange friends. Dr Robson and that Colonel Barrymore. Do you know they were in the same Army unit all those years ago? Now they *still* seem to be in the unit. They meet twice every week. Once here for dinner. On Saturdays. Then for lunch at The Royal Oak in Winsford each Wednesday.'

'Today is Wednesday . . .'

'I know. Which is why Stuart won't be back until late this afternoon at the earliest. So I'm safe. Driving over here in the hope of seeing you. And, Tweed . . .' She leaned close to him and he caught the faintest whiff of perfume. Something expensive. His mind felt dazed. 'They'll all be at The Royal Oak,' she went on in her soft, soothing voice. 'And the weird thing is the colonel – Barrymore – still acts as though he's in command of them. He's creepy. The way he looks at my legs sometimes. I know what he's thinking.'

'Listen to me,' Tweed began briskly. 'Nothing you've

163

said so far explains why you think something awful – that was the word you used – is going to happen.'

'They've all become so guarded – they seem to have closed ranks against some terrible force they fear is coming. Stuart has those dangerous mantraps concealed all round the house . . .'

'Mantraps?'

'Oh, yes.' She held the holder by the tip and waved it with an elegant gesture. 'He says they're to keep out vermin. I don't believe a word of it. The high walls would do that. Those gates are always kept closed. Stuart stays up half the night, pacing in his study. I can hear him as I lie awake. Now, do you see why I need a friend, an ally?'

'Why choose me? You have your brother David . . .'

'We're not close. He's very busy. I once tried to talk with him and he said it was all imaginings – that I should have married a younger man. We had a bit of a row after that.'

'I still say why me?'

'You're Special Branch.' She paused, her lips parted in a warm smile. 'It's more than that. The moment I saw you I felt that I could trust you. Are you going to turn me down flat?'

'I didn't say that. Can't you get away from Exmoor for a while? Spend a little time with a friend. Say in London?'

'Stuart wouldn't stand for it. He *expects* me to stay at Woodside. I'm his wife . . .'

'So talk to him about it – as you have to me . . .'

She shook her head. Her mass of blonde hair swirled in waves. Tweed wondered what it would be like to run his hand through that jungle of blondeness . . . His mouth tightened. Madness. *I want you to remember one thing, Tweed. Never get mixed up with any woman connected with a case you're working on. That is the road to certain disaster.* His mentor when he'd first joined the Yard.

164

'I can't,' she said vehemently. 'He's closed up inside himself. He always was too self-contained. I realized that after we were married. Too late. Can I come to you if things get worse?'

'If I'm still in Somerset. Why are these three men living so close together? Your husband, Robson and Barrymore.'

'Robson is a doctor. He came out of the Army at the end of the war. They kept in touch. When Stuart and Barrymore retired from the Service Robson helped them find homes. I didn't know any of this until after I was married. I never did like such a peculiar set-up. I'd better go now.'

Tweed stood up promptly, checked his watch. 'Actually, I have an appointment. I can't promise you anything . . .'

She slipped on her coat, left it open, stretching her breasts as she threw back her golden hair over the collar. Walking quickly round the table, she hugged him with both arms, pressed her body close to his and kissed him.

'It's early days for you and me,' she said.

Then she was gone.

The phone was ringing when Tweed returned to his room. He ran, knowing the ringing would stop as he reached for the receiver. He lifted it, said 'Hello.' The manager answered, said there was a call for him.

'That you, Tweed?'

Partridge's voice. Sounded as though he'd been hurrying before he used the phone.

'Yes, Sam.' A click, which told him the manager had put down his instrument. 'I think it's all right to speak now. Where are you?'

'Winsford. You take the road out of Dunster where you met me on horseback. Continue on until you come to a signpost on the right. I'll meet you at The Royal Oak Inn for lunch. 12.30 suit you?'

'I'll be there. Stay off the moor, Sam. We'll cooperate. I can tell you something about Masterson . . .'

'Really?' Still sounded in a rush. 'One thing you should know. Antikhana. You know where that is? What happened there a long time ago?'

'I'm with you.' Partridge was exercising caution, not trusting the phone. 'Go on . . .'

'I didn't like the look of Selim, the Sudanese on duty the evening it happened. Humble had questioned him. Superficially. I put him through the wringer. He was hiding something. No doubt about it. Selim vanished shortly afterwards. I think someone used a carrot and stick. The carrot, money. The stick, fear. Never seen again. Rumoured he'd gone back to Khartoum. My bet is he ended up floating down the Nile. Must go now . . .'

'Stay off the moor,' Tweed repeated.

'See you for lunch . . .'

The connection was broken. Tweed replaced the receiver slowly. He felt very unhappy about the call. Hands clasped behind his back, he paced the large room. Later he went out into the garden for some fresh air. He stood on a neat lawn, looking at the old castle which perched above the small town at the other end of the High Street. Beyond the wall at the end of the garden green fields stretched away. An atmosphere of pure peace. And the last thing he was experiencing was peace of mind.

Tweed checked his watch again. Fifteen minutes to twelve. He had studied his map of Exmoor, obtained from a newsagent down the High Street. He calculated thirty minutes would be ample time to drive to Winsford. He would give Paula and Nield until noon to get back from Minehead; if they didn't arrive he would leave a note and drive there alone. Someone tapped softly on his door.

'We were quick,' Paula told him as she entered the room followed by Nield. 'Both windows have been replaced.'

'That *was* quick.'

'I found a Mercedes dealer,' Nield explained. 'With a garage next door. I tipped them well before they started. Four men worked on the job. We're off to Watchet now?'

'No. Something came up . . .'

'She certainly did,' Paula commented, teasing him. 'You've come into close combat with the enemy, I see.'

She reached for Tweed's right shoulder, took something between her fingers off his blue bird's-eye suit and held it up. A long blonde hair. 'Good job we didn't get back earlier.'

'Sit,' Tweed commanded. He was irked by his carelessness. He'd wiped his mouth clean of Jill Kearns' lipstick. He should have checked more thoroughly in the mirror. 'I have a lot to tell – and not much time to tell it. We have to be in Winsford to meet Partridge at 12.30 . . .'

He repeated a concise account of his encounter with Jill Kearns; he had total recall for conversations. Paula and Nield sat and listened while he then went on and told them about the telephone call from Partridge.

'And now you're up to date,' he concluded.

'She doesn't waste much time,' Paula remarked, then clapped her hand to her mouth. 'Sorry, that was pretty catty. She sounds like a very frightened woman. But frightened of what exactly?'

'Or a first-rate actress,' Tweed pointed out. 'Sent by Kearns to probe me, find out what I'm really up to.'

'My own thought,' Nield interjected. 'And why should we assume it was Kearns who sent her? If she's having an affair with one of the other two – Barrymore or Robson?'

'You are a couple of cynics,' Paula observed.

'Pete could be right,' Tweed said. 'Someone may have sent her on a fishing expedition.'

'But what was your real impression?' Paula demanded, leaning forward, staring hard at Tweed.

'Not enough data yet. I'm in a neutral zone. And it's time we set off for Winsford. Same procedure, Pete. Paula comes with me in the Merc. You follow in the Cortina. When we get to The Royal Oak, sit at a separate table. You're not with us. Let's move . . .'

'It's Wednesday,' Paula said suddenly. 'That's the day those three – Barrymore, etc., have lunch at The Royal Oak.'

'And that had occurred to me when Partridge suggested meeting me there. No coincidence I'm sure. Sam knows what he's doing. So, when we arrive we don't recognize him unless he comes up to us. It's his game. Let him play it his way.'

Tweed had taken the right-hand turn off the main road to Dulverton, following the signpost to Winsford. The day was overcast and chilly, the winding road ahead deserted. Paula sat beside Tweed, gazing at the huge brown sweeping ridges of Exmoor towering in the distance.

'Look,' she said, 'it's coming back.'

Tweed glanced to his right. Along the high edge of the ridges a wave curled like a surf-crested sea. The mist crept down, blotting out the upper slopes of the moor, advancing remorselessly. Paula shivered. There was something sinister the way the grey vapour swallowed up the moor.

'I hope to God Partridge has reached Winsford,' Tweed remarked. 'Imagine getting lost in that stuff.'

'You would get lost then?'

'Well, it depends. I guess by now he knows Exmoor pretty well. The amount of time he seems to have spent roaming over it. He probably knows which gulches lead down into Winsford. I just don't like the idea of him being up there at all. Let's hope we find him at The Royal Oak, sitting with a pint in front of him. Then I'll feel better.'

Astride his horse Partridge spotted the first wraiths of mist higher up, wraiths which merged into a solid wave of grey as it rolled towards him. Time to head down for Winsford. Turning his horse, he was about to ride down a gully which would take him on to the main road when he saw the second horse.

It stood riderless, reins draped, head down as it nuzzled tufts of grass. The rider lay sprawled on the ground, face down, his head resting on a boulder. His riding cap was askew, tilted no doubt when the animal had thrown him. Or had he been taken ill, fallen from the horse, his head striking the iron-hard boulder?

Partridge gave a quick glance at the mist which was close now. Dismounting, he strode towards the stricken man. It would be the devil of a job getting him down to Winsford. He'd have to try and fold the unconscious man over his own horse. If he was still alive . . .

The thought made him hurry. At the very least he could have cracked his skull – hitting that boulder. Granite. The hardest of rocks. The mist was floating over the sprawled figure when he reached it. The dampness felt cold on his face. He stood astride the figure, stooped to examine it further . . .

You bloody fool! Suddenly Partridge's instinct for danger flared. *Reins draped* . . . No one falling from a horse had time to do that. He was straightening up when the figure came to life. Mist swirled round Partridge's head as hands like a vice gripped his ankles, toppled him face down. He fell heavily, was winded. He ignored the shock. Started to lift himself on his elbows, to whip over and over. He was seconds too late. He felt a dull ache under his left shoulder

169

blade as the knife was driven home. Then he plunged into a bottomless pit of darkness.

'What a lovely-looking place,' said Paula.

They were approaching The Royal Oak after driving past several thatched cottages. The ancient inn had a steep brown thatched roof. The thatch curved round arched windows close to the inn's sign, a painting of an oak tree. Several cars were parked outside.

Winsford was a sprawling village located at a point where several roads met. It nestled snugly below hilly green fields and as they entered the place Paula saw stately evergreen trees shaped like pepperpots. An oasis of civilization amid the grim unseen moor which loomed behind the mist.

'We'll go inside, get a bite to eat,' Tweed said as he parked the car. In his wing mirror he saw Nield's Cortina arrive and stop on the other side of a small green.

Outside, The Royal Oak was freshly painted, its walls a beige colour. Must have stood there for hundreds of years, Tweed thought as he locked the car and walked with Paula. She pulled up her raincoat collar: there was a chill in the air.

Inside, the large, low-ceilinged room stretched away into separate sections with wide openings leading from one to another. The bar was crowded and behind it a giant of a man in an open-necked shirt served drinks and joked with his customers. Mostly locals, Tweed guessed. A log fire crackled and there was an air of animation.

'Where do they all come from?' Paula whispered.

'I expect they ride or drive in from miles around. You've seen some of the lonely places people live in this part of the world.'

'No sign of Partridge,' she whispered again.

'He'll be along. He's a punctual chap . . .'

She gripped his arm. 'Someone else has arrived.'

Kearns strode in as though on parade. Clad in riding gear – pale grey jodhpurs thrust into boots which gleamed, a drab windcheater – he waved his riding crop at the barman. 'What is it today?'

'Hello, sir. Good to see you again. How about a nice chicken and mushroom pie? And your usual double Scotch?'

'That'll do . . .'

'Here's your drink. I'll send over the food. We've kept your table.'

Paula gribbed Tweed's arm again. 'The clan is gathering.'

Oliver Robson, also dressed in riding gear, but scruffily dressed compared with the CSM, appeared, smiling, exchanging words with several people. The barman spotted him at once, called out again over the heads of the crowd.

'Good morning, Doctor. Don't think you got that tan on the moor. Not this year. Nice to see you back . . .'

He repeated the menu and Robson nodded amiably, said he'd have a glass of white wine. His manner was tentative, Paula was thinking. Like a man who was shy. He took the glass and sat down next to Kearns who sat upright, looking everywhere except in the direction of Tweed and Paula. The two men were sitting at a window table where a third chair remained empty.

'Grab that table,' Tweed advised. 'You're hungry?'

'The chicken and mushroom pie smells good,' she replied as a serving woman passed them with a tray. 'And a glass of the white wine. The third member of the club is joining them . . .'

She sat down at a small round table for two after draping her raincoat over the other chair. Barrymore, also wearing riding gear, had stalked in, his manner stiff. The barman greeted him as 'Colonel' and Barrymore nodded when offered food. He took the chair between Kearns and Robson without saying anything and stared around. Like the chairman of the bloody board, Paula thought.

171

Tweed eased his way to the bar, gave his orders, waited while the wine was poured. Something made him glance over his shoulder. Barrymore had moved quickly. He was standing over Paula, a hand on her shoulder as he spoke. Paula gazed up at him, her expression cold, distant.

Turning back to the bar, Tweed paid the bill. Picking up the two glasses he edged his way out of the crowd in time to see Barrymore sitting down again at his own table. Paula's flawless complexion was slightly flushed. He sensed annoyance.

'You have an admirer,' he teased as he seated himself.

'Saucy swine. He had the nerve to invite me over to Quarme Manor. For afternoon tea, and maybe a drink, he said.'

'I'm sure you coped . . .'

'I told him he could phone me at The Luttrell Arms sometime. They serve tea there.' She paused, drank some wine. 'If you think I might get something out of him I'm quite happy to play along.'

'No! On no account are you to be alone with that man. On the other hand, if he does call you at Dunster, take your own decision. But only meet him in a public place. He's still staring at you.'

'I know. Staring at my legs. I was right. He reminds me of a satyr. And Pete is doing his stuff.'

Nield had perched himself on a stool close to the table where the three men sat. He was drinking a half pint of beer, gazing across the room.

'He identified them quickly,' Paula remarked.

'I gave him a verbal description of them. He has sharp hearing. Even with all this babble going on he'll be able to tell us what they were talking about.' Tweed checked his watch. 'Partridge is late. Very out of character.'

'The mist may have delayed him . . .'

'Not like him, not like him at all.'

They had finished their chicken and mushroom pies,

172

eaten some of the inn's excellent French bread, when the commotion started outside. Voices raised, the sound of running feet. Someone shouting. Tweed stood up.

'Back in a minute. I'll just see what's going on . . .'

'You look grim.' She spoke softly. The babble inside the pub was suddenly hushed. People stared out of the windows. Tweed slipped into the street, throwing on his coat as he walked. He paused to get his bearings. Beyond the small green was parked a Land Rover. A police car, its blue light whirling, was close to it. Uniformed policemen were gently pushing back the gathering crowd. Tweed took his card from his pocket, walked across the green. The grass was soggy underfoot. A uniformed inspector held up his hand.

'Please keep back, sir.'

Tweed, his eyes on the long sheath of folded canvas in the back of the Land Rover, showed the card. The inspector, a short and burly man, took the card, stared at it, compared the photograph with its owner, handed it back.

'Special Branch? We don't see much of you in this part of the world. I'm Inspector Farthing.'

'I may be able to help. What is inside that canvas bundle?'

'Something rather shocking. Brought down from the moor by the chap over there with the corduroy cap. A local, Lock. Goes shooting rabbits on the moor. He found the body inside a rock cleft. Pure luck. Rabbit he'd just shot fell inside the cleft. Nothing in the way of identification. No wallet. No letters.'

'Can I have a look?'

'Of course. I hope you have a strong stomach, sir . . .'

Tweed was moving to the back of the Land Rover when Paula joined him. He warned her it might be unpleasant. She bridled.

'Goes with the territory. Don't treat me like a five-year-old.'

'It's all right,' Tweed assured Farthing who had laid a hand on Paula's arm. 'She's my assistant.'

He heard a retching sound. Lock, the driver, was stooped over a ditch. Nimbly, Tweed leapt up on to the rear of the vehicle open to the sky. Paula followed. Tweed bent down, folded back one end of the canvas. What remained of the face of Partridge stared up at him, eyes open, sightless. He had been savagely slashed many times with a knife. Folds and slivers of flesh hung in flaps. The nose and eyebrows had almost completely disappeared. The clothes as much as anything identified him for Tweed. Paula sucked in her breath. Plunging both hands inside her windcheater, she clenched them into fists.

'I know this man, can identify him,' Tweed said, folding the canvas gently over the brutally ravaged face. He kept his voice low. Farthing crouched to hear him. The crowd of sightseers was still pushing close to the Land Rover. 'Sam Partridge,' Tweed said. He paused. 'A retired Chief Inspector of Homicide at Scotland Yard.'

'Thank God you were here.' Farthing grunted. 'You don't want to see, but all his fingers are missing. Cut off at the base. I'd say they're at the bottom of some other crevice. And all makers' labels have been ripped off the clothes.'

'Someone took trouble in the hope he wouldn't be found quickly – and by the time he was identification wouldn't be easy.'

Farthing breathed heavily. 'Then this case is going to raise one hell of a stink.'

'I'm sure of it. Can I make a suggestion? People rushed out of The Royal Oak to gawk. But three men are still sitting inside at a window table. Colonel Barrymore, Dr Robson and Stuart Kearns. Send a man in to ask them to come out and look at the corpse . . .'

'Study the reactions of each man,' Tweed whispered to Paula when they had moved to the rear of the crowd.

Kearns came out first, strode briskly to the vehicle, climbed into it. Farthing pulled back the canvas, exposed the hideously mutilated face. Kearns stood erect as he gazed down. No trace of emotion showed as he shook his head. 'Never seen him before,' he informed Farthing, jumped down and walked back to the inn.

Robson arrived next and Farthing greeted him more effusively. 'I am glad you were here, Doctor. You're the first medical man to see the victim. He's dead, of course. Do you know him?'

'Let's check before we make assumptions,' Robson replied in a relaxed voice. Tweed could just catch what he said. Robson stooped over the body, felt the pulse at the side of the neck, then nodded. 'He's dead. No doubt about that.'

'An ambulance has been summoned,' Farthing explained. 'But you have given us valuable assistance before. Any idea of the timing of his demise?'

'I could only guess.' Robson frowned. 'Something odd – you see the small amount of blood? Yet the face has been savaged. He was dead before the murderer did that.' His tone was dry and professional as he pulled open the windcheater at the top. 'I suppose you realize the head has almost been severed from the body? Look at that.'

Bile rose in Farthing's mouth as he crouched on his haunches beside Robson. An enormous red gash ran just below the throat, continued out of sight. 'We ought to wait for the forensic team from Taunton before I explore further,' Robson reminded the inspector.

'On the other hand he'll have to be shifted into the ambulance when it arrives,' Farthing pointed out.

'Then we'll go a little further, see if I can find out how he died. Not from that vicious slash across the throat. Again – not enough blood. He was dead when that happened.'

Robson unfolded more canvas to the corpse's waist. Gently he turned the body on its side. The head lolled like

175

the broken neck of a doll. Robson pointed to the back of the windcheater, to a wide rip and crusted blood below the left shoulder blade.

'I would imagine that was the death thrust. He was attacked from behind. A knife was plunged deep upwards, penetrating the heart. That came first.'

He was replacing the body in its original position, folding the canvas back, when the distant sound of a siren came closer. The inspector glanced up. 'Ambulance almost here. Now, Doctor, how long ago?'

'As I said, I can only guess. The Taunton pathologist will be able to give a more accurate diagnosis. During the past two hours I would say. Now, I'd better leave this to you . . .'

He was walking back to The Royal Oak to wash his hands when Colonel Barrymore appeared, strolling towards the crowd, which parted to let him pass through. He levered himself aboard the Land Rover, thrust both hands in his pockets, stared down while Farthing again exposed the face. Ambulance men carrying a stretcher paused behind the vehicle. Tweed stared hard as Barrymore glanced at Partridge's face.

'Must be the work of a lunatic,' he commented sardonically. 'No, I've never seen him.'

Leaping down from the Land Rover, he strolled back to The Royal Oak, presumably to finish his lunch. 'Cold-blooded bastard,' Paula hissed.

'He will have seen a lot of war casualties,' Tweed reminded her.

As they loaded the pathetic canvas bundle aboard a stretcher and carried it to the ambulance Paula stared round. The crowd was dispersing; some heading for The Royal Oak before closing time, others trudging to their homes, while a few men and women stood, unsure what to do next now the show was over.

The quiet country village seemed to have taken on a

macabre atmosphere. She looked up towards the overcast sky, a threatening gloomy pall; towards the moor where the mist was slowly retreating, exposing the sweep of the grim brown ridges. Somewhere up there a frightful murder had taken place. She hated the moor now and turned to Tweed.

'What do we do next? Did you notice anything about the way those three men reacted to looking at poor Partridge?'

'I noticed the absence of something.'

'Don't start talking to me in riddles.' She played with the bracelet composed of Greek key symbols. 'The murder of Partridge is reminiscent of what we heard about that other horrific murder of the Greek in Cairo during the war.'

'Which reminds me of something I should tell Farthing . . .'

He caught up with the inspector who was just about to climb into his car. Farthing looked at him with an impatient expression.

'Bringing those three chaps out of The Royal Oak didn't get us far. What was all that about?'

'They're all locals. I thought they might have seen Partridge. But there's something else you ought to do. Have you a notebook? Good. Note this down.' He gave Partridge's description of Anton Gavalas, spelt his name. 'I should put out an all points for him. Partridge told me he saw him riding all over Exmoor. And there was one occasion when the Greek confronted him, accused Partridge of following him.'

'We'll check . . .' Farthing held a microphone from the radio car in his hand and studied the description he'd noted down.

'I'll be at The Luttrell Arms in Dunster if the CID man put in charge of the case from Taunton wants to talk with me.'

'Roger . . .'

Farthing was issuing an all points bulletin for Gavalas as Tweed and Paula walked back to the Mercedes. Nield strolled out of The Royal Oak towards the Cortina.

Tweed drove back at speed to Dunster, overtaking the ambulance, his expression grim. Paula glanced at him, laid a gentle hand on his arm. He showed no emotion but she sensed he was concealing a feeling of deep shock.

'You're upset, aren't you?'

'I worked with Sam at the Yard once. He was a good friend and my mentor. I learned a lot from him. Facts, he used to say, concentrate on *facts*. Then the solution will come sooner or later. He was generous with professional advice. Not always the case. Now I have to hunt down the man – or men – who killed Sam and Harry Masterson. Whatever it takes.'

She was disturbed. She had never heard him express himself with such vehemence; almost as though he were prepared to throw away the rule book. 'I have a feeling this is important.' She dangled her bracelet. 'Harry wouldn't have sent this Greek key bracelet unless it pointed to something. I wish we knew what it means.'

It began to rain. Tweed turned on the windscreen wipers. The moor was lost in a veil of fine drizzle, disappearing like a monster retreating to its lair, Paula thought. A beastly day – in every way. Wet, chilly, a nightmare day. Tweed made the remark as they reached Dunster.

He turned into the High Street, the cobbled areas like sweating stones. No one about; people were huddled indoors. He swung the Mercedes into one of the parking spaces opposite the hotel.

'You could be right,' he muttered. 'Maybe the answer lies not here but in Greece. Let's hope Newman and Marler get lucky.'

178

PART TWO

Devil's Valley

16

11 a.m. 104°F. 40°C. The heat scorched them like a burning glass. The cloudless sky above the ferry was a molten blue. Newman lifted his hand, wiped his forehead. He was dripping with sweat. His shirt was sodden. The car ferry bound for Siros edged away from its berth at Piraeus, turned slowly through ninety degrees, headed out into the gulf.

Newman stood at the bow of the vessel, elevated above the car deck and below the bridge. The ferry to Siros was small compared with the giant five-deckers which plied between Piraeus and Crete and Rhodes. Below the bridge and stretching to the stern, trucks and cars were parked three abreast, filling the ferry which was open to the sky.

Nick had had to back the Mercedes on to the ferry up the ramp so, like the other vehicles, he faced the ramp for ultimate disembarkation at Siros. Marler, wearing an open-necked shirt loose outside his khaki drill trousers, appeared alongside Newman and grinned.

'Enjoying the weather, old chap? A super day for the trip.'

'If you say so, and not so much of the old chap.'

'Just an expression, old boy. Don't mind me . . .'

'I won't.'

Marler, damn him, looked as cool as a cucumber. Resting his hands on the rail, Marler stared ahead at the millpond sea where the sun reflected like wavelets of mercury. Newman had earlier rested his own hands briefly on that rail. Very briefly. Like touching a red-hot iron.

'What's the object of our trip to Siros?' Marler enquired. 'That is, assuming I'm permitted to be put in the picture.'

'No need for sarcasm,' Newman growled.

'Irony, not sarcasm. Big difference. Why the change of plan at a moment's notice? Sort of thing Tweed would do. We were going to check out Cape Sounion where Harry Masterson took his dive.'

'You have such a subtle turn of phrase, Marler. The enemy – whoever they may be – would expect us to follow Masterson's trail. Instead we're going to Siros – where over forty years ago a man called Gavalas was murdered during a commando raid. I want to see the place where it happened.'

'You think there's a link with Masterson's death?'

'Tweed said it was a possibility. And that commando raid came up in conversation when Harry visited that chap at the MOD.'

'And how on earth are we going to find the spot where Gavalas was killed on Siros?'

'Nick. He knows the island well, has friends there. But we'll have to watch ourselves every step of the way . . .'

'Which is why, I suppose, you had Nick kit us up?'

'That's why,' Newman agreed. He tilted his wide-brimmed straw hat to shield his eyes. Marler, who seemed impervious to the torrid heat, was hatless, his fair hair gleaming in the sunlight. 'Watch it,' Newman warned, 'Nick's coming.'

'It's very hot,' Nick complained as he hauled himself up the companionway leading from the car deck and stood mopping his neck with a large handkerchief which was already limp with moisture. 'You can get a drink inside. The only way to avoid dehydration. I came up for a breath of air. There isn't any.'

'Join us,' Newman suggested.

'No.' Nick shook his head. 'I'll get a bottle of orange juice, take it back. I'd better stay with the Merc. You know why . . .'

Ten minutes later Newman stood alone on the bow deck, a fresh bottle of orange juice in his hand. Four more unopened bottles stood on a nearby seat. He'd have drunk gallons of the stuff by the time they reached Siros, two hours' sailing time away. *You know why* . . . He recalled Nick's words.

It was Newman's idea that they travel to Siros armed. He had not forgotten the bullet fired at them at the port of Zea. And Siros, he suspected, was a sensitive area for someone. He felt confident they had slipped the leash by boarding the ferry at the last moment, but he was not a man to take unnecessary chances.

Hence the guns and ammo Nick had obtained from God knew where. A sniperscope rifle for Marler, one of Europe's top marksmen; a Lee Enfield .303 rifle for himself; a Smith & Wesson .38 revolver for Nick. And all concealed, carefully taped to the underside of the chassis of the Mercedes. Which was why Nick was staying down on the car deck. To keep an eye on the car and its hidden cargo.

An hour later the ferry was moving at speed across the surface of the incredible sapphire blue of the Mediterranean. It almost hurt Newman's eyes to stare at it as he maintained his vigil, thinking, planning his moves when they landed. Over to the port side he made out the tip of Cape Sounion where Masterson had died. He raised the field glasses looped round his neck and focused them.

Perched at its summit the near-intact temple of Poseidon, guardian of the sea, came up in the lenses. A vision of perfection. Newman sighed, dropped the glasses, looked ahead. He'd liked Masterson.

Passing the Cape, the ferry headed south-east direct for the Cyclades group of islands. Siros was the closest of the group but was still out of sight. Peace, perfect peace, Newman thought as the ferry ploughed on through a shimmering heat haze. Probably their tour of Siros would also be peaceful, quite uneventful.

Deep in the heart of Devil's Valley, not twenty miles north of Cape Sounion, Petros Gavalas sat on the veranda of his headquarters farm. He had just put down the telephone. A summer hum of insects drifting above the grass was the only sound.

The farm was huddled under a looming limestone crag, almost hidden from the air, nestled in a wide defile between scrub-studded hills rising like cliffs. Shifting in his cane seat, Petros yelled his instruction hoarsely in Greek.

'Dimitrios! Christina! Get out here fast. And tell Constantine to be ready to take off in the helicopter. Come on! You should be here now, damn you!'

He waited until his two grandchildren stood before him. Christina, clad in tight-fitting denims and a flowered blouse, looked down at him, took a cigarette out of her mouth and ran a hand through her long dark hair.

'Was that Anton?' she enquired anxiously. 'He is on his way back from England?'

'No. And Anton can look after himself. He has a job to do. So have both of you.'

He studied the thin-faced Dimitrios, who often acted as his driver. Forty-four years old, he had Petros' dark eyes, his cruel mouth. With more training, another five years, Dimitrios might become as ruthless as Petros himself, although the old man doubted it. He twisted his hawk-nosed profile, stared hard at Christina.

'That Englishman, Marler, you got information from. Did you sleep with him, you whore?'

'Of course not,' she lied smoothly, refusing to lose her temper with the old bastard. God, she thought, he's still living in 1947. The world has changed since then. But he'll never know it. Petros leaned towards her, reached out a

184

gnarled hand to grasp her arm, to twist it. She was too quick for him: she stepped out of his reach.

'I told you once. That's enough,' she snapped. 'What job? Who phoned you?'

'Pavlos – from Piraeus.' Petros slumped in his chair with disgust. 'He had trouble getting through on the phone. Nothing works in this country any more. Since the colonels went . . .'

'Don't start that again,' she rapped back. 'What has happened?'

'Oh, nothing much.' He made a sarcastic gesture with his hands. 'Just that the two English – Newman and your Marler – are at this moment aboard a ferry bound for Siros. The chopper will get you to Siros ahead of them. The ferry left Piraeus at eleven this morning and arrives soon after one o'clock. It is now noon – so move your leaden feet. Christina, you will stay out of sight. If Dimitrios decides, you can meet your Marler and lure him into a trap.'

'He is not my Marler. You have said that twice. Say it a third time and I will not go . . .'

'You try to disobey me?' Petros heaved himself out of the chair, clenched his fist and moved towards her. 'I will beat you until you cannot move . . .'

'No more!' she shouted back. From the sheath attached to her belt she whipped out a long-bladed knife and waved it in front of her. 'Come one step nearer and I'll cut you open . . .'

Petros stood stunned. He couldn't believe what was happening. A woman was threatening him. Aware that Dimitrios was watching him closely, that he must not lose face to a mere female, he changed tactics. Slapping his thigh, he raised his large head, roared with laughter, then gestured at Dimitrios.

'You see! She is a true Gavalas. A real spitfire, my little Christina.' He turned back to her. 'Use that knife to cut

185

open this Marler and I will buy you a beautiful dress from Kolonaki. Now, off you go! You are armed, Dimitrios?'

'Constantine has loaded shotguns and rifles aboard the chopper. He guessed it was an emergency . . .'

'Then what are you waiting for? If those two English go near where my son, Andreas, was killed in the war – you kill them.'

He stopped speaking as the sound of a helicopter's rotors starting up drowned all further conversation. He sank back into his chair as Dimitrios and Christina ran off round the side of the house. *Stephen and Andreas, vengeance for your deaths will be mine*, he said to himself. He felt great satisfaction.

He had four descendants – Dimitrios, Constantine, Christina and Anton. He believed all shared his obsession that the killers must be dealt with. He had dinned the idea into them since childhood and worried only about Christina. Women should not think – only obey.

Petros looked around the front of the farm while he waited to see the machine take off for Siros. It was a large building. The veranda ran thirty feet along the front. The once-white walls were grey with dirt. In places they sagged, were held up by huge beams of wood which served as props. Many tiles on the roof were broken. Petros never spent money on repairs unless he simply had to.

This meanness had helped make him rich. Money in the bank. That was *power*. And he owned a second farm way up north in Macedonia. A farm which boasted many scores of head of cattle. They provided the milk the tourists loved. And for making the cheese the tourists staying at the great hotels also loved. Goat's milk, which Petros preferred, was not liked by the visitors bloated with money.

The Sikorsky was airborne, flew along the front of the farm as it gained height. The pilot, Constantine, waved. Petros waved back. They would do the job. And the sight of the Sikorsky made him feel good. War surplus bought by another farmer at a knock-down price.

Petros had coveted the Sikorsky. One night during a heatwave summer he had led his grandsons to the farmer's fields. They had used flaming torches to set fire to his crops. He had been ruined. Only then had Petros approached him with an offer for the Sikorsky – an offer which would not have bought a second-hand car. Desperate for money, the farmer had sold him the machine. I'm a good business-man, Petros told himself. Now I wait, see what happens on Siros.

Aboard the ferry Nick sat behind the wheel of the Mercedes and started up his engine. They were coming in to Siros, the ramp would soon be lowered. Newman stood on the bow deck as the ferry began turning slowly through a half-circle, ready to berth stern first. Alongside him stood Marler, lighting one of his king-size cigarettes.

'Pretty-looking place,' he drawled.

Newman was carefully scanning the waterfront with his glasses, searching for any sign of a reception committee. The island was mountainous, one limestone giant rearing in the distance. Mount Ida, he assumed. The lower slopes were arid, studded with more scrub.

He blinked. The small port of Siros was crammed with stark white-walled two-storey houses. Huddled together and piled up the hill, they glared beneath the burning sun. The shallow-sloped red-tiled rooftops were stepped up the incline. He followed the route of several narrow walled roads which appeared to zigzag upwards. A rabbit warren.

The harbour was sickle-shaped, enclosed by two curving jetties. Inside the entrance a small fleet of fishing vessels and motorized caïques were moored. Along one jetty wall the golden strands of scores of fishing nets hung drying. The tavernas and shops lining the waterfront had a sleepy look.

'It's a working port,' Newman remarked, lowering his glasses. 'Not many tourists find their way here would be my guess. And I still wonder about that chopper which flew over us earlier.'

'Could have landed anywhere,' Marler replied off-handedly. 'I think we'd better join Nick . . .'

There was a bump as the stern touched shore by a stone causeway. The ramp was lowered, vehicles began moving off as Newman ran down the companionway, then slowed his pace. It was like moving inside a red-hot oven.

'You take it easy in Greece, old boy,' Marler needled him, strolling down the steps.

'And you don't let on I speak Greek,' Newman warned. 'That way we may hear something interesting.'

'Sir!' As Newman looked over his shoulder Marler gave a mock salute.

Cocky bastard, Newman thought, then quenched his irritation. He had better watch himself in this inferno. Nick had driven the Mercedes off and was waiting on the waterfront. Small boys were dancing round the gleaming car, touching it and then jumping back as Nick shouted at them.

'Where to first?' Newman asked, climbing in beside Nick while Marler settled himself in a rear seat.

'To meet my friend, Spyros. I sent him a radio message from Athens. He lives high up here in Siros . . .'

The car was moving, turning away from the waterfront into one of the narrow side streets. Almost immediately the street was climbing, twisting round narrow corners over the paved surface. On both sides they were hemmed in by the clean whitewashed walls as they ascended the labyrinth. Sweat started pouring down Newman's back. The tunnel-like streets, the blinding glare off the white walls – everything intensified the hellish heat despite the fact that Nick had opened all the windows.

'Where is everyone?' Newman asked. 'We haven't seen a soul.'

'Indoors. Resting,' Nick replied. 'Even for Siros today is very hot. It helps. If we see someone out we must wonder why. Who they are. Did you see that old Sikorsky with the blurred markings which flew over the ferry?'

'What about it?' Newman asked, glancing at Marler, who looked damnably cool and relaxed as he lolled in his seat.

'A woman passenger wearing dark glasses and a scarf over her hair was checking the ferry through binoculars. I think she was trying to find someone. Maybe us?'

'Cross that bridge when we come to it,' Marler responded.

'This is a good place to stop,' Nick went on. 'Then I can get the guns from under the car . . .'

He had reached a tortuous turn and pulled up half-way round so they had a view both down and up the street which was still deserted. Sliding under the car, he was less than a minute before he handed Marler his sniperscope rifle, followed by Newman's weapon. Scrambling out from under the car, he glanced round as he dumped a hip holster with his revolver on the front passenger seat.

'It's all right,' Newman assured him, 'we watched both up and down the street while you were under the car.'

Nick strapped on the holster while Marler raised his rifle and peered through the sniperscope at a fisherman walking slowly along a jetty far below. Nick slipped on a lightweight linen jacket he kept slung from a hook behind the driving seat. He left it open and grinned at Newman.

'It will be hot wearing this – but it conceals what I carry. You hide your rifles under that travelling rug rolled up on the floor in the back.'

'And now?' Newman asked.

'We meet Spyros who is waiting at the top. He will take us to Mount Ida – to the place where the Greek was murdered during the war . . .'

'They have disappeared,' said Dimitrios. 'One moment the Mercedes is driving up towards us, then it vanishes. What kind of a trick is this?'

'They're probably parked at the corner of the road down there. Where it turns a sharp bend. That church dome hides it from us,' concluded Christina.

She sounded thoroughly rebellious. She shook her dark mane, exasperated with her cousins' slave-like obedience to Petros.

Constantine shrugged his shoulders, irked by her attitude. This was not women's work. Like Dimitrios he was thin and bony and he sported a moustache which curved round the ends of his slit of a mouth. He looked after his moustache proudly: it had made him a big hit with the girls, really rolled them over. On their backs.

They were perched on the roughcast terrace of a house overlooking the port of Siros. Through his binoculars Dimitrios had observed Newman, Marler and Nick coming ashore from the ferry. It was Christina who had earlier confirmed they were aboard when Constantine had overflown the ferry.

The house belonged to Petros and was empty. Today was Wednesday. On each Monday a local woman came to clean up the place. Parked in front of the house was a battered Cadillac, paint peeling from its bodywork. Petros had bought it for a song from a man in need of money. The weapons transported aboard the helicopter were stowed inside the Cadillac. Shrubs sprouting blood-red flowers decorated the terrace in large Ali Baba pots. Christina put on her dark glasses, lit a cigarette.

'You won't need to use the guns,' she told them.

190

'We use them if they go near Mount Ida,' Constantine snapped at her. 'You remember what Petros ordered?'

'Ordered! You are like a couple of puppets he dangles at the end of a string. Harm the Englishmen and everything goes wrong. The police will hunt you down. Sarris himself might come. He only waits for his chance to put you all inside for ever. Then what happens to me? If necessary I will handle Marler, lead him and the others away from where it happened . . .'

Constantine grinned unpleasantly, made an obscene gesture. 'Ah! You and Marler. Petros was right. You will do as we tell you to do . . .'

His left hand gripped her arm. He froze. Her free hand had whipped out the knife from the sheath attached to her belt. He felt its point tickle his throat. Her black eyes blazed with fury.

'Let me go or I'll rip your throat open. God knows how many women you have had, you fornicator . . .'

He released her, stepped back carefully. The fear was written large on his face as she followed him and his back pressed into the terrace wall. It was only as high as his hips and there was a long drop to the paved street below. She rested the point of the knife against his breast bone. He breathed heavily. She was strong; if she pushed the knife a couple of inches more . . .

'You will never use that filthy gesture in front of me again,' she told him. 'You will not use the guns. We will find some other way of diverting them. You understand?'

'Yes, Christina. For God's sake . . .'

She sheathed the knife suddenly, turned away. Her expression was contemptuous. As she had always suspected Constantine was a coward. Dimitrios, careful not to interfere – he had previous experience of Christina's temper – stood staring through his binoculars. He lowered them quickly.

'You were right,' he told her. 'They had hidden behind

191

that corner. Why? Could they have spotted us? Impossible. They are driving this way. We must leave in the Cadillac quickly before they arrive, drive up towards Ida and see what they do next . . .'

Nick turned yet another sharp-angled bend in the zigzag road which went up and up. Newman glanced out of the window on his side. Nick was a superb driver: he had missed scraping the wall of a house by inches. They were very high up now and Newman caught glimpses of the sea which was an incredible mixture of brilliant colours – sapphire, turquoise, *lapis lazuli*. No picture postcard had ever captured this. The car slowed and stopped.

'Spyros,' said Nick.

An old hunchback, clad in peasant clothes and with a face like a wrinkled walnut under his wide-brimmed straw hat, sat perched outside a house. He was whittling a piece of wood with a knife. He stood up, adjusted the angle of his hat, opened the rear door of the car and joined Marler.

Nick drove on as he made introductions. 'Spyros. Sitting next to you is Marler. My other friend is Bob Newman.'

'I am pleased to meet both of you,' Spyros replied in English and with quaint old-world courtesy. 'You take the next fork to the right when we leave Siros port and climb the mountain.'

He opened the cloth he had used to wrap the piece of wood and the knife and continued whittling, careful to keep the pieces carved off on the cloth. Marler stared at the wood. It was beginning to take the shape of a madonna. Spyros kept glancing up as he worked, checking their position.

They emerged from the labyrinth of the port of Siros suddenly. Ahead the road was no longer paved. A track of white dust, it snaked up the mountain which rose sheer

192

above them. Before long they were driving along a ledge just wide enough to take the Mercedes. On Nick's side rose a sheer wall of limestone. Newman peered out on his side and the mountain fell away into a deep precipice. Far below a grove of olive trees spread their stunted branches. Beyond the grove the sea spread into the distance, ink blue.

'You're sure the Merc can get all the way?' Newman enquired in what he hoped was a casual tone.

'Spyros would not have let us come if it was not possible.'

'Good for Spyros . . .'

Newman glanced down again and began to feel the symptoms of vertigo. He averted his gaze, forced himself to concentrate on the track ahead spiralling up and round the mountain. At several points there were tracks leading off through gulches in the mountain. Newman would have given anything to tell Nick to turn into one of the gulches – away from the hideous precipice which was growing deeper and deeper. Had the old Greek sensed his fear? Still whittling at the wood, he said suddenly, 'We are very close now. The country will open out. We shall leave the abyss.'

'And then?' Newman prodded.

'We shall be at the place where Andreas Gavalas died over forty years ago.'

The Cadillac, driven by Dimitrios, had taken the other route on the far side of the mountain. Hidden inside a copse of olive trees, they had seen Nick heading up the seaward road.

'They are going where they shouldn't,' Dimitrios said. 'So, we get there first and wait for them . . .'

He had driven like a madman up the curving road with Constantine beside him, a rifle and shotgun resting in his lap. In the back of the car Christina sat tense and silent.

To her left the ground sloped away steeply but not precipitously. In the distance she could see the white-walled houses of Siros port – looking like a child's model.

'We turn here,' Dimitrios said and swung off the road inside a deep-walled gulch which snaked between lofty heights of limestone. The wheels bumped over rocks, shaking the vehicle.

'Why?' demanded Christina.

'We are now ahead of them,' Dimitrios condescended to explain. 'We will check to see they are going all the way. Then, if they are, we turn round here and go on up the mountain. There is a place where we can look down on them, see what they do.'

He had stopped at a point where the track widened and turned the Cadillac so it faced the way they had come. He had concealed the car out of sight of the gap at the end of the gulch. Daylight showed and way beyond it the intense blue of the sea.

'A place where you can look down on them?' Christina queried. 'You are taking your guns with you? Why?' Her hand clawed at Dimitrios' shirt collar as he was alighting. 'What are you planning to do?'

'You heard what Petros ordered. To shoot them if necessary. Now let go, you treacherous cat. At the end is the other road. We shall see their car pass if they have come this far.'

As Spyros had predicted, they had left the abyss behind. Ahead, below the sheer wall of the mountain, an area of flat scrubland stretched before them. Nick stopped the car, Newman stepped out, stretched and took another swig from the plastic bottle of mineral water. They had six unopened bottles: dehydration, as Nick was never tired of warning, was the greatest danger. Newman grimaced after drinking, replaced the cap. The liquid was tepid, tasteless.

The plateau of arid scrubland projected out from the mountain wall, then sloped steeply downwards. A wide deep parched gully led its winding way towards the distant sea. Its surface was cluttered with limestone boulders and pebbles. In winter, Newman guessed, it would be a gushing torrent. Now it was bone dry.

'Where?' asked Marler in his direct way.

Spyros pointed to the gully with his knife. The rocky gulch lay about two hundred yards away. Shielding his eyes, Marler gazed up at the towering mountain above them.

'What in Hades is that?'

Newman stared up. At the summit of Mount Ida, clinging to the edge of the rock, was perched a huddle of ancient buildings. Built of solid stone, one shallow-roofed building was hanging above another, perched at different levels and all joined in one complex.

'The monastery of Mount Ida,' Spyros told them. 'From there you see all over the island. During the war the German general, Hugo Geiger, established a lookout unit. He respected the monks. He said someone should live in peace in this frightful war.'

'Where?' Marler repeated again. 'Where exactly did this Andreas Gavalas die?'

'Inside the gully.' Spyros pointed the knife. 'I will show you the place . . .'

'Not yet.' Marler placed a hand on the old man's shoulder as he began to walk out into the open. 'Everyone back inside the car,' Marler continued, reaching inside for his rifle. He pocketed the sniperscope sight, picked up several spare magazines. 'Go on, get in quick,' he ordered. 'The lot of you.'

'May I ask why?' Newman enquired.

'You may. A mile or so back coming up the mountain I glanced down one of those side tracks leading into a gulch. I saw movement, a man watching. He dodged back out of

195

sight. Before you venture into the open I'm going up there.'

He looked up the mountain which was fractured with deep fissures, some wide enough to allow passage for one man. Newman sucked in his breath at the prospect, thinking of the vertigo.

'You stay in the back, Bob,' Marler instructed. 'On this side of the car. Keep an eye on me. When I wave my rifle you can go into the open. Only then.'

He looped the rifle over his shoulder, wriggled his feet in his rubber-soled calf-skinned shoes to test their ankle support. 'If I'd known I'd have brought climbing boots. Can't be helped. I'll cope.'

'Watch it – for God's sake,' Newman warned.

'And I never knew you cared . . .'

Typical of Marler to mock just before he was attempting a climb fraught with risk, Newman thought. They settled in the car and Newman peered up. Marler was already a good twenty feet up a narrow fissure, finding a foothold on one side, then on the other.

17

'We climb up here. It looks straight down on the place,' said Dimitrios as he switched off the engine.

He had turned off the mountain road, backing the Cadillac into a cul-de-sac. Christina peered through the rear window. At the end of the cul-de-sac a wide defile led upwards between rocky walls. A primitive staircase carved out of the rock led out of sight.

'What is this? Where does it lead to?' she demanded.

'The monks made it ages ago.' Dimitrios grinned as

196

he gripped his rifle, opened the door and slipped out. Constantine joined him with his shotgun. Dimitrios thrust his head in through the rear window. 'Christina, you wait here. We're going up to a high point which overlooks the place. You hear shots, we will be back soon after. Then we drive back.'

'I told you, Dimitrios . . .'

They were gone, climbing the rough-hewn steps rapidly, Dimitrios in the lead. They disappeared round a corner. She climbed out of the car, left the door open, ran back on to the mountain road. From the view ahead she knew roughly where she was. She began running, jogging at a steady trot up the road.

She wore a lightweight jump suit and trainer shoes. As she ran she hauled her dark glasses out of her pocket, perched them on her nose. The stupid cold-blooded bastards. They liked their work: Petros had trained them well. They were true grandsons of the sadistic old ruffian.

Ten minutes later she was still running uphill, pacing herself. She was close to where the mountain ended, where the ground became flat, spreading out towards the sea on the other side of Ida. Pray God she got there in time . . .

Dimitrios crouched down, settled himself in the nest between massive boulders. He perched his rifle in the cleft of a rock, looked along the sight. Three men were alighting from the Mercedes parked at the edge of the plateau. Beside him Constantine aimed his shotgun.

They were positioned seventy feet above the three men. Both of the Greeks were excellent shots. The place Dimitrios had chosen was a meditation point used by the monks. High above them reared the overhanging monastery. Dimitrios glanced up once, then down again. He was satisfied no one looking down from the summit of Mount Ida would ever see them. An overhang of rock almost completely obscured the view from that height. The over-hang was two hundred feet above where they waited.

'Let them get well out into the open,' Dimitrios warned his brother. 'Then there is nowhere to hide. We can pick them off one by one.'

'Which shall I aim for?' Constantine asked.

'You don't. Leave it to me. If one dashes back for the car, he's your dead meat for today. Any minute now . . .'

'Andreas was found lying dead somewhere near the top of that gully,' Spyros explained.

Newman led the way, avoiding the numerous sharp rocks which littered the ground, often almost hidden by scrub grass. The heat beat down on the back of his neck. He tied a handkerchief round it as he walked. It was very still and silent at this height. No screech of gulls. A stillness which was uncanny – and unsettling. He was the first one to hear the sound of running feet approaching.

Breathing heavily, Christina appeared round the side of the mountain, saw them, increased her pace until she reached them. Holding his rifle loosely in his right hand, Newman stopped and waited, suspicious. What the hell was such an attractive girl doing up here in the wilderness? He didn't like questions to which he had no answer. Nick stepped forward.

'This is Christina Gavalas,' he informed Newman.

'Introduce me. Who is he? Quickly!' Christina demanded.

She was panting from her exertions, her breasts heaving under the jump suit. Newman was careful to keep his eyes on hers. They glowed with life. And she was the enemy.

'Robert Newman,' Nick replied. 'The foreign correspondent . . .'

'And where is Marler?' Christina asked anxiously.

198

'Oh, he's gone to deal with a call of nature,' Newman told her easily. 'What are you doing up . . .'

'You are in great danger. There are men up the mountain with guns . . .'

She broke off as a man appeared from the direction she had come. At least six feet tall, he was clothed in a black robe and wore a black cylindrical hat. A priest. Member of the Greek Orthodox Church, Newman realized. His face was lined with age but he was erect, his movements brisk. He spoke in English.

'Welcome to Mount Ida. You wish to see the monastery? I fear the lady cannot enter.'

Newman took a quick decision. The priest, he estimated, was in his late seventies. Had probably spent all his life in this part of the world. Including the period of German wartime occupation.

'We are looking for the place where – over forty years ago – a Greek citizen called Andreas Gavalas died.'

'Was murdered,' the priest corrected him gravely, stroking his black beard. 'I was here when it happened.'

'You mean you saw what actually took place?' Newman concealed his excitement. 'You know who killed Andreas?'

'Damn that priest. He will have to take his chance.' Dimitrios carefully aimed his rifle at Newman's chest. 'Bull's-eye,' he gloated.

Constantine knocked the rifle barrel upwards. By some miracle Dimitrios avoided pulling the trigger. He glared furiously at his brother. 'Cretin! Why did you do that? Do it again and I will break your arm . . .'

'There is a priest down there,' Constantine protested.

'So? Since when did you go religious? Petros is an atheist – he brought us up to regard the whole Church as a swindle on the people. What does one less priest matter?'

199

'And Christina is down there. Are you mad? If your aim is bad you could hit *her* . . .'

'Since when was my aim bad?' He glanced down. 'Now look what you've done. They have started walking towards the gully – the place Petros said they must not reach.'

'The problem is solved then. Forget it.'

'No, I will not forget it.' Dimitrios grinned evilly, hoisted his rifle and tapped Constantine's jaw gently with the heavy butt. 'Interfere again and you'll need a new jaw. You understand? No distractions this time. A moving target? Bull's-eye. Again . . .'

He repositioned the rifle, rested it firmly in a cleft in the rock, thrust the butt firmly against his shoulder, lined up the sight, took the first pressure. One final squeeze . . .

The bullet slammed into the rock less than an inch from the hand on the trigger. A rock splinter cut Dimitrios' cheekbone. His rifle jerked up. This time it fired. The shot winged into the sky. A second bullet slammed into the rock between the two brothers crouched less than half a foot from each other. The third bullet struck Constantine's shotgun. He let go, yelled. The weapon dropped out of sight over the brink. They were scrambling out of the nest when a fresh bullet nicked the heel of Dimitrios' shoe. He jumped with sheer fright.

A hundred feet above them, perched on a ledge protruding from the mountain wall, Marler reloaded. He aimed down in seconds, pulled the trigger. The fifth bullet ripped a shard of cloth from Dimitrios' right shoulder. Before he followed Constantine, who was scrambling back towards the staircase, he risked a glance upwards.

He saw Marler on the ledge and beneath the huge overhang of rock. Constantine looked back, saw the few seconds when his brother was glancing up.

200

'Come on!' he yelled. 'He missed five times. He'll kill you with his next shot . . .'

'Stupid cretin!' Dimitrios yelled back as he also began to run. 'He aimed to miss . . .' Dimitrios was enough of a marksman to recognize shooting superior to his own. Feeling safe as he ran out of sight of the ledge, he jumped with fright again as a fusillade of bullets peppered the rock walls on all sides, showering him with sharp splinters. How could this be?

'Shoot the bastards!' Christina urged Newman viciously.

Newman was standing, legs braced apart, rifle aimed up at the mountain as he continued shooting at the fleeing figures still in view from below. Christina, eyes blazing, stared up at Marler, now edging his way back along the ledge – at her hated cousins disappearing from sight down the staircase. Newman smiled, lowered his rifle, reloaded.

'You're one lousy shot,' she informed him, her hand pressed into her hip.

'You think so?' He smiled again. 'I aimed to miss – just as Marler did. There's been enough killing. And we don't want to start up a fresh vendetta with your lovely family.'

'Blessed be the merciful,' said the priest.

'I don't know about that, Father.' Newman grinned again. 'I might agree – so long as the merciful are alive. Which isn't often the case if you read history. Now, where was Andreas Gavalas murdered? And what did you see?'

The priest led them to the gully wending its way down to the sea. Near the top, where tufts of bleached grass stood at the edge of the dried-up watercourse, he pointed. A smooth-sided cleft large enough to hide a man. This had been Andreas' temporary grave. The priest, taking a 'walk of solitude', had discovered the body by accident.

The hilt of a knife had protruded from beneath the left

shoulder blade and the man was dead. Hurrying back towards the monastery for help, the priest had met several monks who had accompanied him back to the cleft. The body had vanished.

The priest had reported the incident to General Geiger, the German commander-in-chief. Geiger had checked with the only patrol in the vicinity. Later he had told the priest he was satisfied his men had no knowledge of what had happened.

'Then who took away the body?' Newman asked. 'And did you see the British raiding party approaching up the gully after landing from the sea?'

'Yes. I saw them from the monastery. Perhaps that is why my steps led me this way. Presumptuous curiosity. Not a virtue.'

'How many men in the raiding party?' Newman persisted.

'Four. I watched them through field glasses before starting on my walk down here.'

'Four Greeks, you mean?' Newman asked casually.

'No. Three British soldiers and one man dressed in peasant garb. I presume that was Andreas Gavalas who knew the island. I knew they were British because they wore green camouflage raincoats.'

'Surely they would have been seen by that German lookout unit I heard was established in the monastery?' Newman suggested. 'If you saw them coming, the Germans must have done?'

'The British were clever – and lucky. They landed when a thick winter sea mist was covering this area. When I saw them through my field glasses the mist had parted for a short time. At that moment the watchguard unit was being replaced by new men coming on duty.'

'And have you ever heard a whisper as to who might have removed Andreas' body?'

The priest pulled at his beard, his eyes avoided

Newman's. 'It is a mystery,' he eventually replied. 'And now I must return if you will excuse me.'

'The whole business is peculiar,' Newman responded.

He stared round the scrub-covered platform. Very little cover for a raiding party which must have relied on the mist to reach the shelter of the mountain. Doubtless Andreas had known ways of penetrating the fastness. Marler was walking towards them at a jaunty pace, rifle propped over his shoulder, as Newman stared once again upwards. What a life – confined most of your days inside that fortress-like complex perched half-way to the sky. A large bird, probably an eagle, drifted off a tongue of rock and circled them high up.

'Can you take me back to Athens in that car?' Christina asked Newman. 'My cousins drove me up here in an old Cadillac. I have been abandoned.'

'All the way to Athens?' Newman queried in surprise.

'I'm not going back to the Devil's Valley – to where Petros is waiting to beat hell out of me. I've finished with that life.' She moved closer to him, her eyes enormous. 'I will pay for my passage. The last ferry leaves in two hours. You will take me? Please.'

'And how will you pay me?' Newman enquired ironically, expecting a certain answer. She had lowered her voice so only he could hear her.

'With information. About Harry Masterson.'

'You just bought yourself a one-way ticket.'

Marler arrived, brushed dirt off his jacket, grinned at Christina. 'You get around, little lady.'

She walked slowly up to him, a half-smile on her face. 'We met earlier, you may recall . . .'

'How could I forget?' He smiled sardonically.

'I do not forget either. I have something for you, Marler. A keepsake. Is that not the right word?'

She was still smiling when her right hand whipped up, palm open, and hit him with all her considerable force

203

across the face. The blow jerked his head sideways. She smiled again, watching the red weal which had appeared across his cheek.

'Now we are quits. Is that not the right phrase?' She turned to Newman. 'Now, I am ready when you are.'

The priest had lingered with Spyros a few yards away, as though reluctant to leave. His expression was a study in indecision. He seemed to make up his mind suddenly and walked to within a few feet of Newman. He took a deep breath before he uttered the words and then walked rapidly away towards the mountain.

'The disappearance of that body. There was something else on the island when it vanished. I suggest you look in that direction. I refer to the Greek Key.'

18

Nick drove the Mercedes back along the far side of the mountain, much to Newman's relief when he saw the ground beyond the brink sloped away gradually. It had been his idea to use this route after talking with Christina.

'Those two hard cases, Dimitrios and Constantine,' he pointed out to Marler before they started back, 'will travel in their Cadillac to Siros port. Then they'll ditch the car and fly back in their chopper. They landed on open ground just outside Siros according to Christina. They came here in that machine which overflew our ferry.'

'What's the plan?' Marler demanded.

'If we can catch up with that Cadillac I'd like a few words with them – and I guess you would. This time with our fists. Petros has to be discouraged from sending his jackals after us. I don't want to spend the rest of our time in Greece looking over our shoulders. When we get back to Athens *I* want a quiet talk with Christina on her own. I'm sure she has more information.'

'Why not me? I've known the girl a bit longer . . .'

'Oh, yes!' Newman's tone was ironical. 'You got to know her so well she pasted you one.'

'It was the only way I could hope to get her to talk . . .'

'It was the only way *you* thought you could get her to talk – and she didn't.'

'It's just possible you could be right,' Marler admitted reluctantly. He felt his face. 'She's a beauty but she packs a rare punch . . .'

'Which you richly deserved. Let's get over to the car.'

'May I enquire what is the next object of the exercise with her?'

'Christina met Harry Masterson in London, probably pointed him to Exmoor and those three ex-commandos. Why? Only she can tell me. So, old boy,' Newman went on, mimicking Marler, 'I'd appreciate it if from now on you leave the beauty to me. And on the way back we'd better assume those two thugs may be waiting to ambush us.'

They arranged the seating to anticipate the worst. Marler, loaded rifle across his lap, sat in front next to Nick. In the rear they placed Newman, Christina – sitting in the middle – and Spyros occupied the other corner. The hunchback was apologetic as Nick drove away from the plateau, heading for the far side of the mountain.

'I was not a great help to you, Mr Newman. The priest told you everything.'

'Everything? Are you sure about that? Who took away Andreas' body? And what is the Greek Key?'

'Don't ask me that.' The hunchback shuddered, clasped his veined hands tightly. 'I know nothing about such things.'

'But I do.' Christina pressed her shoulder against Newman, turned and gazed at him. 'Maybe later, when we are alone, the two of us should talk.'

'I'd welcome that.' Newman stared back at her. 'You speak very good English.'

'That was my mother's doing. I was lucky enough to be well-educated. And sometimes I think that is why my cousins – and Petros – hate me. They are still men of the soil. They think like peasants, behave like them. My mother was left money by a distant relative. She banked it secretly. Petros was furious. One night she packed me off to Zurich. To a school. I found I was good at languages. As well as Greek I speak German and English. I took a law degree. Then I made a mistake.'

'Which was?'

'I came back for my mother's funeral. Petros insisted I must pay my respects by staying in Devil's Valley for a time. Like a fool I agreed. Time went by. They all made me think their way. Now I have had enough of them for two lifetimes. We will talk later.'

Spyros had produced something from under his floppy jacket. Newman heard a strange sound, glanced across Christina. Spyros was clicking a length of black worry beads. His expression was anxious. Newman looked out of the window. The view was spectacular: a vast panorama stretching all the way down across the island to the sickle-shaped harbour.

There was tension inside the car. As they approached each bend Marler leaned forward, gripping his rifle, alert for any sign of the Gavalas brothers. He had warned Nick to be ready for an emergency stop at any second. Nick kept wiping a hand dry, then grasping the wheel tightly, staring ahead while he crawled round the bends.

The worry beads stopped clicking. Newman remained quite still. Spyros leaned forward, staring in his direction. Newman went on gazing out of the window as the car

206

continued its steep and tortuous descent. Now he could pick out individual boats berthed in Siros harbour.

'My cousin, Sarantis, is an archaeologist,' Spyros began. 'Is that the right word?'

'He goes on excavations – digging up ancient sites. A lot of them round the Plaka district in Athens,' Newman encouraged him.

'That is so. But Sarantis likes places where there are few of his kind. Like Cape Sounion. The Temple of Poseidon.'

'Sensible chap.' Newman forced himself to stay relaxed. 'So what about Sarantis?'

'He is very old. Like me. But he has a wonderful memory for faces. He was near Cape Sounion when the Englishman, Masterson, was thrown from the cliff not many weeks past.'

'He saw it happen?'

'No. But he did see the two men who went to the temple shortly before the killing.'

'*Two* men? You are sure? You did say he was very old,' Newman reminded him gently.

'Eighty years. He recognized Masterson from the pictures later in the papers – the man thrown from the cliff, he said.'

'And the second man,' Newman probed. 'He could describe him? How does he know Masterson was thrown off – if he didn't see it happen?'

'I think he did, but he felt it was dangerous to admit that. He has a good memory for faces,' Spyros repeated, in the manner of the old.

'He described this second man to you?' Newman enquired.

'No. But you could ask him. He would tell you. He likes the English. Treat him gently, please. He is frightened by what he saw at Cape Sounion.'

'You have his address in Athens?'

'Athens? He lives here on Siros. In a house near the top

207

of the port. We could see him before you take the ferry back to Athens.'

'Let's do that,' Newman agreed. 'Maybe we've stumbled on just what we've been seeking. By pure chance – coming to Siros. I have experienced that when I was a foreign correspondent,' he told Marler, who was watching him in the rear-view mirror. 'A stroke of luck when you least expect it. And it opens up a whole new picture – maybe leading all the way back to Exmoor.'

'Sounds just a shade too easy to me,' Marler commented, switching his gaze to the view beyond the windscreen.

Approaching the outskirts of the port, Nick spoke in Greek to Spyros who gabbled vehemently in reply. Newman was watching the view out of his window, apparently taking no interest in the conversation, his expression blank as he absorbed every word of what was being said. Spyros was having second thoughts about mentioning Sarantis; Nick was reassuring him.

Driving down a narrow paved street, closed in again by the glaring white walls of the stone houses, Nick swung off the street up a curving walled ramp. The house was isolated from the town, grey shutters masked the windows, the brilliant red front door was closed. Marler leapt out of the car, gripping his rifle, and poked his head in the rear window to speak to Spyros.

'Is there a rear way out of this place?' he asked urgently.

Newman noticed he had released the safety catch on his rifle. He was tense, quick-moving. Spyros looked up at him and gestured.

'Round the other side. There is a terrace leading to a door. A flight of steps runs down into the street.'

'What's the matter?' asked Newman as he also left the Mercedes holding his own rifle.

'Something not quite right here,' Marler said tersely.

'What makes you think that?'

'Sixth sense.' Marler spoke to Spyros again. 'This Sarantis. Does he live alone? Any wife, servants?'

'No. By himself. A woman comes in each day . . .'

'Will she be here now?'

Marler was firing the questions. Frequently he glanced at the closed shutters. He frowned as he glanced up at the flat roof. 'Any way to get up there?' he demanded before Spyros answered his first question. Nick, who had switched off the engine, had caught the atmosphere, stood near the front of the car, his right hand under his loose jacket, close to the revolver.

'The woman comes only in the mornings,' Spyros replied. 'And round that corner there is a flight of steps leading to the roof . . .'

'I'll take the roof,' Marler snapped. 'Bob, you take the rear door. Nick, wait by the front door here . . .'

'You wait in the car with Spyros,' Newman warned Christina and ran after Marler.

'The front door is ajar,' Newman warned Nick. 'Synchronize our watches. OK? Eighty seconds from now we both go in. Caution is the word . . .'

Newman ran round the side of the house. Marler was taking the steps to the roof two at a time. The terrace widened overlooking the deserted street. Siesta time. Probably all day. The heat burned his back. The grey shutters were closed over the windows at the back. Newman arrived at a door painted a bright blue.

This door was half-open. Somewhere out of sight further down the street a car started up, sped away. Could mean nothing. He checked his watch. Thirty seconds to go. He stood to one side of the doorway, listening. The sound of the car departing had vanished. A heavy heat-laden silence descended on the terrace. No sound of movement inside the single-storey house. He had the feeling the place was empty. So why were both doors open?

Ten seconds. He took a firm grasp on his rifle, held it at waist level. Raising his right foot he kicked the door wide open, darted inside, pressed his body against a wall.

A drop of at least twenty degrees. Positively cool compared with outside. He was inside a large L-shaped living room. A lot of soft furnishing: armchairs, couches. An arched fireplace took up most of the opposite wall. His eyes swivelled, getting accustomed to the dim light. A desk pushed up against the right-hand wall. Its surface littered with papers. He could hear Nick prowling round out of sight. His eyes were fixed on the desk area.

A chair was overturned. The body of an old man lay sprawled on the tiled floor. He lay very still on his back, his eyes staring at the roughcast ceiling. His right hand stretched out, clawed except for the index finger pointing towards Newman as though in a gesture of protest. Nick appeared, gun in hand, followed by Marler who moved with the silence of a cat.

'Anyone in the place?' Newman asked. Both shook their heads. 'Get Spyros. Warn him. I think we're too late . . .'

'Dead as a dodo,' Marler pronounced in a neutral tone.

He was crouched over the body, had checked the neck pulse. He remained crouched on his haunches, his forehead wrinkled as he looked round. Newman was standing gazing down at the old man. He pointed to a scrape mark on the tiles close to the desk.

'Difficult to say what happened,' he commented. 'That looks like the scrape of his shoe. He could have stood up, slipped, cracked the back of his skull. No, I don't think so. Look at his wrist. It's been broken . . .'

'Which could have happened when he slipped. This floor is very highly polished. Makes for accidents.'

'And he broke his arm as well?' queried Newman.

He could now see the arm was turned at an unnatural

angle – it was fractured close to the elbow. He looked up as Spyros entered, followed by Nick and Christina. Spyros walked slowly to the body and his voice quavered.

'Is he . . .'

'I'm afraid so,' Newman told him. 'He is dead. Who is it?'

'My old friend, Sarantis . . . my oldest friend . . .'

Tears ran down his weathered cheeks. Christina wrapped an arm round his shoulders, hugged him. Taking out a handkerchief she wiped his face, whispering to him in Greek. She led him to one of the couches where he sagged, then looked up at her.

'You are very kind – all of you,' he said in English. 'I will be all right now.'

'I'll take up guard on the roof,' Marler said crisply. 'Keep a lookout. I don't think we should linger here very long.'

Then he was gone. Christina disappeared briefly, returned with a glass of water. Spyros accepted it gratefully, gulped down the contents. Christina, her expression grim, walked over and stared at the body. Her voice was harsh.

'Another killing?' she demanded. 'They tried to make him talk?'

'Who?' Newman enquired, propping his rifle more securely inside an armchair.

'Dimitrios and Constantine, of course.'

'Why "of course"?'

'Because of this.' Stooping, she pulled out a handkerchief from under the body. It was brightly coloured with a diamond-shaped design. On a cream area it was discoloured with something dark reddish which looked like dried blood to Newman. 'Dimitrios has a handkerchief like this,' she said coldly. 'The rotten swine.'

'Is that the only handkerchief of that kind in Greece?' Newman asked.

'Well, no. You can buy them in the shops in Athens . . .'

'Then you can't be sure. Give it to me. Nothing must be disturbed.'

Newman tucked the handkerchief back under the body in the same position she had dragged it from. He checked his watch. Spyros sat very still, staring at Sarantis as though wishing to imprint on his mind this last memory of his friend. A great mistake, Newman thought: and made by so many people.

'They were here,' Christina insisted. 'How did he die?'

'Painfully,' Nick whispered so Spyros shouldn't hear. 'His wrist was broken, then his arm. The shock could have killed him . . .'

'You see!' Christina protested to Newman. 'Sarantis worked up on that platform where we were. They wanted to extract information from him, the brutes . . .'

'We don't know who "they" were,' Newman insisted. 'We don't even know there were two of them . . .'

'Yes we do,' she hissed. Nick nodded as she went on. 'Go in the kitchen. There are the remains of a quick meal – *two* plates on the table, two dirty knives, two pieces of half-eaten cheese and two hunks of bread. Two wine glasses . . .'

Marler appeared, rifle held in both hands. 'I really think we should get away from this place.'

'My own thought,' Newman agreed. He looked at Spyros. 'When I first arrived at the back door I heard a car disappearing towards the port. What time is the next ferry?'

Spyros checked his watch. 'An extra one left about one half hour ago. Today there are a lot of trucks bringing supplies to Siros. You can catch the last ferry for Athens if you leave now. About one half hour for you to drive to the ferry. Then about one quarter of an hour before it leaves.'

'Time for a quick snack at a taverna on the waterfront,' Marler said firmly. 'I'm famished.'

'We inform the police?' asked Christina.

'Not from Siros,' Newman replied. 'We get caught up in this and it could take days, even weeks. We might even be suspected. I don't want to move Sarantis – but we haven't seen the condition of the back of his skull. He could have been hit over the head.' He looked at Spyros. 'Do you think you could keep quiet until the police arrive on their own? Even then, you'd be better to stay out of the whole tragedy. For your own sake.'

'I prefer to mourn in silence . . .'

'Then we'll drop you off at your house. I don't think you'll be bothered. Only that priest knows we were on Siros. I doubt if the police will go all the way up to Mount Ida. Let's move . . .'

'And the police?' Christina persisted.

'I'll make an anonymous call to headquarters from Athens,' Newman replied vaguely. 'We have things to talk about – you and I – when we get back to the city.'

19

Room 318 at the Athens Hilton had a spectacular view from the balcony across the city. In the distance the Parthenon perched on the summit of the Acropolis was silhouetted against a clear evening sky. Her arms folded, Christina stood on the balcony alongside Newman.

'It is very beautiful,' she said, 'especially when you think of man's age-long struggle to become civilized. Two steps forward, one step backward. You know they're going to come looking for me,' she added quietly. 'My horrible family. Petros will see to that.'

'Which is why I brought you here instead of the Grande

Bretagne. And you registered under an assumed name.'

'They will still track me down. They will tour the hotels. A few drachmae will change hands. They have photos they can show a bellboy, a reception clerk.'

'When you arrived dressed so differently? Wearing those huge dark glasses and your hair concealed under a scarf.'

'Maybe you're right, Bob. I wish I could feel as carefree as those people by the pool.'

She looked down to where guests sprawled round the large swimming pool, the water a deep turquoise in the sunlight. Even with the air-conditioning going full blast the large double room behind them was heavy with heat. Newman watched her while she gazed at the pool.

On their return to Piraeus aboard the ferry, Nick had driven them to Kolonaki, the Mayfair and Park Avenue of Athens rolled into one. He had left Newman and Christina there while he took Marler back to the Grande Bretagne. Christina had bought herself several new outfits and nightwear because all her clothes were at Petros' farm. Newman had paid with traveller's cheques and she'd made him promise to accept payment from her.

'I can go to the bank in the morning,' she had insisted. 'My mother left me all the money left her by her relative. There was quite a large sum even after paying for my education . . .'

Newman had braced himself for an ordeal. A woman buying clothes would take forever. He found he was wrong. Christina was decisive, could look quickly at a dozen outfits in her size, pick out one immediately, try it on in minutes, then buy it. They came closer together during the shopping expedition. Newman was always consulted as to whether he liked what she'd chosen. Twice he shook his head and she looked for something else.

Now she was kitted out with one evening dress and an adequate wardrobe for daytime. When she changed out of her jump suit she gave it to him, he rolled it up, took it outside the hotel and rammed it inside a litter bin. They would be looking for her dressed in that.

'Are we having dinner together?' she asked as they stood on the balcony. 'Or is that too forward of me?'

'The nicest possible way to put it. I've been hoping you would join me. We'll try the Ta Nissia here.'

'Super!' Her eyes glowed. 'Now, you've appointed yourself my bodyguard. Can you read a magazine or something while I take a bath?'

'Take your time . . .'

He was sitting by the large picture window spanning the end of the room when someone tapped on the door. He walked rapidly and quietly to the door. Leaving it on the chain, he opened it and Marler waved a hand through the gap.

'Embarrassing moment?' he drawled. 'I can come back. Give you another hour with her?'

'Shut up and come in. She's taking a bath before we have dinner downstairs.'

'The balcony,' Marler said tersely.

He waited until they were outside, then slid the door closed and lit a cigarette. 'No sign of the enemy at the Grande Bretagne yet. And,' he forestalled Newman, 'I wasn't followed. Do you realize you may be walking into a lethal trap?'

'What the hell does that mean?'

'Strikes me you're getting pretty cosy with Christina. That's OK as far as I'm concerned . . .'

'Oh, how very kind,' Newman interrupted ironically. 'Nice to have the Marler *Good Housekeeping* seal of approval . . .'

'Let me finish. It could be a set-up – organized by Petros to lure you into a trap. All this stuff she's been handing out about hating them, that they'll come after her. Has she had a chance to use a phone since you left us?'

'As a matter of fact, no.' Newman held up a hand. 'And before you waste any more breath, did you really think the idea hadn't occurred to me? If it is a trap I'll be walking into it with my eyes wide open – to see where it leads. Tweed has used the tactic very successfully himself in the past.'

'Pardon me for being alive.' Marler gazed down at the illuminated swimming pool. 'Plenty of talent down there. Look at that brown beauty sprawled on the grass. And, while we're on the subject, I did as you suggested. Called in at the British Embassy and contacted Patterson. Bit of a drip, but after seeing my identification he let me call Tweed on scrambler. You have to call him back when you can. Sometime tonight. Remember we are two hours ahead of London.'

'That means my going to the Embassy . . .'

'It's on Sofias Avenue – a ten-minute walk along it from here.'

'I know that, too. The point is Christina must be guarded during my absence. You're elected.'

'We need to fix a time, then. There's a large hall outside this room with armchairs. I can sit there – but I need to know when to be here.'

'Be downstairs by the bank of lifts at ten forty-five. When you see me leave you come straight up . . .'

'Ten forty-five? My, we are looking forward to an athletic evening.'

Newman punched him hard on the arm. 'Just piss off, Marler – and before you go, you told Tweed about our trip to Siros?'

'Of course. He said it was as he'd thought before I called – that the solution to Masterson's death lies out here in Greece.' Marler held up a warning finger. 'Don't forget, the last Englishman who got pally with the glamorous Christina was Harry Masterson. And he ended up as a pancake at the foot of Cape Sounion.'

'Again, your subtle turn of phrase. I liked Harry. Now, Marler, just piss off . . .'

Petros sat in his cane chair on the veranda of the farmhouse in Devil's Valley. His shirt front was open, exposing the hair on his barrel-like chest. Across his lap rested a shot-gun. The sun had sunk behind the cliff-like wall of the mountainside to the west. The valley was dark with shadows like blue smoke.

His son and two grandsons stood outside the veranda, keeping their distance, showing their respect. Anton was the most confident. Still wearing his dark blue English business suit, he had loosened his tie and unbuttoned the collar at the neck.

Compared with his two nephews, Dimitrios and Constantine, who were clad in shabby peasant garb, Anton was small and dapper. He smoked a cigarette while he waited for Petros to speak – something the other two would not have dared do. Petros leaned forward.

'Anton is smart,' he began, his voice grating. 'He has just returned from England and the English don't even know he was there.'

'But Passport Control . . .' Dimitrios began.

'Tell me, tell these simple-minded cretins how you did it,' Petros suggested.

'It was easy. Just like that.' Anton snapped his fingers. 'An English gesture,' he lectured his nephews with a superior smile which infuriated them. 'You are right, Dimitrios. I was able to enter England without any check by Passport Control.' He paused. It amused him that he had fooled Petros, an old brigand – an illiterate who couldn't speak a word of English. Well-educated – at Petros' expense – he secretly despised his father. 'I think it would be unwise to reveal my route – it could be given away by Dimitrios in one of his drunken stupors.'

217

'Now, listen to me, all of you,' Petros growled. 'I taught you, since you were mere children, family honour demands that we revenge ourselves on the killers who dishonoured our family name. Your father, Dimitrios and Constantine, was Stephen, my son who was murdered in Egypt during the war. Christina's father, Andreas, was murdered on Siros. Not that she cares . . .'

'We know this,' Dimitrios muttered in a feeble show of defiance, but Petros heard him.

'Silence! Both of you are in disgrace. You blundered badly on Siros today. More of that later.' He sank back and the chair creaked. Hooding his eyes like a hawk, he spoke again.

'Anton. Tell us what you found in England. Make it brief.'

'There is a lonely area called Exmoor. Also a place like here called the Doone Valley. The three men who went with Andreas on a commando raid to Siros – Barrymore, Kearns and Robson – live close together on that moor. Which is strange. They are not related . . .'

'Tell them about the places where they live,' Petros prodded.

'Each house is well-defended. Like small castles expecting an invasion. One has television cameras watching all approaches. Another is guarded by a fierce dog called Wolf. The third has tall walls topped with barbed wire and a single separate wire. I was suspicious. I scaled a wall carrying a cat. I dropped the cat on the single wire. There was a flash. It screamed, died. Electrified. They are afraid – after all this time . . .'

'How did you find these three men?' asked Dimitrios.

'Christina went to England and used a newspaper advertisement which attracted the attention of a Harry Masterson . . .'

'That's enough,' Petros interrupted, eyes wide open. 'No need to give details. But which of the three is guilty, has our blood on his hands? Or were all three involved in both murders?'

'I don't know.' Anton made a resigned gesture with his manicured hands – hands which contrasted with the roughness of his nephews' who, Petros reflected, were poles apart. 'I made discreet enquiries in the pubs on Exmoor,' Anton continued. 'The three men meet twice every week – for lunch in one place, for dinner in another.' His manner changed, became more nervous as he talked more quickly. 'Then there was the strange incident of the murder of the Englishman, Partridge, on the moor.'

'Partridge, did you say?' asked Dimitrios, quick to sense Anton's change of mood. 'We know an Englishman of that name was poking round Athens, asking questions. That he later visited Siros.'

Anton looked at Petros before replying. The old patriarch nodded agreement for him to continue. 'It was the same man. There was an old picture of him in a newspaper reporting the murder. It is worrying – the report said he was a detective for most of his life with Scotland Yard. The Homicide Branch.'

'There was a man of that name in Cairo when Stephen was killed,' Petros reminded him. 'We found out later. He was one of the military detectives who supposedly investigated Stephen's death. Very young, he was. Is Partridge a common English name?'

'Not as far as I know,' Anton replied. He hurried on. 'That is why I returned here quickly. They were hunting for the killer.'

'And why should they think it was you?' demanded Dimitrios.

Anton hesitated again, looking at Petros. The old man frowned. It was a good question. 'Answer Dimitrios,' he ordered.

'I happened to be riding on a different part of the moor when he was killed,' Anton replied. 'Watching the homes of the three men who were the commandos.'

'I see.' Petros frowned and Anton shuffled his feet.

The old man turned on the two brothers, determined to humiliate them, to exert his authority. 'Now, tell us what a mess you made of things on Siros today. Describe in detail. Anton should know what fools his nephews can be . . .'

Petros sat staring into the distance while Dimitrios recalled the day's events. It was when he came to describe their visit to the home of Sarantis, the archaeologist, that he transferred his gaze to Dimitrios who seemed uncomfortable.

'Constantine,' he broke in suddenly, 'do you agree with all that Dimitrios has said?'

'Yes.' The more passive brother paused. 'We tried to make him talk, to tell us what he knew about where Andreas died. We broke his wrist, then his arm. The old fool slipped on the polished floor, fell over backwards and cracked his skull on the tiles.'

'Go on.'

'We decided to leave quickly aboard the chopper. We knew you would not want us to be tangled up with a police investigation . . .'

'So, you leave in the kitchen the cutlery and things you used to eat a quick meal. With your fingerprints on them, of course.'

'No, Petros! We wiped everything clean. Knives, the glasses. We would have put them away but we were afraid someone would arrive.'

'You ate when you first questioned him, then took him into the living room to apply more pressure?'

'That is how it happened.'

'I wonder whether to believe you.' He was silent for a moment. 'And these two Englishmen Christina reported on – Newman and Marler. You fouled that up as well. No information from Sarantis.' He raised his voice to a shout. 'Do I have to be everywhere to make sure you do the right thing? All of you, get out of my sight. No, wait!

Christina has disappeared. Last seen with those English.'
His tone was venomous. 'Tomorrow you go to Athens,
find her. Do not let her see you. Follow her and tell me
what she does, where she goes. Later I decide what to do
about her. Now, go! Prepare the meal. If you can do that
properly . . .'

Petros sat alone on the veranda, a grim smile of satisfaction
on his lined face. Frequently it was necessary to crack the
whip to remind his family who was the chief. He looked
up as Anton appeared and spoke, his voice low.

'While I have been away, Papa, has anyone been seen
near the silver mine?'

'No.' He smiled bleakly. 'You worry too much. Leave
me alone. I have to think.'

Despite the mild rebuke, Petros approved: it showed
Anton was using his brain. At least one of the litter had
turned out well. Odd it should be his second wife's only
son. The wife who had died from overwork like the first –
driven on by Petros' insistence they run the farm. Early
in Anton's childhood Petros had realized he was the bright
one. How he had scrimped and saved to educate the
boy.

While Dimitrios and Constantine had worked in the
fields, Anton had been sent to a select school near Berne
in Switzerland – away from the fleshpots of Athens. A
school where discipline was strong, where he had learned
to speak English and German.

But Petros had taken the precaution of bringing him
home during the holidays for Petros' own kind of discipline.
He had hammered into the boy's head that his half-
brothers, Andreas and Stephen, had been murdered – that
the family must take their revenge. A cloud of poisonous
hatred hung over Devil's Valley.

It had been a long struggle. First the Civil War from

221

1946 to 1949 between the Communists and the anti-Communists. Breaking out soon after World War Two had ended, it had gone on until the Communist guerrillas were defeated. So many wasted years.

Only recently had Petros been able to devote all his efforts to his vendetta. He had reached the stage where he was quite unable to realize it had become an obsession, filling his every waking moment. A stray thought crossed his mind. The Communists.

Why – after all these years – had the Russian, Oleg Savinkov, reappeared in Athens? He was one of the old school, a Stalinist. And the new man, Gorbachev, was a very different leader, they said. Savinkov, once called The Executioner, did not fit the new pattern Petros heard about in the cafés of the village he visited. To play checkers, to listen to the gossip. Above all to get the first hint of a farmer in trouble. Someone whose land or stock he might buy for a pittance.

Why had Savinkov changed his name to Florakis? The Russian did speak Greek fluently. And he had bought a small farm adjacent to Petros on the coast. But why had he made a point of meeting him when Petros was sitting alone in a café? The Russian had handed him an envelope crammed with drachmae. A large sum – so large Petros, greedy for money, had not accepted at once.

'What do you expect me to do for this?' he had asked bluntly.

'Only one thing – which fits in with your own purposes. You make sure no Englishmen visit the island of Siros and poke around up near Mount Ida.'

'You expect me to kill them?' Petros had demanded.

'It is up to you.' Savinkov had shrugged. 'Maybe you rough them up a bit. You could sabotage their car – the mountain roads are dangerous.'

'And how do I get in touch with you?' Petros had asked, testing Savinkov. 'Walk across to your farm?'

222

'Never. And you know me only as Florakis. That is why I am paying you . . .'

Since then Petros had kept the money inside the same envelope in his Athens bank. For Petros this was an act of unprecedented willpower. But one day he might wish to sever all connection with the man who had appeared like a ghost. Then he would throw the money back at him.

But why, he asked himself for the twentieth time, should Savinkov take an interest in the murder of Andreas all those years ago?

20

Inside a first-floor room above a taverna in the Plaka, the sole occupant, Oleg Savinkov, was also reflecting on the past. A wiry thin-faced man in his sixties, with blank grey eyes, he sat at a table in his shirt-sleeves and mopped beads of perspiration from his forehead.

The evening heat confined by the rabbit warren of narrow twisting streets was ferocious. He drank more mineral water; years ago he had stopped drinking any kind of alcohol. Years ago . . . In 1946 he had been a young man of twenty, known and feared in Greece as The Russian – or The Executioner. Sent to Greece by Stalin personally because of his talent – his talent for assassination.

1946. Stalin had agreed at Yalta that Greece should come within the British sphere of influence. But when the Greek Communist ELAS movement rose up in revolt and looked like taking over the strategic country – with its potential great Russian naval base at Piraeus – Stalin quietly betrayed his promise.

Savinkov had been smuggled into Greece from Bulgaria. His mission had been brutally simple: to assassinate all the leaders of the Greek right-wing EDES movement fighting the Communists. He had succeeded – up to a point. Five top EDES leaders fell victims to his high-powered rifle. Hence his nicknames – The Russian and The Executioner.

But he had failed to take out the chief EDES leaders. Enough remained at the head of their troops to defeat the Communist uprising eventually. Savinkov had decided wisely not to return to Russia: Stalin demanded one hundred per cent success.

By this time Savinkov had learned Greek fluently and he merged with the landscape, working on a remote farm in Macedonia. The years passed and he seemed to have become the forgotten man. That was until he received discreet word from the Soviet Embassy that someone important wished to meet him.

The visit of General Lucharsky, a Deputy Chief of the Soviet General Staff, to Greece was never reported in the press. By 1986 Savinkov was settled in the Cape Sounion area, owning a small farm growing figs and olives. He had saved money, obtained from a small bank a mortgage to buy the property. He had applied for the loan in the name of Stavros Florakis. Over the years he had obtained sufficient forged papers to establish a new identity as a Greek citizen.

Here he had taken a risk. After some hesitation he had contacted one of the Communist ELAS leaders who had gone underground, the man with whose group he was working when the whole revolt fell apart. It was a greater risk than he realized since this benefactor kept a discreet and distant line of communication open with the Soviet Embassy in Athens. But this man had seen no reason to inform on Savinkov – his own relations with the Russians had been precarious. Until 1986 . . .

Florakis-Savinkov drank more mineral water. He wouldn't sleep, he knew. The oppressive heat would last all night long. Plus the babble of voices and *bouzouki* playing which drifted upwards through the dense humidity and through the open window.

1986. He had been visited at his farm late one evening by the ELAS leader who had provided him with the papers of a Greek citizen. The man's arrival had been a shock – it was Savinkov's first intimation that he had been watched, that they knew where he was.

He had been invited to meet an 'important visitor' to Athens. That was after he had been asked a number of questions about his reaction to the change of leadership in Russia. Savinkov had been frank – thinking that if he was candid the invitation which worried him might be withdrawn.

No, he did not approve of Gorbachev's *glasnost*. This was not the real Communism he had risked his life for during the Civil War. It was a dangerous departure from Lenin's creed, and so on. To his surprise an appointment had been made for that same evening. His visitor would drive him to Athens.

His destination turned out to be the Hilton Hotel. He was escorted to a room on the second floor where a man wearing a lightweight grey business suit had opened the door and ushered him inside. Tall and lean with the face of a fox, he wore a pair of dark glasses and offered Savinkov vodka. He refused, mentioned that he had not touched alcohol for forty years.

'I am Colonel Gerasimov of the GRU,' his host said as they sat facing each other across a small round table.

General Lucharsky was confident his deception would

never be penetrated. His photograph had never appeared in a newspaper and the general public abroad didn't know of his existence. He was weighing up his guest as he poured himself a glass of the vodka, a fact Savinkov was aware of. Mention of the GRU had reassured him – as intended – since it was a GRU colonel who had accompanied him to the Bulgarian border in 1946.

'We are very worried about General Secretary Gorbachev and his crazy *glasnost*,' Lucharsky commented.

He had no doubts about coming straight to the point: Doganis, who had brought Savinkov to him, would have checked his outlook. And for a man of sixty-one Savinkov looked very fit – more like forty. Already Lucharsky was fairly sure they had selected the right man.

'He is ruining Lenin's work,' Savinkov agreed, 'but why am I here?'

He spoke slowly. It was many years since he had conversed in his native language. But he had taken the precaution of reading novels in Russian and he found the language coming back fast.

'You were once trained as a radio operator,' Lucharsky said. 'Is that not so?'

'Yes. Before I came to Greece to do a job in 1946 . . .'

'To kill reactionary Greek leaders.' Lucharsky leaned forward. 'We need a liaison man who can communicate by radio in English. I understand you are fluent in that language?'

'I learned it in the days when I served as a waiter in hotels here to make money to buy my farm. I keep it up by talking with English people during the tourist season . . .'

'Good. You are just the man we need.' Lucharsky smiled. His wide mouth made him look even foxier. A conspirator type, Savinkov was thinking. 'You will have to operate the latest type of transceiver. Doganis will train you in the use of the instrument, will give you the codes, the wavebands, the times for transmission. England, you see, is two hours behind Greece.'

England? Savinkov was startled. In the old days he used to think very fast and he found his brain moving into high gear again. The man watching him from behind the tinted glasses would be in his forties. He would show him he was not dealing with some dumb peasant.

'There could be a technical problem. Transmitting over that distance.'

'Doganis tells me you have high mountains, very lonely, near your farm. You could use one of your donkeys to take the transceiver to a peak. From there transmission will be top-class.'

'Yes, it would.' They had thought this out very carefully. Which gave Savinkov confidence. But he needed to know exactly what he was doing – and why. He sat up straight, staring at the glasses.

'In the old days I never operated in the dark. I must know what this is all about, Colonel.'

'An independent type. Good,' Lucharsky repeated. 'Really I have already told you. Gorbachev must be removed before he can do any more damage. There is a group inside Russia – high up – which is determined to replace him by a correct type of leader. The trouble is we have to be very careful. He has ears everywhere – inside Russia. So we have reactivated an organization outside the motherland. Partly here in Greece, partly in England. You will be the link. Doganis will deliver the messages you must send. At other times our associate in England will send you signals at certain times arranged in advance. That's it. And Doganis is your sole contact. Never go near the Soviet Embassy here.'

'Who am I communicating with in England?'

'The codename is La Jolla – a small place in America.

227

Doganis will explain everything. Oh, by the way, when you leave here he will drive you to a room we have rented for you over a taverna in the Plaka. I think that is all.' Lucharsky glanced at his watch.

'I don't see how this is going to bring down Gorbachev. And I will be risking my freedom. Greek counter-intelligence could trap me and I would be a spy.'

'You are right.' Lucharsky pursed his thin lips. They had reported Savinkov was intelligent and self-reliant. A thought occurred to him. 'You are not married, we know. What do you do for a woman when you need one? Any permanent girlfriend?'

'None. I would have had to entrust her with my secret. If we had quarrelled one day she might have betrayed me. I have an old woman who comes daily to the farm to cook for me and two men who work on the land. When I need a woman I go into the city here and pick one up. Always a different one. That way, no complications.'

'You are very well organized. And now you will excuse me?'

'I still don't see how you are going to replace Gorbachev – even operating a group safely from outside.'

This was the crunch. By now Lucharsky had made up his mind – time had not eroded Savinkov's training, his reliability, his faith in the cause. Lucharsky waved a hand as though swatting a fly.

'If necessary we await our opportunity – preferably when he is abroad – and kill him. You object to that?'

'Why should I? In the past I have killed enemies of the cause.'

Doganis had been waiting for him outside the room and had led him to a Citroën parked in front of the taxi rank outside the hotel. It had been a baking evening as Savinkov stared at the car.

228

'What happened to the Peugeot you drove me to Athens in?'

'We change cars. Frequently. It is good security. Get in. Now we will go to the Plaka. Inside the locked boot there is an old suitcase. Inside that is the transceiver. You start training tonight . . .'

And, Savinkov thought as he poured yet more mineral water, it was inside this room a year ago that Doganis had produced from a worn, shabby suitcase a superb large transceiver. They had practised half the night, Savinkov tapping the key while the machine was switched off. He had been surprised how quickly he had mastered the machine – so different from the one he had used in 1946.

Later that week Doganis had again visited his farm and the training had continued until Savinkov could operate it blindfold. His greatest shock had come that first evening here in this room when he had tackled Doganis about the clandestine organization working outside Russia.

'Colonel Gerasimov told me they have reactivated an organization – an apparatus – outside the motherland. What does that mean? I do need to know what I am doing,' he concluded aggressively.

'You might as well know. We may have to send a stranger to you with a message. This will identify him. The apparatus which has come alive again is the Greek Key.'

21

Newman escorted Christina through the large bar at the Hilton and down the staircase leading to the Ta Nissia, the main restaurant. It was located at a lower level from the vast entrance hall paved with solid marble. Christina paused at the bottom step and grasped Newman's arm.

'Oh, look, that tempts my taste buds madly.'

Facing them was a vast open fireplace and over the fire spits revolved slowly, cooking the food. The lower spit supported a whole roasting pig. On the long spit above it chickens were turning slowly and an appetising aroma drifted towards them.

'No need to consult the menu,' Newman joked. 'I've reserved a corner table . . .' He gave his name to the maitre d' who escorted them past a huge cold buffet table into a spacious room shut off from the outside world.

They settled themselves at the table and Newman sat alongside Christina on a red velvet banquette, his back to the wall so he could watch the whole room. He glanced at her as she studied the menu. 'You're looking superb in that dress, what there is of it. It suits your figure.'

She glanced at him wickedly. 'Maybe a little too revealing.'

'I'm happy.'

It was the one item of clothing they had purchased in Kolonaki she had not allowed him to see. A strapless, low-cut dress of black velvet, it hugged her closely. 'You'll have to be careful not to drop anything down the front,' he remarked, with a quick look at the upper half of her well-formed breasts.

'You would think of that.' She giggled. 'I've decided. No starter. Spit-roast chicken for me. And it's nice to have a man who's so well-organized.' She nodded towards the ice bucket where a bottle of champagne rested half-concealed beneath a white napkin.

'Veuve Cliquot.' He looked at the waiter standing to take their orders. 'We'll start on the champagne right away – and we can order now . . .'

She waited until they were alone. 'Are these the opening moves in an attempted seduction?'

230

'You brought the subject up.' He lowered his glass. 'First I need to hear all about Harry Masterson.'

'I thought there'd be a catch.' She sighed. 'What do you want to know?'

'Everything. From the very beginning. How you met him would be a good opening.'

'I like this place. It's the first time I've been here. Silly, isn't it?' She gave him a bewitching smile. 'I suppose it is because I live here. A strange room, very cleverly designed.'

He looked round. The walls were constructed of very solid rough brown stone. Set back into the walls at intervals were alcoves containing Greek pottery – beautifully shaped vases and jugs. A soft glow illuminated the room and the windows were high up and recessed into the solid stone. At 8 p.m. there were only a few tables taken, but more guests were filtering in. Newman refilled their glasses.

'Now, about Harry Masterson,' he said firmly.

'What a persistent man you are. Well, it's a long story . . .'

'We have all evening.'

'Petros still had me under his thumb. He persuaded me it was my duty to help find who killed Andreas and Stephen. We Greeks call it *philotimo*, a matter of family honour.'

'Go on.'

'He went about it deviously – like he does everything. I had to fly to Zurich. There I stayed overnight and bought a return air ticket to London. I'd flown to Zurich by Swissair. I used British Airways to fly on to London. When I got there I stayed at the Strand Palace. I then inserted a personal advertisement in *The Times* newspaper.' She paused. 'Petros had written the words. The advertisement read, *Will anyone interested in the Greek Key and who knows about Antikhana please contact me. Irene.*'

Newman sipped champagne to conceal the shock he had

received. Harry Masterson had been Tweed's sector chief for the Balkans, and that zone included Greece. Newman was also recalling that among the items Masterson had posted back to Tweed was a bracelet – a bracelet from which was suspended a symbol. The Greek key.

'What happened next?' he enquired amiably.

'Petros thought I might be contacted by one of three men – the men who were part of the commando raid on Siros when Andreas was murdered. A Colonel Barrymore, Captain Robson and Kearns, a company sergeant major. Whoever answered the advertisement was likely to be the murderer. So Petros thought. He felt sure they would have to find out who was enquiring after all these years.'

'I don't understand the Greek key bit.'

'I'm not talking about that. Too dangerous. For you . . .'

'There's no limit on danger.'

'Don't you want to know who got in touch with the phone number I put in the advertisement?' she asked.

'Go on,' he repeated, confident he already knew the answer.

'Harry Masterson. I was very taken aback. Then I thought it could be one of the three men using a false name. Especially because of the precautions he told me to take when he arranged to meet me.'

'What precautions?'

'I had to meet him at a certain place in Lincoln's Inn – where all the British lawyers are. It frightened me when I arrived at eleven in the morning. No one about. All those ancient courtyards. I thought it was a trap. I'd armed myself with an aerosol. He was very clever. The appointment was for the same morning he phoned. I only had less than an hour to get there.'

Yes, very clever, Newman thought. So typical of Harry – to select a rendezvous where he could watch her approach,

232

make sure no one was following her. A thought occurred to him.

'How would he know it was you?'

'On the phone he asked me where I was and to give a description of myself, what I would be wearing. I waited for ten minutes and decided no one was coming. At that moment he came round a corner. Again he was clever. I realized he couldn't be one of the three men – he was too young. But I thought one of them might have sent him. He took me a short walk to a public place in Fleet Street, The Cheshire Cheese pub. Lots of people about. I felt safe then.'

She paused and drank half a glass of champagne. The restaurant was filling up. As he listened Newman kept a check on the new faces; for one especially. The face of Petros. He'd recognize him: from the picture Sarris, the police chief, had shown him; and even more from that moment he had spotted Petros inside the black Mercedes when they had returned early in the morning from police HQ.

'We're inside The Cheshire Cheese,' he reminded her after their meals of spit-roasted chicken had been served.

'Harry had a way with women. I felt he was OK but I still asked who he was, what he did. He said he was with Special Branch, the British secret police. I asked him to prove it and he showed me a card with his photograph. I found myself telling him about the murders of Andreas and Stephen, why I'd come to London, about Barrymore, Kearns and Robson. He said he had ways of tracing them. I couldn't believe my luck. I asked him what his interest was.'

'And he told you?' Newman was intrigued to learn what piece of fiction Harry had invented to cover that question.

'He said it might just link up with a case he had investigated and never solved. We arranged to meet the following day after he'd made certain enquiries. I've no idea where he went . . .'

I have, thought Newman. To pump Brigadier Willie Davies at the Ministry of Defence. He let her eat her meal while he traced in his mind what had happened. It was all becoming horribly clear now – the tragedy of Harry Masterson.

Harry had been given a month's leave. Unmarried, Harry detested holidays, got bored within twenty-four hours. He'd seen the advertisement Christina had placed in *The Times* and reacted to it for a lark – anything to occupy his time.

The moment he'd met Christina he'd been hooked – but cautious – by her story, by Christina herself. Harry liked the ladies. He had still kept up his guard by pretending to be a Special Branch officer. That had impressed Christina, had given her confidence he could help her. But at any time Harry could pull out, pleading call of duty with another case.

'What happened next?' he asked as she pushed her empty plate to one side. 'And we need more champagne . . .' He mimed the request to their waiter.

'When he arrived next morning at the Strand Palace he was carrying a small case. He told me to pack, that we were going on a journey, that he'd traced not only Barry-more, but Kearns and Robson, too. I was shaken to the core. He said we had to drive to the West Country, to a place called Exmoor . . .'

She went on to explain how they had put up at a hotel in Dunster near the coast. Harry had then driven off to visit the three men now he knew their addresses.

'He made appointments?' Newman asked.

'No, he was devious. He phoned each of the three men and said he was making an enquiry on behalf of the Ministry

234

of Defence, that he would be with them shortly. Then he put the phone down before they could ask any questions. That way he knew they'd be where they lived when he arrived.'

'You'd told him everything you knew about the two murders – one in Cairo, one on Siros? And about Petros' vendetta?'

'Yes.' She smiled ruefully. 'Harry could get any secret out of a woman. I told him more than I intended to.'

'So what happened after he'd seen the ex-commandos?'

'He was suspicious of one of them. He wouldn't tell me which one. He told each of them the identity of the murderer was now known, that he was on his way to Athens to check with the chief of police. He thought the guilty one would follow us.'

Oh God, Newman realized, and he succeeded. At the cost of his own life. No back-up. That had been Harry's fatal blunder. But he had always been a lone wolf, brimming with self-confidence. Had he left behind a clue?

'Did he say anything about how the three men received him?'

'He was very amusing about Colonel Barrymore who tried to treat him like a common soldier. They had a violent argument. Harry ended up by telling him that if they'd had many colonels like him they would have lost the war. Then we flew out here.'

'What came next?'

'I don't really know.' For the first time she sounded depressed. 'We booked in at the Astir Palace at Vouliagmeni. That's a sea resort on the way to Cape Sounion . . .' Which is why we weren't able to locate where he stayed, Newman thought grimly. She continued as he watched her closely. 'He said he was going to see Chief Inspector Sarris. I don't know whether he ever did. He changed his mind a lot.' She sipped more champagne and leaned against him. 'I'm getting a bit tiddly. Lovely.'

235

He changed his mind a lot. Newman knew why Harry had done that: to keep Christina off balance in case she was passing on information to someone. He had never completely let down his guard with her.

'Then what happened?' Newman prodded.

'He told me over early breakfast one morning he was visiting Devil's Valley. He wouldn't say why. I'd told him about the silver mine. I think he was going to try and find it. I feel awful about that. I may be responsible for what happened to him.'

'What silver mine?'

'It's near the top of a mountain in Devil's Valley. Nobody has worked it for years. It's abandoned – but Petros forbids anyone to go near it. I don't know why. He has even told his shepherds who work near it to shoot anyone they see prowling in that area.'

'Which is against the law,' Newman remarked.

'Petros makes his own law. Harry was intrigued by that silver mine – why it was forbidden territory. I've never been near the place.' She shuddered, drank more champagne.

'So, when Harry set out on his last journey that morning he was trying to locate this abandoned mine. Any idea what the place is like?'

'Dimitrios once told me something when he was drunk. The shaft is still open. It goes down a long way, a vertical drop with the old cage which took down miners still suspended at the top. It sounded horribly sinister to me. But at the last minute before he left Harry changed his mind again. He received a phone call when he was getting ready to leave his bedroom. He said he might go first to Cape Sounion to meet the Englishman.'

'What Englishman? What time in the morning was this?'

Newman was watching her closely. Was she spinning him an elaborate yarn? Setting the same trap for him she'd set for Harry? She was such a beauty with her mane of

236

black glossy hair; by the light of the single lighted candle on their table her bare shoulders gleamed. A girl to dazzle any man.

'We'd had breakfast at six,' she continued. 'Neither of us could sleep that night. The phone call must have come through before seven in the morning. Harry went up to his room to take it. He looked pleased when he came back, said his ruse had worked. I presume he meant telling those three ex-commandos he was flying to Greece while we were on Exmoor. The caller had disguised his voice but Harry was sure he knew who it was. He wouldn't give me even a hint. Said it was dangerous . . .'

And it had been dangerous, Newman reflected grimly. It had ended in Harry's death. But what she had told him was confusing. Had Harry tried to locate the silver mine first before going on to Cape Sounion?

'Christina, did Harry know the exact location of the worked-out silver mine?'

'Yes. He had a map of the area he bought in Athens. He asked me to mark its precise location on the map, which I did. Afterwards I wished I hadn't done that. Harry could be very persuasive.'

'So can I.' He produced a large-scale map he'd purchased of the huge peninsular area stretching between Athens and Cape Sounion. 'Mark the location for me.'

She pushed back her empty plate, clasped her hands in her lap, turned to face him. 'No. The last time I did that a man died. I'm growing fond of you, Bob . . .'

'Cut that out,' he said brutally. 'Mark the bloody map. Now!'

'It's your funeral.' Her eyes flashed. 'And don't ever use that tone to me again.' She spread out the map, took the pen he offered, studied the map, then drew a cross at the top of a mountain.

'Petros is crazy,' she warned. 'You'd be crazy too if you went anywhere near Devil's Valley.'

'When was the last time you saw Harry? Alive, I mean,' he persisted, his voice cold.

'You bastard . . .' Her voice trembled. She was on the verge of tears. 'When he left the breakfast room and went straight to his hired car . . .' She fiddled in her envelope-shaped handbag for a handkerchief.

He put an arm round her back, rested his hand on her shoulder. 'No need to get uptight, Christina. But I knew Harry well. I have to know everything he did – planned to do. What about a spot of dessert? The strawberry gâteau looks pretty good – forget about your figure for tonight, even if I can't . . .'

'Flattery could get you somewhere.' She recovered her poise as he squeezed her shoulder. 'And I'd love some gâteau. And more champagne.'

He waited until dessert was served, until she was tucking into the huge quantity with gusto. 'To sum up,' he began, 'you went to London at Petros' command, inserted the advertisement, made contact with Harry. OK so far?'

'On the nose,' she assured him and winked.

'He drove you to Exmoor, after tracing Barrymore, Robson and Kearns. He went to see each man, told them he was flying soon to Greece. You arrived with him. What was your mood about the mission Petros had sent you on when you got back here?'

'Bloody bolshie. I'd had Petros up to here. The trip to London – and spending time with Harry – had snapped any bonds with Petros. I didn't care any more who had killed Stephen, Andreas. I'd never even known them. I was worried about Harry. Now I'm worried about you. If it's not a secret, what are you going to do next? Please . . .'

She laid a hand on his arm. Then she waited until he turned towards her and kissed him full on the mouth. 'Please,' she repeated. 'I've been honest with you.'

'Fair enough. I'm going to phone a man in London I

238

know after I've packed you off to bed. And Marler will stand guard. Outside your room.'

'Who are you phoning?' she pressed.

'My editor,' he lied. 'I am a foreign correspondent. Remember?'

22

Newman arrived at the British Embassy at eleven, well after dark. The large villa on Sofias Avenue was surrounded by a stone wall, looming up behind a Turkish-style church. Patterson, his contact, was a pain in the neck.

Impatiently, Newman waited in the hall as the round-faced man in his forties carefully examined his press card and then his passport. A typical bureaucrat, Newman thought: inflated with a sense of his own importance. Smooth-faced, he turned the passport pages with irritating slowness.

'For God's sake,' Newman snapped. 'You knew I was coming. Tweed warned you.'

'It is my responsibility who uses the phone,' Patterson responded in his bland voice.

'It's just a phone . . .'

'It's the scrambler,' Patterson reminded him pompously. 'I have to log all calls, be very careful who uses it. You have no diplomatic status . . .'

'*You* won't have any if I report you're obstructing me. You're on probation, don't forget.'

The blow struck home. Patterson's well-padded face flushed, he ran a manicured hand over his slick black hair. 'No need to be rude,' he bleated.

'Just realistic. Let's get on with it. Now. Tweed is waiting. Or have you forgotten London is two hours behind us? He likes to get home early to work on files,' Newman lied.

The phone was in a small room in the basement. A table, chairs pushed under it, the phone with the red button the only object on the table top. Newman sat down, reached for the phone, then looked up at Patterson who still stood waiting.

'Piss off, there's a good chap. This is confidential. Leave the card and passport on the table. Shut the door on your way out.'

Pressing the red button, he dialled Park Crescent. Paula came on the line within seconds. She sounded relieved to hear his voice.

'We wondered what the devil was happening to you . . .'

'Nice to be loved. Tweed about? I'm on scrambler from the Embassy in Athens.'

'He's here. Take care . . .'

Tweed sounded as fresh as sea air at nine in the evening. Newman plunged straight into a terse report of what had taken place since his arrival. Tweed listened without interrupting. At the end of five minutes Newman concluded his story.

'That brings you up to date. Doesn't really take us any further as to who killed Harry.'

'It might have done. You have a pipeline into this weird Gavalas clan – Christina. Whether she can be trusted is for you to assess. What do you think?'

'I'm leaning to the idea she has broken with the whole crew. But only leaning – she's pretty street-wise and could be a first-rate actress. Pity Harry hadn't told her who the mysterious Englishman who phoned him was. Could it have been one of the commando trio?'

'Yes. All three I visited had just returned from separate holidays abroad. All had a deep suntan – which they could

240

have picked up in Greece. The timing is right, too. One of them could have been out there at exactly the time Masterson was killed. I have the feeling the solution lies in Greece. That raid on Siros all those years ago. What intrigues me is the missing body – who took the dead Andreas away from that gulch? And why? I may fly out to join you when the right moment comes. What's your next move?'

'To explore that old silver mine in Devil's Valley. Something very strange about that – the way Petros takes such precautions to keep strangers away from the place . . .'

'Don't!' Tweed's tone was sharp. 'I don't like the sound of Mr Petros one bit. We may do it together later. You need plenty of back-up to go into a place like that. Harry Butler and Pete Nield would be useful. Plus Marler. At the moment Butler and Nield are on Exmoor, nosing around and picking up gossip about Barrymore, Kearns and Robson. How are you finding Marler?' Tweed asked casually.

'A pain. But I can handle him. One thing I will give him – he's a good man to go into the jungle with. I'll keep you in touch . . .'

'Don't go.' A pause. 'At this stage it seems like a vendetta directed by Petros against whoever killed his two sons, Andreas and Stephen. His main suspects being on Exmoor. Is that how you see it?'

'With the little data we have to go on yet, yes. Especially now you've told me about this Anton character. Christina hasn't mentioned him, which I find odd. Butler and Nield are on the lookout for Anton, too, I assume?'

'Anton has disappeared. I suspect he's flown by some secret route back to Greece. He didn't pass through London Airport – I've had the security chief there check the passenger manifests.'

'But it backs up the vendetta theory.' Newman paused and Tweed said nothing. 'Or is there something more?'

'I think this business could be much bigger, far more

serious than we realize. I can't figure out the link between Exmoor and Greece.'

'There has to be one?'

'If there isn't, then we're wasting our time. But who pushed Masterson over a Greek cliff?' Tweed paused again. 'After he'd visited Exmoor. We're missing something . . .'

Florakis – Oleg Savinkov, The Executioner – crouched at the top of the mountain above his farm. It was 2 a.m. and earlier he had received a coded signal he suspected emanated from inside the Soviet Embassy in Athens.

His suspicions were correct. But he would have been surprised had he known the hand which tapped out the message was that of Colonel Rykovsky, military attaché. Rykovsky had waited until the Embassy staff had gone home: hence the arrangement made via Doganis for Savinkov to be ready to receive the signal at two in the morning.

Savinkov had placed the powerful transceiver given to him in a small depression at the mountain summit. The telescopic aerial was extended as he checked his watch by the light of a pencil torch. Time to retransmit the message to England. And for that elevation was needed to cover the long distance.

His bony face was tense with concentration as he sent out the call signal, received immediate acknowledgement. He began tapping out the coded message, keeping an eye on his watch as he operated. Three minutes was the maximum agreed time for any transmission.

It was unlikely Greek counter-espionage would have detector vans as far south as this remote wilderness, but Doganis had emphasized the importance of security.

'Take no chances. You are the linchpin of the whole operation.'

'What operation?' Savinkov had asked.

'I don't know, but it's big, very big. It could change the whole course of history. That's all I've been told.'

The words echoed in Savinkov's brain as he completed tapping out the signal. He felt excited as he depressed the aerial, lifted the heavy transceiver back inside the shabby suitcase. It was a long climb back down the mountain to the farm but he would be there long before daylight.

One thousand six hundred-odd miles to the north-west another hand on Exmoor was already beginning the task of decoding the signal which had just come in from Greece. The unbreakable one-time code had been used, the novel the series of numbers referred to was Sinclair Lewis' *Main Street*. Half an hour later the message was decoded, written on the pad which had a sheet of protective plastic beneath the sheet to avoid any risk of an impression of the wording reproducing itself on the sheet beneath the plastic.

All equipment and preparations should be made immediately. Possible that target will land in Britain on way to or when returning from Washington summit. Potential timing September or October this year. The Greek Key.

23

'Gorbachev must go, he is destroying the military supremacy we have taken so many years to build up. His crazy *glasnost* will be the ruin of the Soviet state,' General Lucharsky said vehemently.

By which he meant the power of the Red Army, his faithful aide, Colonel Volkov, thought as they strolled side by side in full uniform in the Moscow park. Children played ball games on the grass in the warmth of the sunlight round them as they followed one of the many twisting paths.

Lucharsky had chosen the park for this conversation because it was impossible for them to be overheard. He walked very erect, hands clasped behind him, head bowed in thought. Volkov asked the question tentatively. He was not sure Lucharsky wanted to reveal details of the plan but his curiosity drove him on.

'How can we ever hope to achieve his replacement? The Politburo is now packed with a majority in his favour . . .'

'Ligachev,' the General said tersely. 'He is Number Two. He does not agree with the new madness. Once Gorbachev has been removed he will take over and the yes-men in the Politburo will swing behind him.'

'But how can the present General Secretary be removed?'

'He can be killed.'

The cold-blooded audacity of the statement astounded Volkov and he was silent for a few minutes as they continued their stroll. Lucharsky took off his peaked cap and ran his hand through his blond hair, enjoying the feel of the sun on his forehead.

'But it must be done outside Russia,' Lucharsky continued, 'at a suitable moment. I set the wheels in motion when I made my unofficial visit to Greece. There are plenty of hard men in the Politburo who will welcome a return to the good old days. Fortunately, Comrade Gorbachev is playing into our hands. He agrees we must do everything possible to spread our influence in the Mediterranean. But by peaceful means. You, Comrade, have been chosen to follow up my visit to Athens. Like me, you will travel there in civilian clothes – on an unofficial visit. We are offering the Greek government special trade concessions. While you are there you will carry verbal orders from me to Colonel Rykovsky, the military attaché at the Athens

244

Embassy. I will give you those orders just before you fly to Athens via Zurich.'

'Why Greece? What is happening there?'

Lucharsky changed direction, headed for a path which twisted through a wooded area of birch trees. He had spotted two men in plain clothes who had KGB written all over them. One had a pair of field glasses slung round his neck. He might be a lip-reader. They entered the wood.

'Because,' Lucharsky explained, 'it is too dangerous to plan a coup inside the motherland. Gorbachev is no fool. He knows he faces opposition and has eyes and ears everywhere. We must not underestimate him. So, we have reactivated an organization outside Russia, one which has not operated for years. It is composed of men who worked for Stalin, who have been forgotten. Shadow men.'

'And Greece is this base?'

'One of them,' Lucharsky replied enigmatically. 'We are using the KGB cell system. Only what you need to know is told to you. There is great dissatisfaction inside the Red Army, as you know. When Gorbachev has gone the Army will again wield all the power it once did after Stalin died.'

'But you implied this organization outside the motherland is made up of Stalinists,' Volkov reminded him. He was bewildered.

'So it is. We use them, then discard them. They may well be the scapegoat for the assassination of Comrade Mikhail if that proves necessary.'

'You mean they do the job for us and then we accuse them of being responsible?'

'Possibly. It would be better if we could spread rumours once Gorbachev has gone that he was the victim of hardliners inside the Pentagon. We will play our cards as the game progresses. We wait for our opportunity – which may come within a few months. Our only chance to liquidate the mad dog is while he is outside Russia. There our allies can operate more safely.'

245

'I am at your service, Comrade General,' Volkov, a round-faced ball of a man replied.

'Who knows?' Lucharsky commented, adjusting his cap to a more jaunty angle. 'It might end up in promotion for you.'

Always dangle the carrot in front of the donkey, he thought. No point in explaining that those who helped would also have to be eliminated when the coup succeeded.

Inside his office at Park Crescent Tweed sat behind his desk staring into the distance. The desk-top was covered with neat piles of documents which he had just examined for the third time. The items Masterson had posted him from Greece and the notebook of Partridge he had collected from the safety deposit in Knightsbridge.

Paula sat at her desk checking through a file. Every now and again she glanced up at her chief. In another corner Monica bent her head over a card index, her dark hair tied behind her neck in a bun.

'Are we getting anywhere?' Paula ventured. 'After that phone call from Bob last night?'

'Listen, both of you.' Tweed sat upright in his swivel chair, hands clasped in his lap, his eyes alert behind his glasses. 'Let's go over what we have briefly. Damn all, as far as I can see.'

'Maybe more than we know,' Paula suggested. 'Basically it all appears to have started with two murders a long way off and a long time ago. Andreas Gavalas on Siros Island, Stephen Ionides – now revealed as Stephen Gavalas. Someone is trying to bury both killings.' She caught Monica's expression. 'Sorry – that sounded a bit callous . . .'

'But it may be true,' Tweed agreed. 'Go on.'

He was, Monica realized, conducting in reverse an exercise he'd often carried out with her. At a certain point of an operation he would sum up the main points, using

Monica to bounce off his ideas, to test their relevance.

With Paula he was listening to how she saw the situation – seeking a key element they had overlooked. Something simple; maybe a factor which didn't fit what they knew. Paula went on.

'We have met Barrymore, Robson and Kearns – the three men who were with Andreas when he was killed. The same three men were back in Cairo when Stephen was brutally murdered at the Antikhana Building. Both victims were brothers. It really stretches the long arm of coincidence to breaking-point – that the commando trio were in the vicinity of two murders. OK so far?'

'Go on . . .' Tweed had relaxed, listening with his eyes closed as he visualized what she was saying.

'Now we have two odd complications – which don't link up with what I've said so far. The mysterious disappearance of Andreas' body from Siros the night he was killed. And the arrival of Anton Gavalas on Exmoor making enquiries about the ex-commandos.'

'Something else odd about Anton,' Tweed pointed out. 'The way he vanished without leaving a trace of the route he used. We checked with the harbourmaster at Watchet. No ship left for anywhere when Anton pulled off his vanishing act.'

'Anything in Partridge's notebook?' Paula asked.

'Yes. According to Partridge Anton is well-educated and speaks fluent English. Yet Newman told me his nephews – Dimitrios and Constantine – are peasant types. And what game is Anton playing? In his notebook Partridge records Anton is a lone wolf with plenty of money at his disposal. Newman also said Christina hadn't mentioned Anton. They seem to want him to be the invisible man.' He paused and Monica asked who 'they' were.

'That is what we need to find out. Anton could be acting independently of old Petros. This vendetta business is complex, reeks of a long and dangerous hatred. You know,

I'm getting the impression someone is using the vendetta as a smokescreen – to hide something far more deadly. And who killed Masterson?'

It was Saturday night at The Luttrell Arms in Dunster. They always dined together on Saturdays. At the corner table at the far end of the dining room Colonel Barrymore occupied a seat facing the room with his back to the wall. Dr Robson sat beside him while Kearns was seated opposite the two men. They were at the coffee stage.

'Another large Scotch,' Robson called out.

'Of course, sir. Coming right away,' the manager assured him as he passed their table.

'Pushing the boat out a bit, aren't we?' Barrymore commented in a supercilious tone, glancing at his companion.

Robson's complexion had lost most of its suntan and was now a ruddy colour like a setting sun. It was his fourth double plus several glasses of Beaujolais. He stroked his thatch of brown hair, pulled at his straggle of a moustache, grinned amiably. As usual he was in high good humour.

'Thought we were here to enjoy the evening. Ever known me to be half seas over?'

'There's always a first time,' Barrymore continued in a lofty tone. 'And we have serious business to discuss. See that chap with the dark moustache, black hair, a hearing aid? Caught him watching Quarme Manor this morning. I challenged him.'

'You did?' Robson sounded amused and Barrymore glared at him. 'Where was he?'

'Up on the ridge behind the manor. Riding a horse.'

'Free country – in case you've forgotten.' He chuckled. His blue eyes lit up as his drink arrived. 'Thank you.' Lifting the glass, he swallowed half the contents. 'That's better.' He turned to Barrymore. 'So what happened when you *challenged* the chappie? Sounds like the corporal of the guard.' He grinned at Kearns who stared back, blank-faced, ramrod-backed.

'Had the insolence to tell me he was bird-watching,' Barrymore continued. 'Hence the field glasses trained on Quarme Manor. Rode off pretty sharp, I can tell you.' His tone changed, became silky. 'Gentlemen, I smell trouble. There was the Greek you encountered, Kearns.'

'And how can you be sure he was Greek?' Robson chaffed the ex-CSM. 'Wearing his *Evzone* outfit, was he?'

'No laughing matter,' Barrymore snapped. 'Tell him,' he ordered Kearns.

'Well, sir,' Kearns began, gazing at the colonel, 'his appearance for one thing. Olive-skinned, the facial bone structure. I've seen enough of them to recognize the breed. When I spoke to him he replied in English but with a slight accent. Greek.'

'Not Bulgarian or Yugoslav?' Robson enquired. He grinned again, drank more whisky. 'Would you know the difference?'

'Yes, I think I would,' Kearns responded stiffly.

'And what was he doing? More bird-watching?'

'Said he was on holiday, that he liked wild places. Asked me the way to the nearest pub. Told him Simonsbath, miles away from where we met. To test him. Later I saw him riding down a gully towards Winsford. Which *was* the way to the nearest pub. See what I mean, sir?'

'He knew the moor, tried to pretend he didn't. That's what I want to talk about. The enemy could be closing in. Need to take more precautions.'

Barrymore sipped his cognac and Robson glanced at the balloon glass. 'Time I had one of those . . .'

Pete Nield, sitting with Harry Butler three tables away, adjusted his earpiece. A snappy dresser, he wore a navy blue business suit and a large jewelled tie-pin in his pale red tie. The tie-pin, shaped like a flower, was a directional microphone. The wire attached to it behind his striped shirt led to the miniaturized tape recorder in his jacket pocket. He spooned more fruit salad into his mouth as he listened.

Harry Butler, heavily built and clean-shaven, was dressed informally in a tweed sports jacket with leather elbow patches and a pair of grey slacks. He leaned over to whisper in Nield's 'good' ear.

'Reception OK?'

'Picking up every word,' Nield replied in an undertone and fingered his neat moustache.

The Engine Room wizards at Park Crescent had excelled themselves. Despite the presence of people at four other tables the directional mike was recording every word of the conversation at Barrymore's table. It had been easy for Nield to 'point' the microphone in the correct direction. A man fiddling with his tie-pin attracted no attention . . .

'You're not going to have a cognac on top of all you've had?' Barrymore enquired sardonically. 'You do have to drive home.'

'I'll get there.' Robson grinned again. 'I always do.' He signalled to the manager, pointing to the colonel's glass and then himself. The manager smiled, acknowledging the request. 'The other chappie,' Robson continued, 'the bigger one with the thin one you *challenged* . . .' His tone was mocking. 'Was he on the moor as well?'

'Never seen him before. As I was saying . . .'

'Had the thin one that hearing aid when you met him?' Robson persisted with the geniality of a man who has imbibed well.

Barrymore frowned, trying to recall the scene. 'Don't think he had. But he wouldn't need it, would he? Not out on the moor. Now, for the third time, I think we should review our defences. Too many people poking around. There was that Tweed who barged in on us all.'

'Special Branch,' Kearns remarked. 'I thought that rather strange. Despite the yarn he spun. Seemed to me

250

he had an ulterior motive for calling on me. That man worried me.'

'Oh, just one of the horde of bureaucrats justifying his fat salary at the expense of the taxpayer.' Barrymore waved a languid hand. 'Wish I'd had him in the battalion. He'd have had to jump to it.'

'I suspect, sir,' Kearns persisted quietly, 'Tweed has had a spell in the Army. Something about his manner. And he'd done his homework. Knew about the raid on Siros. And the murder of that Greek chap, Ionides, at the Antikhana . . .'

'Hardly relevant.' Barrymore made a dismissive gesture.

'Are you certain, sir? Did anything strike you as weird about that body they brought down off the moor at Winsford?'

'Should it have?' The colonel was clipping the tip from a cigar. He lit it with a bookmatch as Kearns continued.

'The savagery of the attack.' Kearns paused. 'He was slashed to pieces. Just like Ionides all those years ago.' He turned his attention to Robson. 'You examined the body inside the Land Rover. Surely I have a point?'

'Somebody had really done a job on the poor chap. A broad-bladed knife would be my guess. Mind you, it was a brief examination.' Robson's tone suddenly sounded sober, professional. 'Fail to see the connection with Ionides.' He drank more of his large cognac. 'Thought we were assembled here to enjoy ourselves.' He chuckled. 'But you Army types never slough off your skin.'

'The fact remains,' Barrymore intervened irritably, 'we now have possible enemies on two fronts. The Greeks and this Special Branch lot. I just hope to God it isn't the Greek Key.'

'After all these years?' Robson scoffed and grinned. 'Come off it. Not like you to suffer an attack of nerves, Barrymore.'

'I never suffer an attack of nerves, as you put it,' the

251

colonel replied coolly. 'I'm just saying we should look to our defences. Just in case.'

'Put up more barbed wire,' Robson joked. 'Lay a minefield round Quarme Manor.' He hiccuped. 'Call out the guard!'

'I'm serious,' Barrymore said coldly.

'I fear you are. As for me, business as usual. Carry on with my local practice. Did you know the local paper is doing an article on me? *The Only Doctor in the Country who Rides to See Patients* will be the headline. Rather good.'

'Jill has gone up to London,' Kearns said suddenly.

'Why?' Barrymore demanded.

'To pick up a few things from the shops she said.'

'You should have stopped her.' Barrymore sounded angry.

'Well, sir, that isn't the easiest thing in the world . . .'

'You made the mistake of marrying a younger woman,' the colonel told him brutally. 'Wives should be kept under heel. In the Army they knew their place . . .'

At his table Pete Nield finished his coffee, glanced round the dining room. A couple was just leaving. Which left only the trio at the end of the room and his table occupied. He leaned close to Butler.

'Time to go, wouldn't you say? We're going to look conspicuous.'

'Agreed. Let's move the feet now.'

Nield waited until they were in the deserted hall and suggested a breath of fresh air. They wandered out under the ancient portal into a deserted High Street. Opposite the entrance the old Yarn Market with its many-sided roof was shrouded in shadow. A moon cast a pale glow over the silence. Barrymore's Daimler was parked across the road.

'How's the recording?' Butler enquired, thrusting his hands into his trouser pockets.

'Let's check. Inside the Yarn Market would be a good place . . .'

Taking the recorder out of his pocket, Nield turned the volume to 'low' as they stood under the roof. He pressed the button which reversed the tape. Then he switched on the sound and together they listened.

Another large Scotch . . . Of course, sir. Coming right away . . . Pushing the boat out a bit, aren't we . . .

Nield switched off. He gazed through one of the arched openings to the far end of the town. The eerie silhouette of the brooding castle loomed above the buildings. The sudden silence of night was uncanny.

'Perfect,' Butler commented. 'The voice tone is good. You can tell who is talking.'

'I think I ought to drive up to London tonight,' Nield suggested. 'Then Tweed can hear the tape in the morning. I can drive back here tomorrow if that's OK.'

'Do it,' Butler agreed. 'While you're away I think I'll keep an eye on the colonel.'

'Why choose him?'

'Sixth sense. As Tweed would say . . .'

24

Three people were seated round Tweed's desk as he listened to the tape for the third time. Monica sat crouched forward, her head turned to one side, her forehead crinkled with concentration.

Paula sat upright, notebook in her lap as she made notes. On the third replay she ignored the notebook, staring out of the window as she visualized the faces of the three men whose conversation was reeling out as they had talked over dinner at The Luttrell Arms.

Tweed was the most relaxed. He sat back in the swivel chair, his hands resting on the desk-top, no particular expression on his face. He glanced at Pete Nield, seated behind Paula's desk, who was smoking a cigarette while he watched the others. The recording ended, Tweed switched off the machine.

'Very interesting, most revealing. What they said. And the relationship between those three men.'

'The reference to the Greek Key?' Paula suggested.

'That possibly, but something else. Pete, describe to me how they were seated. You came in with Harry to find them starting dinner?'

'No. We carefully did it the other way round – to avoid calling attention to ourselves. Harry asked one of the staff when they normally arrived for their weekly dinner. So we were at our table when they came in. Other tables were occupied with guests so we merged with the background.'

'And how were they seated in relationship to the two of you?' Tweed repeated.

Paula looked puzzled. She couldn't fathom the reason behind the question.

'They came into the dining room about ten minutes later,' explained Nield. 'They walked past us. We had our backs towards them as they entered. You know the corner table where they sit?' Tweed nodded and Nield went on. 'Barrymore and Robson faced us. Kearns had his back to us the whole time. Which is why his voice comes across quieter.'

'I thought it was like that. Something said in their conversation could be very significant. I may have the lead I've been waiting for.'

'And you wouldn't care to tell us what that is?' Paula enquired.

254

'Not for the moment. In case I'm wrong.' Tweed smiled. 'Listen to the tape on your own a few times. You might get it.'

Paula glanced down at her notes, then clenched her fists with a gesture of frustration. 'You'll drive me crazy with your hints one of these days.'

Monica nodded sympathetically. 'I know just what you mean. He's been doing it with me for years.'

'If you agree,' Nield said, 'I plan to drive straight back to join Butler again on Exmoor. Have there been any developments at this end?'

'Bob Newman called from Athens . . .' Tweed gave him a concise account of their conversation, picking out the main elements of the data Newman had passed on. 'Does anyone spot something odd about what he told me? Bearing in mind the clear description he gave of the topography of where Andreas Gavalas was killed?'

Three blank faces stared back at him. Paula pursed her full lips and sighed. 'Here we go again – more mysterious hints. I give up.'

'I have two questions I'd dearly love answers to,' Tweed told them as he perched his elbows on the desk. 'The raid on Siros. The three-man commando team – with Andreas – land on a hostile coast. They make their way up a twisting gulch. That gulch is overlooked by a monastery perched on Mount Ida like the nest of an eagle. The Germans have established a permanently manned lookout post on top of that monastery looking straight down the gulch. Why, then, in heaven's name, did the raiding party choose that point to climb up the island? There must have been scores of other places safer for them to choose.'

'Does sound very strange,' Paula agreed. 'Plus the fact that the body went missing.'

'My second question,' Tweed went on, 'is what happened to the cache of diamonds Andreas was carrying to hand over to Greek Resistance fighters on Siros? In those days

255

they were worth about one hundred thousand pounds – so Brigadier Willie Davies at the MOD told me.'

'Stolen by the man who murdered Andreas,' Paula said promptly. 'Maybe we're dealing with a case of simple robbery.'

'I don't think so,' Tweed objected. 'And I've been to see a leading diamond merchant in Hatton Garden I know. I asked him what a parcel of diamonds worth a hundred thousand back in 1944 would be worth today. I got a shock.' He paused, looked round. 'Any estimates? No? My contact could only make a rough guess. Something in the region of one million pounds sterling.'

There was a stunned silence in his office. Nield screwed up his eyes, thinking hard. Paula crossed her legs, tapped her pen against her teeth, then reacted.

'So we may be looking for something – or someone – showing signs of great wealth? What about Barrymore and Quarme Manor?'

Tweed shook his head. 'He bought it years ago. Probably for a song.'

'He has a Daimler,' Paula persisted.

'An old job,' Nield interjected. 'Looks glitzy but wouldn't fetch all that much. A cool million? The only thing I've seen in the area is that modern little estate of de luxe bungalows near Kearns' place . . .'

'We're looking for something pointing to one of those three men we've listened to on the tape,' Paula objected.

Tweed was hardly listening. 'That business of where they landed on Siros. And the missing body. The priest told Newman they had asked the commander of the German occupation troops about Andreas. None of his patrols knew a thing. And Geiger was convinced they were telling the truth. So who else on the island could have spirited away the body? There's only one answer.'

'Which is?' Paula asked.

'It had to be some of the Greek Resistance people. But which lot? And why on earth would they do that? Now our next job is to pay a visit to Guy Seton-Charles. You come with me, Paula.'

'And who might he be?' she enquired.

'A name in Partridge's notebook. A professor of Greek Studies at Bristol University. The intriguing fact is he was based in the Antikhana Building at the time of Ionides' murder.'

'How could he help?' Paula persisted. 'After all this time?'

'That's what I want to find out.' Tweed swung in his chair to face Nield. 'You come with us to Bristol in a separate car – then later return to Exmoor to provide Butler with back-up. I want those three men to be aware of your presence. It will put pressure on them, may force one of them to make a wrong move.'

'You've used that tactic before,' Monica commented. 'And it worked. You're doing the same thing with this Seton-Charles, aren't you?'

'Partridge found out something,' Tweed remarked sombrely. 'I am certain he was murdered because he approached the wrong man. Which man?'

The timing was better than Tweed could have hoped for. He was approaching Professor Seton-Charles' room when the door opened and a brunette in her early twenties rushed out. She was in such a rush she almost collided with Paula who was walking alongside Tweed. The door automatically closed behind her on spring-loaded hinges. Very slim, her intelligent face flushed, she stopped abruptly, clutching a green folder.

'I'm dreadfully sorry. I could have knocked you down.'

'I'm pretty sturdy . . .' Paula began, and smiled.

'You look really upset,' Tweed said quickly. 'Professor in a bad mood?'

'The sarcastic bastard! I'm not attending any more classes he takes . . .' The girl flushed again. 'Oh, Lord, I'm sorry. Are you friends of his . . .'

'Hardly.' Tweed acted on instinct. 'We've come to investigate him. Special Branch. What's the matter with him?' he asked persuasively.

'Everything! He's a bloody Trotskyite. Tries to brainwash us . . .' She paused. 'God, I'm saying all the wrong things.'

'Don't worry, we won't quote you.' He squeezed her arm. 'Do me a favour. We were never here. Agreed?'

'My pleasure. I'd better push off now.' She turned back for a last word. 'And I can keep my mouth shut. Give him hell.'

Tweed waited until she had disappeared round a corner at the end of the corridor. Then he knocked on the door which carried a name in gilt lettering. *Prof. Guy Seton-Charles*. The door opened swiftly. A man started talking and then stopped when he saw them.

'That's my last word, Louise. You have an IQ of minus . . .'

'Special Branch.' Tweed showed his card. 'You're alone. Good. May we come in . . .' He was walking forward as he spoke while the man backed away and Paula followed, closing the door. 'You are Professor Seton-Charles? This is Miss Grey, my assistant, who will take notes during the interview.'

'Interview about what?'

'The unsolved murder of a Greek called Ionides in Cairo over forty years ago. We can sit round that table. If anyone arrives to interrupt the interview please tell them you're busy, get rid of them.'

Tweed was at his most officious. He fetched two fold-up chairs from several rows arranged beyond the table. The

258

room was furnished starkly; walls bare, painted off-white; the table for the lecturer to sit behind and address his class; windows on the far wall which looked out on to a roughcast concrete wall.

Guy Seton-Charles was a slimly built man in his early sixties, Tweed estimated. His face was plump and pale, and perched on his Roman nose was a pair of rimless glasses. The eyes which stared at them were cold and bleak and wary. He had thinning brown hair, was clean-shaven, his mouth was pouched in a superior expression. Prototype of the self-conscious intellectual, Tweed decided.

He was dressed informally in a loose-fitting check sports jacket, a cream shirt, a blue woollen tie and baggy grey slacks. Not a man who gave much attention to his personal appearance.

'This is an unwarranted invasion of privacy,' Seton-Charles protested in a high-pitched voice.

'Oh, I can get a warrant,' Tweed assured him, 'but then we'd have to hold the interview in London at headquarters. Might not be possible to avoid a certain amount of publicity . . .'

'There's going to be publicity,' the Professor spluttered. 'I can promise you that . . .'

'About a murder investigation in which you might be involved? No skin off my nose.' Tweed was seated on one of the fold-up chairs. He pointed to the chair behind the desk. 'Unless you want to sit down and hear why we are here. Make up your mind.'

'Murder investigation? About Ionides? You're a bit late in the day, aren't you?'

His tone was truculent, sneering, but Tweed noted he had sat in his chair, a significant concession. He frowned as Paula sat in the other chair, produced her notebook, rested it on her lap and waited, pen poised.

'Is she going to record my answers? A bit bureaucratic and official.'

'Oh, it's official.' Tweed's expression was grim.

'All about a forty-year-old murder?'

'Which may be directly linked with two more very recent murders.'

Behind the rimless glasses Seton-Charles' greenish eyes flickered. Tweed had the impression he was thrown off balance. He recovered quickly.

'Which murders? If I am permitted to ask. It all sounds so melodramatic.' A tinge of sarcasm in his voice now.

'We may come to that later. Let's go back to Greece – and Cairo during the war. You had a job and an office inside the Antikhana as a young man. Why weren't you in the Forces?'

'Didn't pass the physical, if you must know. My eyesight.'

'What was your job? Start talking, Professor. I'm a very good listener. It's your job – talking.'

'Even as a young man I had an interest in Greece. It's my subject,' he added pedantically. 'They said I could do my bit for the war effort by going to the Mid-East. I was packed off aboard a troopship round the Cape and landed up in Cairo. My job was to create propaganda to encourage the Greek Resistance . . .'

'Which side?' Tweed snapped.

'Oh, you know about that battle in high places? The SOE lot – Special Operations Executive – in Cairo had a fetish for backing the right-wing crowd. Wanted to bring back the King after the Germans were defeated. Wrong side altogether. The EDES people. The London end were brighter – possibly as a result of reading my reports.' He preened himself with a knowing smile. 'It was the ELAS organization who were killing Germans by the score . . .'

'The Communists, you mean,' Tweed interjected. 'After Russia had been attacked by Hitler, of course.'

'No need to be snide . . .'

'Merely stating a fact. You supported the idea of switching the airdrop of arms to the Communists. That right?'

'Yes. As I told you, they were really fighting the enemy – and London agreed. Churchill himself took the decision, so I heard. Killing Germans was his main aim in life in those days . . .'

'And Ionides was the man you worked closely with,' Tweed guessed.

'I wrote the text for leaflets in English. Ionides translated them into perfect Greek. I wasn't up to that then. I didn't know him at all well. We worked through secretaries. Hardly ever spoke a word to him. Very close-mouthed, our Mr Ionides.'

'Who do you think killed him so savagely? And why?'

'No idea. My billet was an apartment in another part of Cairo. I wasn't there the night it happened.'

'Quite so.' Tweed gazed at the concrete wall beyond the window, switched the topic suddenly. 'Where do you live, Professor?'

'You do jump about . . .'

'Just answer the question, please.'

'I bought a bungalow on a new estate near Simonsbath on Exmoor. Rather exclusive . . .'

'You work here in Bristol, yet you live on Exmoor?' Tweed's tone expressed disbelief. 'Why?'

Seton-Charles sighed heavily as though his patience was wearing thin. He spoke as though explaining a simple point to a child. 'With the motorway a lot of people commute between a home on Exmoor and Bristol. Businessmen as well as university professors, amazing as it may seem. My hobby is walking. I like the open country, the moor. Would you like a list of some other people who live exactly as I do? Your assistant could take down names, help to fill out your report.'

'Might be helpful,' Tweed agreed equably. 'Plus the occupation or profession of everyone living on that bungalow estate.'

Seton-Charles' expression went blank. Something like venom flashed behind the glasses, then disappeared. Tweed was puzzled so he kept silent, forcing the other man to react.

'I don't know anyone on the estate,' the Professor snapped. 'I keep to myself. I take students' papers home to work on. Any free time I walk the moors, as I've already told you. I was referring to the *bourgeoisie* who live in luxury pads near Taunton.'

'That bungalow you live in must have cost a packet,' Tweed observed in the same level tone.

'I have a huge mortgage, if it's any concern of yours. The colonel was very helpful.'

'The colonel?'

Tweed was careful not to look at Paula. He sensed she had frozen, pen poised in mid-air. Only for seconds then she relaxed as Tweed waited again. Seton-Charles was answering more slowly.

'Colonel Winterton. He owned the land the estate was built on – had some old barns pulled down. That was why he was permitted to build. With a restriction the houses should be one storey high.'

'Where can I find this Winterton?'

'No idea. I never met him. I dealt with his staff at an office he had in Taunton. It was a package deal – he arranged the mortgages where required. He was fussy about who he sold the properties to. You had to qualify.'

'How?' Tweed pressed.

'I don't know about the others. When he heard I was a professor in Greek Studies he accepted me. I think the other residents are brokers, solicitors – boring things like that. They leave for work before me, I get back when they've got home. We don't mix.'

'So you could give me the address of Winterton's office based in Taunton? I'd like that.'

'You're welcome to it. Except it's no longer there.'

262

'What do you mean? Stop playing the half-smart intellectual with me.'

'You don't know everything . . .' Seton-Charles paused. Paula could have sworn he changed like a chameleon, then recovered, changed back again. Something about the cold glint in the eyes. 'Once he'd sold all the properties he closed down the office and the whole outfit vanished.'

'Vanished?' Tweed's tone was sharp. 'Explain that.'

'The staff weren't local. They disappeared. The rumour was that Winterton pocketed his profits and went to live abroad.'

'The whole outfit didn't vanish,' Tweed objected. 'Who do you pay your mortgage interest and repayments to?'

'Oh, we found out that was handled by the Pitlochry Insurance Company. Winterton had simply acted as middleman, taken his commission. That's it. End of the trail.'

Was there a smug note in Seton-Charles' voice? Paula couldn't be certain. He sat behind the table, smooth-skinned hands linked together. Like a man satisfied he had closed all the loopholes.

'You visit Greece frequently?' Tweed said suddenly.

'I go to Athens spasmodically.' He was frowning as though he hadn't expected this thrust. 'I have links with the university there. Take seminars . . .'

'Your last visit was when?'

'A few weeks ago. I thought we started out with the murder of Ionides over forty years ago.'

'We did.' Tweed stood up. 'Which makes a good point at which to end our first interview.'

'Our *first* interview?'

'That's what I said,' Tweed replied and walked out.

They waited in the Mercedes loaned by Newman, waited in the car park. Tweed sat behind the wheel, Paula stirred

263

restlessly beside him. There was no one else about and they were hedged in by cars on either side.

'What do you think of him?' Paula asked. 'And why did you insult him with that half-smart intellectual crack? Not your normal style.'

'To rattle him. I think it worked. *You don't know everything.* He got that far and stopped what he had been going on to say. Something funny about that new estate of bungalows near where Kearns lives. And Pete Nield, who often hits the nail on the head, remarked that estate was the only thing he'd seen on Exmoor worth a cool million. Something like that.'

'Where is Pete? He followed us down here from Park Crescent as you suggested, then dropped out of sight.'

'He's parked in the Cortina up the road. Again as I suggested. I want to see if Seton-Charles takes the bait.'

'Don't understand.' She gave a rueful smile. 'Par for the course – working with you. I still don't see why there should be something funny about the bungalow estate.'

'There may not be – but Seton-Charles is an experienced lecturer, used to fielding the sort of questions I threw at him. He answered fairly tersely, then went out of his way to explain a lot about the estate. I don't think he liked my asking where he lived. Now, who have we here?'

'Professor Seton-Charles – and in one devil of a hurry.'

In the distance the Professor was wending his way among the army of parked vehicles. He carried a briefcase and his hair was flurried in a breeze. For a man in his sixties he moved with great agility.

'Maybe it has worked,' Tweed commented. 'Pressure. Everyone remembers the last thing you say. I mentioned this was the first interview, suggesting I'd be back. One odd thing about our conversation. He only made a brief comment on my reference to two more recent murders. The *absence* of something so often goes unnoticed.'

'Well I didn't notice it, but I was taking notes. Are you going all mysterious on me again?'

'The absence of any later comment by the Professor. You'd expect almost anyone to come back to that – to ask again what I'd been talking about. Whose murders? He didn't . . .'

'He's getting into a Volvo station wagon. Do we follow?'

'No, too obvious . . .'

'He's a professor. His mind will probably be miles away while he's driving.'

'Seton-Charles,' Tweed told her, 'has a mind like a steel trap. He may have nothing to do with what we're looking for, but he has to be checked out. And carefully . . .'

Tweed waited until the Volvo was moving towards the exit, then turned on his ignition. He drove out of the slot slowly, turned into the main aisle as Seton-Charles shot at speed for the exit. 'Speedy Gonzalez,' Paula commented. Tweed arrived at the exit seconds after the Volvo had swung left. Perching with the nose of the Mercedes at the exit, he flashed his lights. Seconds later Nield drove past the exit, following the Volvo in Tweed's Cortina.

'There, it worked,' Tweed said with some satisfaction.

'You arranged with Pete to park outside?'

'Yes. I foresaw I might get lucky, pressure Seton-Charles into leaving. Pete will see where he heads for, who he meets, and report back to me.' He checked his watch. 'Three o'clock – we can make Park Crescent by early evening. We'll be driving into London when the commuters are pouring out.'

'Pressure all round,' Paula remarked as they left the car park. 'Butler and Nield showing themselves to the ex-commando trio. After Nield has tracked Seton-Charles. You think we're getting somewhere?'

'Time will tell. I'm waiting for someone to crack. Here – or in Greece.'

Monica looked up as they entered Tweed's office. 'Nield called ten minutes ago . . .' The phone started ringing. 'Maybe that's him.' A brief exchange, she nodded towards Tweed's phone.

'Just got in, Pete,' Tweed said. 'Any news?'

'Subject drives straight back to Exmoor, makes a call from a public box near Simonsbath. Which is strange.'

'Why?'

'He has a phone in his bungalow. They have overhead wires out here. A three-minute call – and he checks his watch.'

'And then?'

'Drives back to the estate and into his garage. He has one of those electronic devices so you can open it from inside the car. Something else odd I noticed. Perched on the roof of his bungalow is one of the most complex aerial systems I've ever seen – plus a satellite dish. A whole mess of technical gear. Change of subject. Gossip in the pubs reports a dog ferreting on Exmoor came home with Partridge's wallet in its mouth. A hundred pounds, all in tenners, intact. Banknote numbers in sequence. That's it.'

'You've done well. Get back to Butler in Dunster. Start a campaign of harassing all three men. Put on the pressure – but from a distance. And watch your backs.'

'Will do. 'Bye, Chief.'

Tweed put down the receiver, jumped up from his desk and began pacing the office as he rubbed his hands with satisfaction.

'Things are moving. It worked, Paula. Seton-Charles called someone from a public booth. Reporting my interrogation of him, I'm sure. We're on the right track.'

'At last,' said Monica.

'And I want you to call Inspector Farthing of Dunster police,' he told her. 'Partridge's wallet has been found. I'd like a list of everything inside that wallet. Someone may just have made the fatal mistake I've been waiting for.'

At the summit of the mountain where he used his transceiver Florakis-Savinkov completed sending the latest coded message to England. The pace was hotting up. Earlier he had been instructed to receive the signals from Athens weekly. Now it was twice a week. The radio traffic was increasing.

He was about to sign off when he was amazed to receive an order given in clear English. He blinked as he recorded the message. *From now on call sign changed to Colonel Winter.*

25

Newman was in shirt-sleeves as he drove along the coast road which twisted and turned and was empty of other traffic. It was twilight time, the most torrid period of the day as the earth gave up its heat and the atmosphere was cloying and humid. Nick sat beside him with a worried frown; beyond him the Mediterranean was indigo, a smooth sheet of water stretching away towards the hulk of a huge rock rearing up out of the water.

In the distance a toy-like temple perched at the summit of a cliff was silhouetted against a purple sky: the pencil-thin columns of the Temple of Poseidon where Harry Masterson had died. In the rear of the car Christina pulled at the tops of her slacks thrust inside climbing boots. She was perspiring all over. It had been one hell of a hot day and her nerves were twanging at what they planned to do.

'Tell me when to stop,' Newman called over his shoulder. 'We must be near now.'

'Round the next two bends. That structure we're passing is on the land of a farmer called Florakis. He sold it to a developer.'

Newman glanced at the ruin-like structure on the landward side. In the half-light it looked like an abandoned building site, as though the developer had run out of money.

'What is that place?' he asked.

'The beginning of a new hotel complex,' Nick replied. 'They are spoiling the whole coast with new tourist developments.'

The structure had a weird skeletal look. Two storeys high, it consisted of a steel framework for several buildings and he could see right through it to the hillside beyond, like staring through the bones of a Martian-type skeleton eroded by time.

'I still don't like the idea of you going with Christina into Devil's Valley,' Nick said for the second time. 'Petros has armed shepherds patrolling the area night and day. They all carry rifles. Tourists, amateur mountaineers who have gone in there never came out. They had "accidents". They fell over precipices, God knows what. I must warn you . . .'

'Thanks, Nick. You have warned me. You've done all you can.'

'Then stay away from that old silver mine. Please.'

'Of course. The idea never entered my head.'

Christina bit her knuckles to stop herself protesting. Newman *was* going into Devil's Valley with the sole idea of locating the silver mine. He had concealed his plan from Marler as well as from Nick. At first she demurred at his suggestion to act as his guide into the Valley. But he had

268

the map she had marked when they had dinner at the Hilton two weeks ago.

'Stop the car round the next bend,' she called out. 'You can park it well off the road on a flat area. It is part of Florakis' land but farmers go to bed early because they rise at dawn.'

Newman pulled in, turned the car in a wide half-circle so it faced the way they had come. He switched off the engine. A brooding silence fell over the mountains which rose close to the road. In the back Christina shivered at the lack of sound. A moon was rising, casting a pale illumination over the arid mountain slopes, the still, endless sea.

'Nick,' Newman told him, 'I think the car would be concealed much better if you drove it back to that building site.' He looked at Christina who had climbed out and was standing alongside him. 'We could find that on the way back easily with the moon up, I assume?'

'Yes. It would be a good landmark . . .'

'And exactly where do we go to find the entrance to Devil's Valley?'

'Straight up that gulch. It's on Florakis' land but only for a short distance. I can show you on the map.'

Newman slipped on his sports jacket, took a pencil torch attached to the breast pocket, shielded it with his hand and opened the map. Christina traced the route up the gulch, showed where it led to the entrance to Devil's Valley. Newman held his hand so Nick couldn't see the cross which marked the silver mine.

'We'd better get moving,' he said. He checked his watch. Well after ten o'clock. He opened the glove compartment, took out Nick's revolver, slid it inside his hip holster, pocketed spare ammo. 'You won't fall asleep?' he asked Nick. 'We'll be away for some time.'

'Not me. I can stay awake all night. And I'll drive back to the hotel development and wait for you there.'

'See you. The rifle is in the back – just in case.'

'It will be in my hands until you return,' Nick promised.

Parked in the shadows of the steel framework, Nick was careful. He smoked the cigarette inside his cupped hand. The headlights of the car approaching from the Athens direction appeared only five minutes after he had arrived. He stubbed out the cigarette. It was the first vehicle he had seen for over an hour.

The headlights swung over the building site as the car slowed. They swept over his Mercedes. He opened the door, took a firmer grip on the rifle, the muzzle aimed through the gap. The car was stopping.

It backed slowly, very slowly. For the second time the headlights played over the Mercedes, for a longer period. Nick sat very still, raised the muzzle slightly, slipped off the safety catch. The car had stopped now. The headlights stayed on, beamed at an angle beyond his own vehicle, glaring on the building site, which took on a surrealist quality in the dazzle.

Nick had acute hearing. He listened in the heavy silence – for the opening of a car door, the crunch of feet on the loose stones covering the ground. Nothing. The silence grew heavier. Sweat began trickling down his neck. He sat immobile as a Greek statue. Nothing. The driver couldn't be a ghost . . .

'Hello, Nick. I could have shot you rather dead.'

Marler's voice, speaking through the open passenger seat window. How the hell could a man move so silently?

'Come on, Nick, where have they gone? Newman and Christina? I followed you from Athens, so where are they? Exploring Devil's Valley?'

270

Nick reached for the bottle of mineral water, took a long swig. He was in a state of shock. And couldn't decide whether to tell Marler the truth. Marler seemed to read his mind as he leant an elbow on the open window.

'Loyalty is a virtue. Especially for a Greek. I know that. I also know you wouldn't want something to happen to Newman – something fatal. The last man who made friends with Christina ended up at the bottom of a cliff. She's all Gavalas. So, tell me – Newman needs back-up. Desperately. We're talking about Devil's Valley.'

'Christina is guiding him to the entrance to the Valley. He is going to find the old silver mine. I know it. He said he wasn't but I know he was. They went up a gulch two bends further down the road.'

'Show me. And mark the location of that silver mine.'

Marler dropped a large-scale map of the area into Nick's lap. 'I don't know the exact location of the mine . . .' Nick protested.

'Do the best you can. Hurry. I'm driving my car alongside yours. Back in a minute . . .'

He parked his vehicle a few feet away from Nick's, doused the lights and walked to the boot. He appeared at Nick's window and the Greek stared. Marler wore mountaineer boots, had a long loop of rope coiled over one shoulder, an Armalite rifle over the other.

'You came equipped?' Nick said.

'I saw Newman and Christina buying boots in a shop. I guessed the rest. I'm a good guesser. Marked the map yet?'

He studied the map Nick had marked by the overhead light. He nodded, took the map, refolded it, shoved it inside his pocket.

'I'm off on my travels now. See you.'

'It could be dangerous . . .'

'I agree. For anyone I meet up there.'

*   *   *

271

Newman led the way up the gulch with Christina close behind. The moonlight helped. He was careful where he placed his feet: the gulch was littered with loose rocks. Sound carried a long way at night. He was relieved to hear no sound from Christina as she plodded up behind him. Which is why he heard the faint tumble of stones slithering.

He stopped, turned, grasped Christina by the arm, raised one finger to his lips. Unlike some women she didn't ask questions: she simply raised one thick eyebrow. He crouched down behind a boulder, pressing her down, and her shoulder rested against his.

'Someone else on the mountain,' he whispered.

'I didn't hear anything – and I have good hearing . . .'

Another slither of stones. One came over the side of the gulch and touched Newman's right boot. Christina nodded. Newman had been right. Someone was approaching and very close.

They were crouched behind the large boulder at a point where the gulch began to turn sharply above them to the left. Whoever was on the prowl couldn't be descending the gulch, thank God, Newman thought. For the stone to have slithered from immediately above them the intruder had to be moving higher up the slope. Could he see down inside the gulch? Newman slipped the revolver out of the holster and Christina gripped his other arm. He looked up and froze. He hardly dared breathe. He held his body tense – for fear of dislodging even a pebble.

Along the crest of the ridge above, the silhouette of a man was moving. In the moonlight Newman could clearly see the bony profile, the prominent nose, the sunken cheeks beneath prominent cheekbones, the curve of the mouth. Over one shoulder was looped a rifle. He was carrying something in the other hand – something heavy. Newman frowned and then felt his right leg begin to cramp. He gritted his teeth.

Christina, hunched beside him, kept perfectly still.

272

Newman was staring at the heavy bag the man was carrying as he climbed the mountain – he knew it was heavy from the way the figure sagged to one side. But it wasn't a bag. It was rectangular-shaped, like a metal box. Newman was certain it was a high-powered transceiver – and that size meant it was capable of transmitting over long distance. The silhouette disappeared behind the ridge.

'That was Florakis,' Christina whispered. 'Someone pointed him out to me in the Plaka.'

'You're sure? In this light . . .'

'Positive. I could see his profile clearly. And he is walking on his own land. What on earth can he be doing at this time of night?'

'No idea,' Newman lied. 'Let's get moving. How much further to Devil's Valley?'

'We're nearly there. Another hundred feet up this gulch and we cross the pass. Then it's downhill . . .'

They climbed higher up the gulch inside its shadow, the ground levelled out and Christina pointed. Beyond, a track descended into an arid steep-sided valley, the slopes studded with scrub. The crest of the far side was lower and, following the line of her extended arm, Newman saw a weird structure perched on the crest. It looked like a large shack, but there were no walls. Between the supporting pillars at each corner there was open space and moonlit sky beyond the apertures.

'The old silver mine,' Christina said. 'A track from that huddle of boulders down there leads straight up to it. Mules used to bring the ore from the mine down that track years ago.'

'You know your way back?' Newman enquired casually.

'I know every inch of this country. As a child I used to roam all over it. I liked to go down that gulch so I could cross the highway and swim in the sea.'

'Sorry about this. It's for your own good . . .' Newman swung round and clipped her on the jaw. He caught her as she sagged and laid her carefully on the ground, placing her head on a soft tuft of grass as a pillow. He checked her pulse, found it was regular. Taking out the note he had prepared earlier, he tucked it inside the top of her slacks. Then he hoisted the rifle on his shoulder and started the descent, heading for the silver mine.

'There is someone coming up the track,' said Dimitrios and he slipped the safety catch off his rifle.

'You are imagining it,' objected Constantine. 'You see ghosts everywhere. Because of what is in the mine . . .'

'Someone is climbing that track,' Dimitrios insisted. 'I tell you I saw something move.'

'Now he says he *saw* something,' Constantine scoffed. 'In the past tense. Sure, he saw something move – a goat, maybe?'

Petros had sent them out as he did regularly – as another form of discipline, of keeping them under his thick thumb. And forcing them to stay up all night in the open toughened them. Petros had a dozen reasons for exerting his authority.

'Tonight you will go up and guard the mine,' he had ordered. 'One day there will be an intruder. Too many have been poking their snouts into my valley. And all accursed English. First there was Partridge – and he gave you the slip. Then came Masterson. Now we have more. This Newman, this Marler. Why so many so suddenly? Am I the only one who can scent danger? You go tonight . . .'

So they had climbed to the summit of the ridge close to where the mine reared up like a hideous eyeless monument. Constantine peered over the edge to where he could see stretches of the track as it mounted up to a point a quarter of a mile from where they waited.

Parts of the track were clearly illuminated by the moon; other parts were obscured by overhangs of rock, by the blackest of shadows. He could see nothing. From his ragged

274

jacket pocket he pulled the bottle of *ouzo*. He handed it towards Dimitrios as he sneered at his brother.

'Drink some. It will steady the nerves of an old woman . . .'

'You talk to me like that and I break your scrawny neck, wring it like a chicken's.'

But Dimitrios snatched the bottle, tore out the cork and upended it. The liquid gurgled down his throat. That was better. He recorked the bottle, looked at Constantine and stiffened.

'What is it, cretin?'

'There is someone down there now coming up the track – a man with a rifle. A well-built man used to rough country.'

'Where?'

Dimitrios peered over the edge, saw nothing – only the wending track which came and went. Into the moonlight. Back into the shadows. He leaned over further, his mouth a thin slit, shoved the bottle into his own jacket, rested both hands on the rock, still staring down.

'Now you see ghosts.' He glanced at his brother. 'What are you doing?'

Constantine, always the quieter, the calmer of the two brothers, was checking his shotgun. He nodded with satisfaction. Then looked at Dimitrios.

'Inside ten minutes he will appear at the top of the track. We move now to that point. That is where we prepare the ambush.'

'And we drop the body down the mine . . .'

Marler had taken a short cut from the hotel site where Nick was waiting with the parked cars. He had scaled the almost sheer face of the mountain, working his way up a chimney hollowed out of the limestone. The map had shown him he would reach the pass far more quickly

275

than by following the route Newman and Christina had taken.

Now he heaved himself over the top and the pass was thirty feet below. He descended rapidly, reached the entrance to the pass, stopped, head cocked to one side. The rope was again looped over one shoulder, the rifle over the other. Someone was coming. He heard the stealthy movement of feet padding among the bed of pebbles. A thick needle-shaped column of rock rose up near the track. He slipped behind it.

Christina was in a cold fury. Her jaw was sore, but that was nothing. When she regained consciousness she had found the note tucked inside the top of her slacks. Its message was clear – to the point. *Christina, this expedition is too dangerous for me to take you any further. Sorry for the tap on the chin. Go straight back to Nick. I'll join you there. Later. Bob.*

The stupid swine. She could have helped him find the mine, showed him where to veer off the track so he reached it more quickly. She *knew* the country. He didn't. And her sharp eyes could have spotted any shepherd guards lurking . . .

The arm came round the back of her neck, lifted her off her feet. She used her elbows to thud into the midriff of her attacker, her feet to kick back at his shins. She wriggled like a snake and the pressure on her throat increased. The voice whispered in her ear.

'Don't want to strangle you. Relax. Go limp. I'll let you go. Be quiet. There may be others about. Ready?'

Marler's voice. She stopped struggling. He released her. She turned round. His expression was bleak. She swung her right hand with the speed of a striking snake. The flat of her hand slapped hard into the side of his face. His head didn't move.

'Make you feel better? Jezebel . . .'

'Why call me that, you bastard?'

276

'Because you've just led Newman into another trap – the way you did with Masterson . . .'

'You bloody idiot!' She waved Newman's note at him. 'Better read that. He socked me one, left me behind because he was worried about me . . .'

'Worried you'd betray him . . .'

'Read the bloody note.'

He shrugged, took the note, read it, then looked at her. 'OK. Tell me where he's gone.'

'To the silver mine. The crazy idiot. He's a suicide case.'

'Hardly. At least I hope not. Care to tell me exactly where this mine is?'

'You can see it from the end of the pass. I'll show you . . .'

Her long legs covered the ground in minutes. Marler had collected the rifle and rope he had left behind the needle of rock and hurried to catch up with her. At the end of the pass again she pointed, indicating the position of the silver mine. Marler frowned, then turned to her. She waited, hands on her hips, her expression contemptuous, eyes flashing. He lifted a hand and his slim fingers closed round her chin. She gritted her teeth, determined not to wince. The gentle way he handled her was a surprise. He turned her chin to examine it by the light of the moon.

'Sorry. I was checking to see how hard he'd hit you. Scarcely a bruise. Just enough to put you out. How long ago do you think he left you?'

She looked at her watch. 'I checked it just before we got here. I must have been out cold ten minutes. No more than fifteen.'

'Then I have to hurry. Anything you can tell me to help?'

She repeated what she had told Newman. She pointed out where the track ran up to the mine. But this time she tried to show where Marler could veer off three-quarters of the way up, cutting across direct to a point just below the mine.

277

'Got it,' Marler said. 'Do me a favour. Go back to Nick. I think I can make it faster on my own. And I don't want to have to worry about you.'

'I'm popular with the men tonight, aren't I? Marler, why are you waiting? Get there fast . . .'

Newman had caught the faintest hint of movement high up and out of the corner of his eye. Imagination? He remembered the man he'd only known as Sarge. The time when he'd trained with the SAS – the Special Air Service – Britain's élite strike force, so he could write a series of articles on them. Sarge had put him through the full course. And he'd survived it. Just.

If you even suspect you've seen something, heard something, smelt something – *assume the worst.* You've been seen. Sarge, the toughest man Newman had ever known, the sergeant who'd put him through his paces, had said something else. Get inside the enemy's mind. Sit in *his* chair. What would you do *if you were him*? Out-think the bastard . . .

Newman moved into the shadows out of the moonlight. He paused, took out the compact pair of night glasses he'd bought in Athens. His mouth was parched with thirst, with fear. His boots, his clothes, were coated with limestone dust from his journey up the track. Slinging the glasses from his neck, he took the opportunity to relieve himself against a rock. Then he took a swig from the small bottle of mineral water in his pocket. Now . . .

He leant against the side of the rock and raised the glasses, aiming them where he thought he'd seen something move at the top of the ridge to the right of the track. He moved the glasses slowly, scanning the whole ridge. He stopped. Silhouetted against the night sky was the outline of a man, a man peering over a rock parapet. Got you. He held the glasses very still. No doubt about it. One of the

278

shepherd guards. And he held the high ground. Time to rethink.

Assume the worst. He'd been spotted. Coming up the track. So what would the enemy do? Wait for him where the track emerged at the top. The solution? Get off the track. Move up to the left. However rough the going. Head diagonally straight for the mine. He put the glasses back into his pocket. Began climbing higher, so long as he kept in the shadow. He nearly missed the defile spiralling up to his left.

It looked pretty steep, but rock projections formed a kind of ladder. He entered the defile, felt safe from observation. It was exactly like climbing a ladder. He placed his boots on each projection, hauled himself higher and higher. He began to feel the strain on his calf muscles. He was sweating litres with the effort. Keep going. He must be close to the top.

His head and shoulders projected above the defile without warning. He remained perfectly still. Listening. Sniffing. For the smell of a mule. The shepherd might well be patrolling on an animal. He turned his head very slowly. He had emerged just below the crest of the ridge. Keep below it. That was the mistake the shepherd had made. He could see the spectral outline of the mine. No more than a hundred yards to his left.

No sign or sound of anyone else. He rubbed the calves of both legs. No time to get cramp. He hefted the Smith & Wesson out of the holster, moved towards the mine in a crouch, placing his feet carefully. The ground was powdered dust. Easy to slip on. The mine came closer.

'The bastard has tricked us.'

Dimitrios stood at the top of a huge crag which gave him a view of the whole length of the ridge. Below him

Constantine waited, gripping his shotgun. Dimitrios clambered down and joined his brother.

'What do you mean?' Constantine asked.

'I saw him moving. He's nearly reached the mine. We'll have to hurry. He left the track, came up a different way.'

'Then let's get moving. If we lose him Petros will go mad.'

'Petros is mad. Maybe we don't tell him what happened. That shaft goes down forever. Who is to know? So long as you keep your big mouth shut. I lead, you follow. We've got him cornered.'

Newman approached the weird structure cautiously. There could be another guard hidden and waiting. Resisting the temptation to peer inside the shaft, he crawled slowly round, pausing at each of the four corners. The structure reminded him of a ruined Greek temple constructed of rusting iron. He peered round the final corner. Nothing.

He had completed one circuit round the mine. He chose the side furthest away from the head of the track, from where he had seen the immobile silhouette on the ridge. Straightening up, he looked into the mine.

No cage. Christina had said there was a cage at the top. But she had never been up here. Someone must have told her about a cage, had lied. He was looking down into an immense bucket made of iron. It was suspended by a chain windlass coiled at the top. He switched on his pencil torch, his hand well below the surface of the mine. At its base he saw remnants of ore. He thought his light reflected off veins of silver, but it could have been his imagination.

Newman was baffled. Why should Petros make such a fuss about no one going near the mine? Between the huge bucket – large enough to hide a crouching man – and the side of the shaft was a wide gap. He shone the torch down the shaft. The light penetrated only a short distance into bottomless blackness. A musty aroma drifted up to his nostrils. He swivelled the light and saw a huge chain dangling beneath the bucket. And something else he couldn't identify . . .

He heard the shuffle of feet hurrying across rock-strewn ground. He peered through the aperture and saw two men coming, still several hundred yards away. From the direction of the track. They dropped out of view, presumably into a dip in the ground. But he had seen the long barrels perched over their shoulders. Men with rifles. He glanced round quickly.

No cover. Anywhere. The ridge behind him was open, as exposed as the slope which fell away from it. And they could out-range him with those rifles. A handgun was useless except for closer quarters. He went very cold, thinking. He leaned over into the mine, took hold of the rim of the bucket, tried to move it. The bucket was so heavy he couldn't shift it a centimetre. He flashed his light on to the windlass chain holding it. The links in the chain were enormous. He recalled it had been built to hold God knew what tonnage of ore.

He slipped on the pair of gloves he had used when scaling the defile. Without them his hands would have been bloodied raw – clutching at razor-edged rocks to heave himself upwards. He gave one more brief glance to where he'd seen the two men approaching. Any moment now and they would climb up out of the dip into view. He lowered himself into the shaft, hanging on to the rim of the bucket. It remained immovable as the Rock of Gibraltar. Now for the tricky part.

Engulfed in the darkness of the shaft, he held on to the rim with his left hand, felt down with his right for the dangling chain attached to the base of the bucket. He was just able to clutch it. Every muscle in his body strained as he jerked the chain with all his strength, testing it. It held. He took a deep breath, let go of the rim and fell. He whipped his right hand round the huge chain a second before the full weight of his body pulled at him. Now he had two hands gripping the length of chain which continued at least seven feet below him. He could tell that because he'd used both feet to get a hold on the chain lower down. His right foot rested on one of the enormous links. His left foot slipped, dangled in space. He forced it upwards, felt for a foothold, found it opposite the other foot and hung there suspended. The bucket had still not moved. But something light but unyielding had brushed his face. He couldn't identify it. He took another chance.

Holding on with his right hand, he felt for his pencil torch with his left. Sweating like a bull, he switched it on. He estimated the two men would not yet have arrived in the vicinity of the mine. What he saw by the light so frightened him he nearly lost his grip.

Suspended by a separate chain from beneath the bucket was a man-sized skeleton. The skull was inches from Newman's cheek. A gibbering skull with one eye intact.

Inside the gloves his hands were suddenly greasy with sweat. He gripped the chain more tightly, scared stiff his hands would slip out of them, plunging him down the shaft. The eye twitched and Newman nearly had a bowel movement. Then he saw it was an insect perched in the hollow eye socket, something like a praying mantis. The light had disturbed it. The insect twitched again, then flew upwards. Newman switched off the torch, rammed it in his pocket, gripped the chain with his free hand. Just in time. The strain on his right hand was becoming unendurable.

In the brief seconds while the light had been on he noticed the skeleton was wired together, which explained how it could hang there. Jesus! What a companion to hang suspended next to. Newman concentrated on securing his

282

grip with his hands, his feet. Then he heard movement at the top of the mine.

Two voices. Talking excitedly. Leaning over to peer down into the shaft. Now they were moving round as though to get a better view. Still chattering.

Then the beam of a powerful flashlight shone down into the darkness. The light swung slowly, probing the shadows. The angle of the light changed, penetrated deeper. Newman looked down and cursed inwardly. The flashlight was shining on the lower part of his dangling legs, illuminating them from the knees downwards. More chatter. Then silence. Followed by a metallic click. Newman recognized the sound. The release of a safety catch. The flashlight beam remained very steady now, shining on his legs. He realized his teeth were clenched tightly. The bastards were going to shoot him in the legs. Not one damned thing he could do. Except wait for the impact, the slipping of his hands from the chain, the plunge down the shaft until his body smashed against the base, however far that might be . . .

Marler, smaller than either man, held the rifle at a horizontal angle, level with his nose. He swung the butt to his left. It smashed into the back of Dimitrios' skull. He was collapsing when Constantine began to turn round. Marler reversed the swing and the barrel thudded with all his strength against Constantine's forehead. The Greek sagged to the ground, dropping his shotgun. Dimitrios' flashlight had vanished down the mine.

Marler leaned over, switched on his own flashlight. He called down. 'Anyone at home?'

'Me, for God's sake. Hanging on to a chain under the bucket.'

'Hang about. I need a minute. You can last that out?'

'What the hell can you do?'

283

'Haul you up.' As he had started talking Marler had picked up the looped rope he had laid quietly on the ground before creeping up behind the two Greeks. He was creating a large loop with a slipknot. He tested the knot, then picked his flashlight off the parapet, shone it down.

'I'm lowering a rope with a big loop. Plus a slipknot. I can see your lower legs. Can you slide them inside the loop? I'll haul it up slowly. You have to get it round your chest, under your armpits. Think you can manage that simple exercise?'

'Give it a go. Soon as you're ready. I have company . . .'

Marler ignored the cryptic remark, held the torch in his right hand, lowered the loop with his left. When it was level with Newman's dangling feet he had to swing it away from the wall of the shaft. Newman saw what he was doing in the beam of the flashlight, waited for what he hoped was the right moment and swung his feet off the chain. Marler jerked the loop up and it ringed Newman's legs. He warned that the light would go out and took the rope in both hands. He hauled it up slowly and Newman called out that it was sliding up over his body.

'Tell me when it's under your arms, there's a good chap . . .'

'Now . . .'

'Tricky bit coming,' Marler called out. 'I need both hands to haul you up. When you let go you'll swing against the side of the shaft. Try and cushion yourself. Piece of cake. If you're lucky.'

'Thanks for the vote of confidence . . .'

Marler had his feet and knees braced against the side of the mine. He had knotted the rope in a few places to ward off as much rope burn on his hands as possible. And Newman weighed a few more pounds than he did. He called down that he was OK and waited for the considerable increase in weight. Newman called back that he was letting go.

284

The rope had slid up under his armpits, the loop had tightened. He let go of the chain and swung outwards, his right hand palm up. It slammed into the wall. His hand stung horribly from the impact. For a moment he hadn't the strength to call up.

'OK to haul you in? Tell me, for Pete's sake,' Marler rasped.

The weight was greater than he'd expected. His knees were pulverized with the pressure against the side of the mine. Newman said something he couldn't catch. Can't mess around any longer, Marler told himself and began to haul up the excruciating weight.

Newman came up facing the curve of the wall, hands pressed into it to steady his ascent. His head appeared over the top, Marler arched his body backwards, gave one last heave. Newman's hands scrabbled at the edge of the mine, then he came over the top like a cork out of a bottle and flopped on the ground beside the two unconscious Greeks.

'This one with the shotgun was going to pepper you,' Marler remarked as he stooped over the unconscious Greek. 'I heard the charming conversation when I came up behind them. Relieved to be back in the land of the living?'

'You could say that. Who are these two jokers?' Newman eased his back up, rested it against the side of the mine, took off his gloves and flexed his aching fingers. 'Did you do a real job on them – or will they come round? If so, maybe I'd better put a bullet in their skulls.'

'Tweed said you'd become a hard man after that trip behind the lines in East Germany.' As he spoke he was searching the Greeks. He pulled out a bottle, uncapped it, sniffed, used his handkerchief to wipe the top and handed it to Newman.

'You need a pick-me-up. Drink. *Ouzo*.'

'Thanks.' Newman upended the bottle, swallowed, choked a little. He took another swig when he'd recovered. His whole body was aching. Legs, arms, hands, shoulders. 'Who are the bastards?' he asked again.

Marler was scanning a photo he'd taken from a grubby envelope. 'This one, as I thought, is Dimitrios. Taken with a girlfriend. Rather crudely erotic. I was pretty sure I recognized him from our little escapade on Siros. The other is Constantine. Meet the Gavalas brothers.'

'Let's hope I don't – on the streets of Athens. For their sake.'

'Feeling better? You have a hike. Back down the track to where Nick is waiting with the cars.'

Newman forced himself to stand, supporting himself with a hand on the wall of the mine. He drank a little more *ouzo*. Marler took the bottle off him.

'That's enough. We don't want you drunk. I'll be ready to go in a minute.'

Marler was emptying the rifle. He threw the cartridges down the slope, then held the rifle poised over the well. 'Might interest you to listen to this . . .' He let go and the rifle plunged down past the bucket into the black hole. Newman waited and his hand tightened on the wall. Seconds passed before they both heard the faintest of thuds. Marler looked at him.

'You could have sprained an ankle if you'd gone down there.'

'Ended up as a jelly. Safe to leave these two thugs?'

Marler was stooping over the Greeks, lifting an eyelid of both men. He straightened up. 'Out for the count for a while yet. Maybe I split a skull.' He emptied the shotgun, sent it down after the rifle. Dimitrios was wearing a sheathed knife under his jacket. Marler was about to toss it into the well when Newman stopped him.

'Let me look at that.'

He held the knife up to the moonlight and his voice was

grim. 'This is a standard-issue commando knife. I'd like to know how he got hold of that.' He dropped it inside the well. 'While I remember, thanks for saving my life . . .'

'All part of the Austin Reed service. You're an idiot, you know that? Coming up here by yourself. I followed you from Athens. Had an idea what you were up to, you crazy loon.'

'You could be right. Let's make with the feet. But I discovered the secret of the mine.'

'That's what I like. A bit of melodrama. Back to the track . . .'

26

Florakis lowered the transceiver into the cavity, concealed it with a flat rock, picked up the shotgun he had left inside the cavity before climbing the mountain. The transceiver was heavy. Now to investigate the two cars parked on his land down by the hotel site . . .

Dawn was breaking over the Mediterranean shore, flooding the unruffled sea with a variety of fantastic colours. Behind the wheel of his Mercedes Nick sat smoking another cigarette. The ash tray was crammed with stubs. Disgusting. He hauled it out from under the spring clip, stepped out of the car, then reached back in for his rifle. You never knew.

Christina was curled up on the back seat like a cat, fast asleep. Nick walked quietly across to a pile of rocks, lifted a few and emptied the ash tray, then replaced the stones. Crouched over, he froze. Someone was approaching from behind the steel framework. He remained crouched, aimed the rifle.

Florakis came round the corner, shotgun held in both hands. He stopped abruptly when he saw Nick, who straightened up, rifle still pointed. 'Good morning to you,' Nick called out in Greek.

'What are you doing on my land?' snapped Florakis.

'Parking off the road. You see any damage we've done?'

'We?'

Christina had woken, had heard the exchange. Running her hands through her mane, she sat up and looked out of the open window. Florakis glanced in her direction, grinned lewdly and turned his attention back to Nick.

'I charge a fee for screwing on my land . . .'

'Watch your mouth,' Nick responded sharply. 'Who the hell are you?'

'Stavros Florakis. I own this land,' he repeated. 'I'm telling you to shove off now before I blow a hole in you . . .'

'Keep very still,' Nick warned. 'You forgot your back.'

Florakis stiffened as he felt the muzzle of Marler's rifle press into the nape of his neck. Marler nodded again at Nick, who understood. 'Place that shotgun carefully on the ground, step over it towards me. A dozen paces will do, then stop.'

Florakis bent forward, laid the weapon down, did as Nick had ordered. He stood in the open as Newman walked past him, keeping out of Nick's line of fire. He went towards the Mercedes and called out to Christina. 'Give me the mineral water. I'm parched.'

He drank from the bottle, turned round, leaned against the car. He smiled as Florakis stared back bleakly. Yes, Newman thought, this is the man we saw on our way up the gulch, the man carrying a heavy transceiver.

'What's his name?' he called out to Nick. 'I couldn't quite get it.'

'Stavros Florakis. He owns Greece,' Nick replied in English.

A tough, wiry individual, Newman was thinking. Self-contained. A typical Greek shepherd. Except that he carried a transceiver up the mountain. The lined face suggested he was in his sixties. Newman's mind wandered. In his sixties. Weren't they all – Barrymore, Kearns and Robson. And Tweed had rabbited on about the missing link with Greece – between Athens and Exmoor. So, during World War Two Florakis would have been about twenty. Old enough to be in the Resistance. Which one? The instinct which had made him one of the world's best foreign correspondents was working again.

He took out his handkerchief, wiped the mouth of the bottle, turned as though to say something to Christina, and wiped the rest of the bottle clean. He turned round and smiled.

'Nick, I think we ought to apologize for trespassing on Mr Florakis' land.' He began to walk towards the Greek, holding the bottle by the neck, still smiling. 'It's thirsty weather. As a token of our regret I'd like to offer him a drink. Translate for me.'

Nothing in Florakis' neutral expression showed he'd understood every word Newman had said. He listened patiently as Nick spoke in Greek. Florakis was nervous: all these people appearing, seeing him out and about at dawn. The last thing he wanted was any talk of his nocturnal activities to reach Athens.

Newman extended the bottle, holding it by the neck. Florakis was also bone dry: he had forgotten to bring his water bottle. He nodded his thanks, grasped the bottle, took a good long drink, handed it back to Newman, who again grasped it by the neck and wandered back to the car.

'Nick,' he called over his shoulder as he reached the car, 'let him know we're leaving now. That if we come this way again we'll park elsewhere.'

While Nick translated Newman leaned in the window. 'Christina,' he whispered, 'give me that paper bag the bottle came in.' He slid the bottle inside the bag, holding it by the neck, then he pressed the top of the paper bag inside the neck and capped it. He now had Florakis' fingerprints.

'What was all that business about the bottle?' asked Christina as Nick drove them at speed back along the coast road to Athens.

Newman sat beside her in the rear of the Mercedes while Marler followed close behind in his own car. Newman was staring out of the window as the sun came up from behind the mountains and bathed the Mediterranean in its fierce light. The sea was now a smooth sheet of pure mother-of-pearl. An amazing country.

'Just fooling around,' he replied.

'And how was the fooling around in Devil's Valley? Marler did find you. Did you find the mine? And thanks for the sock on the jaw. I love you too.'

'Quiz time,' Newman said jocularly. 'So many questions.' He looked at her chin. 'No sign of a bruise. Just a gentle tap. Marvellous, isn't it? You save a girl from what could be a death-trap and she hates your guts.'

She looped her arm inside his, nestled against him so he could feel the firmness of her breast pressing into his body. 'Don't remember saying anything about hating your guts. And you evaded answering my questions.'

'I do believe I did.'

He looked out of the window again. They were covering the distance to Athens, seventy kilometres from Cape Sounion, in record time. They passed a hotel at the edge of the shore and tourists were walking the beach, swimming in the placid water.

'They make use of every minute,' he called out to Nick.

290

'They know what they do,' he replied. 'Later in the morning no feet will be able to touch that beach. The sand will be so hot it will burn them like a red-hot stove. They'll retire to their rooms, lie on their beds and sweat it out with nothing on.'

'What a lovely idea,' Christina whispered. 'Maybe we could lie on my bed at the Hilton with nothing on, sweat it out?'

'I'm dumping you there,' Newman said abruptly. 'Nick, make for the Hilton. Then have breakfast with Christina. When she goes to her room would you please sit in the lobby outside to guard her till I get back? A large tip will be my thanks.'

'Forget the tip, I take care of her.'

'Thanks a lot,' Christina snapped, her eyes flashing. She pulled away from him and stared out of her window.

'I have business to attend to, an editor to keep quiet,' Newman told her. 'And you may be in even greater danger now after what has happened. And don't ask me what.'

'Did you tell Christina about the skeleton?' Marler asked as he drove away from the Hilton.

'Nary a word. Nor about the mine . . .'

'Which means you're getting smart. *You* don't trust her.'

'Can it, Marler. Information like that is dangerous. You do realize who that skeleton is?'

'I think so. You tell me.'

'The missing Andreas. My guess is Petros was on Siros when the commando raid took place. He took the body of his son. He's stark raving mad. He must have had it buried, then after the war the bones were removed to Devil's Valley. Wired together – hidden in the mine. You know Greece well. Tell me again about *philotimo*.'

'And you're sure this is a smart move – what we're doing

291

now? Driving to police headquarters to see Chief Inspector Sarris?'

'I want Florakis' fingerprints checked against their records. Look, a sixty-year-old Greek, tough as they come, lugs a transceiver up a mountain. He's gaining altitude. That suggests long-distance transmission. Who is he contacting? So secretly? I've had this lucky break before as a correspondent. You are working on one thing, you stumble across something much bigger. Yes, I think it's a smart move.'

Very little traffic at seven in the morning. They were coming close to Alexandras Avenue below the soaring peak of Mount Lycabettus. Close to the new police headquarters.

'*Philotimo*,' Marler began, 'is the Greek code of ethics which rules family life. No one must dishonour the family. If they do, the disgrace must be wiped out. In extreme cases by killing the culprit. Even if it is a member of that family. Only then can the family have peace of mind. Petros is just the type of man to be soaked in the creed – in the crudest and most old-fashioned way. Just the man to go to extreme lengths.'

'Just the man to go right over the edge,' Newman commented. 'I think Petros is taking the attitude Andreas cannot be finally buried until his murderer is identified and executed. Petros is crazy as a coot. Revenge is the most self-destructive force that can take hold of a man.'

'And this is the main reason we're going to see friend Sarris?'

'No. I want the fingerprints on this bottle checked. We may have stumbled into something even more diabolical than Petros' desire for revenge.'

The Thin Man. The hawk-nosed, dark-haired Sarris sat listening behind his desk. His eyes never left Newman's.

He smoked one cigarette after another. But he listened without interruption.

'That's it,' Newman ended, his voice hoarse from talking, from his ordeal at the mine. 'The skeleton at the mine, the bottle on your desk with Florakis' fingerprints. The transceiver I saw Florakis carrying up the mountain.'

'Petros has committed no crime,' Sarris responded, stubbing a cigarette. 'Yet. Funny you should come to me with this news of a possible transceiver . . .'

'Possible?'

'You have no proof that was the object Florakis carried. But, as I say, it is funny you come to me at this moment. Have you ever noticed weeks, months, can go by with no clues in a case? Then, bingo! Within hours the clues pour in.'

'What are you talking about? I'm damned tired.'

'Have more coffee.' Sarris poured as he went on. 'A friend of mine is what you call in England . . . a radio ham. Is that right?'

'Yes. An amateur radio operator. Sometimes they're helpful – pick up Mayday calls over long distances. That sort of thing.'

'My friend picked up something strange on the airwaves. Someone transmitting a series of numbers – sounds like a coded signal. At the end there are a few words in English – from the man receiving the coded signal.' Sarris leaned forward. 'So maybe the operator sending the coded signal was transmitting to England.'

'A big assumption,' Newman objected. 'English is a universal language these days . . .'

'Judge for yourself. My friend has a tape recorder. He recorded the entire signal. You might like to hear it . . .'

Sarris pressed a lever on his intercom, spoke rapidly in Greek, sat back, lit a fresh cigarette. 'The cassette will be here in a moment.'

He was wearing a pale linen suit and even at that early

hour he looked alert. He watched his two visitors until a uniformed policeman brought in a cassette. Sarris picked up the cassette, inserted it inside a machine on a side table. 'Listen,' he commanded.

The cassette reeled out a string of pure gibberish for Newman. He glanced at Marler who was staring out of the window, showing no apparent interest in the proceedings. Sarris was checking his watch. After two and a half minutes he raised a warning hand.

The gibberish stopped. There was a pause. Then it came through loud and clear. In English. *From now on call sign changed to Colonel Winter*. Staring at Newman, Sarris switched off the machine.

'You have heard of this Colonel Winter?'

'No. Doesn't mean a thing to me.'

'Pity. I am thinking of informing the Drug Squad. The traffickers are becoming very sophisticated. Using coded radio signals to warn of a shipment on its way. The Drug Squad has radio detector vans. Maybe they'll send a couple down to Cape Sounion, try to get a fix on this Florakis.'

'And the fingerprints on that bottle?'

'We'll check them through our records. That could take time.'

'You can isolate Florakis' prints? I gave you that postcard I showed Christina while we were driving back. You've taken my prints. The card gives you Christina's. Eliminate hers and mine and you're left with Florakis.'

'I had worked that out for myself.' Sarris rose from behind his desk. 'Thank you for the information. Now I expect you'll want to get back to the Grande Bretagne, have a shave, some breakfast, then maybe some sleep. You've been up all night.'

'I had hoped for more from you,' Newman said as he stood up.

'I gave you the radio signal – which may link up with Florakis.' He paused. 'I will give you something more. I said earlier all the clues seemed to pour in at once. Yesterday we had a woman here with a weird story. A Mrs Florakis. About sixty and recently she took a bus tour to Cape Sounion. A widow, by the way. Married very young.' He smiled thinly. 'I see I have your attention?'

'Go on.'

'Her husband, Stavros Florakis, was killed in 1947 during the Civil War. In a battle with the Communist ELAS forces. It so happened a woman friend saw him die near Salonika. This woman also saw the Communists search the body, take his papers, then they incinerated the corpse. Something Mrs Florakis never understood. Still intrigued?'

'Stop tantalizing. You sound like my editor.'

'As I said, Mrs Florakis takes this bus tour. The bus stops off the road close to a new hotel building site. To let them get a good view of Poseidon. A man appears with a shotgun. He threatens the driver, tells him to get off his land. The bus driver argues. Mrs Florakis then hears the man with the shotgun shout, "I am Stavros Florakis. I own this land and you are trespassing." She gets a good view of this man. She gets a shock. He is not a bit like her husband. Then she remembers what happened to him. All this flashes through her mind in a few seconds. Then the bus moves off. She tells her story to me very clearly, but I am not impressed. We get so many crazies wandering in here. For good public relations I let her make a formal statement, which we filed. Now you tell me something that makes me think maybe I was wrong.'

'Florakis is an impostor,' Newman observed. 'So who is he?'

'Maybe – just maybe – the fingerprints you cleverly obtained can unlock his true identity.' He shook hands with Newman and Marler. 'Let us keep in touch, gentlemen . . .'

* * *

'So that covers what Newman told me, Kalos,' Sarris concluded as he clasped his hands behind his neck and relaxed in his chair. 'What do you make of it all?'

Kalos, his trusted assistant, was very different physically from his chief. Small and stocky, with thick legs and arms, he had a long head and intelligent eyes. In his early forties, he had been passed over for promotion several times but bore no grudge. It was Sarris' private opinion that it was Kalos' lack of height which had held him back. Most unfair, and Sarris had done his best to help him up the ladder. But who said life was fair?

'We've had a lucky break again,' Kalos decided. 'We ignored the Florakis woman – but she may have fingered the key link in the organization the Drug Squad is trying to locate. With no success. Unless it's political,' he mused. 'Not drugs.'

Sarris sat up straight. 'What does that mean?'

'My mind roams.' Kalos smiled drily. 'As you know there are people higher up who don't approve of a man who lets his mind roam. Never get fixated on one theory. My inflexible maxim, and stuff them upstairs.'

'You said unless it's political. Please elaborate.'

'Last year,' Kalos began, fitting his bulk inside the arms of a chrome-plated chair, 'a so-called Colonel Gerasimov visited us from Moscow. We were asked to guard him like royalty – but discreetly with plain-clothes operatives. He spent very little of his visit at the Soviet Embassy, a lot of it at the Hilton. He had three rooms booked and switched from one to another. I got curious and had him secretly photographed . . .'

'Without my permission,' Sarris chided him.

'You know me. When I visited Belgrade unofficially about this drugs problem I showed that picture to a Yugoslav – a Croat called Pavelic in the security services. I got him drunk and showed him the picture. He laughed when I said it was a photo of Colonel Gerasimov of the

GRU. He told me it was General Lucharsky, a Deputy Chief of the Soviet General Staff.'

'I remember. Do continue,' Sarris urged him with a quizzical smile.

'Yugoslavia is sensitive to power movements inside the Kremlin. Gorbachev suits the Belgrade Government fine. Pavelic, though, is a hardliner. He told me Lucharsky was "one of ours".'

'You didn't tell me that bit,' Sarris snapped.

'Why raise hares? You were up to your eyes in work. While in Athens the man at the Soviet Embassy Lucharsky spent most time with was Colonel Rykovsky, the military attaché. And an expert in communications.'

'How do you know that?'

'The Greek cleaning woman they employ when their menial staff is on holiday happens to clean my apartment.'

'Purely by chance, of course?' Sarris was leaning forward now, taking in every word. 'You do realize you are far exceeding the scope of your duties, my friend?'

'I like to know what is really going on.' Kalos ran a stubby finger round his open-necked collar and smiled drily again. 'It is hardly likely to affect my promotion prospects. And now we hear a Colonel Volkov will soon visit us from Moscow. Odd.'

'Why?'

'Pavelic, the Croat, was *very* drunk when we talked alone. He said to me, "I would not be surprised if you receive another visitor in Athens one of these days. Lucharsky's aide and confidant. A Colonel Volkov. Another sound man." Translation – another hardliner. These are not pro-Gorbachev men. So why do they travel to Athens, I wonder?'

Sarris sat thinking. Yugoslavia was a 'federation' of six different nationalities. A racial mix, and not all of them loving each other. Croatia, the Yugoslav state in the north, was the most rebellious, the most pro-Russian, the one

297

closest to the real hard men in the Kremlin. Gorbachev's opponents.

'This is all speculation,' he suggested, testing his assistant.

Kalos ran a hand over the thin brown stubble which covered the dome of his head. 'You are right. Up to now. There is one more thing. When off duty I often amuse myself by following the military attaché, Colonel Rykovsky. He likes wandering inside the Plaka. He thinks he has lost anyone who might just be tailing him. Then he meets and spends time with Doganis.'

'Doganis?'

'A leading member of the Greek Key.'

27

'Where to now?' Marler asked as they climbed into his car.

'British Embassy. I'll rout that fat slob, Patterson, out of bed if necessary.'

'Be it on your own head.' Marler nodded towards the clock on the dashboard. 'Eight in the morning here is six o'clock back in London. Who will be at Park Crescent apart from the guard?'

'Tweed would be my bet. I think he's reached the camp bed stage by now.'

They both knew what that meant. Tweed started investigating a fresh case slowly. Then the tempo built up. He unfolded the camp bed kept in his office and took up a permanent vigil at his desk, often working well into the night.

At the Embassy on Sofias Avenue Patterson greeted

them in his shirt-sleeves, unshaven, sullen. He let them inside the hall without a word. No one else was about as Newman rubbed both hands together vigorously.

'The scrambler phone. It's an emergency.'

'When isn't it? And you might have shaved before invading the precincts of Her Majesty's Embassy.'

Ye Gods! Newman thought. How bloody pompous can you get? He grinned at Patterson. 'You look pretty rough yourself. Late night on the town?'

'I don't indulge. Like some people. I'll unlock the door – you know the drill. He can't come with you.' He jerked his thumb at Marler.

Marler said nothing. He produced his Secret Service card, held it under Patterson's nose, withdrew it when Patterson reached for it. The official bit his lip, made no further comment, produced a bunch of keys and unlocked the door leading to the basement. Newman ran down the steps after switching on the light.

Marler pulled out a chair as Newman sat down and pulled the phone towards him. Upstairs Patterson slammed the door shut with great force. Newman pressed the red button, dialled the Park Crescent number.

'Who is calling?' Tweed's voice, very alert.

'Newman here. Sorry to call at this hour.'

'That's all right. Very glad to hear from you. I was worrying. I slept here, got up with the dawn. Paula's here – she couldn't sleep and has just arrived. In case you need data taking down. Now, I'm listening . . .'

He listened without saying a word for ten minutes as Newman reported everything that had happened since they last spoke – including the trip into Devil's Valley and how Marler had saved his life. Glancing across the table he saw Marler spread his hands in a *What the hell* gesture.

'You shouldn't have gone in alone,' Tweed told him.

'I know that now. OK, I'll behave in future. Nowhere tricky without my chaperon. Now you know the lot.'

'And maybe we've come a long way – with the information you've given me and what I've gleaned at this end. A lot more of the pieces in my hands. Now I have to try and fit them together. I'd better warn you, I'll be phoning Peter Sarris to try and stop him taking any action. Yet. I'll cover you. What's the next move you plan?'

'Grilling Christina again about her relationship and movements with Masterson. That's what I came out for – to find out what really happened to Masterson. It looks like the Greeks to me. Petros and his vendetta. He's mad as a hatter.'

'And dangerous. Tread carefully. He'll be turning Athens upside down to locate Christina. But don't be too sure you've got to the bottom of anything. Someone may be using Petros as a gigantic smokescreen – to divert our attention.'

'From what?' Newman asked.

'I don't know. Just a sixth sense. There are some pretty peculiar characters involved. Including a Professor Guy Seton-Charles. At the moment he's in the West Country, holds a position at Bristol University. But he takes seminars at the university in Athens. Greek Studies.'

'Description?'

'Early sixties, looks younger. Slim build. Clean-shaven, thinning brown hair, Roman nose. About five feet eight. Intellectual type. Conceited manner. Most distinctive feature the rimless glasses he wears. Informal dress.'

'I'll recognize him. Early sixties again. So many of them are. Barrymore, Robson, Kearns, Florakis . . .'

'Which could be significant. Takes them back to World War Two – where all this started, I suspect. Another point about this Seton-Charles. He was stationed in the Antikhana Building in Cairo at the time of the Ionides murder.'

'A pattern is beginning to form,' Newman suggested.

'Yes, but it's like a kaleidoscope. New events shake it

300

up, give a fresh picture. One more thing before I go. And warn Marler – he can be impulsive. Petros is a very dangerous man. That crazy business about the skeleton in the mine. I'm sure you're right. It is the remains of Andreas. Watch your step, both of you. And has something else struck you just before I go?'

'I expect not, since you phrase it like that.'

'From your description Florakis' land adjoins Petros' – that is a strange coincidence. Might be worth following up. But cautiously. Keep in touch . . .'

As Tweed put down the phone the door opened and Monica came in. She greeted Paula, took off her raincoat, said she would be making coffee for everyone. Tweed waited until she returned with the tray and asked for black coffee. He was still working on automatic pilot, struggling to throw off the remnants of sleep.

'I woke early,' Monica said as she filled their cups. 'It was all going round and round in my head.'

'I can give you more – enough to make your head spin. Newman just called . . .'

He gave them both a concise résumé of the data Newman had provided. The two women listened intently. Paula made a few notes in her book. Monica absorbed it in her encyclopaedic memory. Tweed leaned back in his chair as he concluded.

'So what do you make of all that?'

'Florakis seems to be the key,' Paula said promptly. 'You've been looking for a link between Greece and England. The fact that he appears to be sending coded signals to somewhere here may be the missing link. That reference to Colonel Winter intrigues me. Colonel Barrymore?'

'Not necessarily . . .'

'But the thing I got from that tape recording Pete made

301

of the conversation at The Luttrell Arms was Barrymore still treats his two companions as though he's in charge.'

'Colonel Winterton,' said Monica. 'The man Seton-Charles told you had handled the property transactions for that bungalow estate near Kearns' house. Colonel Winterton, who disappeared once all the properties were sold. The Invisible Man.'

'Have you contacted Pitlochry Insurance then?' Tweed enquired. 'They were the outfit which actually loaned the mortgages.'

'I managed to get through after you left yesterday afternoon. I had trouble getting the manager to part with the information. I used our General & Cumbria Insurance cover to get him to open up. Said we'd had an enquiry from a Colonel Winterton about a property deal, that he'd given Pitlochry as a reference and . . .' She began choking. 'Coffee . . . went down the wrong way.'

Paula jumped up, accompanied her to the ladies' room. Tweed sat thinking. The plate at the front entrance read General & Cumbria Insurance Co. The cover had worked well. They pretended to be a specialized company dealing with top security protection for private individuals of great wealth. Officially, they also dealt with kidnapping insurance, negotiating with the kidnappers if a client was snatched. This explained all the trips abroad made by Tweed and his sector chiefs. They were even a member of the insurance industry's association – to complete the cover. Monica came back with Paula, dabbing at her mouth with a handkerchief.

'I'm all right now,' she said, sitting down behind her desk. 'I was telling you about Pitlochry. The manager said they'd found Colonel Winterton sound and businesslike. He confirmed that Winterton had simply acted as a middleman between clients buying those bungalows and Pitlochry supplying the mortgages.'

'He met him?'

302

'No, that was the odd thing. Odd to me. All the transactions were carried out by correspondence from the Taunton office and Winterton on the phone.'

'Did you manage to get any idea how he sounded?'

'Yes, by cracking a joke. Winterton had a very upper crust way of talking. Very much the colonel addressing the battalion – the manager's phrase.'

'Any forwarding address?'

'None. No one at Pitlochry has any idea where he is nowadays.'

'The Invisible Man,' said Paula.

'Another cul-de-sac,' Tweed remarked. 'Which reminds me – we still have no idea what Masterson meant by his note referring to *Endstation*. I feel certain that's a major pointer – either here or in Greece. Masterson was the cleverest interrogator I ever met. He was trying to tell me something. But what?'

'Dead end for the moment,' Paula said briskly. 'But I've come up with something.' There was a note of triumph in her tone which made Tweed and Monica stare at her. 'I didn't tell you while we were there. I thought I'd follow something up for myself.'

'Which was?' asked Tweed.

'You remember the evening we visited Colonel Barrymore when you interviewed him? I was sitting to one side. He had his copy of *The Times* folded back to the personal advertisement section. I memorized the date. Yesterday I went off to Wapping, checked their files. What do you think I found?'

'She's playing you at your own game,' Monica said and chuckled. 'Teasing you.'

'So I'll play along. What did you find?'

'An advertisement placed at the time Christina Gavalas was in England, the time when Harry Masterson was going around with her over here. The advertisement was this.' She read from a small pocket diary. '*Will anyone interested*

303

in the Greek Key and knows about Antikhana please contact me. Irene. It gives a phone number for contact. I phoned the number. Turned out to be the Strand Palace. I phoned the hotel, said I was the sister of Christina Gavalas. Had she stayed at the hotel? They wouldn't play. So I jumped in a taxi and went down to the Strand. I sexed up the reservations clerk – naughty of me, I think he thought he had a date. He looked up their records. Christina stayed there at the relevant time.'

'But Irene is the wrong name,' Monica observed.

'I think she did that to protect herself. Not knowing who would come looking for her.'

'I agree,' Tweed said. 'Type out that ad with the date and add it to the file. You did a good job. Actually,' he admitted, 'I knew about the advertisement. Newman told me over the phone that Christina had explained to him during dinner that was how she met Masterson. He saw the ad and contacted her.'

'Thanks a lot!' Paula threw down her pencil. 'So I wasted my time.'

'Hardly. I didn't spot that newspaper in Barrymore's study – which shows he was interested. And in the near future I think you and I should drive down again to Exmoor to see how Butler and Nield are getting on. We know more than we did last time.'

He stopped as the phone rang. Monica grabbed her receiver and spoke briefly. Putting her hand over the mouthpiece she looked at Tweed.

'Talk of the devil. Pete Nield on the phone for you.'

'Sorry to phone you so early. I called on the off chance,' Nield explained. 'I'm talking from a public box. We put the pressure on and guess what's happened. The hunters have become the hunted. Harry and I are being watched by Barrymore and Kearns.'

'What do you mean?' Tweed's tone was sharp, alarmed.

'We each took one of them in turn and let them spot us

304

– riding on the moor. Now when we get up there they appear out of nowhere and stalk us! It's uncanny . . .'

'They know the moor better than you'll ever do. What was their routine before they turned the tables on you?'

'Robson rode to see patients during the day. He can go for ages without food or drink. His patients are scattered over a large area. Evenings he has a meal, presumably prepared by his sister. Then he retires up to that conning tower place and reads. After dark he draws the curtains. Goes to bed late.'

'And Kearns?'

'He rides the moor a lot. His wife, Jill, never appears. She hasn't been seen by either of us. Maybe he locks her up. As for Kearns, he rides up to the summit of Dunkery Beacon. Stays up there at night. God knows what he's doing. Can't get close enough. Weird bloke. A solitary.'

'Dunkery Beacon? That's the highest point on Exmoor . . .'

'That's right. Like to know about Barrymore?'

'Of course.'

'He's about one hundred feet from where I'm talking. Inside a newspaper shop that opens early. He's standing by the window, half-pretending to read a paper. But he's watching me. He came into the village on a horse tethered further down the High Street. He's also got a rifle in a scabbard attached to the saddle.'

Tweed thought quickly. 'Now listen to me. Butler is inside The Luttrell Arms? Good. This is what you do. The unexpected. You vanish. Pay your bills. Then both of you drive to Taunton. The colonel can't follow you on a horse. Hire fresh cars in Taunton. Quite different models. Book into the main hotel in Taunton, using assumed names. Change your clothes – buy new ones which completely change your appearance. Then switch your attentions to Professor Guy Seton-Charles. Track him night and day. Don't let him know you're on his tail. You can pick him up tomorrow morning at his bungalow on that estate. Understood?'

'Will do.'

'And let Monica know the name of your new hotel, how we can contact you. Now, move!'

Tweed slammed down the phone. He started cleaning his glasses on his handkerchief. Monica watched, winked at Paula. She recognized the signs.

'Something has happened?' she ventured.

'Yes. The pressure worked . . .' He told them what had happened. 'Maybe crisis time is approaching.'

'And the object of the new exercise is?' Paula asked.

'To throw Barrymore and Kearns off balance. One moment they're being tracked by Butler and Nield. Suddenly the trackers disappear. I'll bet for the next week Barrymore and Kearns scour the moors looking for them, wondering where the devil they've gone. Also I'm pulling Butler and Nield out of the firing line. Maybe literally.'

'Don't follow,' Paula said.

'I didn't like the sound of the rifle Barrymore is carrying. You get shooting accidents on moors. And no one can prove it wasn't just that. And it's psychological warfare.'

'Don't follow that,' Paula said.

'We'll leave Exmoor alone for a week. Just when the hunters think they've scared off the opposition you and I arrive – asking more questions.'

They had breakfast brought in by the day guard, George. Sandwiches and coffee which they consumed at their desks. It was ten o'clock when Tweed asked Monica to put in a call to Chief Inspector Sarris of Athens Homicide.

'I met him once at a security conference in Geneva. He's very bright, but I have to try and stop him doing something. The timing is wrong. If he's not there, ask for Kalos . . .' Tweed spelt it out for her. 'He is Sarris' clever assistant.

306

Has a mind like a computer – especially where Greek history is concerned.'

Tweed returned to studying the file headed *Ionides*. Monica reported all the lines to Greece were busy. 'Probably travel agents booking holidays. I'll keep trying.'

'Fair enough. Meantime, try Brown's Hotel again. In Dunster I made an arrangement with Jill Kearns that if she came up to London we'd meet. I said I'd keep in touch with the hotel so I'd know when she was here.'

'I'm calling daily. She wasn't there yesterday . . .'

'Nield told me she's disappeared from Exmoor, that they haven't seen her for some time. Try now . . .'

'She's on the line,' Monica told him a few minutes later.

'Tweed here. When did you arrive?'

'Darling, how absolutely marvellous to hear your voice. So reassuring. I'm on my own. God, am I glad to be back in civilization. I was going out of my mind on that dreadful moor.'

'Can we meet today?' Tweed asked, stemming the flood.

'You asked me when I arrived. Late yesterday. Just in time to have tea. It's out of this world, tea at Brown's. Why don't we do that?'

'Good idea. I could get there about three-thirty. Would that suit you?'

'Gorgeous. I'll count the minutes. Don't be late. They have the most scrumptious strawberry cake. But it goes quickly. Oh,' she added as an afterthought, 'I'll have something interesting to tell you. Not over the phone, darling.'

'Three-thirty then. Goodbye . . .'

Tweed put down the phone as though it were hot. He sighed, took out his handkerchief, mopped his forehead in mock horror. 'Good job you didn't take that conversation down.'

'She's very attractive,' Paula said in a thoughtful tone.

307

'Swarms all over you.' He looked at Monica. 'But you did tape-record the conversation I had with Nield?'

'Yes, I saw you nod twice. It's recorded for all time. Want to hear it played back?'

'Later. Something Nield said was significant and now it's gone. I was concentrating on getting them out of Dunster. Damned if I can remember what it was. You listen to it, Paula. See whether something strikes you. Monica, try Peter Sarris again.'

'Chief Inspector Sarris? London calling. Mr Tweed of Special Branch would like a word with you . . .'

Tweed spent little time over exchanging greetings. 'Robert Newman, the foreign correspondent, has told me of his conversation with you, Peter. He's fully vetted . . .'

'He works for you these days?' Sarris enquired.

'No, he doesn't. But when he's after a story and comes across something he feels affects national security he tells me.' That covered Newman. 'I have a big favour to ask you. Hold off any action on this character Stavros Florakis. Give him enough rope and he'll hang himself. I'm at the early stages of the investigation.'

'What investigation is that? If I may ask.'

'You may. I'm investigating the death of one of my top men – Harry Masterson. Can't tell you what it's about yet. Point is Florakis' farm is close to Cape Sounion where Masterson died in suspicious circumstances.'

'Official verdict is an accident.'

'And the unofficial? I'm on scrambler.'

'So am I,' Sarris assured him. 'We had it installed when drugs became a major problem. Unofficially? I'm only expressing my personal opinion. There are people higher up who wouldn't like this . . .'

'Don't worry. This chat is totally confidential.'

'Masterson was murdered. I went to the Cape myself,

looked over the ground. No sane man could have stumbled over the edge. And Masterson was very sane – I saw him once at the Hilton. So, you want me to hold off the cavalry?'

'Please. We're at an early stage, Peter. I'm not sure at which end the key lies yet – yours or mine. Talking about keys, have you ever heard of the Greek Key?'

Sarris hesitated. Only for a second or two, but Tweed caught it.

'Doesn't mean a thing to me. Will we be seeing you out here?' he continued.

'Hard to say just now. How is Kalos? I remember him well at that security conference in Geneva. You have a clever assistant there.'

'Ah, but you are shrewder than some people here on the higher floors.' Sarris hesitated, this time for longer. Tweed waited, sensing the Greek was making up his mind about something. 'It is interesting you mentioned Kalos. He has made an important discovery. As you may know, Newman obtained Florakis' fingerprints. We were putting them through the computer. Kalos – as always – went his own way. He checked back through a card index of old records going back to 1946.'

'Sounds like Kalos,' Tweed commented.

'He came up trumps. An hour ago we were comparing the fingerprints of Stavros Florakis with another set under the magnifier. They matched.'

'Who is he really?' Tweed kept the excitement out of his voice.

'A certain Oleg Savinkov. Sent in by Stalin to murder leaders of EDES, the right-wing group fighting the Communists during the Civil War. Are you with me?'

'I have read about it. Go on.'

'Savinkov was nicknamed The Executioner, sometimes The Russian. So what is he doing as an impostor back in Greece? Someone has reactivated him. Can't be

Gorbachev. He's in the détente business. You still want me to hold off the dogs?'

'More than ever. And I will definitely be flying to Greece as soon as I can . . .'

28

Newman knew there was something wrong the moment he stepped out of the elevator on Christina's floor. Nick was sitting in an armchair on guard. He was smoking a cigarette and the ash tray on the marble-topped table was filled with discarded butts.

But it was Nick's reaction as soon as the elevator doors opened which warned Newman. Nick stood up abruptly and his right hand slid inside his jacket towards the Smith & Wesson revolver Newman had returned to him. When he saw who it was Nick converted the movement into scratching his armpit.

'Is she safe?' Newman asked.

'OK. But we have a problem, a crisis. Anton, one of her relatives, has arrived. He came up to this floor, then wandered off down that corridor when he saw me. Later he came back and went down into the lobby again. Could still be there.'

'A good moment for me to have a little talk with Christina.'

'Maybe not. She's very touchy. Like a bomb that could blow up in your face. It's Anton that did it. I told her. Felt I had to . . .'

'You did right.'

Newman went to her door, rapped in the special way

they had agreed. She opened the door after removing the chain and Newman realized she was in a bad mood. Her eyes looked larger than ever, she didn't smile, she turned her back on him and walked towards the balcony, arms folded under her breasts.

'Anton is here. They've found me,' she snapped before he could say a word.

'You haven't told me about Anton. Talk. And keep away from the balcony. If he's by the pool he could see you.'

'What difference does it make? He knows I'm here.'

'We'll handle that.' He took hold of her by the shoulders and turned her round, sat her down on the edge of the bed. 'Stay put.' He lifted the half-empty glass on the table, sipped it. 'Champagne. Bit early in the day.'

'I needed something to settle my nerves. The bottle's in the fridge. Fill it up for me.'

'Anything the lady wants, the lady gets.'

'Anything?' she asked as he brought back the refilled glass, handed it to her. She was wearing a cream blouse with the top three buttons undone. She wore no bra.

'Not that now,' he said. 'I have questions to ask.'

'Your eyes said something different.'

He moved away to a chair. She also wore a short pleated cream skirt. Her legs were stunning. Get your mind on the business in hand, he told himself.

'Stop it,' he snapped. 'Tell me about Anton. The full *curriculum vitae*. That means his life from the day he was born.'

'I know. I'm not illiterate – like Dimitrios and Constantine.' She sipped her champagne. 'Nor is Anton. He is Petros' son by his second wife – who was worked to death like the first wife. That makes Anton, six years younger than me, my uncle, for God's sake. Petros spotted he was bright. He spent money on his education, every drachma that was available.'

311

'What kind of education?'

'A good school in Athens. Anton was always top of the class. So he went on to a school in Switzerland. As well as Greek, he can speak German and English fluently. He's a natural linguist. An expert horseman – he learned to ride in Germany, then went on to Vienna for dressage. Petros wanted a gentleman in the family, someone who could mix at all levels of society. He's also a crack shot with any kind of rifle or handgun.'

'Where did he learn that? In Devil's Valley?'

'You're joking. When he came back here Dimitrios and Constantine hated him. The one thing they could do to make him look useless was to shoot. Anton flew to England, joined a shooting club. When he came back he could make Dimitrios and Constantine look like children with guns.'

'Happy families. How old is he?'

'Thirty-eight. He looks ten years younger. He dresses smartly. Oh, I've left a bit out. When he came back from Geneva he had a spell at Athens University. He came under the influence of an English professor. He still attends his seminars when this professor comes here in summer.'

'You know the name of this professor?'

She screwed up her thick eyebrows. 'A double-barrelled name. I met him once. Didn't like him. He reeks with conceit and self-satisfaction. But he's clever.'

'Try and think of his name.'

'Got it. Guy Seton-Charles . . .'

Newman had a word with Nick, who went straight down to the lobby by elevator. Returning to the bedroom, he found Christina sitting in front of the dressing table, brushing her hair. A bottle of mineral water and a glass stood next to her cosmetics.

'I've sobered up,' she announced. 'I drank two glasses of water. Do you think this is a good idea – my going down to the lobby with you if Anton is still there?'

'Part of the plan. If he's hanging about I want him to see you. And I want to see him – so I'll know him in future.'

'He's the most dangerous of my relatives. Because I'm well-educated too he resents me. And he has pots of money of his own. Money is power he says.'

'Where does it come from?'

'He runs a chain of shops in Athens and Salonika. They sell expensive television, video and radio equipment. Imported, of course. We Greeks don't make anything – except silverware. Anton is clever technically, too. He can build the most complicated high-powered radio equipment.'

'That's interesting,' Newman commented to himself. He went to the door as he heard the agreed rapping signal. It was Nick.

'Anton is still here. He's strolling round the lobby below the elevators. With a bit of luck we could see him by looking down. Without him seeing us.'

'That's not the idea. Come with us. Ready, Christina?'

'If you insist.'

They crossed the first-floor lobby. Nick had pressed the button, the elevator doors opened and they stepped inside. Newman gave Christina's arm a squeeze as the elevator descended. She made a moue, stiffened herself, stood erect.

'To hell with Anton,' she said.

'That's my girl,' Newman responded.

They stepped out into the main entrance hall. Below them, beyond a waist-high wall, was a deep well, a large reception area approached by steps from the even vaster marble-floored hall leading to the street. 'Over to your left, behind the pillar,' Nick whispered.

313

Several couples occupied some of the spacious couches at the lower level. A small man stepped from behind a pillar, lifted a small object to his eyes, held it there, then replaced it in his pocket.

Marler sat in an armchair at the lower level. He had a newspaper in front of his face. He dropped the paper, stood up, wandered over to where Anton was lighting a cigarette. Marler brushed past him, looking the other way. 'Excuse me,' he said in English and walked on a few paces. He took the camera he'd filched from Anton's pocket, fiddled with it, snapped it closed again and tucked it down inside the side of his slacks.

Anton still stood by the pillar. A small compact man wearing an expensive lightweight blue suit which Marler suspected was made of silk. He had a blue-striped shirt and a pale blue tie. Very dressy, Mr Anton. His pale face was plump and his black hair was brushed back over his high forehead. No parting.

As Marler approached he was feeling in his jacket pocket. He looked up, put out a hand to detain Marler, who stepped behind the pillar. 'A word with you,' Anton said, following the Englishman. 'You've just stolen my camera.' His right hand gripped Marler's arm and there was strength in the hand.

Marler wrenched his arm loose, shook himself, his expression bleak. 'Don't do that again.' He glanced down on the floor, pointed. 'Your bloody camera is down there. You dropped it, you stupid little man.'

Anton stooped with agility, retrieved the camera. As he stood up Marler hit him hard on the jaw with his clenched fist. No one sitting in the reception area could see behind the pillar. Anton sagged, the back of his head caught the pillar, he lay on the ground.

Marler hurried to the steps, ran up to the higher level where Newman waited with Christina and Nick. 'He's out cold. Time to move her. I'll inform the reception desk . . .'

314

'Nick, go out to the car. Be ready to drive us to the Grande Bretagne . . .'

Newman grasped Christina by the arm, guided her into a waiting elevator, pressed the button. As it ascended he talked fast. 'You kept most of your case packed as I suggested?'

'Yes. I can dump my cosmetic stuff inside in its sachet and be ready in two minutes.'

'Make it one . . .'

In the main lobby Marler was talking to the chief receptionist. 'A chap has collapsed behind a pillar down there. Just keeled over. May have had a heart attack.' He waited until the receptionist phoned for a doctor and rushed off, then asked a girl for the bill for Christina's room.

'Everything's paid up,' he announced as Newman emerged from an elevator, carrying a bag with Christina by his side. Behind him he heard the same girl receptionist call out. 'Phone for you, Mr Newman . . .'

'Take Christina to the car,' Newman ordered Marler. 'I'll be with you in a minute. God knows who this could be.' The girl behind the counter handed him the phone.

'Tweed here, Bob. There's an emergency. Call me back safely within the hour. No later . . .'

'Thanks a bundle.' Newman lowered his voice. 'We have a crisis at this end. I'll call back.' He slammed down the phone.

Nick was waiting outside at the end of a queue of taxis. He opened the rear door of his Mercedes and Christina dived in, followed by Newman. As Nick dumped her bag inside the boot Marler appeared at the rear window. 'Follow us to the Grande Bretagne,' Newman told him. 'Reserve a room for Christina in the name of Mrs Charles. Take over. Nick will be taking me back to the Embassy.'

'Will do.'

Nick turned into the traffic. Christina was producing a large silk scarf from her handbag. She carefully wrapped

315

it round her hair so it was concealed. Next she donned a pair of dark wrap-round glasses, then looked at Newman.

'Do I pass inspection?'

'Unrecognizable.' Newman felt relieved. Everyone was getting into the swing of quick escapes. And Nick was driving a devious route to the Grande Bretagne. Christina looped her arm inside Newman's and snuggled up against him as he glanced through the rear window. Marler was close behind.

'How the devil did Anton find me?' Christina wondered.

'Probably by showing a photograph of you to a member of the staff short of folding money . . .'

'But I arrived at the Hilton disguised.'

'And then paraded yourself on the balcony. There were loads of staff serving drinks to the sun-worshippers round that pool. I should have thought of that. I should also have thought of telling you to wear your scarf and glasses when we had dinner at the Ta Nissia restaurant. We'll be more careful at the Grande Bretagne.'

'And maybe,' Nick called over his shoulder, 'I should park this car at the Astir Palace across the road from the Grande Bretagne. They'll have the registration number by now. It means booking a room . . .'

'Book one. In a different name. Buy a case and a few clothes, including one of those peaked caps the Germans like to wear. We want to sink out of sight – and that includes you. And sleep in the Astir Palace room, if that's OK. Then you're available on the dot when we need you. Unless your wife would object?'

'Glad to see the back of me.' Nick grinned. 'Sorry about the traffic snarl-up, but no one can follow us into this.'

They had arrived at Omonia Square, the Piccadilly Circus or Times Square of Athens. Everywhere intersecting roads converged, the traffic was solid. The square was surrounded with second-class hotels, department stores. Nick tapped his hand on the wheel as he waited.

316

'Refugees from abroad flock to this area. The police don't mind. They know where to look if they're after someone. Miracles will never cease. We're on the move again . . .'

On the veranda of his farm deep inside Devil's Valley Petros was lecturing his two grandsons viciously. He gestured with a heavy fly-swatter as they stood in front of him.

'You, Dimitrios, are telling me again that several men crept up behind you that night at the mine, then clubbed both of you. Is that still your story?'

'It is the way it happened . . .'

'Liar! Cheat!' Petros moved with savage speed. The end of the fly-swatter whacked Dimitrios across the back of his left hand. Reinforced with leather, the swatter brought up an ugly weal. And Petros was still sitting in his chair. 'You lie in your teeth,' he snarled.

'It was like that . . .' Constantine began, then stopped when Petros turned to him. He braced himself for the blow but Petros relaxed in his chair, studying the end of the fly-swatter as he talked in a calm tone.

'You were both staring down inside the mine. You saw the legs of a man protruding from under the bucket. Had you shot him without hesitation – as I would – you would have turned round and seen the single man coming up behind you, the man one of you probably glimpsed before he knocked you both out. Clumsy fools.'

'Why do you say that?' Dimitrios ventured. He sucked his injured hand.

'Because I know the mine, know that for hundreds of yards it is surrounded with loose rock chippings. One man trained in field warfare, one very clever man, might make his way silently across those rocks without making a sound. One man,' he repeated. 'I refuse to believe that several

317

men managed it. You are covering up for your idiocy. It was a trap, you realize that?'

'A trap?' Constantine sounded genuinely puzzled.

'Of course. One man – the man inside the mine – lets you see him. He leads you to the mine. His companion then creeps up behind you both. Constantine, you said you saw a rifle barrel just before it struck you. He did it like this.' Holding the fly-swatter by the middle of the handle, Petros swung it first one way, then the other. 'Were they the English?' he growled. 'You saw one man coming up the track.'

'Too far away to see him at all clearly,' Dimitrios broke in before Constantine could reply. It was a relief to be able to tell the truth.

'And you did a lousy job of not finding Christina,' Petros sneered. He was enjoying himself, taking them down a peg, showing who was boss.

'We did our best,' Dimitrios protested. 'So many hotels . . .'

'Oho! Your best. Your worst, you mean. You walk into the Hilton and try to bribe the chief receptionist! He knows it is not worth risking his fat salary to give out information. I would have gone after the menials – people like yourselves. A chambermaid, a cleaner. Someone who needs the money, someone who goes into every bedroom. Well, at least Anton is now looking. He will find her.'

'We could go back, try again,' Constantine suggested eagerly.

'Now you grovel.' Petros spat beyond the veranda. They took all the insults he heaped on them, he was thinking. It was a tribute to the power of his personality. His huge body emanated physical magnetism. He waved towards the scrub-studded mountains.

'Get out there in the sun. Tend the sheep. Make sure the other shepherds are not sleeping behind rocks. If you catch one, kick hell out of him.' He paused. 'That was curious that you should see Florakis climbing a mountain

318

at that hour. Keep an eye on him, too. Report to me when you find out what he is up to.' Petros could not resist one last dig. 'And forget about Christina – let Anton find her. Anton has brains.'

When Dimitrios and Constantine had left the farm, climbing up the track even a goat might find trouble negotiating, kicking up limestone dust which filled their nostrils, sweating in the afternoon sun, Petros remained on the veranda. His leonine head sunk on his barrel-like chest, he remained awake, thinking.

Always the hated English. Newman and Marler – those were the two English Giorgos had reported as registering at the Grande Bretagne. Giorgos who had ended rammed inside a cask of wine upside down in the Plaka.

Without any formal education, Petros possessed a native cunning, the devious mind of a peasant which sometimes could out-think the well-educated. Newman and Marler who had seduced Christina into joining them. They had been sent by whichever of the three men had killed Andreas on Siros all those years ago.

Which one? Colonel Barrymore, Captain Robson or Company Sergeant Major Kearns? Could all three be involved in the bestial murders? Because later – when the war was over – Petros had visited Cairo to learn what he could of the murder of his other son, Stephen, masquerading as Ionides. An Egyptian who worked as a cleaner at the Antikhana Building had told him. The same three men had been based in the building. In some way one of them had penetrated Ionides' real identity, had discovered he was the brother of Andreas.

Which one? Petros asked himself the question he had pondered a thousand times. Now Anton – clever Anton – had located them at some place called Exmoor. Why were they all living so close together?

It didn't matter! Petros heaved himself out of the chair, went into the farmhouse, returned with the box he kept hidden. He opened it. Inside, wrapped in newspaper, was the commando knife, the knife he had used all his strength to heave out of Andreas' back. The knife he would one day use to kill the murderer of his two sons.

Dapper and assured, despite his experience, Anton thanked the chief receptionist and walked out of the Hilton. The doctor they had summoned had been a nuisance. Anton had assured him he'd fainted, caught his jaw against the side of the pillar. He had also handled the chief receptionist cleverly. Just before he left he made the remark casually.

'It was the heat. I must have fainted just before my friends left the hotel . . .' He described Christina, Newman and Marler. 'Did they say which hotel they were moving to? Maybe not – as they left in a rush.'

'No, they didn't. As you say, they were in a hurry,' the chief receptionist had replied.

Which confirmed Anton's suspicions. He shrugged as he walked into the blazing heat, hardly noticing the change in temperature. He had found her once, he would find her again. But first there was more urgent business to attend to. He checked his watch – he was late for his appointment.

Let the bastard wait. He would be so relieved when he saw Anton arrive. He ignored the taxis. Their drivers had good memories. He made his way over the complicated crossing and walked briskly down Avenue Sofias towards Syntagma Square where the Grande Bretagne was located.

Anton smiled to himself as he thought how livid Petros would be if he knew where he was going, who he was going to meet and why. The old ruffian was living in the past.

Had no idea of what was really going on in the world. Wouldn't he be surprised one day when he found Anton was a Cabinet Minister? The Ministry of the Interior for preference. There you had real power.

Half an hour later he was walking through the maze of alleys and streets which made up the honeycomb of the Plaka. Was the plan already beginning to work? Sooner or later the man he was going to see would have to tell him what was happening. The clod who was still important to Anton. For the present. The man called Doganis. The Athens chief of the Greek Key.

'You're late,' Doganis greeted him. 'Why?'

Anton sat in a rush-covered chair in the room above a taverna, took his time about lighting a cigarette. He disliked this hulking brute but was astute enough to conceal his distaste. Doganis, a man in his sixties, was heavily built with broad shoulders and a large head of greying hair. His hooded eyes regarded Anton with a cold expression.

Anton studied his chief, careful to betray nothing of the contempt he felt. The huge soft hands holding a circular ebony ruler, the sagging jowls, the barrel-like stomach. Out of condition, out of touch with the modern world. One of the Old Guard. A gross monument of the Civil War days.

Doganis was also studying the dapper Anton. Ambitious, ruthless. A young upstart who had to be kept in his place. Dressed like a gigolo. Doganis had been ordered to tell him the next move in the operation; personally he thought it premature.

'You are going back to England soon,' he informed him. 'You'll be taking letters to Captain Robson, Sergeant Major Kearns and Colonel Barrymore. Two of the letters will be meaningless. The third you will have the honour of delivering to Jupiter.'

'Jupiter? Who is that?'

'The man who is reactivating the organization. Do not ask who he is.'

'Jupiter is a Roman god, not a Greek,' Anton remarked, feeling his way.

'Which confuses the issue, protects his identity. You travel to England again in a few weeks' time – after we have received an important visitor from abroad.' Doganis paused. At least they hadn't told him to reveal yet to Anton that the visitor was Colonel Volkov, aide to General Lucharsky. 'You can travel there by the secret route again, I assume? Again there must be no record of your visit to England.'

'It worked before, it will work again,' Anton told him boldly. 'You do your job, I'll do mine . . .'

There was a sudden cracking sound. Anton stared. Doganis, who constantly held something in his restless hands, had split the ebony ruler in two in his fury.

Anton was astounded. The grotesque obese Doganis he had put down as effete had enormous strength in his apparently flabby hands. Strangler's hands. Doganis pointed the jagged end of one half of the ruler at him. His voice was more sinister for its soft tone.

'Listen to me, Gavalas. We have laid a tremendous responsibility on your immature shoulders. I have only to report you have lost my confidence and you are dead in twenty-four hours. You have displayed arrogance. I find that disturbing.'

Anton swallowed. The room was dimly illuminated by an oil lamp on a side table. Doganis' huge shadow suddenly seemed to fill the room. He forced himself to speak respectfully. 'I apologize, Comrade. I wished to assure you all will go well.'

'And remember this,' Doganis continued, ignoring the apology, 'I may introduce you to our visitor. He may wish to brief you himself. Treat him with reverence. Phone me daily from a public call box.' He changed the subject

322

without warning, watching the other man closely. 'Is every-thing quiet down at Cape Sounion? No sign of anyone becoming curious about Florakis?'

'No sign at all,' Anton assured him.

'You replied too quickly. What about Petros?'

'He is still planning his mad revenge on the English murderers of his two sons. He thinks of nothing else.'

'Useful. He will divert the attention of those two English-men, Newman and Marler. Go now. Your future depends on obedience to the cause.'

Anton stood up quickly, glad to leave the presence of this man who now frightened him. He hurried down the narrow staircase leading direct to the street. He paused before he walked into the deserted street.

He did not see the small stocky man with a stubble of brown hair waiting in the shadow of a doorway across the street. For the simple reason that Kalos did not want to be seen. Kalos wore a stained old jacket and baggy trousers. He raised the camera with the infra-red lens and snapped off three shots. Anton turned left and walked rapidly away.

I'm lucky, thought Kalos. Whoever he is left the building when the tourists and the locals are eating and drinking inside the tavernas. He already had inside his camera two shots of Doganis. At least he had known this senior member of the Greek Key.

Kalos had waited over an hour outside the apartment Doganis rented in the Plaka, then had followed him to this new rendezvous above a taverna. Maybe Sarris would identify the younger man who had just left after spending half an hour with Doganis. The Greek Key was apparently recruiting younger members. A bad sign. And Kalos won-dered who, where, and how they were finding fresh recruits.

323

29

'Bob, what crisis?' Tweed asked. 'Where are you talking from?'

'The Embassy. On scrambler phone. Now, you listen . . .' Newman explained tersely what had happened. He was alone in the basement room: Patterson had pushed off after unlocking the door.

'So your main task,' Tweed said, 'is to guard Christina, hide her away from Petros . . .'

'Our main objective is to find out who killed Masterson. And the last person we've found yet who saw him alive is Christina. It may be significant that Petros – through Anton – is doing his damnedest to track her down. What's your problem?'

'*Your* problem now,' Tweed told him. 'I had Butler and Nield on Exmoor, tailing Professor Guy Seton-Charles. An hour ago I had an emergency call from Butler. He was at London Airport. Seton-Charles suddenly took off. Left his bungalow with a case, drove a devious route to the airport . . .'

'Devious?'

'He took the main road to London, then cut off down a side turning. Nield followed him and Butler cruised on along the highway. Later Butler saw Seton-Charles come back down a slip road. From that point Butler and Nield leapfrogged so the target wouldn't spot them. At London Airport Nield stood behind Seton-Charles as he booked a first-class return to Athens. He's in mid-air now. British Airways flight 456, departed London 2.35 p.m., arrives at

Athens 8 p.m. Both local times. Can you get to the airport and track him? Remember his description?'

'Perfectly. And I've loads of time.'

'I need to know who he *contacts*. Something very funny about the professor.'

'Leave it to me . . .'

The BA flight from London touched down at Athens Airport at 8 p.m. Newman, lounging in a seat near the exit, spotted him at once – Seton-Charles wore a light-weight linen suit crumpled from sitting inside the aircraft. The professor climbed into a taxi. Newman got inside the next taxi.

'I'm a detective,' he told the driver. 'Don't lose that taxi – and here's a thousand drachmae as a tip.'

'What has he done?' asked the Greek.

'That's what I'm trying to find out . . .'

Settling back in his seat, Newman took off his jacket, mopped his forehead. The interior of the vehicle was like a sweat box. He recalled a headline blazoned on a newsstand. *Killer Heatwave Hits Greece*. And the character who wrote that one up wasn't joking, he thought.

Half an hour later, after passing between endless rows of white-walled two-storeyed houses backed by arid hillsides, they entered the city. Seton-Charles' taxi pulled up outside its destination. The occupant got out, paid off the driver and without a backward glance carried his bag inside the Hilton Hotel.

Tweed had phoned Jill Kearns at Brown's Hotel an hour before he was due to have tea with her. He had explained something urgent had come up, an emergency he had to cope with personally. Would she forgive him? Could they make a fresh date for tea in a couple of days' time?

325

Jill had shown no signs of resentment, said she certainly understood he had a difficult job. She would look forward even more to their being together now she would have to wait a little longer to see him. He put down the phone and looked at Monica.

'She's still keen to see me. Meantime we'll see where she goes, how she spends her time, who she meets. I fixed this up while you were out.'

'Fixed up what?'

'At this moment Paula is sitting in the lobby of Brown's. Jill can't get out of either the Albemarle Street or the Dover Street exit without Paula spotting her. When she leaves, Paula follows.'

'Paula will recognize her?'

'You've forgotten.' Tweed relaxed in his chair, pleased with the way things were developing. 'Paula,' he reminded her, 'was with me when I visited Kearns on Exmoor at his horrible old house near that bungalow estate where Seton-Charles lives. Jill sat in the room during my interview with Kearns – as did Paula. They sat within six feet of each other.'

'Is this Jill bright?'

'A very attractive blonde, in her thirties, and very bright.'

'Then she may well spot Paula following her,' Monica objected.

'You think so? Before Paula left here she altered her hair style. I loaned her a pair of glasses with blank lenses. It's amazing how a pair of glasses alters a person's appearance. On top of that she left early enough to call at Simpsons in Piccadilly – to do some shopping.'

'What shopping? You can be so exasperating. You're enjoying keeping me in suspense.'

'She went to buy a white raincoat, one with a large collar which buttons up to the neck. You may have observed it is drizzling on and off. In that outfit Jill will never recognize her.'

'And what's your motive in this devious – typically devious, if I may say . . .'

'You just did.' Tweed grinned.

'Devious ploy I was going to say if you'd let me finish just one sentence.'

'I'm suspicious of the glamorous Jill Kearns. She may be acting on her husband's instructions. I'm giving her enough rope – two days of it – to hang herself.'

'You don't trust anyone, do you?'

'Especially not attractive blondes who flatter me, try to make out they think I'm the cat's whiskers.'

'Maybe for her you are.' Monica doodled on her note-pad. 'She may be just what you need . . .'

She stopped speaking, feeling she'd gone too far. Tweed's wife had left him several years ago, had walked out to take up living with a Greek shipping magnate. Last heard of in Rio. Tweed showed no sign of having heard her.

'Now we're on our own, let's check the facts we have so far, what we're doing. I'm a good listener as you know.'

He relaxed in his chair, hands clasped in his lap, eyes half-shut. Monica began her survey of recent events, reciting from memory.

'Object of the exercise – to track down the killer of Harry Masterson . . .'

'I'm going to get that bastard,' Tweed said half to himself.

Monica paused, surprised by the vehemence of his tone, then went on. 'Harry was going on holiday, bored stiff with the idea. He sees the ad Christina Gavalas placed in *The Times*, signing herself Irene. Intriguing reference to the Greek Key, which is a mystery to us still. Christina tells the story of the murder of Andreas and Stephen during the war. Harry gets interested, fools her into thinking he's a detective. Together they visit Exmoor. OK so far?'

'Go on.'

'Harry visits each of the three men, one of whom the Gavalas family is convinced is the murderer. Robson, Barrymore and Kearns. Harry is probably the shrewdest interrogator we've ever had – so maybe he spots the bad apple. He then, God save his soul, lays a trap. He tells each of the three he's flying to Greece. Which he then does with Christina. Harry is killed at Cape Sounion.'

'And,' Tweed added, 'by the time Paula and I do the same run Harry did – visit those three on Exmoor – they've all been on holiday and have suntans. Which means one of them could have been to Greece while Harry was there.'

'What I just can't see is who could have tricked Harry and pushed him over that three-hundred-feet cliff.' Monica shivered. 'The big question is who could have gained Harry's trust?'

'Christina is the obvious answer. The obvious is often correct.'

'There is an alternative,' Monica mused. 'Someone else Harry had no reason to fear but who got the better of him.'

Tweed opened his eyes. 'That's a new idea you have there. Someone he met in Greece?'

'Doesn't seem likely,' Monica disagreed. 'Next thing, Newman and Marler go out to Greece, make contact with Christina, who seems to have changed sides. But that could be another ploy, this time to trap Newman. That woman worries me. I sense she's clever.'

'Not clever enough to fool Newman,' Tweed assured her.

'She may have fooled Harry. I gather she's very attractive.'

'Harry,' Tweed recalled, 'was a great one for the girls. After his wife divorced him because he wasn't home every night, Harry made hay, was a devil with women.'

'Bob Newman is single again,' Monica reminded him.

'After that brutal murder of his French wife in the Baltic.'

'No woman ever fooled Bob,' Tweed insisted. 'He might *pretend* to go all starry-eyed over someone like Christina – but he'd be fooling her. Go on with your summary.'

'Newman and Marler contact Christina. They hear about this old villain, Petros – obsessed with tracking down his sons' killers over forty years afterwards. An impossible mission . . .'

'Theoretically,' Tweed interjected. 'But his son, Anton, does find his way to Exmoor – and locates all three ex-commandos. Petros must be a man with a deep peasant cunning. Obsessed, I agree. An impossible mission? Maybe not. And those three on Exmoor are scared of something. Look how Paula and I found all three were living inside fortresses. As I said to Paula, they're like men waiting for Nemesis.'

'Next development,' Monica continued, 'we get all this weird data from Newman. And weird it is – Andreas' skeleton hanging inside that old silver mine. Macabre. Petros is obsessed.'

'No proof it is Andreas. Probable, yes. Certain, no.'

'Plus the strange trip to the island of Siros. Dimitrios and Constantine – according to Christina – tried to shoot Newman. And,' she pressed on, 'this is the hairbrained place where the three commandos landed – with a German lookout point perched in that monastery above them. Back to the present day, we have the murder of Giorgos – who worked for the Grande Bretagne and spied on Newman and Marler. Also macabre – ending head down in a cask.'

'I think the solution lies in Greece.' Tweed, suddenly alert, walked over to the window and gazed towards the trees of distant Regent's Park.

'Looks like it,' Monica agreed. 'That's further reinforced by this peculiar Seton-Charles character hurtling off to Athens. That might mean nothing – except for the devious

329

route he took to London Airport. Harry and Pete handled that cleverly. But what do they do now?'

'They're already doing it. While you were out when Butler called from London Airport I sent them both back to cover Exmoor. Robson, Barrymore and Kearns are still holed up there. Change of tactics again. Butler and Nield will have gone back to checking on that curious trio. Later, I'll fly out to Greece. I want to question Petros.'

'That could be dangerous. Newman nearly got killed venturing into Devil's Valley.'

'Sometimes you have to take chances.' He was pacing restlessly. 'Harry was murdered at Cape Sounion. That's close to this Devil's Valley. And some swine murdered Sam Partridge on Exmoor. That Greek, Anton, was floating about when it happened. Two scores I have to settle. Someone is going to pay the price.'

Monica again was disturbed by the ferocity of his language, his bitter tone. She spoke quietly.

'Be careful. Don't get obsessed – like old Petros. You're losing your normal sense of detachment. You always said that was the fatal mistake . . .'

'Stop nagging me, woman.' Tweed stared at her. 'I'll work it out in my own way without your advice . . .'

He stopped, appalled at Monica's expression. She looked like a woman who had been whipped across the face. In all their long relationship he had never spoken to her like that.

'I'm dreadfully sorry,' he apologized. 'I do rely on your judgement – maybe more than you've ever realized. I feel like a man walking in a fog, a tired man,' he admitted. He stuffed his briefcase with tape recordings and files. 'I think I'll spend a couple of days in my flat, sitting in an armchair, thinking. I need something to happen which points the way.'

'It always does.' Monica smiled. 'Now you're following your usual method. Don't worry. You're under pressure.

I'm amazed you haven't blown your top before. And there's a lot of personal feelings you've had to grapple with. Go home, get some rest – or would you like some coffee first?'

Tweed said thank you but he wanted to get straight off. He put on his shabby Burberry, squeezed her shoulder and walked out with his briefcase. Monica stood up, went to the window to watch him walk round Park Crescent through the net curtains. She was frightened. Tweed was acting like a man obsessed with his problems.

He left the building. He paused on the front steps to button up the raincoat, glancing all round the Crescent in case there were hostile watchers. Then he headed for the taxi rank.

On the way he passed a newspaper seller with a poster propped against the garden railings. Tweed didn't even notice it – he was thinking about Monica. It read, *Reagan–Gorbachev Summit in Washington?*

30

'I'm scared stiff. I need someone to confide in.' Jill Kearns laid a hand on Tweed's knee. It was two days later.

Tea at Brown's. Tweed looked round the room, admired the wooden wall panelling, the moulded ceiling. The atmosphere of the place created an air of intimacy. Especially when you were with a woman.

They sat at a table in an arched alcove at the end of the lounge. Behind them was a fireplace and they were isolated from the other guests taking tea. He twisted round in his deep armchair to look at Jill. She was worth the effort.

331

She had twirled her blonde hair into a single long plait looped over her shoulder. And she was dressed for London. A pair of tight-fitting leather trousers thrust into boots which displayed her well-shaped legs. She also wore a tunic of some black material splashed with vivid-coloured oriental flowers. Tweed drank some tea before replying.

'What exactly is worrying you?'

'Stuart, for one thing . . .'

'And for another?'

Tweed helped himself to a scrambled egg roll, bit off half of it. On the table in front of them stood a four-tier stand of some of the best food he'd ever enjoyed. The lowest tier had delicate little sandwiches with the crusts removed; on the second and third tiers were selections of bread and more sandwiches. Logically, the top tier held a variety of cakes, including some chocolate eclairs. You worked your way up.

'The company he keeps,' Jill replied, squeezing his leg. She used the other hand to eat and drink. The room was full of couples and quartets whose conversation muffled what Jill was saying. 'Those two men, Captain – Dr – Robson, and Colonel Barrymore. The colonel gives me the creeps.'

'Why?'

'He seems to mesmerize my husband and Robson. You'd think they were all still in the Army and Barrymore was their CO – the way he talks to them. Loathsome sarcastic bastard.'

'I take it you don't like him . . .'

'Don't make fun of me.' She looped her hand round his left hand he'd rested on the arm of the chair. 'You'll help me, won't you, Tweed? I wish I could get you on the telephone. Give me your number. It would be nice if we could have dinner. More cosy.'

All in a rush. She'll proposition me soon, Tweed thought. I wish to God I knew what she's really up to. He asked a question to throw her off balance.

'How do you know all this – how Barrymore talks to them? I thought they met by themselves for dinner once a week at The Luttrell Arms.'

'Sometimes they come over to our place and talk half the night in the study. I eavesdrop.'

'A bit naughty, that.' He smiled to take the sting out of the comment.

'You've got a lovely smile,' she said.

'You overheard something that frightened you,' he probed.

Outwardly impassive, Tweed wasn't feeling too comfortable. A woman had come in and sat down at a small table at the side of the room. She had folded her raincoat and parked it on the other chair. She was watching them briefly over the top of her glasses with a cynical expression. Paula. She hadn't, he knew, missed the fact that Jill was clasping his hand.

'Stuart is reinforcing the defences, as he put it. He's even laid some of those beastly steel-teethed traps outside the walls of our house. Barrymore advised that. They're all strengthening their security. Just as though they were expecting a raid.'

'Perhaps they are. By who?'

She hesitated, pushed two fingers under his shirt cuff. 'I've no idea. I feel like a prisoner.'

'You escaped for now. You're sitting here, in the middle of London. Not on Exmoor.' He poured more tea and she leaned over to hold the teapot lid in place, her breasts brushing his arm. 'You're confiding in me, as you put it, although I can't imagine why.'

She released her hand, flopped back in her armchair, her long leather-clad legs stretched out in front of her. Paula raised her glasses higher up the bridge of her nose, adjusted her beret and looked away. Tweed wished she'd stop sending signals.

'Because,' Jill said, 'you put the wind up all three when

333

you came to see them. I heard Stuart talking to Barrymore on the phone after you'd left. He was agitated. He started to say "This man Tweed is dangerous," then he slammed the door of his study and I couldn't catch any more. If you can put the wind up those three you're the man for me, my ally.'

She remained flopped in the chair but still looked elegant as she spoke in a coaxing tone.

'What about dinner here tonight? Say eight o'clock. And you haven't given me your phone number yet.'

'Can't do that – give you a number. Security. What I can do is to have you called daily in case you've got a message for me . . .'

'And dinner?'

'I expect to be working till midnight. Dinner will be sandwiches at my desk. Sorry.'

'If you agreed to dinner . . .' She crossed her legs and watched him through her lashes. 'I might have more news to pass on to you.'

'I can't promise to be an ally,' he warned. 'And if you've really more to tell me, do it now.' He decided an eclair was pushing it and took another scrambled egg roll.

She took a pack of cigarettes from her large handbag, extracted a king-size cigarette when he shook his head, and lit it with a gold-plated lighter. In the mellow light her beautiful bone structure stood out clearly. He was tempted to change his mind, to say he could make it for dinner. She's a devil, he was thinking. Blowing out a stream of smoke, she smiled.

'I can read your mind, Tweed. You're reconsidering your decision about dinner.'

There was an aura about her which drew him to her. In her thirties, he reflected. Not such a huge difference in their ages. He drank half a cup of strong tea to get a grip on himself.

'How long have you and Stuart been married?'

334

'Ten long years. Oh, it was fun to start with. He's a good-looking bastard. I met him soon after he'd left the Army – at a party in Taunton. He had a sense of humour in those days. Then he became cold – and spent more time with Barrymore and Robson. That's when he started turning the house into the Tower of London – like the others. I could leave him any day now for the right man.'

'That might be traumatic . . .'

'No more traumatic than the way we live now. At nights he spends half his time riding over the moor up to Dunkery Beacon. He's not back by midnight.' She looked at him with a certain expression. 'So I make a point of pretending to be fast asleep when my lord and master rolls in.'

'Dunkery Beacon? That's the highest point on Exmoor. And it's pretty rough country. How does he manage in the dark?'

'He doesn't.' She leaned forward to straighten his tie. 'He only goes up there half the month – not before there's a half moon waxing. I spend my evenings watching the television rubbish. I lead the most exciting life.'

'At least he seems generous,' Tweed remarked. 'Your clothes, that lighter . . .'

'Paid for out of a big legacy my favourite uncle left me.'

Tweed checked his watch. 'Sorry, but I have to go . . .'

She sat up straight and her face was close to his. 'All right, I'll tell you. One night when the three of them were talking they left the study door open a bit. A few nights ago. I crept down the stairs. Do you want to know what I heard?'

'Up to you.'

'My reward for telling is you have dinner with me soon. Promise?'

'I'll think about it.'

'The trouble was I only heard a bit. Then one of the

treads on the staircase creaked. Barrymore came to the door and slammed it shut. I froze, still as a mouse.'

'Did he see you?' Tweed kept the anxiety out of his voice.

'I'm not sure. Before that happened Robson said they'd better watch out. He sensed that the Greek Key might arrive soon on Exmoor, that he'd heard Petros – I think that was the name – was looking for them . . .'

Tweed was getting anxious: it was after 7 p.m. and there was still no sign of Paula. Monica, who worked all hours, saw him check his watch.

'She'll be all right. Paula can look after herself.'

The phone rang, she picked it up, spoke briefly. She nodded towards Tweed's phone.

'It's Harry Butler. Says it's an emergency. Not like him . . .'

Tweed lifted the receiver. 'Hello, Harry. Where are you calling from?'

'From a public phone box in Minehead on the coast. We're staying at a tiny place called Porlock Weir, also on the coast. End of the road. Literally. It stops there. I decided we needed a new base. Not Dunster, not Taunton. Porlock Weir is tucked away. Has a toy harbour for boats. The only way west is to walk along the rocky shore. I can hear the tide coming in at night. High tide around midnight. Got a pencil handy? Good. We're staying at The Anchor Hotel. I'm in Room Three, Pete has Room Two. Telephone number is 0643 862753. Got it?'

'Yes. Something's happened?'

'The ex-commando lot have disappeared. All three. Robson, Kearns and Barrymore. They've left Exmoor . . .'

'How do you know that?' Tweed felt a chill creeping up his spine.

'I took Barrymore and Robson's residences – because

336

they're close together. Pete watched Kearns. We kept in contact with our car radios. Careful what we said. Not a sign of them. I decided to use bull-at-gate method.'

'What did you do next?'

'Called at each address after buying new outfits. Country stuff. Pete shaved off his moustache – after a lot of pressure from me. I wore a polo-necked sweater and a pair of tinted glasses. Not foolproof, but if one of them opened the door we'd know at least they were there.'

'And the result?'

'At Quarme Manor that old bat of a housekeeper, Mrs Atyeo, tells me the Colonel is not at home. Can't say when he'll be back. I chatted her up, but let's skip that. So I drove on to Captain Robson at his posh bungalow. His sister – when I coax her – says her brother is away in London. Pete had a rougher time at CSM Kearns' place. No answer to the bell-push so he scrambles over the gate. The dog comes at him – ruddy Alsatian type. Pete coped, bashed the beast on the nose with the barrel of his gun. They don't like that – a hefty bonk on the nose. Pete prowled round the place. It was after dark. No lights. No one home. That's it. They've gone. To London maybe. Robson could have lied to his sister. We feel we should have seen one of them go.'

'Not necessarily. Harry, both of you stay on at The Anchor – and pick up any gossip on the three men. Call Monica if there's a fresh twist. In any case, call daily. Take care.'

Tweed sat staring into the distance after putting down the phone. Monica watched him as she removed the cassette which had recorded Butler's conversation.

'He said something which triggered off a memory,' Tweed told her after a few minutes. 'Can't put my finger on it. We'll play it back later, see if I can spot what it was.'

He walked over to the wall where three maps had been

attached – maps carrying flags with names. A map of Exmoor. A map of the Greek area stretching from Athens to Cape Sounion. And a map of Athens which Monica had obtained.

On the Exmoor map flags with names located the homes of Barrymore, Robson and Kearns, the bungalow estate, Professor Seton-Charles' residence, The Royal Oak at Winsford and The Luttrell Arms – the two places where the trio met weekly for lunch or dinner. One flag pressed in close to Winsford carried the name Sam Partridge. Tweed picked up two more from a tray on a table and wrote Butler and Nield on each. He pressed these in over Porlock Weir.

The map of Greece carried fewer flags. One for Petros in Devil's Valley, another close by for Florakis. A third, perched at the edge of Cape Sounion, carried what amounted to an obituary. Harry Masterson.

The street plan of Athens was becoming crowded. At the corner of Syntagma Square where the Grande Bretagne was situated, three more names: Christina Gavalas, Newman, Marler. At the other end of Avenue Sofias a flag for Professor Seton-Charles at the Hilton. And, finally, at the police headquarters building on Alexandras, Peter Sarris and Kalos.

'Who is Kalos?' Monica asked.

'The Dormouse.'

'Sorry? Did I hear you aright?'

'You did. I met Kalos, Sarris' loyal assistant, at the security conference in Geneva. A small, stocky chap with a stubble of light brown hair peppered over his head. I nicknamed him The Dormouse – because that's what he looks like. We got on well together. When I go to Athens he's the man I'm hoping will tell me anything they know. Sarris is more cautious. Another reason for my respecting The Dormouse is his uncanny ability to track a suspect while merging with his background. Sarris told me that.'

'Maybe you'd better fly to Greece soon,' Monica suggested.

'All in good time.' He looked at the wall maps again. 'At least we have our forces well distributed – Newman and Marler in Greece, Butler and Nield on Exmoor. There's a name missing.'

'Who's that?'

'Anton. Trouble is he's a will o' the wisp. First he was back in Greece, then he slips into this country by some unknown means before slipping out again. I'd like to know how he managed that.'

After parking his car at The Anchor Butler went for a walk westward along the coast. It was dark and he passed several isolated cottages with lights burning inside. To his right he could hear the slap of the incoming sea hitting the rocks. He turned round, went back to The Anchor and into the bar. Nield was chatting to the barman, a young chap who polished glasses as he talked.

'They have a ghost prowling the beaches at night,' Nield said to Harry, who ordered half a pint. 'Meet John, the barman. Local.'

'Not exactly a ghost,' John told Butler as he served him. 'A few weeks ago the old crone, Mrs Larcombe – lives in the end cottage – swears she saw flashing lights out at sea. Then another light flashing further west along the coast. Can't take her seriously.'

'Bats in the belfry?' suggested Butler, only half-listening.

'Hardly. Sharp as a tack. Local nosey parker. It was about the time that Portuguese ship, *Oporto*, was due to berth at Watchet.'

Butler frowned. 'Surely not at night – no ship could get inside Watchet except in broad daylight.'

'They said it missed the tide, had to heave to offshore all night.'

Butler nodded, said to Nield he was hungry. Time for dinner.

Paula arrived back at nine o'clock. She took off her raincoat, sagged into the secretarial chair behind her desk, kicked off her shoes. Monica said she was making coffee. Paula grinned. 'Bless you.' Tweed leaned back in his chair, studying her.

'You look all in – and you're still wearing those glasses.'

'So I am. I'd forgotten them. Thank the Lord I was wearing my flatties. That Jill Kearns has the stamina of a goat.' Waiting until Monica had left the room, she looked at Tweed quizzically. 'I'm sure you could have ended up in bed with her. She's ravishing. And she's after you. You do know that?'

'The thought crossed my mind. Don't push it. Give me a report. About her movements.'

'Window-shopping for three days. Didn't buy a thing. Went all over the West End . . .'

'She didn't spot you?'

'Of course not. I wore that beret I had on in Brown's, took it off from time to time. Switched round my reversible raincoat – every conceivable variation . . .'

'But did she at any time use a public call box?' Tweed asked.

'Definitely not. This evening she had early dinner – at Brown's. Then went up to her room. I thought it was time to return. To report to "Sir",' she added with mock solemnity.

'And that's it?' Tweed sounded disappointed.

'Except I found out she always stays at Brown's when she comes to town.'

'How did you discover that?'

'I chatted up the hall porter.' She looked at Monica who had come back with a tray. 'You're an angel.' She drank half her cup of black coffee, then gazed at Tweed. 'Now, what did you find – apart from the fact that Jill has wandering fingers?'

Tweed gave her a concise summary of his conversation with Jill. 'Well, did you notice anything interesting or significant she told me?'

'Robson's reference to the Greek Key,' Paula said promptly. 'I also spotted it's the first time we've heard any of the Exmoor trio mention Petros – linking him to the Greek Key. Surely that is significant?'

Tweed pursed his lips. 'Significant of what? But Robson seems to have changed his mind. On Nield's tape – recorded during their dinner talk that night at The Luttrell Arms – Robson scoffed at Barrymore's mention of the Greek Key.'

'And now he's linked Petros with it – whatever "it" may be.'

'So I simply must confront Petros – interrogate him – sooner or later.' He caught Monica's dubious glance and looked away. 'I have something else to do urgently. Monica, try and get Jill at Brown's for me. She could be in great danger.'

'Why?' asked Paula.

'She always stays at Brown's – you just told me. They'll know that on Exmoor and I've just heard all three ex-commandos have disappeared. That they may have come to London . . .'

He broke off as Monica signalled she had Jill on the line. He took a deep breath and began talking. She must pack at once, book a room at the Stafford Hotel in St James's Place, pay her bill and take a taxi there. Yes, tonight. At once. He put the phone down and sighed with relief.

'Thank God for a woman who does what you ask without questions.'

'Proves what I said earlier,' Paula remarked and winked at Tweed.

341

He turned to Monica. 'Could you play back that recorded talk I had on the phone from Minehead with Butler? Paula, listen carefully to what he says.'

Paula rested her elbow on her desk, cupped her chin in her hand, concentrated. Butler's cool voice came through loud and clear. As the tape ended Tweed asked his question. 'Anything strike you as interesting – bearing in mind that jumble of clues Masterson sent me in a cigar box from Athens?'

'Nothing. I must be thick. And I'm tired and hungry. So what did I miss?'

'Probably nothing, as you said. It was a wisp of an idea I had. I wanted to see if it hit you in the same way. And I'm taking you out to dinner. Monica has stuffed herself with sandwiches – fortunately.'

'Wild exaggeration,' Monica protested. 'But I have eaten. And why "fortunately"?'

'Because I want to locate Barrymore, Robson and Kearns. May, Robson's sister, let slip he'd gone to London. Start phoning hotels. Those three will be together.'

'What makes you so sure?' Paula asked. 'Before I pop along to the bathroom to fix my face. I feel a wreck.'

'Because those three have stuck together for years – trapped by the past and their fear it may come back. They're haunted men.'

'The two murders forty years ago? You think they were all involved?'

'I doubt that,' Tweed replied. 'Put yourself in their places. I suspect two out of three are wondering which of them committed the murders. I also suspect the guilty man is cleverly manipulating the other two. Listen again sometime to the tape recorded by Nield at The Luttrell Arms. Now, hurry up – I have a raging appetite too!'

He went on talking as he put on his Burberry after Paula had gone to the washroom.

'We'll wait a week or two longer before I fly to Greece – wait and see if anything breaks. Newman and Marler will be pretty active out there. Their rooting around may provoke someone to make a false move, to surface. There's something going on we've missed. I sense it.'

'Take-off time coming,' Monica observed. 'Your usual method. First gathering all the data – which can take ages. Suddenly it will be all action. I'm starting already. What kind of hotel might those ex-commandos be staying at?'

'Not Claridge's or The Ritz.' Tweed had his eyes half-closed as he thought. 'One of them stole the present-day equivalent of a million pounds in diamonds after killing Andreas. So he won't throw it around, show he's loaded. Try the hotels in the medium-priced range. Maybe somewhere in Kensington.'

'You don't ask much, do you?' She was reaching for the yellow pages when Paula reappeared. 'This job could take forever.'

'You may get lucky. We must try,' Tweed said as he opened the door for Paula. 'One more point. From now on we'll codename the murderer Winterton, the ghost who sold those bungalows on Exmoor.'

31

Moscow. General Lucharsky was walking in the park again with his aide, Colonel Volkov. Both men wore civilian clothes and Volkov had to quicken his pace to keep up with the long strides Lucharsky was taking. The sunlight cast thin shadows from the trunks of birch trees. Mothers pushed prams with babies along the lower path as

Lucharsky headed for a dense copse of trees, mounting a curving path.

'You leave for Athens tomorrow,' he reminded Volkov.

'I am fully prepared, Comrade General . . .'

'I should hope so,' Lucharsky snapped as they entered the copse. 'Everything depends on your passing on the verbal orders to Colonel Rykovsky, to Doganis and Anton, the Greeks. Events are moving quickly. I hear the Gorbachev–Reagan summit will take place in Washington. More important, the British Prime Minister has invited the General Secretary to land in England en route for America. A stroke of incredible luck.'

'What is the position now?' Volkov enquired.

'Gorbachev has gone too far. He is signing a treaty in Washington for the withdrawal of intermediate missiles from Europe. If we let him do that he will go on for more disarmament. The Red Army's power will fade instead of growing. And we have some powerful allies. Elements high up in the KGB are worried. They yearn for the return of the days of Brezhnev.'

'So it is something drastic?' Volkov suggested as he pushed aside foliage from his pasty plump face. The path they were following was getting overgrown, was rarely used.

'Gorbachev will be assassinated,' Lucharsky announced in his calm clipped voice. 'The Troika took the decision last night.'

'That will be difficult, and who will take over? What is this Troika?'

'A lot of questions, Comrade. First, you remember that document I handed you yesterday when I was wearing gloves? An incriminating document.'

'Yes.' Volkov felt a chill crawl up his spine despite the humid heat which enveloped Moscow that day.

'I put it in your safe after you had read it. I locked the safe and said I would keep the key. You do recall this?'

Lucharsky asked in a mocking tone which had reduced subordinates to jelly. 'I only check your memory because you had drunk a lot of vodka.'

'At your urging . . .'

'I am a good host, although I stick to mineral water since the new General Secretary's expression of dislike for hard drinking. That document – locked away in your own safe – carries only your fingerprints. You would be shot within a week if that document was placed before the Politburo.'

'Why do you threaten me, Comrade?'

'Just in case you thought you could obtain swift promotion by betraying the Troika which, officially, does not exist.' Lucharsky stopped, faced his companion, gave him a Siberian smile. 'Of course we know you would never dream of betraying us. Now, you asked certain questions. Who will take over from Gorbachev? Answer: Yigor Ligachev, his Number Two in the Politburo. He has openly disagreed with *perestroika* and *glasnost*. He does not know what we plan, but once the seat is vacant he will be compelled to become the new General Secretary.'

'And the Troika?'

'The three-man council of high-ranking Red Army officers who have decided Gorbachev must be removed. I am their liaison with the men in the field who will do the job.'

Which was a lie. No point in letting Volkov know that Lucharsky was the top man among the three generals who made up the Troika.

'But who will carry out the assassination?' pressed Volkov, anxious to know the plan would really work.

Lucharsky folded his arms, swung again on his heels, staring through the foliage which surrounded them. On no account must they be observed. And Volkov's anxieties were transparently clear to the General. He must reassure him for the moment.

'The assassination will apparently be carried out by two Arab fundamentalists. Those fanatics are capable of any

345

mad action. And relations between Moscow and Iran are deteriorating. That way we avoid any danger of a confrontation with the Americans – in case rumours spread it was the work of the CIA. We need the time to establish Ligachev in power, to turn back the clock to Lenin's age. To renew the great military build-up.'

'Arab fundamentalists? That is clever,' Volkov agreed.

'So tomorrow you travel with the instructions inside your head to Athens,' said Lucharsky, resuming his walk over the path encumbered with undergrowth. 'Doganis is controlling the operation – although he doesn't know what is really involved.'

'And what does he think he's getting out of all this?'

'A shrewd question, Comrade. We have hinted at support for a new Communist uprising in Greece. Doganis sees himself as a future Prime Minister. It won't happen that way, of course.'

'But, Comrade, I speak no Greek,' Volkov protested.

'Which is why you are chosen. While at the London Embassy you perfected your English. Doganis speaks the same language.'

'Everything has been thought of,' Volkov remarked, impressed by the efficiency of the planning. Then something struck him. 'I don't see how British security – which is good – will be penetrated? What weapons will be used?'

'No more questions.' Lucharsky increased his pace. 'But I can tell you the special weapons needed are at this moment on their way to their destination. Now I leave you, as last time. Go to your mistress's apartment. That gives you a reason for sneaking into Moscow if you are recognized. Give me five minutes to get back to my car.'

He turned round before leaving the copse, stood looking down at Volkov. 'And don't forget that document plastered with your fingerprints, locked away in your own safe. The KGB would not treat you with kid gloves – not after reading that document. *Bon voyage*, Comrade . . .'

Lucharsky emerged cautiously from the trees, standing to glance round like a man enjoying the warmth of the sunshine. Then he hurried back to his car parked in a deserted side street. It stood outside the block which contained the apartment of a well-known general he knew to be on holiday at a Black Sea resort. A further precaution – just in case a KGB patrol noted down the registration number.

Once inside the Chaika, Lucharsky took a pouch from his pocket, selected a specially designed tool. It took him only five minutes to turn back the odometer fifty kilometres. His chauffeur logged all journeys and recorded the precise distance. There was now no record he had ever made this trip from the barracks.

Everything has been thought of. Volkov didn't know the half of it. Lucharsky had earlier decided that after Gorbachev had been eliminated all his collaborating subordinates would go the same way. Rykovsky and Volkov would die in a helicopter crash over the Caspian Sea. Florakis would be ordered to take out Doganis and the other members of the Greek Key. Then Lucharsky would send someone from Moscow to liquidate Florakis.

Yes, everything had been thought of.

Kalos took the call at police headquarters the following day when Sarris was absent from his office. It came from the chief of security at Athens Airport.

'That you, Kalos? Stefanides here. Your target just arrived. Colonel Volkov. In person.'

'Hold him till I get there. Make out you've received threats against Russian personnel. That you're bringing in a bullet-proof limo from Athens. I'll fix that before I leave. Hold him.'

'Will do. See you . . .'

Kalos followed the limo, driving an unmarked police car

347

himself. It took forty minutes to reach the airport. Damned hot, Kalos thought as they arrived. Late afternoon. Like a furnace. He watched Stefanides escorting a stocky man clad in a pale grey lightweight suit to the limo. He had thick black hair, was clean-shaven, a pair of large rimless glasses very like those Gorbachev wore. In many ways he was like a pocket version of the General Secretary. And his face was pasty and plump – making him stand out as a new arrival. An easy man to follow.

Kalos watched a porter dump two suitcases in the boot, started his own engine as the boot was slammed shut. The limo glided away along the main road into Athens. Kalos followed.

Destination: the Soviet Embassy. As Kalos had expected. He parked the Saab behind another car, settled down to wait. Kalos was good at waiting. He watched Volkov disappear inside the building, followed by the chauffeur carrying the bags. Ages would now pass while Volkov conferred with Colonel Rykovsky.

Kalos radioed in to his assistant at police headquarters that he was on surveillance, that it might take all night. There was no request for information as to where he was. Surveillance meant secrecy. And he didn't want Sarris to know what he was up to. Yet.

Twenty minutes later Kalos had a surprise. Two men emerged and started walking down the street towards him on the far side. Volkov had changed into a linen suit, wore a straw hat. The glasses and the walk confirmed to Kalos it was Volkov. They were smarter than he'd anticipated. Never underestimate the enemy: Sarris' favourite maxim.

The second man, also short but slimmer, wore a similar linen suit and a peaked cap favoured by German students. A beak of a nose with a dark smear of a moustache, neatly

348

trimmed, a man who made quick gestures with his hands. Colonel Rykovsky.

They hailed a passing taxi, climbed inside. Kalos waited until he saw the taxi moving in his wing mirror, did an illegal U-turn, tracked the taxi. In Omonia Square they paid off the taxi, gazed into a department store's windows. Not normal behaviour. Kalos felt a glow of satisfaction as he pulled into a parking slot which a woman had just vacated.

The two Russians moved slowly along the pavement, stopping to stare inside another window. Rykovsky glanced over his shoulder, scanning the street. Kalos was slumped behind the wheel, eyes almost closed. A taxi stopped, dropped a fare and both Russians moved.

As Volkov climbed into the rear Rykovsky gave the driver his instructions and followed his companion. The taxi pulled out into a gap in the traffic. Kalos grinned to himself as he turned out, one vehicle behind the taxi. Who were they going to meet so secretly was the $60,000 question.

Inside ten minutes the taxi entered the Plaka, driving slowly, wending its way amid the labyrinth of twisting streets. The two Russians alighted outside a taverna. *Papadedes.* That made sense, Kalos thought, as he watched the couple disappear up a staircase alongside the taverna. Papa made a nice income on the side out of that first-floor room sealed off from the taverna.

He rented it out at exorbitant prices to Athenian businessmen who took their mistresses there. The room was nicely furnished, including one of those sofas you could convert into a bed. Papa also supplied his clients with drinks – at only four times the price charged in the taverna.

Kalos turned into a side street, parked his car on the one-man wide pavement and the cobbled street. He felt in his pocket. Yes, he had the compact Voigtlander camera he always carried. He got out, took up a position in a doorway where he could see the staircase entrance.

Something serious was going on. Why couldn't they have had their meeting inside the Soviet Embassy? That puzzled Kalos. And he was damn sure Volkov had disguised himself. OK, it was pretty warm. And the Russian had just flown in from Moscow. But that straw hat had been well pulled down over his face – and they'd spent very little time outside.

He was about to light a cigarette when he stiffened, reached for his camera, the unlit cigarette clamped between his lips. A tall heavily built figure was strolling towards the taverna. The Fat Man. An open-necked shirt, clothes hanging loosely from his body. Doganis. Senior member of the committee that controlled the Greek Key.

Kalos raised his camera, cupped inside his hand, waited. Doganis stopped suddenly, turned on the pavement, a woman collided with his huge bulk. He ignored her as he glanced down the street the way he'd come. Then he plodded on in his large trainer shoes, paused again to look back in front of the staircase entrance as though not sure of his whereabouts. Kalos took three quick shots as the Greek swivelled his outsize head. Full-face, profile – and behind him the name over the taverna. Then Doganis vanished. He'd slipped up the staircase towards the room where the Russians had gone. For a large man he moved with great agility.

Kalos pocketed the camera and frowned. He was disturbed. This looked even more serious than he'd suspected.

Inside the expensively furnished room Doganis stood gazing at the two Russians who sat at a highly polished English antique round table. A tray – brought up by a waiter from the taverna before anyone had arrived – stood on the table.

350

Two bottles of vodka, three cut glasses. Both men had a glass in front of them.

Doganis nodded to himself. Free of the anti-alcohol restrictions imposed by Gorbachev, they were indulging themselves. The slim supercilious Colonel Rykovsky stood up to make introductions. Doganis shook hands with Volkov, squeezing his hand in a vice-like grip. The Russian had trouble avoiding grimacing at the pressure.

'Vodka?' Rykovsky offered.

Doganis shook his head, lowered his bulk into the third chair at the table. He wanted a clear head dealing with these goddamn Russians who had let down Greece in 1946 during the Civil War: they had not supplied the weapons needed. Later the US President, Truman, had sent a military mission, arms by the ton. That was what had defeated them. Rykovsky remained on his feet, downed the full glass of vodka, and explained.

'I am leaving you now with Colonel Volkov,' he continued, speaking in English. 'He has a long message to give you. It must be transmitted by Florakis to Jupiter tonight. The first part, that is. The signal is so long it has to be divided into three parts – sent on three successive nights. You have a good memory?'

'You know I have,' Doganis growled, his large paws clasped on the table-top. 'Get on with it.'

'Volkov will tell you where one section ends, the next begins. When he has passed on the complete message Volkov will leave. Give him five minutes. Then go yourself, drive at once down to Cape Sounion. Florakis will be expecting you. I have already phoned him. I am now returning to the Embassy to call him and confirm you are coming. He will wait for you at that site where they are constructing a new hotel complex. You know it?'

'I do.'

'They have stopped work on it for the moment. Something to do with waiting for fresh materials.' Rykovsky waved an elegant hand. 'The main point is the complex is deserted. When you get back to Athens, call me at the Embassy. Use your normal codename. Simply tell me you have found a further supply of mineral water – despite the shortage owing to this infernal heatwave. Remember, all calls are monitored, recorded . . .'

'I know that.'

'And get down to Cape Sounion as soon as you can. Florakis will need time to code the message. Understood?'

'Yes.'

Rykovsky told Volkov he would see him back at the Embassy later. He was leaving when he turned back.

'Doganis, you do have transport to drive to Sounion?'

'My car is parked a quarter of a mile away. I know what I am doing.'

Rykovsky nodded, bit his lip, decided to say no more. The Greeks were a touchy lot. He was glad to get out of the room. Doganis was glad to see him go. He turned to Volkov. 'I am listening.'

The stocky Volkov knocked back another glass of vodka, saw the Greek's expression and refrained from refilling his glass.

'This is the message. I will say it slowly. There is a lot to remember. The first part concerns furniture vans . . .'

Kalos took two photographs of Rykovsky as he hovered at the exit from the staircase, looking to left and right. The Russian then walked briskly away to the left. Doubtless searching for a taxi. In his notebook Kalos noted down the precise time, as he had done when Doganis had arrived.

He was growing more puzzled. That left the gross pig, Doganis, upstairs with the new arrival to Athens, Volkov. Most peculiar. It was half an hour later before a second figure appeared. Volkov. He walked straight into the street in the same direction, straw hat rammed down concealing

352

the upper half of his face. He stopped suddenly, lifted the hat as he stared round. Kalos took two more shots, waited until Volkov had disappeared, noted down the time. He had been precisely thirty minutes alone with Doganis. Most mysterious.

Unless he had been passing detailed instructions to Doganis – but why had Rykovsky not remained present? My God, Kalos was thinking: maybe Moscow doesn't even trust Rykovsky to hear what Volkov was saying. The cell system – carried to these lengths! The instructions must be incredibly secret.

Five minutes later, exactly, Doganis stood at the exit, lounging against the side, lighting a cigarette, scanning the street. A real professional, the overweight slug. Kalos risked it, took another photograph. Without a glance in his direction, Doganis walked off.

Kalos memorized the time, ran to his car, backed it into the main street, crawled after Doganis. That had been a difficult decision Kalos had wrestled with. Who to follow? Since they had met so furtively, he'd decided the Russians would probably return to the Embassy. You're my meat, he thought as he trailed after Doganis.

Kalos found he could drop back well behind his target. Among the tourists and locals crowding the Plaka Doganis loomed up among the other heads like a bear lumbering forward. He had parked his battered old Renault on an open stretch of ground. Kalos waited until he had eased his bulk behind the wheel and started moving. Then he followed him.

'Repeat the whole message back to me. Indicate where one section stops, another begins,' said Doganis.

'Get stuffed. I've memorized it perfectly,' Florakis snapped.

'Prove it.'

'I said get stuffed . . .'

The two men sat in the front seats of Doganis' Renault parked in the shade thrown by the skeletal structure of the new hotel complex. Florakis, wearing his shepherd's garb, cast a sneering glance at the bloated jelly beside him, reached for the door handle.

'I said prove it,' Doganis said in a quiet voice. 'That comes from the top. I have to tell them you've really grasped the message.'

'Play with yourself, you overblown melon . . .'

Doganis grasped Florakis by his arm below the elbow. He squeezed as Florakis swore and struggled to get free. There was a brief tussle, then Florakis' face twisted in agony. He was staggered by the strength of that fat man who he'd imagined was soft as a jelly. Doganis, with no expression, began to bend the arm. Florakis stifled a scream of pain.

'Now, let's try again, shall we?' Doganis suggested, releasing his grip.

'You stupid bastard,' railed Florakis. 'There's no feeling in my arm. And I have to tap out your bloody signal . . .'

'You're right-handed,' Doganis said mildly, gazing out of the window where an opening in the building structure framed the sizzling blue of the sea. 'I remembered that when I twisted your left arm. In any case, you'll be OK by nightfall when you do the job. Going to repeat the message? Word by word?'

'Blast you! Yes . . .' Florakis took a hold of himself, let his rage evaporate, then began reciting carefully.

'That's pretty good,' Doganis said fifteen minutes later. 'One more thing before you ride your donkey back to that cesspit you call a farm.'

'What's that?' Florakis asked sullenly.

'In future don't ever again forget I'm the boss. Now push off. I'll give you ten minutes to get clear before I drive back to Athens . . .'

354

Behind a boulder a short distance up the arid hillside under the scorching sun Kalos was watching. He peered through the field glasses he'd taken from his glove compartment. He'd followed Doganis all the way from Athens, keeping well back when he realized his quarry was taking the coast road.

He'd crested a hill with a clear view of the Temple of Poseidon atop Cape Sounion when he saw the Renault swing off the road behind the building site. Immediately he'd turned off the main road himself, jouncing over the rough ground into one of the many gulches which ended near the coastal highway. Parking his car well inside the gulch, he had climbed high enough to stare down at the site.

His glasses had brought up clearly the two men seated inside the stationary car. Kalos had recognized Florakis and he recalled finding the fingerprints which exposed Florakis' real identity. Oleg Savinkov: The Russian, The Executioner of the Civil War.

He waited until Doganis had driven over the crest on his way back towards Athens, then drove after him. He didn't expect to discover any new twist but he followed Doganis all the way back to the city. His eyes narrowed as he grasped that Doganis was heading back into the Plaka. He was even more startled when Doganis parked his car on the same open space and got out, then checked his watch and waited, lighting a cheroot. Kalos parked illegally in a one-way street and waited.

Thirty minutes passed before Doganis made his way on foot to the same street where he had arrived earlier in the day. Kalos guessed his destination was the room over Papadedes taverna and watched him disappear inside the entrance to the staircase.

Kalos parked his own vehicle in the side street he had used before. Standing in the doorway, he saw Colonel Volkov arrive five minutes later. He noted down the time below his record of Doganis' entering the building.

Very curious. This meeting was taking place without the presence of Rykovsky. He blinked and only took his camera out in time when a third figure walked down the street, paused by the entrance, glanced confidently around and vanished inside.

He wrote down the arrival time of Anton Gavalas. What the hell was going on?

32

'This is political dynamite,' Sarris snapped, staring at his assistant. He waved the file containing Kalos' report. 'We have to bury it. You want us both to lose our jobs?'

Kalos ran a hand over his stubble of hair, unperturbed by his chief's outburst. He clasped his hands and spoke with great deliberation, gazing out of the window where night was falling over Mount Lycabettus.

'Point One. We know Doganis is the most powerful figure on the so-called committee running the Greek Key. An organization of fanatical Communists which has lain fallow for a long time. In that file there is photographic proof that Doganis met with Colonel Rykovsky and the new man from Moscow, Colonel Volkov . . .'

'That's what I'm talking about,' Sarris protested. 'Our government hopes for closer relations with Russia now Gorbachev has proclaimed his policy of *glasnost* . . .'

'These people are not *glasnost*,' Kalos interjected in the same calm tone. 'They are hardliners – anti-Gorbachev. That swine, Pavelic the Croat, said as much to me when I was in Belgrade. He also let drop the name General Lucharsky – who visited us last year as Colonel Gerasimov of the GRU. I stole his photograph from Pavelic's file when he was dead drunk. I followed him to the Hilton Hotel where he interviewed Florakis.'

'And now you've put Lucharsky in your report! I hadn't finished when you interrupted me. I don't make our government's policy. I think they may be a bit over-hopeful . . .'

'To the point of idiocy,' Kalos commented.

'Keep quiet. Our government hopes for more trade with Moscow. Maybe even sophisticated military equipment to make our army stronger than the Turks . . .'

'It won't happen. Let me go on,' persisted Kalos. 'Point Two. Rykovsky leaves Doganis alone with Volkov – which suggests even he is not permitted to hear some highly secret message from Moscow – from Lucharsky, maybe. Point Three. After that meeting I follow Doganis. To where? Another subversive rendezvous – this time with Oleg Savinkov, alias Florakis. Peter, this is a conspiracy I have uncovered.'

'That's an assumption . . .'

'And there is more – also backed up with photographic evidence in that file. Doganis drives back to Athens, to the same rendezvous in the Plaka. What happens now? Colonel Volkov arrives on his own – again Rykovsky is not privy to this clandestine meeting. Who else arrives? Anton Gavalas. Where does he fit in? He's supposed to be helping his crazy father – to locate the man who committed two murders over forty years ago. I repeat, it is a deadly conspiracy.'

'And I repeat I cannot show this to the Minister. He will blow his top.' Sarris softened his tone. 'Kalos, you know I'm right. If I thought there was the slightest chance the Minister would let us follow this up I'd hand him the file.'

'You're the boss.'

Kalos sat, motionless, still gazing out of the window. He

knew Sarris had judged the situation correctly. He was frustrated beyond belief. Sarris rose from behind his desk, took the report out of the file, separated the photographs.

'Kalos, I'm sorry about this. It really is to protect you as well as me.'

He went over to the shredding machine. Kalos watched impassively as Sarris fed in the photographs, then the typed sheets Kalos had produced on his own typewriter. A mess of shredded fragments showered into the plastic bag. The job done, Sarris sat behind his desk.

'I had no choice. Forgive me.'

'You are ordering me to cease my investigations?'

Sarris chewed his lower lip. 'I don't recall saying that. And you have an excellent memory. Just be careful, for God's sake. For ours . . .'

Kalos nodded, left the room and went back to his own office. He locked the door, went to his desk, unlocked a lower drawer and took out the duplicate file of the report Sarris had destroyed. There were also copies of the photographs: Kalos had developed them himself in his own darkroom in his apartment on the edge of the Plaka.

With the file tucked under his arm, he crouched down and turned the numbered combination on the door of his safe. Opening it, he used a screwdriver to prise open the slim secret drawer at the bottom. Dropping the file inside, he closed the drawer, shut the safe, spun the combination lock.

As he straightened up he thought how curious it was that Sarris had not asked him for the negatives: Sarris, who never missed a trick.

After witnessing the meeting between Doganis and Anton Gavalas, Kalos had again been faced with a difficult decision. Which of the two men to follow? They had left the building separately: Doganis had emerged first. Kalos let him go.

Ten minutes later Anton had appeared. Kalos had followed him. He was surprised when his quarry took a taxi which dropped him outside the Astir Palace Hotel on Sofias Avenue, only a short distance from the Grande Bretagne.

There was nothing else he could do about that so he returned to present his report to Sarris.

Inside his room Anton sat on the bed and dialled the number of Petros' farm in Devil's Valley. He had to wait some time before they made the connection with that remote area.

'Anton here . . .'

'You have found Christina?' growled Petros.

'Found her and lost her . . .' Anton explained briefly his experience earlier that day at the Hilton. He expected Petros to explode. Instead the old man said he needed a minute to think. Anton jumped in quickly.

'Isn't it time I returned to England? We should know what the commando killers are doing on Exmoor. This time I may find out whether all three were guilty – or whether it was only one of them.' He went on talking quickly. 'I have ideas for harassing them. As I told you, they already live in terror. They've barricaded themselves in their homes like men scared witless.'

'But we must find Christina . . .'

'Let those lazy sons-of-bitches Dimitrios and Constantine come back to Athens. She's here somewhere. All the idiots have to do is to bribe cleaning women, show them her photograph. Not approach the chief receptionist like that cretin, Dimitrios, did. Which is more important?' he pressed on. 'Tracking down Christina or tracking down the killer of your sons? I could be in England in a few days. This time I will be more aggressive.'

The word 'aggressive' decided Petros. He liked the sound of that. It appealed to his temperament. It was how he went about problems.

'Very well,' he said. 'When will you leave? You have plenty of clothes?'

'Probably tomorrow. And I packed a case before I came to Athens. In any case, I have money. Keep Dimitrios and Constantine down there for two days, then kick their asses, send them, tell them they can't come back until they've found her.'

Splendid, Petros thought. Anton was becoming more like himself every day. Very aggressive.

'You can use the special route to England you mentioned?'

'Absolutely.' Anton was standing up now, his voice vibrant with confidence. 'Don't worry if I'm away for a while. This time the job must be done . . .'

Anton put down the phone, realized he was sweating profusely. It wasn't the heat – although the room felt like an oven. He had managed to persuade Petros, the old fool, to agree. Now he was ready to carry out the orders Volkov had passed to him.

Anton was pleased so much responsibility had been heaped on him. It augured well for the future. He saw a top Cabinet post in a Greek Communist government in his grasp. Who knew? Maybe one day he would be Prime Minister.

Extracting a Swissair timetable from his case, he sat down, checked flight times. Flight SR 303 left Athens at 5 p.m., arrived at Zurich 6.45 p.m., local time. He needed a late flight: there was some more work to do before he left Athens in the morning. He turned the pages.

From Zurich another non-stop flight, SR 690, departed Zurich at 12.10 p.m., reaching Lisbon in Portugal at 1.55 p.m. Again local times. That meant spending only one night in Zurich. He always stayed at top hotels: with luck he'd find some willing married woman on her own to spend the night with.

Anton was careful with women. The married ones, away

from their husbands and out for a fling, were safest. No comebacks. No risk of some annoying entanglement. He checked the dates in his diary. His memory had served him well.

The freighter, *Oporto*, was not due to sail for several days. Then it would leave Portugal with its holds full of cork, bound for the Somerset port of Watchet. Later it would return with a load of wastepaper.

Plenty of time to get in touch with the skipper, Gomez. To warn him this time there would be a special cargo as well as himself. And to call Jupiter at the agreed time to have someone ready for the rendezvous at sea. The phone number, he felt sure, was a public phone booth. Most important of all, time for him to contact the arms dealer in Lisbon, to collect from him the special weapons which would go aboard the *Oporto*.

Anton called room service. 'Send me up a double Scotch. No ice. No lemon. Plus a bottle of mineral water.'

He sat down, tired from the concentration. Now the only remaining task was to contact Professor Seton-Charles at his seminar at the Hilton in the morning. He'd go along as a student. Pass on the instruction Volkov had given him for the Professor.

33

Seton-Charles had held three seminars for Greek students over a period of two weeks. Newman and Marler had taken it in turns to monitor his movements. The seminars were held in a conference room inside the Hilton. They were advertised on a board in the vast lobby, giving the whole two-week programme. Subject: The Greek Civil War, 1946–1949.

The tension was rising between Newman and Marler. Security on Christina had been tightened up to the hilt: they had learned from their experience at the Hilton. Well-disguised, a scarf concealing her hair and wearing her outsize tinted glasses, she had registered as Mrs Irene Charles at the Grande Bretagne.

Booked into a suite, she stayed there. All meals were sent up by room service. Newman kept her supplied with books and magazines. 'This is marvellous, Bob,' she told him one day. 'The first real rest I've had in years – and I'm reading like mad . . .'

To keep up their watch on Seton-Charles, Newman and Marler had very little sleep. They exchanged surveillance duty at the Hilton; one staying with Christina, the other eating and keeping an eye open at the Hilton. Marler complained after a few days of this ritual.

'I feel locked in. I'd like to be outside, trying to find more data on what happened to Harry Masterson. Maybe take a trip to Cape Sounion, see what's going on down there.'

'Feeling the heat?' Newman grinned as he used a sodden handkerchief to mop his neck.

'No. You're the one who can't stand it. Doesn't affect me.'

'I can stand the waiting better than you can,' Newman told him. 'We're doing what Tweed asked. Checking on Seton-Charles and guarding Christina.'

'And as far as we can tell the Professor hasn't gone outside the Hilton. Which is pretty weird. Maybe he uses the phone in his room.'

'Not for any calls we'd want to know about. He'll know they'd go through the hotel switchboard.'

'So maybe he sneaks out in the middle of the night.'

'I have a feeling any message will be smuggled to him

by someone attending one of those seminars. Probably he doesn't like the heat. He looks the type. I saw him go outside once and he came straight in again, glad to return to the air-conditioning. Patience, Marler.'

'You know where you can stuff that. As for waiting, you spent your life waiting as a foreign correspondent. Mostly holding up bars, from what I've heard.'

'Which shows your ignorance,' Newman rapped back. 'I was moving about, searching for fresh contacts. Time you got back to the Hilton. Don't fall asleep . . .'

'Up yours, chum.'

They had been drinking mineral water at the Grande Bretagne bar. It was eleven at night: Newman had come back sometime after he'd seen Seton-Charles go up to bed. He mopped his sticky hands when Marler left. It was going to be another torrid night.

They had booked two rooms at the Hilton. Whoever was on duty stayed up until he was pretty sure Seton-Charles had retired for the night. He then waited another two hours, sitting in the lobby. Just on the off-chance S-C reappeared. Then he went to his room, set the alarm for five o'clock. After taking a shower, he put out his outfit to wear in the morning. Which meant the man on duty fell into bed at about 2 a.m. For three hours of sleep. No wonder the relationship – never good at the best of times – was growing strained.

It was Newman who spotted Anton Gavalas attending the final seminar eleven days later.

Christina had shown him a group photograph. Petros flanked by his family at the farm, occupying the central position, sitting on the veranda.

'Looking like God Almighty,' Christina had remarked venomously. 'Dimitrios and Constantine are there – on either side. As you see, I'm relegated to the outside – the proper position for a female. And that . . .' She had pointed to a slim man standing with his hand on Petros'

363

shoulder. '. . . is Anton. Petros' favourite, the smooth bastard.'

Newman borrowed the photograph. He showed it to Marler at the first opportunity, pointing out Anton.

'Cocky-looking sod,' was Marler's only comment.

Eleven days later Newman was 'on duty' at the Hilton. He had eaten breakfast in the ground-floor restaurant, sitting four tables away from Seton-Charles who was looking limp from the heatwave.

Now he sat in the lobby on a couch close to the entrance to the conference room where the third and final seminar was taking place in half an hour's time. Newman wore a short-sleeved shirt, open-necked, a pair of loud check slacks. He was smoking a cigar, reading the *New York Times*. He looked like one of the many American tourists staying at the hotel.

Students – men and girls – began arriving, standing round, chatting. Age range: sixteen to twenty-five, Newman estimated. Some carried briefcases, others clutched files. Newman stretched out his legs, crossed them at the ankles. He wore green socks decorated with white diamonds, a pair of loafers.

Seton-Charles arrived in his shirt-sleeves, a pair of creaseless powder-blue slacks. Newman puffed at his cigar, glanced up as he turned to a fresh page. For a moment he glanced at the Professor, who looked down at him. Behind the rimless glasses perched on his Roman nose eyes as hard as diamonds skimmed over the seated man. Newman had a shock.

This was the first time they had looked straight at each other. The first time Newman had noticed those eyes. You're a cold-blooded bastard, he thought.

Then Seton-Charles was leading the students inside the conference room. Like a shepherd leading lambs to the slaughter. Why had that thought entered Newman's mind? He settled down, then glanced up again as a latecomer arrived, hurrying inside the conference room. Newman froze inside as the slim, smartly dressed man passed him. Anton Gavalas . . .

He stood up and wandered to a seat on the far side of the lobby. Startled as he was by Anton's appearance, Newman still noticed what else was going on.

A moment after the Greek had disappeared he observed a man who had been lingering outside the entrance come into the hotel. A small stocky man who reminded him of a dormouse. The newcomer also took a seat against the wall, settled himself, crossed his fat legs and began reading a Greek newspaper.

Newman forgot about him as he sat down to wait. He'd have given a lot to be an invisible witness to what was happening inside the conference room.

When Anton walked into the seminar the students were sitting down in the rows of chairs facing the dais where the Professor stood behind a table, arranging papers in neat piles. He paused, Seton-Charles looked up, Anton walked across the room and mounted the dais.

'Good morning,' he whispered. 'Jupiter has sent me with information . . .'

He had been going to say 'instructions', but then he looked at the eyes behind the rimless glasses. No sign of recognition. Ice-cold, they seemed to assess him at a glance. Anton began to wonder how high up in the power structure this man might be.

'Take a seat in the back row. Record a few things in this notebook. Make sure you're still here when the last student has left.'

The back row was empty. Anton sat down, perched the notebook he had been given on his knee, took out his

365

gold Parker pen and listened as Seton-Charles began to lecture.

Seton-Charles was a natural orator, reminding Anton of newsreels he'd seen of Hitler. He started slowly, then worked himself up to a pitch of fanaticism, waving his arms. When he stopped the students applauded vigorously, then filed out. Anton pretended to make more notes until they were alone.

He stood up, approached Seton-Charles, who was gathering up his papers and stuffing them into a file. Again Anton mounted the dais. The Professor's hair was dishevelled from his oration and he was sweating profusely from his efforts and the heat.

'Yes?' he said without looking up.

Anton felt it was important to address this man respectfully. 'You are requested to catch Swissair flight 303 today to fly to Zurich. It departs at 5 p.m. Then tomorrow you fly on to London and return to Exmoor. That is the message.'

'That means they have managed it,' Seton-Charles said, half to himself.

He looked up and stared at Anton as though photographing his appearance on his memory. Anton felt he dare not ask what they had managed, who they were.

'So you are not surprised, I shall be on the same flight,' he explained.

'I shan't even notice you. Hadn't you better go now? At once . . .'

Anton flushed at the tone of curt dismissal. Without another word he left the room. His feelings were a mixture of fury and fear.

In the lobby Newman watched Anton leave. He wished he could have followed him. But his task was to keep up the watch on Seton-Charles. Tweed had made that very clear.

366

Newman observed the quick short steps Anton took as he crossed the marble floor and left the hotel.

He lowered his eyes to his newspaper when out of the corner of his eye he saw movement. The dormouse-like man had folded his newspaper, shoved it inside his pocket and was also leaving. It looked very much as though he had Anton Gavalas under surveillance.

Outside the Hilton Anton climbed into a cab, slammed the door. Kalos ran to his Saab parked a few yards away and dived behind the wheel after unlocking the door with one deft movement.

He followed the taxi into the traffic, his bead-like little eyes gleaming with interest. The route was back along Sofias Avenue, past the British Embassy, and round Syntagma Square. The taxi returned to the opposite side of Sofias and Anton paid the driver, disappearing inside the Astir Palace Hotel. The same place where Kalos had followed Anton after his rendezvous at Papadedes.

Several days earlier Kalos had decided a piece was missing from his report. He had phoned the Astir Palace and obtained confirmation that Anton *was* registered at that hotel. He could hardly use a false name: he was too well known in Athens.

Since then Kalos had endured a long vigil patiently. Anton had stayed inside day and night – until this morning. Now a fresh link was established – of a sort. Anton had a connection with one of the students attending the seminars; maybe even with the crazy-looking Professor Seton-Charles. The latter seemed unlikely.

Parking his car, Kalos wandered into the vestibule of the modern-looking hotel, a black glass block which did not fit in with the more traditional surrounding architecture. He arrived in time to hear Anton giving the receptionist instructions in Greek.

'I shall want my bill ready immediately after lunch. Then

you must arrange a car to get me to the airport by 3.30 p.m. The car must not be late.'

'Of course not, Mr Gavalas,' the receptionist assured him. 'I will deal with everything myself . . .'

He tailed off. His guest had walked away, was heading for the elevators. Kalos pursed his lips, wondering where Anton was flying to. Well, he would be there in good time to find that out.

In his room Anton called room service, ordered a large Scotch. The plane was leaving at 5 p.m. but he had deliberately arranged to arrive at the airport very early. The last thing he wanted was to bump into Seton-Charles.

Anton, a ruthless, hard man, had met some tough characters during his wanderings as a youth. But there was something about the Professor which disturbed him. The man reminded him of a cobra.

In the late afternoon Newman was driving a hired car towards the airport. He had seen Seton-Charles collect a travel folder from the reception desk in mid-morning. The Professor had returned to his room, reappearing for lunch. When he stepped out of the elevator he was carrying a case which he deposited with reception.

Newman had phoned Marler, phrasing his message carefully over the hotel phone. 'I'm tied up. Urgent business suddenly cropped up. Be with you this evening. Can you hang on there?'

'My pleasure . . .'

Arriving at the airport, Newman parked two vehicles behind the taxi Seton-Charles was travelling in. He stood behind him in the queue for checking in, heard the Professor being booked aboard Swissair flight 303 to Zurich, left the queue. Tweed must be informed at once.

Leaning against a wall, Kalos watched, took a quick picture of Newman. Earlier he had done the same thing

368

when Anton arrived. Anton was flying to Zurich. Why? He waited until the queue had evaporated, approached the check-in girl.

'That Englishman with the thinning brown hair, rimless glasses. Where is he flying to?'

'I'm afraid we can't give out information . . .'

Kalos placed his police identity card in front of her, waited.

'Oh, I suppose that's different.' She hesitated, Kalos waited.

'He's a Professor Seton-Charles,' she said. 'First-class seat on Swissair flight 303. Departs 5 p.m., arrives Zurich 6.45 p.m.'

'Thank you,' said Kalos.

He thought about what he had learned as he drove back to police headquarters. Anton had arrived three-quarters of an hour ahead of Seton-Charles. A trick. Kalos was certain the two men were collaborators: they had taken the precaution of not appearing to know each other. They'd sit in different sections of the plane to keep up the masquerade. But Anton had attended the Professor's seminar.

He tapped his fingers on the wheel as he waited at a red traffic light. What the hell could he do now to find out where they had gone? Then he had an idea. Switzerland . . .

Arriving in his office, Kalos locked the door before he made the call to Berne, capital of Switzerland – and headquarters of the Federal Police. He was lucky. Arthur Beck, chief of the organization, was in his office.

Kalos spoke tersely, explained what had happened, gave details of the flight. He described both Anton and Seton-Charles. Could Beck help?

'Something to do with drugs?' Beck enquired, still speaking in English.

'Could be,' Kalos replied non-committally.

'I'll go myself,' Beck decided. 'Anything to help Peter Sarris. I have time to get a chopper from the local airport, Belp, fly to Kloten Airport outside Zurich. I'll be there to watch the passengers disembarking. Which is most important?'

'Anton,' Kalos said after a moment's thought. 'Maybe you will call me back. Sarris is up to his ears.'

'Consider it done,' Beck replied and broke the connection.

Kalos put down the phone. Sarris had no idea what he'd started, and Kalos had no intention of letting him know. If it all blew up in his face, Sarris could disclaim all knowledge of what his assistant had been up to. As he began to record the latest details in his secret file Kalos was worried. Had he been right to give Beck priority in watching Anton?

34

'Newman here, speaking on the Embassy phone. Can you hear me?'

'Very clearly, Bob,' Tweed assured him. 'What's happened?'

'Seton-Charles is on his way back to England. At least, I assume he is . . .' He gave an account of his recent discoveries, including the appearance of Anton.

'You're probably right,' Tweed agreed. 'He's a devious so-and-so. Remember how he tried to make sure he wasn't followed to London Airport on his way out. My guess is he'll catch another flight back here tomorrow. At least that means you only have to guard Christina. One of you can start poking around again. How are you and Marler getting on?'

'Like two long-lost brothers.' He nearly added, 'who hate the sight of each other,' but kept his mouth shut. 'First I'm going to have another talk with Christina about Anton. Do you really need both of us to stay on in this inferno?'

'Yes. If you can stand the heat.' Tweed paused. 'You see, when the right moment arrives I'm flying out there. I may need back-up. I must grill that scoundrel, Petros.'

'Be it on your own head. He's got armed shepherds patrolling the whole area.'

'We'll cope. Keep in touch . . .'

Tweed sat back and looked at Monica and Paula. 'One bit of good news. Anton still seems to be floating round Athens. I didn't like the idea of that Greek on the prowl over here. And Seton-Charles is probably on his way back to Exmoor. I sense things are hotting up. Monica, warn Butler at Porlock Weir about the Professor possibly returning. Maybe at long last we're getting somewhere.'

The grim news reached them the following day.

In her room at the Stafford Hotel Jill Kearns checked herself in the mirror. Her bedside clock registered 6.25 a.m. She eyed herself critically, fiddled with her single golden plait. That would have to do. And how many people would be about at this hour? Not the point, she thought: never appear in public except at your best.

She was wearing a form-fitting pale green sweater, a white pleated skirt and flat-heeled shoes. Just the outfit for her early morning walk before breakfast.

A girl of firm routines, she always walked on the moor every morning before breakfast. Always left the house at precisely 6.30 a.m. Stuart, for some unknown reason, found her routine irritating. 'Should be in the bloody Army,' he'd told her. He never accompanied her; at least he hadn't for the last few years.

She said 'Good morning' to the hall porter and went out of the hotel, turning left into St James's Place. No one else about, thank God. It was a fresh morning, was going to be one of those rare fine days with the sun shining and the warmth on your face.

Reaching the end of the deserted street, she came out into St James's Street. Again no one in sight. Only a Jaguar parked by the kerb a score of yards further down the street, facing her way, the engine ticking over. She took a deep breath and made for the pedestrian crossing.

She was half-way across it when she heard the Jag coming. It had started moving the moment she stepped off the pavement. She glanced to her right, then froze in horror. The car was driving straight at her.

She began to run, taking a diagonal course to cross the whole street. Glancing again over her shoulder as she reached a point just midway across where a side street opposite entered from St James's Square, she had a glimpse of the driver behind the tinted glass.

He wore a chauffeur's cap pulled well down over his head and a pair of tinted goggles like motorbike riders affected. She ran faster, thanking her lucky stars she was wearing her flat-heeled shoes. The Jag was turning now, coming at tremendous speed.

The radiator slammed into her, lifted her whole body and threw it against the railings of a basement area on the far side of the street. She twisted under the immense impact. Then her lifeless body lay sagged against the railings. Blood from her smashed jaw flowed down over her green sweater, spreading like a lake.

The Jaguar picked up more speed, vanished in the distance as it turned into St James's Square. Suddenly it was very quiet.

35

'You're not going to like this.' Monica, who had rushed into Tweed's office, paused for breath. In her hands she clutched a copy of the *Evening Standard*.

'You're back early from lunch,' said Tweed as Paula jerked her head up from the file she was studying.

'It's awful,' Monica went on, sinking into her seat. 'I know how you liked her.'

'What is it?' Tweed asked, very alert.

'It's in the stop press. A Mrs Stuart Kearns, staying at the Stafford Hotel, was killed by a hit-and-run driver early this morning.'

'Show me.' Tweed's tone was bleak. He read the item, looked at Monica. 'Let's get this in the right sequence. Which hotel did you track those three down to? Something like a theatre.'

'Barrymore, Kearns and Robson are staying at the Lyceum Hotel. A modest place just off the Strand, close to Trafalgar Square.'

'And it says here the so-called accident occurred in St James's Street. Not very far from the Lyceum. Phone up the place. I want to know if they're still there.'

He stood up, shoved his hands inside his jacket pockets, began pacing up and down close to the window, his brow furrowed.

'They've checked out,' Monica told him as she put down the phone. 'All three left mid-morning. No forwarding address.'

'Get Chief Superintendent Walton of Special Branch. Urgently.'

'Why did you say "so-called accident"?' enquired Paula.

'Because I don't believe it. Jill Kearns had all her marbles. That newspaper item says it happened before seven in the morning. How much traffic is about at that hour?'

He broke off to take the call. 'That you, Bill? Tweed here.'

'You on scrambler? Good.' Walton's voice was its normal buoyant tone. 'Are you still forging my Special Branch identity cards in that Engine Room? I don't know why I let you get away with it.'

'You supplied the original model for copying,' Tweed reminded him. 'We agreed total secrecy could only be maintained if we did the job. And if anyone queries one they'll be put through to you.'

'Someone has queried one,' Walton warned him. 'Recently. A Colonel Barrymore. I told him you belonged to my department, that he'd better answer any questions you put to him. Very supercilious, he was. Plummy-voiced type. Now, what can I do for you?'

'Early this morning a Mrs Stuart Kearns, staying at the Stafford Hotel, was killed by an alleged hit-and-run driver. There's a stop press in the *Standard*. I think it was murder. I'm going to give you details of three possible suspects. They were staying last night at the Lyceum Hotel off the Strand. I'd like you to phone Chief Inspector Jarvis of Homicide at the Yard. Warn him, but don't mention me.'

'Why not?' Walton enquired. 'You and Bernard were pals during your old days at the Yard.'

'Because I need to maintain a low profile. Here are the details, including the addresses of the three men. Incidentally, they've left the Lyceum . . .'

He read out where Barrymore, Robson and Kearns lived on Exmoor. Walton said OK, he'd call the Yard. Say he'd had a tip from a very reliable source. And they must have lunch one day.

'What are you up to?' asked Paula when Tweed had finished the call.

'Pressure. I want maximum pressure put on those three. It's possible one – or all – of them will break. Though I doubt it.'

'You really think they ran down poor Jill?'

Tweed began cleaning his glasses with his handkerchief. 'It's a long coincidence. The morning Jill is killed the three of them are staying at a hotel about half a mile away.'

'But you moved her to the Stafford for safety – and they only knew she always stayed at Brown's. How could any of them have found her?'

'I'm afraid I blundered. I may even be responsible for her death. By mistake, anyway. I think she was being watched during that afternoon I went to Brown's for tea. Someone got frightened of what she might have told me. I suspect I was followed when I walked up Albemarle Street and didn't notice.'

'That's ridiculous,' burst out Monica. 'You always check . . .'

'On the other hand,' Paula said quietly, 'I was following her for three days. I could have been spotted. And I was with Tweed when he visited all three men on Exmoor.'

'Pure surmise.'

Tweed dismissed the idea with a wave of his hand. Secretly he was pretty sure she was right. But it was not something he wanted on Paula's conscience.

'Then,' Paula continued, 'they would have seen her change her hotel to the Stafford. And I bet that was a morning habit of hers on Exmoor. To stroll over the moor. Always at the same time.'

'Forget it!' Tweed snapped. 'We have to decide what to do next.'

'What do you suggest?' asked Monica.

375

She sensed an atmosphere of depression in the room. Worse, a mood of guilt that one – or both – of her colleagues had caused the killing of Jill Kearns. Paula had sunk into a brooding silence, so unlike her normal buoyancy. It was Tweed who changed the mood.

'We take action. Monica, call The Anchor at Porlock Weir. Tell Butler – or Nield – to call me back urgently. He'll know what that means – use a public phone box. I want to find out if Barrymore and Co. have returned to Exmoor. Then we'll move.'

'How?' asked Paula, lifting her head.

'You and I will drive down there at once. Partridge was murdered on Exmoor while those three were there. Jill was murdered in London – while they were here. I'm going to ask each of them a lot of tough questions.'

Monica was already dialling The Anchor. She spoke for a short time, then put down the phone. 'Both of them are out,' she told Tweed.

'Keep trying at intervals until you get one of them. I want to be at their throats before they've had time to settle in.'

Monica nodded. Again she didn't like the vehemence with which Tweed had spoken. If he'd still been a Chief Superintendent at Scotland Yard in Homicide, they'd have taken him off the case. Too much personal involvement.

Zurich. Arthur Beck could pass in the street for any profession. Except that of Chief of Federal Police. In his mid-forties, he wore a light blue business suit, a cream shirt, a blue tie which carried a kingfisher emblem woven into the fabric. Plump-faced, his most prominent feature was his alert grey eyes beneath thick dark brows the same colour as his hair.

He sat alone in an office at Zurich police headquarters with a window overlooking the River Limmat, the university perched on the hill rising steeply from the opposite shore. Lifting the phone, he dialled Kalos' number. The Greek answered quickly.

'Beck here. I have some data on your Anton Gavalas. Ready?'

'That was quick. It was only yesterday. Go ahead.'

'Anton disembarked from the Athens flight, caught a taxi to the Hotel Schweizerhof which faces the main station. He had early dinner, then wandered down the Bahnhofstrasse to the lake. He sat on a seat watching the boats come and go. No one approached him. He made no phone calls from the hotel – I found that out after he'd left.'

'Left for where?'

'Let me tell you in my own way,' the Swiss said precisely. 'I checked with the porter after he'd returned from his walk. He went straight to bed. This morning he has a leisurely breakfast. Again, no one approached him. Then he leaves by cab for Kloten Airport, where he arrived. A model citizen, Mr Anton Gavalas. Always well-dressed. Walking down the Bahnhofstrasse he could be mistaken for a Swiss – except for his dark suntan.'

'What happened next?' Kalos asked.

'He produces a first-class ticket, checks in his luggage for the SR 690 flight bound for Lisbon . . .'

'Lisbon?' Kalos sounded surprised.

'Lisbon in Portugal,' Beck continued genially. 'The 12.10 p.m. that reaches Lisbon at 1.55 p.m. That's Portuguese time. Which means you can alert someone in Lisbon to meet the flight if you wish. End of report.'

'I'm very grateful.' Kalos paused. 'It almost sounds as though you followed him everywhere yourself.'

'But I did. My dear Kalos, when you're trapped behind a desk in Berne most of the time, reading files, it does you good to get out on the streets again. Stops you getting rusty – your mind going to sleep.' He added the last bit in case Kalos' English was not up to the colloquialism.

'I really am grateful,' Kalos repeated. 'I owe you one.'

'Indeed you do. But that's for the future. Good hunting . . .'

In his Athens office Kalos put down the phone and mopped his forehead. The heatwave was getting worse. There was a real shortage of mineral water.

Lisbon? Kalos was baffled. He added the data to his secret file. What could the connection be? And he had no way of checking, no link with Portugal he could use without Sarris' cooperation.

36

Anton landed at Portela Airport, changed a sum of Swiss franc high-denomination banknotes into escudos, the local currency. He never used traveller's cheques while moving about secretly: they left a trail which could be followed. Inside the taxi he opened his case, used the raised lid to conceal what he was doing from the driver.

Inside the suitcase was an executive case crammed with Swiss banknotes. He had been handed this by a woman who visited his room at the Schweizerhof in Zurich. An incident Arthur Beck had no chance of observing; the woman had reserved her own room at the hotel for the night.

Anton collected the equivalent of £5,000 in escudos, tucked the bundle into an envelope. He then counted out the equivalent of £10,000 in Swiss banknotes, transferred them to a second envelope and put them in another pocket. When he closed the lid, the executive case contained £100,000 in Swiss notes. He looked out of the window.

Lisbon was a galaxy of colour-washed houses: pink, blue, green and all of them pastel shades. The side streets were narrow and twisting. He paid off the driver outside the Ritz Hotel.

Speaking perfect English, he registered under the name Hunter, using the forged passport Doganis had supplied for his previous trip. The Portuguese were strict about examining passports. Inside his room he checked the time and ordered mineral water from room service. He would need a clear head for coping with the arms dealer.

He ate a quick dinner in the restaurant, keeping an eye on the time. It was still light when he took a taxi to Cascais, a resort and fishing village on the coast. The air was sultry, but nothing compared with the burning heat of Greece. He paid off the taxi on the promenade, found a cheap clothing shop and bought a large fisherman's pullover, a pair of trousers. His feet were shod in trainer's shoes which fitted him comfortably. Footwear was important: you never knew when you would have to move fast.

Checking the time again, he walked along the front, the package of wrapped clothes under one arm, the other holding the executive case which was well-worn and had a grubby look. He found a *fado* café which was crowded, went inside, sat at a table and ordered a glass of wine which he paid for.

He drank half the glass, asked the waiter for the washroom, disappeared inside it. He locked the door of the cubicle, undid the parcel. Within a minute he had pulled the trousers up over his own pair and donned the turtle-necked pullover. Flushing the toilet, he stuffed the wrappings behind it and walked out carrying the case.

He made a point of finishing the glass of wine, standing at the table as people pushed past him. The place was a babble of voices with a background of mournful *fado* music.

379

Personally, Anton preferred the *bouzouki*. He checked the time once more.

He walked along the front and it was dark now. Lights sparkled in the clear air, the Atlantic rolled in, threw its gentle waves on the shore. Carlos, a gnarled wiry fisherman, was waiting with his boat moored, a lamp shining in the tiny wheelhouse.

'Mr Hunter,' he greeted, 'my wife had your phone message, passed it to me.' Clambering ashore, he pointed. 'Everything is with us when you need.'

He was pointing at a donkey cart half-filled with hay, a donkey between the shafts and fastened to them with traces. Anton frowned, put his free hand on the animal's shoulders. The head peered round.

'She has to carry a weight,' he commented. 'And also stay by herself for some time.'

'She is good. You take the cart. Look at wheels. She carries weight. When you come back I take you with cargo to *Oporto*.'

'The freighter is at the harbour now? Gomez is expecting me?'

'All is ready, Mr Hunter. We take cargo aboard in the night. The *Oporto* sails when the sun rises. One day from this day. Sails for England.'

'Here you are, Carlos. I'll be back later.' Anton handed him the envelope containing £5,000 in escudos. 'Don't open that envelope until you're inside the wheelhouse. And turn down the lamp.'

'I'll do that. All the time God gives us. I nearly do not know you in those clothes . . .'

Anton led the donkey cart along the front back the way he had come. He had no trouble controlling the animal. He'd had a lot of experience in handling the creatures on Petros' farm. The main thing was that it was docile.

From the cafés he was passing came more *fado* music, the voices of men and women who had consumed large

380

quantities of wine. It was not a night when anyone was interested in what was happening on the deserted front. Arriving at a narrow side street, he guided the donkey across the road, parked it outside a shop which sold swimwear and which was closed. Just beyond was the entrance to the dimly lit Rua Garrett. The address Volkov had given him.

He left the bright lights and plunged into Stygian darkness as he picked his way over the uneven cobbles of Rua Garrett. One place was still open, double doors thrown back. He strolled past it, glancing inside. A big place with a cracked concrete floor – a service garage on one side, a ship's chandler on the other.

His glance showed him a gloomy cavern lit by oil lamps. On the garage side a car was perched on an elevated platform about a foot above a service pit. He walked in when he was satisfied only one person was inside.

'Mr Gallagher?'

'That's me. What do you want?'

'I've come to collect the merchandise, the type with a sting in its tail.'

'So, you're the one? Brought the money?'

'Of course.'

Gallagher was six feet tall and broad-shouldered. He spoke with an American accent. In his late thirties, his manner was offhand and he moved silently. Like a big cat. Anton studied the insolent expression, the restless eyes. The arms dealer was not a man Anton liked the look of. Still, he had come prepared.

Gallagher held out a large hand. He made the universal gesture with thumb and forefinger.

'I'd like to see the colour of your money first.'

'That is reasonable.'

'Wait! We need a little privacy for our business transaction.'

He walked over to the wall, pressed a switch and the

381

double doors closed automatically. The place was not so down at heel as Anton had thought. Sealed inside the cavern, the stench of petrol and oil grew stronger. Anton laid his case on the table, unlocked it, raised the lid and stood back. While Gallagher walked back to the case and picked up bundles at random, riffling through the banknotes, Anton hoisted his pullover a little higher.

'Just how much is here?' Gallagher demanded.

He had the flattened nose of an ex-boxer, a mass of untidy hair the colour of ripened wheat, a hard jaw. His pale eyes watched Anton, waiting for an answer.

'One hundred thousand pounds in Swiss francs. The agreed price in the agreed currency. For three Stingers. Plus six missiles.'

'Price just went up,' Gallagher informed him. 'Law of supply and demand. Been a heavy call for Stingers. IRA, Angolan rebels, Iranian nutcases. People like that. £145,000 is the going rate. Take it or leave it.'

'But the price was agreed,' Anton protested coldly. Volkov had been very clear on that. 'Your reputation rests on keeping to a deal once concluded.'

'Grow up, buddy boy. I said the going rate is the price. You can't raise it? Get lost.'

'I didn't say I hadn't got that much,' Anton replied. 'Since you insist, I'll pay it. But first I want to see the weapons.'

'You need to go to the bank?' Gallagher pressed, arms folded. 'Or is it in there?' He nodded towards the case Anton had shut and relocked. 'You came ready for the bad news? *I heard it on the grapevine*,' he sang the old melody and then laughed.

'I hid more money in the Rua Garrett earlier,' Anton told him. 'You'll never find it – but it's within a hundred yards of where you're standing. Now, show me the weapons.'

'Good to do business with a gentleman.' Gallagher grinned and walked back to the bank of switches and buttons on the wall. He pressed one and the elevated platform supporting the car rose up four more feet. The arms dealer lowered himself into the pit, pressed a switch which illuminated the darkness. Against one wall was a large canvas bundle. He unstrapped it, rolled back the canvas with care, exposing three Stingers and six missiles. He looked up.

'Satisfied?'

'Bring one up, plus one missile. No – take the middle ones in each case.'

'Leery sort of bastard, aren't you?'

Gallagher placed a Stinger and a missile on the garage floor, hauled himself up. 'Show you how it works.' He grinned again. 'You get value for money here. It's shoulder-launched by one man. Weighs only thirty pounds. It has a hundred per cent hit rate – mainly due to its infra-red heat-seeking system, plus its amazingly accurate aiming system. You fire in the direction of the aircraft and leave it to do the rest – home in on the target. God knows how many Soviet fighters it's wiped out back in Afghanistan. Take hold of it.'

Anton balanced the weight in both hands, surprised at its lightness. It looked like a mobile telescope with a wide muzzle at the front tapering to a slimmer barrel resting on his shoulder. To his right as he held it was a large rectangular plate. He peered through the aiming system.

'This is how you load it,' Gallagher said, inserting a missile. 'Don't pull the trigger or we'll both end up as red goulash.'

'I want a demonstration,' Anton remarked as he handed back the weapon. 'Don't argue. For £145,000 I'm entitled to check the damned thing works . . .'

Gallagher had driven them in his Volvo station wagon into the hills. Leaving Rua Garrett, Anton had noted the donkey still stood patiently with the cart where he had parked it; it looked as though it would stay there all night.

Gallagher pulled up at a lonely spot overlooking the sea. Getting out, he grasped the Stinger and the single missile concealed under a travelling rug. They picked their way past a cactus grove and Gallagher halted at the top of a cliff. Out at sea a lone fishing vessel was returning to port, navigation lights twinkling. Gallagher handed weapon and missile to Anton.

'There's your target. There's always one comes crawling back late.'

'I don't understand.'

'That fishing vessel. Get on with it. It's about two miles away. How far will your target be in the air?'

'Less than two miles. I still don't understand . . .'

'Oh, for Christ's sake! The missile is heat-seeking. That boat has a boiler in the engine room. Aim straight for it.'

'Won't there be an enquiry?' Anton inserted the missile, raised the Stinger, cuddling it into his shoulder. 'The police might start searching – when they realize what did it.'

'Except they won't. A month ago a similar fishing vessel blew up – the boilers they use are ancient as these hills. It will be recorded as another case of inefficient maintenance. They don't bother that much round here.'

Anton aimed at a point well below the wheelhouse. He squeezed the trigger, the missile left the launcher, curved in a low arc above the Atlantic at such speed he didn't see its flight. A dull boom echoed in the humid night. The fishing vessel turned into a pillar of flame after a brief flash. The flame died fast.

Lowering the Stinger, Anton gazed at the smooth surface of the sea. The fishing vessel had vanished. He lifted the Stinger, peered through the aiming device. He could see no trace of any wreckage.

'Satisfied?' Gallagher demanded. 'If so, let's get back to the garage.'

'How many in the crew?'

'Roughly half a dozen. Plenty more where they came from . . .'

'Drop me at the entrance to the Rua Garrett,' Anton told the arms dealer as they drove along the front. 'I have to bring my transport.'

'That the transport?' Gallagher enquired as Anton, carrying his executive case, alighted by the donkey cart. 'You'll get a long way with that. And I bet I know where you hid the balance of the money. In that mess of a hillside at the end of the street.'

'And you could search for years and never find it. See you at the garage. Don't wrap the merchandise until I'm there.'

'Anything you say, buddy boy . . .'

I don't think he's American at all, Anton was thinking as he led the donkey cart into the side street, following the Volvo. Under the accent, the over-use of American slang, he had detected traces of some unidentifiable Mittel-European language.

He left the donkey cart outside the open garage doors. Inside Gallagher had lowered the elevated car back over the pit. A careful man, Mr Gallagher. Anton continued down the dark tunnel of the narrow street.

He'd noticed when he first arrived that at the end the street stopped where a steep hill rose, its slopes covered with undergrowth and trees. He found a narrow path twisting up and followed it a short distance. Crouching down, he unlocked the case, lifted the lid.

He took a number of bundles of banknotes and stuffed them inside his pockets until his pullover bulged in an ugly manner. This would appear to be the extra money. He

385

locked the case, made his way back down the tortuous path, walked back to the garage.

'Looks like you're going to have a baby,' Gallagher commented.

He stood by the control panel, pressed one switch, watched the garage doors slowly close, pressed another and the platform elevated above the service pit. Anton put the case down on a table, hoisted his pullover a few inches as he asked the question casually.

'Supposing I want to come back and ask you a question tomorrow. About the operation of the Stingers. You'll be here?'

'No. Anything you want to ask, ask now.' He lowered himself into the pit. 'I'll be away for a week in another country. A fresh deal.'

'Your regular customers – for servicing cars – will be pleased.'

'They know me. The doors are closed, I'm not here. Give me a hand. Take these, put them on that big table, the one with the sheet of canvas.'

When the three launchers and five missiles were laid on the top of the table, Gallagher hauled himself out of the pit. He towered over Anton. He spent the next ten minutes working rapidly, wrapping each launcher and missile in polythene sheets; then he arranged them on the large canvas already spread out. Rolling up the canvas, he fetched some straps and began securing the bundle. 'You can start relieving yourself of that money,' he suggested.

Anton pulled out the bundles of banknotes, laid them in stacks on the table-top. Gallagher was fastening the last strap when the Greek stepped back to pick up the case he'd stowed under the table. Gallagher had his back to him, stooped over the canvas-wrapped weapons.

Anton took out a handkerchief, blew his nose, kept the handkerchief in his hand, grasped the handle of the commando knife inside its sheath fastened to the belt under

386

his pullover. He drew it out, stepped forward and rammed it with all his strength into Gallagher just below the left shoulder blade. Gallagher gasped, made a muted gurgling sound and slumped forward across the table.

'You really should keep to an agreed price,' Anton said.

Anton used two of the straps as makeshift handles to carry the canvas bundle to the donkey cart. At that, he staggered under the weight which must have been between a hundred and fifty and two hundred pounds. And Anton kept himself fit.

He dropped it into the cart and moved the hay to conceal the weapons. He hauled large handfuls close to the bundle, which caused it to sink, then dumped the hay on top. It took him a good five minutes to complete the job. Returning to the garage, he repacked the stacks of banknotes in the case, locked it and buried it under the hay.

Half an hour later he was leading the donkey along the deserted front. The cafés and discotheques were going full blast. From open windows the sound of guitars being strummed, of girls singing *fado*, drifted. At least it guaranteed an empty waterfront.

He had acted quickly clearing up the garage behind closed doors. Gallagher's dead body had been heaved into the pit. Anton had found an oil-stained canvas sheet to cover the corpse. Then he had pressed the button and lowered the elevated platform. He had doused the three oil lamps. Fortunately the control panel was near the doors: he had pressed the switch and dived into the street before they closed.

Carlos leapt on to the jetty when he arrived. Between them they lowered the weapons into his fishing boat. The Portuguese hid them under a pile of fishing nets. He wiped his hands on his trousers and looked at Anton, who asked the question.

'What about the donkey and the cart?'

'Will wait until I return from the *Oporto*. Then I go home. I saw a fishing boat out there die.'

'Sorry?'

'It blew up. Boom! They do not take care with boilers. I am careful. It is my living . . .'

'Has the coastguard gone out?'

It was an important question. Anton was thinking police launches might be prowling around.

'No.' Carlos spread his hands. 'They will not make the hurry. Maybe when the sun rises. Are we good to leave for the *Oporto*?'

'As soon as you can get under way . . .'

Anton felt relieved as he saw the shoreline receding. It would be a week before anyone started worrying about Gallagher's closed garage. That had been a bit of luck. As the boat chugged steadily towards the main harbour Anton wiped his forehead. They were away.

Gomez, skipper of the freighter *Oporto*, was well-organized. A short fat jolly man, he helped to bring the canvas-wrapped cargo aboard up a gangway lowered on the far side from the jetty where his ship was moored. Anton waited until Carlos was guiding his fishing vessel back to Cascais, then handed Gomez the envelope containing £10,000 in Swiss banknotes.

'The same amount as before. Where is the crew?'

'Below decks. I invented work for them when I saw Carlos coming. What they don't see, they don't know. Better I hide this in a safe place?'

'Very safe.' He knew Gomez would assume he was smuggling drugs. 'When do you sail? I have to complete some business.'

'At dawn the day after tomorrow.' He checked his watch. 'It is eleven-thirty. Yes, not tomorrow, the day after. That is OK?'

'Perfectly.' Anton, holding his executive case, decided to take it with him. He had to return to The Ritz, act normally, sleep there, have breakfast, then pay his bill. 'I would prefer it if I could slip aboard tomorrow and stay under cover until you sail.'

'What time? Your cabin is ready now.'

'Probably about midday. You can time arrival at our destination as you did when you took me before? At eleven o'clock at night? Again someone will be waiting to take me ashore.'

'There is a problem.' Gomez, his weatherbeaten face making him look more like sixty than forty, scratched his head. 'Last time I told the harbourmaster at Watchet we had engine trouble. Ah! I have it. This time, after you leave us, we will steam back a way down the Bristol Channel, turn round, and berth during the morning.'

'I'm counting on you.'

'Of course. You will be put ashore at Porlock Weir just as you were before.'

37

'I've never seen anything like this place,' Tweed said as they walked out of The Anchor. He had Paula on one side, Butler on the other. 'It's fascinating. A tiny world on its own.'

Tweed had driven down with Paula to Porlock Weir after he had warned Butler they were coming. 'Book us two rooms at The Anchor,' he had told Butler. 'I want to avoid The Luttrell Arms in Dunster this time. The idea is to surprise Barrymore and Co. You said they've all returned to Exmoor?'

Butler had confirmed the three men had arrived back the previous day. As they left The Anchor after a satisfying lunch he explained.

'Nield and I each have our own hired cars. We spent our time touring the whole area, checking for any sign of life at their residences. We split up, went to pubs to catch any gossip. It's common knowledge the three men took a trip away from Exmoor. You can't go to the loo down here without everyone knowing. Nield is out having another look-see.'

They crossed a narrow wired-fenced footbridge over seventeen-feet lock gates. A notice warned, *Closed Spring Tide*. Tweed paused, gazing at the oyster-shaped harbour behind the gates. Low tide. The harbour was a basin of sodden mud. A trickle of water ran under the footbridge out of the basin. Expensive power cruisers, moored to buoys, heeled over at drunken angles.

No one else was about as they followed a footpath past a small row of three terraced houses; all of them old, one with a thatched roof. Beyond, a shoal of pebbles led steeply down to a calm grey sea. Tweed stopped, taking in the atmosphere.

He looked back at the gabled hotel which was combined with The Ship Inn. Gulls drifted in the overcast sky, crying mournfully. Behind the coast the hillside, covered with dense trees, climbed. To the west the rocky coast stretched away and everywhere was a feeling of desolation.

'A quiet hideaway,' Tweed commented. 'Like the end of the world.'

'That reminds me.' Paula sounded excited as she delved inside her handbag. 'I found this in a pocket in my suitcase when I was packing to come down here. A brochure I picked up at The Luttrell Arms.'

She handed him a coloured brochure headed *Take*

the West Somerset Railway to Minehead. Below was a picture of an old-fashioned steam train. He opened it up and looked at the map inside as Butler peered over his shoulder.

The steam train started at Minehead, ran along the coast through the port of Watchet and later turned inland over the Quantock Hills, ending at Taunton. It began running on 29 March and shut down for winter on 29 October.

'*Endstation,*' said Paula. 'That clue Masterson gave you inside the cigar box he posted from Athens. He was drawing your attention to that old privately run railway.'

'And which is *Endstation*?' Tweed asked. 'Minehead or Taunton?'

'No idea. Don't you think I'm right?'

'Maybe.' Tweed folded up the brochure, handed it back to her. 'Hang on to it. It goes through Watchet, I see. The port where Anton probably came ashore from that Portuguese freighter.'

'Except he didn't,' Butler said. 'I checked that out. A two-storey building looking straight down on the harbour there is Customs and the harbourmaster. I followed him into a pub and got chatting. Told him a cock-and-bull story about how a friend had boasted he'd come ashore from that freighter without being spotted. The harbourmaster said bullshit. They keep a sharp lookout for suspicious characters trying to sneak ashore. It's this drugs problem. He was a solid ex-seaman type. Said it was impossible. I believe him.'

'Another theory gone down the drain. Let's wander west along the coast a bit. Looks pretty lonely.'

Butler led the way back across the footbridge and they walked down a road a short distance. It stopped abruptly and they had to pick their way across a treacherous surface of pebbles and small rocks.

'It really is the end of the world out here,' Tweed remarked.

'Maybe that's what Masterson meant when he wrote *Endstation*,' Butler suggested. Wearing a thick woollen pullover as protection against the damp sea mist drifting in, he walked with his hands inside his trouser pockets. 'There's an old dear back in one of those cottages who says she's seen ghosts – and lights flashing late at night. The barman told me so I called on her. A Mrs Larcombe. In her late seventies, but sharp as a tack.'

'I don't think you're right,' Paula objected. '*Endstation* is one of those two terminal stations on that railway – Taunton or Minehead.'

'What's got into him?' Butler asked her.

Tweed was striding ahead, peering at the ground, his Burberry collar buttoned to the neck. He seemed totally absorbed in his thoughts.

Paula told Butler about the death of Jill Kearns. He listened as she explained Monica's anxiety about Tweed becoming obsessed. 'And now his mind is full of three deaths,' she went on. 'Masterson's, of course, and Sam Partridge and Jill.'

'Don't see how they link up. One in Greece, one on Exmoor, one in London.'

'That's what he's trying to do – link them all together. Drop the subject, he's coming back . . .'

'I found traces of a wheeled vehicle,' Tweed announced. 'In a patch where sand showed.'

'No vehicle would cross that terrain,' commented Butler.

'And on the way back, could we call on Mrs Larcombe if she's at home? I'd like a word with her . . .'

The cottage was built of stone, roofed with red tiles mellowed by the years. Swagged lace curtains draped the windows, the front garden was barely three feet wide but the lavender borders were trimmed and there was not a weed in sight.

Approaching the cottage, Tweed noted there was an end window facing west where he had walked. Butler raised the highly polished brass knocker shaped like a dolphin and rapped it twice. A nameboard on the picket gate carried the legend *Dolphin Cottage*.

A tall sharp-faced woman opened the door. Her nose was prominent, she was long-jawed, her eyes alert, her mass of hair grey neatly brushed. Butler spoke to her for a moment, then gestured for Tweed and Paula to enter. Mrs Larcombe led them into what she called 'the parlour', invited them to sit down and Butler made the introductions.

'What can I do for you, Mr Tweed?' she asked, seating herself in a chintz-covered armchair.

'I'm in insurance. No, I'm not trying to sell you any policy. I'm Chief Claims Investigator for my company. A holidaymaker called Burns disappeared here a few weeks ago. Last seen late at night walking that way.' He twisted in his chair, pointed west. 'We've had a claim on the basis presumed dead. Since no body has been found I'm puzzled.'

'Funny goings-on round here.' Her eyes glistened, bird-like. 'No one believes me. They think I'm seeing ghosts. I know what I saw and heard.' She sat more erect.

'Could you tell me a little more?' Tweed asked quietly.

'It would be a few weeks ago – about the time your Mr Burns disappeared. Can't fix it exactly. Yes, I can. About the time the Customs at Watchet practically took that Portuguese freighter apart. Didn't find anything except a lot of cork. The rumour was it was carrying drugs.'

'What did you see and hear?'

'Close to midnight it was. I don't sleep well. I was looking out of my bedroom window which faces the way you pointed. I saw a light flashing out at sea. Like someone signalling. Then another light flashing from the shore. There was a ship at sea, a fairish way out.'

'You had your bedroom light on?' Tweed enquired.

'No, I didn't. I'd got out of bed in the dark and put on my dressing gown. I know where all the furniture is. I had the window open. It was a sticky night.'

'This ship you saw – it had navigation lights? Which is how you came to see it?'

'No, it didn't. But my sight is very good. No glasses, as you see. I saw it as a vague silhouette. I thought that was funny. What you've just mentioned. No navigation lights.'

'And that was all?'

She stiffened. She wore an old-fashioned black dress with a lace collar pinned with a brooch. 'You don't believe me?'

'Yes, I do. Because your night vision would be good – since you hadn't put a light on. Was there something else?'

'I went back to bed, leaving the window open for some air. I fell asleep quickly. Then I was wakened by a noise. I felt fuddled but I got up again. It was the engine noise of some vehicle approaching – from the same direction. I thought that funny. No cars drive over those pebbles. By the time I got to the window it was passing my gate. No lights. I ran to the front window because the noise stopped. I was worried – it sounded to have stopped by my front gate. I made a racket opening the front window – the thing sticks. As I looked out the engine started and the vehicle disappeared towards Porlock.'

'Without lights?' Tweed asked gently.

'No. As it passed the harbour the lights came on. The red ones at the back and dimmed headlights in front. Then it was gone.' She leaned forward, her eyes shrewd. 'Could it have been your Mr Burns?'

'Possibly,' said Tweed. 'No way of telling for sure. Could you describe what sort of vehicle it was? Even in the dark?'

'An odd-looking beast.' She frowned with concentration. 'High up off the ground. Behind the cab it was squarish. At a guess, canvas-covered.'

'Colour?'

'Couldn't tell.'

'White or cream?' Tweed suggested.

'Definitely not. It would have shown up more. A darkish colour. No idea who was driving – I was looking down on it, you see.'

Tweed stood up, took his glasses case out of his pocket, fumbled, dropped it on the dark floral-patterned carpet. The room was dim. He put his hand behind him, stopped Paula searching for it. He almost knocked over a vase of dried flowers. Mrs Larcombe stepped forward, took hold of the case, handed it to him.

'You'll be lost without this.'

'Thank you. And thank you for giving us your time. Your help is greatly appreciated.'

'*You* do believe me then?' Mrs Larcombe asked as she stood up to see them out.

'Oh, yes, I believe you.'

'Well, I'm glad someone doesn't think I've lost my marbles . . .'

Paula waited until they were walking back to The Anchor before asking the question. 'What was that business about your glasses case? There was no need to take it out of your pocket.'

'A final test on her eyesight. My case is dark-coloured. Even I couldn't see where it had dropped – it merged with the carpet. Mrs Larcombe has exceptional eyesight.'

'What do you think she saw then?'

'Some kind of covered jeep or four-wheel-drive vehicle which could negotiate that pebble ground easily. Now I'm phoning Colonel Barrymore. He's first on the list for some hard interrogation. His reaction to my calling him will be interesting.'

Inside his room at The Anchor Paula looked out of the window while Tweed made his call. She had a view down over the road which ended a short distance to the west, and the harbour with the dried-up channel where the sea would come flooding in.

Tweed's conversation with Barrymore was brief. He spoke tersely and concluded by saying, 'Then I will call you back within the hour.'

'He says he has to try and cancel an appointment,' Tweed told her. 'I think he's up to something. Let's have some coffee sent up and review what we've discovered. Butler is taking a well-earned rest . . .'

He called back exactly one hour later. This time the conversation was longer. Tweed's manner was even more abrupt. He closed by saying, 'Very well, if you insist. It will save me time.'

He looked grim as he replaced the receiver. 'I was right – he was up to something. He's phoned Robson and Kearns and invited them to join him at Quarme Manor. We'll be confronted by the three of them.'

'Including Kearns? But surely he must be distraught so soon after the death of his wife?'

'We'll see, won't we?'

38

Colonel Barrymore did not bother to receive them. When they arrived at Quarme Manor the door was unchained and opened by Mrs Atyeo. She ushered them into the hall and then indicated the door to the study.

'They'se waitin' for you in there.'

'Thank you,' Tweed said pleasantly. Followed by Paula, he opened the door without knocking. They were seated round a large oak table in the bay window. Barrymore,

Kearns and Robson. The colonel had his back to the window with Robson at his left and Kearns on his right. Tweed instantly realized that the seating arrangement forced Paula and himself to face the light while the others had their back to it. An old tactic. Barrymore remained seated, launched his onslaught as soon as they were inside the room.

'I see you've brought that girl again. This time I won't have her taking notes. You sit there and there.'

'Paula Grey is my assistant,' Tweed rapped back. 'She will take notes of the entire interrogation.' He sat down and dropped his bomb. 'Now we are investigating four murders which may all have security implications.'

'Four? What on earth are you talking about?' Barrymore demanded in his most commanding voice.

'One, Ionides at the Antikhana during the war.' Tweed waited to see if anyone would correct him, say 'Gavalas'. Three blank faces stared back at him. 'Two, Andreas Gavalas on Siros when you made your commando raid. Three, ex-Chief Inspector Partridge here on Exmoor.' He paused.

Paula was watching Kearns. He sat very stiffly, motionless, and his face was drained of colour, chalk-white. Tweed turned to him.

'Four, your wife, Jill. My condolences.'

'She was knocked down by some hit-and-run bastard,' Barrymore protested. 'And that's pretty bad form to raise the subject – to call it murder is madness.'

'Then why is Scotland Yard investigating it as a case of murder?'

'How do you know that?' Barrymore snapped.

'I have contacts. I'm Special Branch. You know that. You checked up on the phone with my chief, Walton.'

Robson, wearing a loose-fitting brown shirt, a plain brown tie, the knot slack below his throat, and an old check sports jacket, stirred. He turned to face Barrymore.

'You didn't tell me that.'

'Must have slipped my mind,' the colonel replied curtly.

Robson tugged at his straggly moustache, turned back to face Tweed. His pale blue eyes studied him for a moment.

'What makes you think Jill was murdered?'

'A cleaning woman inside one of the St James's Street clubs saw a Jaguar waiting by the kerb with its engine running. The moment Jill started to cross the street the man behind the wheel headed straight for her. Cold-blooded murder.'

Tweed waited again. Before leaving London he had changed his mind, had phoned Chief Inspector Jarvis in charge of the case. No description of the driver worth a damn. The silence inside the room became oppressive.

Paula was studying Kearns. He sat like a statue. Not a blink of an eyelid at Tweed's statement. Years of iron self-discipline as a CSM, she thought. Never show your emotions however tough the situation. She felt Tweed was treating him inconsiderately.

'Why have you come to see us?' Robson asked, leaning forward, gazing at Tweed as though deciding on a diagnosis.

'Because you're all suspects, of course . . .'

'How dare you!' Barrymore burst out. 'Are you accusing us? And what evidence have you to base that slanderous statement on? I want an answer.'

'I'll give you one. You were all members of the commando raid on Siros. Andreas Gavalas was murdered. A fortune in diamonds he was carrying for the Greek Resistance was stolen. You were all based at the Antikhana Building in Cairo. You had returned from the raid. Ionides was murdered. You were all here on Exmoor a good few weeks ago. Partridge was murdered. You were all staying in London at the Lyceum Hotel – only a short distance from St James's Street. Jill Kearns was murdered. How much more coincidence do you think I can swallow?'

Robson laid a restraining hand on Barrymore's arm. He asked the question in the manner of a doctor enquiring about a patient's symptoms.

'Why do you think that Jill was murdered?'

'Because someone who knew she always stayed at Brown's saw me having tea with her. Whoever it was became worried she might tell me too much.'

'Stretching it a bit, aren't you?'

'Possibly. Until I link it up with the fact you must all have known she made a habit of staying at Brown's, that she made a habit of going out for a walk at that time every single day of her life. The killer followed her to the Stafford where I asked her to go, hoping to ensure her safety. Where were you all at 6.30 a.m. that fatal morning?'

Barrymore opened his mouth to protest. 'What damned impudence. I'll see you in hell before . . .'

'Best to reply,' Robson intervened. 'We all got up early – the habit of a lifetime. Goes back to Army days. By early I mean about 5.30 a.m. None of us have breakfast. There were tea-making facilities in the bedrooms. I spent my time packing, then studied some medical journals. No one to verify that.' His smile was wintry. 'Barrymore had gone for a walk – I know that because I went to his room and there was no reply. Kearns was also out walking. It was a fine day. Doesn't help a lot, does it?'

'Not a lot,' Tweed agreed. 'You were out for a walk, Barrymore?'

'You heard what Captain Robson said. I'm getting a trifle fed up with you . . .'

'And I'm fed up with the fact that my old friend, Sam Partridge, was foully murdered,' blazed Tweed. 'I'll move heaven and earth to find out who did that.'

Paula glanced at Tweed in surprise. She'd never known such an outburst during an interrogation. Then she saw the supercilious smile of satisfaction on Barrymore's face. He'd needled Tweed. She glanced back as Tweed began cleaning his glasses on his handkerchief and nearly sucked in her breath. Tweed had put on an act. She tensed: she was witnessing a duel between Tweed and the three men. Kearns spoke for the first time.

'That cleaning woman. Did she get a description of the driver? And what about tracing the owner of the Jaguar?'

'Stolen from outside a night club near the Lyceum Hotel where you stayed. Some fool of a yuppie got drunk, left the keys in the ignition, was persuaded to walk back to his flat in case he was stopped by the police.'

Tweed stood up and Paula closed her notebook, which carried a complete record of the conversation. Barrymore remained seated, his voice sardonic.

'You know your own way out. Mrs Atyeo will be waiting to lock up after you leave the premises. Don't come back.'

Tweed sat behind the wheel of the Mercedes where he had parked it in a lay-by twenty yards or so away before arriving at Quarme Manor. Butler, who had followed them from Porlock Weir, then waited, parked behind the Mercedes, appeared at Tweed's window.

'Next move?' he enquired.

'I want to ask Robson something on his own. His Saab is in the courtyard. Let's hope he comes out soon. You wait here. Then if Barrymore appears, follow him.'

'There's a better place for me to wait. I can back my car just a short distance and into a field. That way I won't be conspicuous if he comes this way.' Butler paused. 'Is it a good idea my leaving you? I'm the one with the gun.'

'It's broad daylight still. Not to worry. You back your car – and where is Nield?'

'No idea. We'll see him sometime at The Anchor when he's good and ready. Does Barrymore know where you're staying?'

400

'No. I said I'd phone him back when he wanted to call me.'

Paula stretched her arms to ease the tension out of herself as Butler left them. 'Did you get anything out of that interview? It was a bit fraught at times.'

'Two things you might have noticed. The absence of one of them asking a question. And someone else did say something.'

'And now you're going to leave me dangling. I'll ask you again. You think they're all in it together? Or just one of them?'

'Just one.'

'I'm too smart to ask which. Lord, it's getting darker.'

Earlier there had been hazy sunshine during their drive to the Manor. Now low heavy clouds were rolling in, obscuring the crests and higher slopes of the moor. It began to spot with rain the windscreen. Then the Saab came out, turned in the other direction and drove off.

'We've got him,' said Tweed and followed as the Saab vanished round a bend. He drove slowly and when they reached Endpoint Robson had disappeared. The Saab was parked just below the terrace and Tweed gazed towards the Doone Valley. When he got out he stretched his legs, pacing up and down.

'Time to beard the lion in his den,' he remarked and they walked up the steep drive. It was very quiet, a silence Tweed felt pressing down on him. Then he stopped. The drive continued round the right-hand side of the bungalow. Parked next to the end of the building was a canvas-covered four-wheel-drive vehicle. Dark-coloured.

Robson's sister, May, opened the door, welcomed them inside and showed them into the sitting room. She asked them to sit down.

'Oliver is writing out his medical records in the conning tower. I'll just fetch him.'

'Conning tower?' Tweed asked.

'Well, I think it looks more like a lighthouse – the tower at the end. But Oliver calls it the conning tower. Back in just a minute.'

Her thick hair seemed even greyer in the daylight. She wore a flowered print dress over her ample form. On this second visit Tweed noticed she had the same pale blue eyes as her brother, eyes which had a remoteness about them.

Robson appeared quickly, gave his shy smile. He took out his pipe as he sat down and began to fill it with tobacco from an old leather pouch.

'Something else?' he enquired.

'Yes. Sorry to trouble you again – but it was Barrymore's idea I met all three of you at his place. Going back to that morning at the Lyceum Hotel, you said you went along to the colonel's room and he was out for a walk. How did you know he was out?'

'First there was a *Do Not Disturb* notice hanging from the handle of his door. He always does that when he goes out – very security conscious, our CO. That way any burglar will assume someone is sleeping inside. Don't bother myself.'

'You said "first". What else was there?' Tweed persisted.

'I wanted to ask him something. So I banged on his door to make sure. He's a light sleeper, like most Army types. He was definitely not there. You sound like a detective.' He smiled to take any sting out of his remark.

'I used to be one.' Tweed paused. 'With Homicide at the Yard.' Robson nodded and puffed at his pipe as Tweed continued. 'What did the three of you do the night before in the evening – after you'd arrived at the Lyceum?'

'Barrymore had some business to transact. Kearns and I went to Rules for dinner. The colonel joined us later.'

'And after your meal you did what?'

402

'Kearns and I went back to the hotel. Barrymore went for a walk. Said he felt like a breath of fresh air. He's a keep fit sort of chap.'

Tweed stood up. 'Well, thank you. Sorry to disturb your work.'

'That's all right. Do you mind if May shows you out? I've quite a workload to get through. There's a bug going round and I've been rushed off my feet. I make quick notes after seeing a patient. Then when I get the time I make a proper record. Ah, here is May.'

'I was going to ask if anyone would like coffee?' she said.

'They're just leaving. Perhaps you'd show them out . . .'

She accompanied them to the front door, Tweed said 'Goodbye,' and she closed the door.

Tweed walked down the steps off the terrace and strolled round to the end of the bungalow. Paula followed as he stood looking at the four-wheel-drive vehicle. Along the bodywork of the passenger seat side at the front was painted a word. *Renegade.*

'Can't be the same one,' Paula whispered. 'Mrs Larcombe would have noticed that word. It's in huge letters and painted white.'

'No, she wouldn't have done,' he observed, 'it's painted on the far side – the wrong side when she looked out of her window.'

'Can I help you?'

It was May who stood just behind them. Neither had heard her approach on the tarred drive. Tweed smiled and indicated the vehicle. 'We were just admiring it. In bad weather it must be a godsend.'

'Oh, that isn't Oliver's. He borrows it from Mr Kearns.'

Inside the isolated public call box near Simonsbath Seton-Charles pulled at his lips with his thumb and forefinger. He was waiting for the phone to ring, had been waiting a good ten minutes. Jupiter insisted he arrived in good time.

His car was parked off the road amid a clump of trees: an empty car left in the middle of nowhere in full view could attract attention. He looked round through the windows for the fifth time. The deserted road spiralled away up on to the moor. Mist curled down over the ridges. If the call didn't come soon it was going to be a difficult drive back to his bungalow.

He shivered. The chill seemed to penetrate the box. He felt the cold after his stay in Athens. He grabbed the phone when it began to ring.

'Clement here,' he said. 'Speaking from . . .' He gave the number of the call box, reversing the last two digits.

The voice began speaking immediately, the tone clipped, the accent upper-crust. No time wasted on greetings. Straight into the instructions.

'We need two furniture vans for the move. In Norwich there's a firm called Camelford Removals. Just gone bankrupt. Selling everything off. Purchase two vehicles, large ones. Pay in cash to save time. Store them in the barn at Cherry Farm in Hampshire. Make sure the doors are double padlocked. Two sets of keys. I want you to drive there tonight after dark. Put up at a hotel in Norwich.'

'I can't drive two vans back myself . . .'

'Think, man. Store one in a garage in the Norwich

area tomorrow. Drive the other to Cherry Farm. With a motorbike inside. Use the bike to get back to Norwich. Then drive the second van back to the farm. The bike is expendable. I want both vehicles at the farm two days from now. Camelford Removals' address is . . . Got it?'

'Yes,' said Seton-Charles. 'You're sure the vans will still be available? Not already sold?'

'My dear chap, the advertisement said they have six vans they want to shift. Bound to be at least two left, providing you're in Norwich first thing tomorrow. That's it . . .'

The connection was broken. Seton-Charles hurried back to his Volvo station wagon, backed it on to the road, started driving for his home on the bungalow estate.

He had no idea of the identity of the man who had called him. He thought the codename Jupiter rather pretentious, but driving along he realized Jupiter was a first-rate organizer. Now he'd drive to Norwich during the late evening, find a hotel. He'd have to park his Volvo in a lock-up, buy a second-hand motorcycle.

When he'd purchased the two furniture vans he'd park the motorbike inside one, then drive it to Cherry Farm, an uninhabited farmhouse he'd visited earlier. Next he'd ride the bike back to Norwich, collect the second van, drive it to the farm. Finally, he could use the bike to ride back again to Norwich to pick up his Volvo. The bike would be dumped in some convenient wood. Job done.

But what could Jupiter want with a couple of furniture vans? He couldn't even guess. But the operation – whatever it might be – was under way. And there had been a hint of urgency in the way he'd been given his instructions.

'Do go easy on Kearns,' Paula said as Tweed parked the Mercedes just short of Woodside House. 'Remember, his wife has just been killed.' She looked up. 'Good Lord, it's Pete.'

Nield leant on the edge of Tweed's window. He looked very tired. He winked at Paula and then spoke to Tweed.

'It's a small world, as they say. Seton-Charles has come back from Greece. I've been checking for days. He's just returned to that bungalow of his at the end of the cul-de-sac after making a covert phone call.'

'Covert?'

'I saw his Volvo parked outside his bungalow so I hung around. He has his own phone, as you know. So what does he do? Drives to a public call box near Simonsbath.'

'A long call?' Tweed asked.

'Let me tell it my way. I follow him. He hides his Volvo in some trees, walks into the box, then waits at least ten minutes.'

'That sounds like a professional. He has an arrangement to be at a certain call box at a specific time. Go on.'

'The phone rings. He snatches it. Conversation lasts precisely ninety seconds. Then he drives back here. His car is inside his garage. What do you think?'

'He bears watching.' Tweed looked closely at Nield. 'You've had a long day, I'd say.'

'Bit frayed. I could do with a sit-down and a half pint.'

'Then drive back to The Anchor now. If Seton-Charles put his car away it doesn't look as though he's going anywhere tonight. We'll see you for dinner. Go and relax.'

'Thanks. You're still prowling?'

'We're calling on friend Kearns. If he's home.'

'He is. I saw him ride in on his horse a while ago. I'll get moving . . .'

'Wait for that beastly dog to appear,' Paula said as Tweed pressed the bell-push beside the gates.

A light came on over the distant porch. Kearns came out slowly. He was carrying a heavy stick. He shone a

406

flashlight and the powerful beam reached the gate, blinding Paula. Tweed half-shut his eyes.

'No dog,' Paula whispered. 'Funny.'

'It's you,' Kearns greeted them. 'I suppose you'd better come in. I'd like it kept brief, whatever it is.'

'Of course,' replied Tweed.

They followed him carefully up the centre of the path, keeping clear of the rough grass and the mantraps it concealed. Kearns led them into the dimly lit hall. Outside it was twilight; dusk was gathering over the moors. Paula dropped her handbag, scrabbled on the floor and picked it up.

Tweed hardly noticed: he was thinking Kearns was getting careless about security. The inner heavy wooden slab doors had been open when they arrived; only the grille gates were closed. Where was the dog?

There was a sudden ferocious snarl from behind a closed door as Kearns passed it. A heavy thud, as though the Alsatian had hurled its bulk against the far side. Kearns hammered a clenched fist against the door.

'Shut it!' he growled.

The first sign of tension – of emotion – he had shown. He took them into the same dining room with the oak table and the panelled walls. Again the lighting was dim. White-faced, Kearns sat at the opposite side, gestured for them to join him on the far side.

'What is it now?' he demanded.

'I know this is a grim time for you,' Tweed began, 'but we need as much information as we can get about your wife's murder. And memory has a habit of fading fast . . .'

'You are convinced it was murder?' Kearns asked, his large hands clenched, the knuckles showing white. His brown marble-like eyes stared at Tweed.

'Yes, I think it was. It's not much consolation – but since the Yard is also convinced they'll do their best to hunt down the killer. An ordinary hit-and-run driver who's probably never caught can cause even more anguish.' He looked round the room. 'The place looks well looked after. Have you got someone in to help?'

'I've done it myself.' Kearns stiffened his back. 'I don't want any other woman inside the house now Jill's gone.'

'I understand. Incidentally, at Quarme Manor I gathered you went for an early morning walk the day you left the Lyceum Hotel. So did Barrymore – on his own. Did you by chance see him while you were out?'

'Strangely enough, no.'

'Why "strangely"?'

'Because,' Kearns explained, 'he always walks in St James's Park when we're in town. Which is where I went. No one else about at that hour. I didn't see any trace of him.'

'One more question, then we'll leave you in peace. I called in on Dr Robson while I was on my way here. He had a four-wheel-drive vehicle parked by the side of his bungalow. It's got the word *Renegade* painted on the side opposite to the driver's seat. Said he'd borrowed it from you.'

'That's right. But it isn't mine. I borrow it from a chap called Foster. Stockbroker type. Lives in the bungalow nearest the main road – on the left as you face the cul-de-sac. We do a lot of that on Exmoor – exchange things on loan. It saves money.'

'How old would this Foster be?' asked Tweed.

Kearns looked surprised at the question, but answered. 'I'd say about forty. Like most of them on that estate.'

'And when did they all move into those bungalows?'

'Fifteen years ago.'

Tweed stood up. 'Thank you for bearing with me. You have some friends you can talk to? I know myself what it's like – stuck on your own in a house when your wife is gone.'

Paula glanced quickly at him. She realized Tweed was

408

recalling the time when his own wife had left him for a Greek shipping magnate.

'Oh, yes. In Winsford,' Kearns replied. 'I'll survive. Let me show you out.'

As they crossed the hall they heard the Alsatian. Now it was moaning and whining behind the closed door. Tweed thought that it sounded as if it were mourning the death of its mistress.

It was dark as Kearns used his flashlight to guide them to the exit. He said 'Goodnight', locked the grille gates and walked slowly back to the house. Tweed and Paula returned to the car. He sank behind the wheel, took a packet out of the glove compartment and smoked one of his rare cigarettes. Paula kept silent for a few minutes before she spoke.

'You're ruminating.'

'A lot to think about. That four-wheel-drive vehicle, *Renegade*. First it seems to belong to Robson, then Kearns and now this man, Foster. The question is, who drove it along the coast near Porlock Weir about midnight? No way of telling.'

'So we can't pursue that line of enquiry – assuming that it's worth pursuing.'

'Then there's the weird psychological set-up between the three men – Robson, Barrymore and Kearns. That must be quite something.'

'I'm not following you.'

'Use your imagination. Three men take part in that commando raid on Siros all those years ago. Andreas Gavalas is murdered with a commando knife. One of them did it . . .'

'But Barrymore checked their weapons after they found the body.'

'So, the killer carried an extra knife, knowing what he was going to do in advance. A hundred thousand pounds' worth of diamonds – now worth a million – went missing.

409

When Barrymore and Kearns leave the Army they settle on Exmoor, close to Robson – who found accommodation for them. I don't think the three of them conspired to murder Andreas. Just one of them.'

'I'm being dim – what about the psychological set-up?'

'It's diabolical, like something out of a Tennessee Williams play. Nobody knows who did it. But two out of the three *know* they didn't. So two of them who are innocent must have wondered all these years which man was a murderer. That makes for almost unbearable tension.'

'So why stay together?'

'That's the truly diabolical part. There's another factor locking them together – fear of Petros and the Gavalas clan coming to Exmoor for revenge. They're trying to protect one another.'

'You're right,' Paula said slowly, 'it's a macabre relationship.'

'Let's get moving.' Tweed shook himself alert. 'I want to take a quick look at that bungalow estate down the road.'

He parked near the bottom of the hill with the engine still running. In the night they had a good view of the six bungalows with whitewashed walls, three on either side of the cul-de-sac. Curtains were closed. Behind them lights shone. The coach lamps in the porches were all lit. No sign of life.

Each dwelling had a low wall, also whitewashed, bordering a trim lawn inside. All the gardens had the grass cut. No cars were parked either in the road or on a drive. All neatly tucked away inside the garages attached to the bungalows. On the roofs of five of them were the same conventional television masts. Only Seton-Charles had the complex structure with a satellite dish.

'I tell you again,' Paula said, 'it doesn't look real. If robots walked out I'd hardly be surprised.'

'Best get back to The Anchor . . .'

He was releasing the brake after moving the gear into drive when she touched his arm. He put the brake back on and turned to her.

'What is it?'

'This.' She was holding a small white stick she'd taken out of her handbag. 'Remember when we arrived at Kearns' place – I pretended to be clumsy and dropped my handbag on the floor. I'd seen this on the woodblocks.'

'What is it?'

'I'm pretty sure it's French chalk. Let me test it.' She held the stick, rubbed it on the cuff of her cotton blouse. A white mark appeared. She brushed at it with her fingers and it vanished. Opening the glove flap, she balanced the makeshift shelf on her knee, rubbed the stick across it. The substance appeared as small grains of powder. She bent forward, sniffed at it. 'No smell.' Moistening her index finger, she dabbed it in the powder, tasted it. 'No taste. It is French chalk.'

'I fail to see the significance.'

'You know I make some of my dresses. I use it for marking. And there's another purpose it could be used for.'

'Now you're keeping me dangling.'

'Kearns' complexion – normally ruddy when the suntan has worn off – is white. We put it down to grief. I think he used this stick of French chalk to alter his complexion, to simulate grief. It must have dropped out of his pocket. I think he used it to touch up the effect just before he appeared at the door. There is a mirror in the hall. And I noticed traces of white powder on his jacket lapel.'

'My God!' said Tweed. 'And Howard still thinks I'm wrong to introduce women into the Service.'

40

They arrived back at The Anchor and found Butler and Nield having a drink in the bar. Nield sat at the corner table with his head leant against the wall, his eyes half-closed. It was early for business: they had the place to themselves.

'Don't get up,' Paula said as Nield stirred. 'You look all in.'

'Application to the job in hand.' Nield smiled. 'Your boss expects non-stop action,' he said as Tweed arrived with the drinks: mineral water for himself, a glass of white wine for Paula. 'I've been driving over those moors until they seem to start moving.'

'Application!' Butler snorted and drank from his half-pint glass. 'That's what we're here for.' He lowered his voice, speaking to Tweed, who sat next to him. 'Barrymore left Quarme Manor soon after you'd gone. Drove into Minehead. Made a call from a public box. Funny thing to do – he has his phone at home.'

'How long a call?'

'Between one and two minutes. I was going to time it but found my watch had stopped. Then he drives straight back to Quarme Manor.'

'Odd,' Tweed agreed. He looked round the table. 'Does anyone know whether Jill Kearns used to take that Alsatian when she went for her early morning walk on the moor?'

'I do,' Nield said. 'The answer is yes. Came out in a chat I had with the barman over there. She was well-known for those walks. Always started at 6.30 a.m. on the dot. The dog always went with her. For protection as much as company, I imagine. A lonely place, the moor.'

'That means the dog was pining for her,' Tweed remarked. 'And why am I worried about Mrs Larcombe down the road? Something she said. It will come back to me. What is it?'

Paula plucked at his sleeve. 'Look outside.' He twisted round, gazed out of the window. Two men and two girls clad in denims and windcheaters were getting out of a Land Rover covered with a canvas roof. They walked off towards the harbour. 'You see,' she said, 'another of those vehicles.'

Butler nodded. 'Four-wheel drives? They're pretty common – Pete and I have seen a number while we've driven around.'

'And there,' said Tweed, 'goes another theory I had. Every time I think I've got somewhere it turns into a dead end.'

'Like Porlock Weir,' Paula chimed in and sipped more wine.

'One thing I'd like you to do,' Tweed said to Nield, 'is check on the inhabitants of that bungalow estate near Kearns' place. Any titbit you can pick up.'

'First target the electoral register,' Nield replied. 'Then go on from there.'

'Why the interest?' Paula asked.

'Two remarks you made. That it didn't look real. And that you almost expected robots to emerge. Incidentally, the pathologist at Taunton told me Partridge was killed by someone who knew just where to insert the knife. Another thing, Pete,' he went on, 'I need to know whether Kearns still takes those night rides up to the summit of Dunkery Beacon . . .'

'Certainly not at the moment. Only when there's enough moonlight to see his way. Tricky riding those moors at

413

night even for a really experienced horseman.' He drank more beer. 'Well, that should keep my days filled.'

'There's more for you.' Tweed smiled at Nield's expression. 'You'll cope. I'd like you sometime – in daylight – to get up to the top of Dunkery Beacon and poke around up there. With Butler's help you'll manage. Plus, of course, keeping an eye on the other two. I wouldn't want you to have time on your hands, to get bored.' He finished his mineral water and stood up. 'I fancy a breath of fresh air. Want to come, Paula?'

'Lovely idea. Help to work up an appetite for dinner. That remark you made about the pathologist's comment again points the finger at the commandos.'

'Any news from Greece?' Tweed asked Butler as he donned his Burberry. 'You check regularly?'

'As you requested. Not a word. Monica didn't seem worried. She said Newman only calls when he has something solid. Same with Marler.'

'See you.' Tweed nodded to the barman, opened the door, paused. 'Pretty blustery out there.' He took his old waterproof hat off a peg and rammed it over his head. Paula wrapped a scarf round hers.

'Gale warnings round all coasts,' the barman called out.

'Which means a sleepless night,' Tweed remarked to Paula. 'Our bedroom windows both face the front.'

'Harry and Pete will be OK. Theirs face the back. I'm OK . . .'

The wind hit them as they plodded west along the road and then over the track which was still moist from the morning tide. To their right they could hear the crash of the sea against the rocky shoal. Spume, caught by the wind, blew off the wave crests and they felt it on their faces as they walked against the nor'wester.

'Are we staying here long?' Paula asked, her mouth close to his ear.

'I haven't decided. We may push off back to London

414

within a day or two. I've stirred up those three ex-commandos again. One of them may be nudged into making a wrong move. I'm stumped, Paula. And this doesn't seem the right place for any funny goings-on. That vehicle Mrs Larcombe saw would have to drive on through Porlock village even before it could turn up Porlock Hill. Too much risk of being seen.'

'That's not so. Harry told me about the toll road.'

'Told you what?'

'A very lonely road which turns up the hill just outside Porlock Weir. Apparently it turns up and joins the main road to Culbone. Sheer drop on one side. Harry's point was, that is the direct route to Quarme Manor and End-point – even on to our Mr Kearns' place. You take the first left off the main road like we did during our last visit. No one would see you driving that route late at night.'

'I've had enough of this,' said Tweed. 'We'll turn back.'

The wind was hammering them, making it difficult to walk over the sliding pebbles. They reached the track and were hurrying towards The Anchor when Tweed grabbed Paula's arm.

'Let me take a quick look at the harbourmaster's office. It has a notice behind the window.'

He took out a pencil torch, went close up to the deserted building. He shone the beam on the cardboard clock with adjustable hands. *High Tide 10.50 p.m.* The sea was already surging inside the channel which fed the harbour.

'I hope we decide to go back to London,' said Paula. 'If it's going on like this.'

Arriving back in the bar, they hung up their raincoats and got rid of their headgear. Butler and Nield sat at the same table. Tweed offered drinks.

'Not for me,' said Butler. 'I'll stick with this half pint – you may want to send me off somewhere.'

'I'll have a second,' Nield decided. 'I'm not going anywhere. Except to bed after a good dinner.'

'Harry,' Tweed said as he sat down, after calling out the order to the barman, 'have you shown Masterson's photograph to the barman here?'

'No. You told us to keep quiet about him – unless a lead turned up. It didn't.'

Tweed pulled an envelope from his breast pocket, extracted the matt print inside. When the barman arrived with Nield's drink he tapped the print.

'Recognize him? A friend of mine. Said he might stay here a few days. I owe him twenty pounds he lent me when I found I'd left my wallet behind. Can't trace him.'

The barman took hold of the print, studied it with half-closed eyes. He pursed his lips. 'You couldn't add a pair of tinted glasses? And a yachting cap – one of those peaked efforts with gold braid.'

Tweed took back the print, handed it to Paula. 'You're the artist.' She opened her handbag, delved inside, her hand came out holding a felt-tip pen. She frowned for a moment, then started working. She added tinted glasses and a yachting cap. Tweed was startled: it was just the type of gear Masterson would go for. He handed it again to the barman.

'Yes, that's him. Came in here half a dozen times. Thought I knew him when you showed me it first time. Now I'm sure. Had a whizz of a girl with him. Long dark hair and eyes a man could drown in. Spoke good English, but she looked foreign.'

'How long ago was this?' Tweed asked quietly.

'Seems like months ago. A lot of weeks anyway. It's coming back to me. Engaging sort of guy. I remember him asking about the colonel. Did he come in here? I said now and again. Mostly in the evenings.' He handed back the print.

'The colonel?' Tweed queried.

'Yes. Colonel Barrymore. Lives over at Quarme Manor near the Doone Valley. Gloomy old place.'

'Thank you,' said Tweed, and gave him a pound coin.

Paula crossed her legs. She swung one foot up and down. Studying the mud on her shoe, she asked the question.

'Does that mean we'll be staying?'

'I'll sleep on it.'

The *Oporto* mounted a huge wave, the deck tilting at a steep angle. Even in the dark Anton, clinging to the rail, could see its foaming crest. Knowing what was coming, he tightened his grip. The freighter hovered on the crest, then plunged downwards into the chasm. All around him Anton could see giant walls of water which seemed about to overwhelm the vessel. The plunge continued, as though it was heading for the bottom of the ocean. It was pitching and tossing at the same time.

The wind tore at his sodden windcheater, threatening to rip it off his body, howling in his ears. He had just returned from a perilous trip to the hold crammed with baled cork. Twice each day he checked the canvas-covered Stingers, tucked away by Gomez next to the bulkhead.

Anton had taken the precaution of tucking a thread of cotton pulled from a shirt under one of the straps. If anyone fooled around with his precious cargo he would know. The cotton thread was still in position when he made his recent check. As the *Oporto* regained its equilibrium in the trough, Anton ran up to the bridge before it started climbing another mountain.

He opened the door to the wheelhouse and the wind snatched it from his grasp. It took all his strength to pull the door shut. Behind his wheel, Gomez glanced round, his expression impassive as always despite the fury of the storm. Anton hung on to a side rail, ignoring the mate who understood no English.

'Where are we?' he asked.

'Just abreast of Ushant in France. To the east.' Gomez

417

made a quick gesture to his right, then grabbed at the wheel.

The freighter was heading downwards again, its bow flooded with teeming sea. Anton thanked God he was a good sailor. But the view from the bridge was terrifying. An army of tidal-size waves moved towards them from all directions.

'Are we keeping to schedule?' he asked anxiously. 'I mean with this storm.'

'We shall be heaving to off Porlock Weir two days from now. On schedule.' Gomez gave him an evil grin, showing the gold in his teeth. 'If we survive . . .'

Seton-Charles looked like anything but a professor in Greek Studies as he drove back to the Victorian bed-and-breakfast boarding house in Norwich close to midnight. He wore a boiler suit used for gardening. Before leaving his bungalow he had smeared the overalls with a mixture of oil and grease.

He had decided to leave for Norwich early and had driven off ten minutes after Tweed and Paula made their way back to Porlock Weir from Kearns' house. Now he would be in Norwich, ready to visit Camelford Removals, first thing the following day.

Well along the A303 he had seen a truck drivers' café and had pulled in alongside a giant twelve-wheeler. Inside the café he ordered a mug of steaming tea and sat down at a table close to the door. The place was full of drivers, some chatting, others slumped over their own mugs. A juke box playing pop records had added to the noise and the place was filled with blue smoke.

After drinking half the mug of tea, Seton-Charles had left. On his way out he paused to button up his suit at the neck. He eyed the row of caps hanging from wooden hooks. He took a cap with a plastic peak and walked out.

He didn't try it on until he reached a lay-by well clear of the café. It fitted well enough. And for the rimless glasses he normally wore he had substituted his spare pair of horn-rims.

After reserving a room for the night at the boarding house, he ordered a plate of fish and chips and another mug of tea at a cheap café. While he ate he studied the town map he had bought from a newsagent. He decided to take a look at Camelford Removals. He parked the Volvo round the corner from the warehouse, surprised to see lights inside. The figure of a man was silhouetted against a grimy window.

'I've come to take a look at a couple of furniture vans,' he informed a short middle-aged man who introduced himself as Mr Latimer, owner of the bankrupt business. 'They mayn't be what I'm after, but I come on spec . . .'

He slurred his vowels and spoke with a coarse accent. Latimer showed him the four vans still for sale. Seton-Charles chose the two largest, then began haggling over the price, which was expected. He bargained carefully: not offering too little but refusing to agree to Latimer's first price.

They compromised and Seton-Charles pulled a bundle of well-used fifty-pound notes from a pocket in his stained overalls. He paid the agreed deposit and Latimer held several of the notes up to the naked light bulb suspended over a roughened table.

'Done,' he had said. 'You'll collect soon? Pay the balance before you drive them away?'

'Only way to do business. Night . . .'

As he settled between grubby sheets that night Seton-Charles was satisfied. Within two days he'd have both vans hidden away in the barn at Cherry Farm. Although God knew what Jupiter wanted them for.

41

At the Grande Bretagne Newman had caught on to the game Christina was playing. She was holding back on supplying more information to keep him there as a protector against Petros and the Gavalas family. He was on the verge of threatening to leave – to force her hand – when something happened that decided him to be patient a little longer.

The killer heatwave had broken. It was a mere 80°F. September temperature. Marler arrived at 9 a.m. in Newman's room, sprawled on a sofa. He lit a cigarette.

'Well,' said Newman, 'get on with it. What's happened?'

'Patience, chum. You know I've been paying frequent visits to the Cape Sounion area. Object of the exercise to keep an eye on Florakis traipsing up the mountain at night with that transmitter.'

'You're sure it is a transmitter?'

'Absolutely. Took a pair of high-powered night glasses with me. Spent night after night watching him. It's stopped.'

'What has?'

'Do listen. Florakis has stopped making his excursions with the jolly old transmitter. I realized something last night – out of the blue, so to speak. It coincides with no moon.'

'You mean he only transmits when there's a moon? Doesn't make sense.'

'Transmits for about two weeks – when the moon's waxing and waning. Only possible explanation? It's important to the man he's transmitting to. Something else happened. Equally important. Tweed wants to interview friend Petros, I believe?'

'Yes he does. When he can get out here . . .'

'Better make it soon. That snide Dimitrios spotted me watching by the sea shore. Crept up on me. Thought I must be deaf and blind. Put down his rifle, came up behind me, grabbed hold of me. Thought he was going to throttle me, silly ass.'

'So why not tell me what happened next?' Newman asked in a resigned tone.

'Just going to. He ended up flat on the ground, arms pinned to his sides, my knee in his groin. He gave me a splendid opportunity to get him talking. He talked.'

'And how did you accomplish that feat?'

'As I said, we were by the edge. No one about. Still dark. I dragged him to the water's edge. Goes down deep there. Held his head under water three times. He thought I was going to drown him. Which I would have done if he hadn't opened his mouth.'

'Get on with it,' Newman snapped. 'What did you learn?'

'Within two weeks Petros is leaving Devil's Valley. He's owner of a cattle farm in the far north. Macedonia. Tweed would have trouble finding him there. Two weeks,' Marler repeated. 'Up to Tweed, wouldn't you say?'

'I'll call him from the Embassy. But first I'm going back for a word with Christina. You made Dimitrios talk. I'm going to do the same job on her about Anton.' A thought occurred to him as he grasped the door handle. 'Surely you've blown it. Dimitrios will go straight back to Petros and tell him what happened?'

'Doubt that. I warned him. If I heard he'd said anything the next time I saw him would be the last. For him. And he's going to keep quiet for another reason. If he told Petros he'd spilt the beans the old man would kill him.

421

You'll want me to guard Christina when you go to the Embassy, I take it?'

'I'll want you to do just that. Stay with her.'

'Hurry it up, then. I'm short of sleep.'

Christina had just finished drying her washed mane when Newman entered her room. She threw it back over her shoulders.

'How do I look?'

'Never mind that.' His voice was harsh. 'Marler and I will be leaving if you don't start telling me everything you know about Anton. You're on your own.'

'No!' She was appalled. 'Petros will find me. He'll kill me.'

'That's your problem. A family tiff . . .'

'Tiff! Don't you realize yet what he's like?'

'Start telling me then.' Newman perched on the edge of the bed. He folded his arms and stared out of the window, not looking at her as she slumped into a chair.

'I'm frightened. I've told you so much about them already. If Anton found out he'd be even worse than Petros. Anton is cruel.'

'I'm still waiting.' He looked at his wristwatch. 'But not for long.'

'You're a bastard . . .'

'I have diplomas to prove it. Stop stalling.'

She sat down in a large armchair, curled herself inside it like a cat, exposing her long legs. He made a point of not admiring them as she began.

'Anton is one of those people who can do anything. An expert at scuba-diving. Good with boats. Anything mechanical. He can design and build a word processor, a video recorder, a transceiver. And repair them if they break down. He's experienced with hydraulics. He got an estimate for a lift to be installed in his warehouse at Piraeus, thought it too much – so he built the damned thing himself. He's a good horse rider, but I told you that . . .' Once started, she didn't stop. 'He's an expert on handguns and rifles. A crack shot with both. Won some kind of trophy once at Bisley in England. For God's sake, isn't that enough? Oh, and he's a hell-raiser with the women. I think I told you that before.'

'A bit of an all-rounder,' Newman mused.

'He's also good at carpentry. Very good.'

'Carpentry?'

'Building anything out of wood. He made all the furniture for his room at the farm in Devil's Valley. That's the only decently furnished room. The rest is a slum.'

'Why didn't you tell me this before? People must know his many talents.'

'No, not many. He's very secretive. He likes his image of playboy. It amuses him to fool people. I loathe him – and I've never understood him. One more thing, he can fly any kind of light aircraft. Cessnas, Pipers, etc. He belonged to a flying club, then resigned once he'd mastered flying. Said he was bored with it. I think he craves excitement, new worlds to conquer. And he's very ambitious – to become one of the most important men in Greece. I really think I've given you the lot.' She watched him through her eyelashes. 'Do I still get protection?'

'You do. For as long as we can manage it. I have to go out for a short time. Marler will stay with you.'

'He'd better keep his distance,' she said viciously and picked up a hairbrush, 'or I'll crack his skull with this.'

'Argue it out with him while I'm gone.' Newman grinned. 'All I think he wants is kip – sleep. Alone . . .'

Tweed put down his office phone after asking Newman to call him daily. He sat for a few minutes, thinking. Paula and Monica were careful to keep quiet while they worked.

'Paula,' he announced, 'we have to fly to Greece – and soon. Inside the next couple of weeks. Monica, book a couple of first-class return tickets via Zurich. Open date. Bob has just told me Petros is leaving Devil's Valley for some other farm he has up in Macedonia. No one knows the territory up there. Marler and Newman do know Devil's Valley. I need to interrogate the old villain. He's crazed with a lust for vengeance. I want to find out whether he had Masterson killed.'

'How will you go about it?' Paula asked.

'I shall go into Devil's Valley with someone who speaks Greek as an interpreter. I'll grill him at his farm – the only way to get at him. He never comes to Athens – or rarely – so Newman said.'

'That could be dangerous,' Paula protested. 'He sounds mad as a hatter. And Newman told us earlier the area is crawling with armed shepherds.'

'We'll cross that bridge when we come to it.'

'I don't like it,' Paula insisted.

'No one asked you to.' He regretted the words as soon as he had spoken. 'I'm sorry, that was rude. I'm confused about this whole business. There seems no rhyme or reason to it. Unless the whole thing revolves round Petros.'

'You could ask Peter Sarris for help,' Paula suggested.

Tweed shook his head. 'No police until we know what we're getting into. We'll rely on our own resources.' He looked at Monica who had just made the phone call. 'All fixed up?'

'Two open date return tickets via Zurich booked.'

'Is this why we returned here so quickly from Porlock Weir?' enquired Paula.

'Yes. I felt I was getting out of touch with the position in Greece. Butler and Nield can keep a watch on any developments on Exmoor. You have your bag packed, Paula? Good. I may decide to leave suddenly for Athens.'

424

'Why go via Zurich?' Monica asked. 'Instead of flying direct?'

'I want to consult Arthur Beck. We'll call him before we leave. He often knows what's going on. And there are direct flights to Athens from Zurich.' He paused. 'So there are also flights direct from Athens to Zurich.'

'Oh Lord!' Monica groaned. 'He's being enigmatic again.'

Midnight. The storm had abated when the *Oporto* was rounding the tip of Cornwall. The sea now was just choppy as the vessel hove to west of Porlock Weir. On deck on the starboard side Anton held the flashlight and directed the coded signal towards the distant shore. Then he waited.

Gomez stood alongside him close to the gangway which had been lowered over the side. At the foot of the steps waves lapped over the metal platform. The canvas-wrapped Stingers, recovered from the hold, lay at Anton's feet. He wore a waterproof windcheater, thick seaman's trousers tucked inside rubber boots and over this gear a dark green oilskin. His suitcase was protected with another oilskin lashed round it with rope.

'You will need luck to make contact a second time,' Gomez commented.

'The crew are all below decks?' enquired Anton.

'As arranged – except for a lookout who can be trusted.' In the dark he smiled. 'He has been paid to be trusted . . . Look. Over there.'

Anton had already seen the light flashing its return signal from the shore. He checked the number of flashes, then sent a brief final signal, acknowledging, and rammed the flashlight inside a pocket of the oilskin.

'Now we have to wait. But not for long, I suspect . . .'

He was right. As the freighter rocked slowly under the

425

surge of the sea the sound of an engine approaching reached his acute hearing. The night was moonless but soon both could see the white wake of the small boat. Anton reached down and hauled up with both hands the heavy weight of the canvas bundle. Gomez picked up the suitcase with one hand; with the other he raised a pair of night glasses to his eyes, leaning against the rail as he scanned the shoreline. They were two miles out. To the east he picked out the lights of Porlock Weir. He lowered the glasses.

'Be very careful when you go down the gangway. The steps will be slippery. You are carrying a heavy weight.'

'I'll be all right. And when I've left you're turning round and sailing out to sea, ready to come back tomorrow?'

'Do not worry. No one will know we arrived off England earlier.'

The small grey-coloured motorboat, powered by an outboard at its stern, was close. Gomez could make out the figure of the solitary man aboard. As before, he wore a Balaclava helmet under a dark green oilskin. He cut the power, the boat glided forward, bumped against the platform. Balaclava hurled up a mooring rope. Gomez caught it with his free hand, the glasses looped round his neck, made the rope fast to the rail.

Anton stood on the top platform, slowly went down, step by step. He rested the bundle on the rails on either side, letting them take the weight, sliding it down. The moored boat ground up against the *Oporto*'s hull, made a grating sound. Anton was half-way down when the sea lifted the freighter, then dropped it. Anton lost his grip, the bundle tumbled down the remaining steps, landed on the lower platform. He swore in Greek, grabbing the rails to recover his balance.

Balaclava leant forward, took hold of the cargo, heaved it up and lowered it quickly inside the boat. Anton stepped off the platform and joined him. Gomez called down, dropped the mooring rope he had untied and Balaclava hauled it in, dripping, looped round the handle of Anton's suitcase.

Anton sat down as his companion started up the outboard, grabbed the tiller and guided the boat away from the *Oporto*. He was just in time. A large wave lifted the boat, would have hurled it against the freighter, but Balaclava had steered the boat round. He headed for the distant shore.

The motorboat was coming in close to the rock-strewn coast. Behind it cliffs loomed, hiding them from the mainland. Anton was careful not to stare at the eyes which looked out through the slit in the Balaclava helmet.

He had no idea of the identity of his companion. When he had landed on his previous trip to Exmoor the same man had met him, wearing the same gear. Because of the loose flapping oilskin he wore it was impossible for Anton to guess Balaclava's height, build or age. Only the voice was distinctive. Upper-crust, clipped. On the rare occasions when he spoke.

As they approached the shore, the boat pitching and tossing, the engine was cut out. Balaclava crouched over the tiller, peering ahead, steering the craft towards a slope. There was a grinding sound as the keel rode up over rocks and pebbles, stopped.

'Take the weapons, put them in the vehicle.'

Anton heaved up the bundle, stepped out of the boat and staggered to the canvas-covered four-wheel-drive vehicle parked close to the shoreline. He used his shoulder to ease up the flap at the rear, hoisted the bundle higher, lowered it inside on top of a pile of coiled ropes. The wind whipped at his oilskin, blew it round his legs as he let the flap drop and went back for his case.

Balaclava had taken an axe attached to the side and began hammering at the deck. The axe was heavy, its blade

427

honed like a razor. As he worked chips of wood flew up and he protected his eyes by holding one arm across them. He paused as Anton lifted out his case, turned to him.

'The sea goes down a hundred feet here. We have to lose this boat. Don't stand there watching me – keep an eye out along the shore.'

The axe began to sweep down again in thudding arcs. Inside a few minutes the boat was holed. Balaclava went on working, enlarging the gaping cavity. He was only satisfied when the hole was a foot wide, then he hurled the axe into the waves and returned to the vehicle. Climbing into the rear, he shifted the Stingers and covered them with the mass of rope. Jumping back on to the shore he gestured Anton to join him.

'We want to heave the boat over the edge. Give me a hand . . .'

They stood near the bow on either side and pushed with all their strength. The boat slid slowly backwards, the outboard poised over the edge. They straightened up, stretching their strained arms, took hold of the boat again. One more prolonged heave and the boat was floating. It filled rapidly with water, drifting just offshore. Then it went down stern first. The bow hovered above the surface, disappeared.

Balaclava strode towards the vehicle, climbed in behind the wheel and Anton sat beside him. They drove off without lights, heading away from the sea, bumping and jostling over the rough terrain.

The driver switched on his lights as they reached the track past the cottages. He never gave a glance at the darkened dwelling where Mrs Larcombe had talked with Tweed. He drove on along the road at higher speed, passing The Anchor Hotel, continuing towards Porlock.

Reaching the toll road, he swung the vehicle up the steep

428

curving slope. At the top he turned right again along the coast road. Beyond Culbone he turned left off the main road down on to the winding country lane which eventually led to the Doone Valley. For the first time he broke his long silence.

'Here is the key to the small house where you spend the night. It is unoccupied. And here is a pencil flashlight so you can find your way round it. The electricity is cut off. You will find canned meat, a tin opener, a loaf of bread, butter, knife, two bottles of mineral water inside a brown paper parcel in a downstairs room. Also a sleeping bag. The place is unfurnished. We'll park the vehicle in a garage alongside. But take the weapons into the house. Sleep with them by your side. And here is a sheathed knife for protection – to be used only in an emergency.'

Anton took the weapon. 'This is a commando knife,' he commented. 'I brought a couple with me . . .'

'Listen!' Balaclava was concentrating on negotiating the road which dropped as it twisted between high hedges. 'Keep that knife. Now, in the morning you take the weapons to Cherry Farm. You remember how to get there from the drive we took last time?'

'Yes. It's near Liphook in Hampshire.'

Balaclava stopped the vehicle at a bend where he could see in both directions, pulled an ordnance survey map from the door's pocket. 'Use the flashlight and show me the location of Cherry Farm. Your route is marked part of the way in pen – driving along side roads. That way you should avoid all police patrol cars.'

Anton unfolded the map, studied it with the aid of the light. He pointed to an area. 'The track to it turns off about here.'

'Good. Keep the map. Burn it when you get there. And you've plenty to keep you occupied when you do get there. You will find you have company. You give him the password – Sandpiper.'

'What does he say in return?' Anton asked.

'Nothing.' Balaclava chuckled, a hard cynical sound. 'You'll recognize him. Tomorrow morning you drive this contraption to Taunton.' He hauled a slim folder from the same pocket. 'I've marked on this with a light pencil cross the car park where you leave this vehicle about ten in the morning. You park at the very back where there's a thick hedge. Hide the cargo under that hedge while you're away hiring a car from Barton's – they are marked with a pencilled circle. And here is a driving licence in the name of Partridge for hiring the car. Drive it to the car park. Collect the cargo. Then head for Cherry Farm. You leave this vehicle in the car park and you must be on your way by eleven o'clock. I will have the vehicle collected. Understood.'

'Let me check this.' Anton was studying the street plan of Taunton with the aid of the flashlight. He found the cross and the circle. 'All clear. But why can't I drive straight on to Cherry Farm now? Or am I dropping you somewhere?'

'Of course not. I have transport waiting not far from the house where you spend the night. And travelling at night is dangerous. You could be stopped and checked by a patrol car. You should have thought of that yourself.'

'You are right,' Anton agreed quickly. There was something in Balaclava's manner, in his contemptuous tone, which frightened him.

'Needless to say, you burn the Taunton map soon after you have left Taunton behind. Now listen carefully. I said earlier you will have plenty to occupy you at Cherry Farm. Something that will test your skills as a carpenter and hydraulics expert. So *listen*. There are two furniture vans at the farm. This is what you have to do . . .'

By early afternoon the following day Anton was driving his hired Austin Metro close to Liphook in Hampshire.

The Stingers and missiles were in the boot, concealed under a load of groceries he had bought in Glastonbury.

On both sides of the country road the flat fields stretched away beyond low hedges. The sun was shining and he hadn't passed another vehicle for several miles. He drove round a bend and slowed his speed, recognizing he was very close. Anton had the most retentive memory for routes and geography. Across the road were freshly fallen leaves. Autumn was coming. Soon September would become October.

He stopped the car alongside a closed gate with a gravel track beyond. He sat listening for several minutes, listening for the sound of the distant approach of any more traffic. Nothing. He got out, opened the gate which carried the legend *Cherry Farm* in white paint. Driving up the track a few yards, he stopped the car again, got out and went back to close the gate. Attention to detail.

The field alongside the track was spongy grass. As he drove further he passed large lakes, the product of rain which had fallen three days earlier. Poor agricultural land. He followed the curve of the track and Cherry Farm came into view.

A long low two-storey building made of brick with a tiled roof, it had two squat chimney stacks and a large barn to the right of the farmhouse. The place had a deserted look and he drove slowly, his eyes scanning the whole area in search of a sign of life.

Beyond the large barn stood two long sheds with corrugated iron roofs. The doors to both were closed. As he drove closer he saw the farm had an abandoned look. Undergrowth was smothering the tiny garden in front. Ivy creeper sprawled up the brickwork like a giant spider, its tentacles crawling over the closed shutters.

Had something gone wrong? Where was the man he was supposed to meet? He drove on round the back of the farmhouse, parked the car in a muddy yard, switched off the engine and listened again. There is no silence more eerie than that of a deserted countryside.

Anton remained behind the wheel, checked the knife in the sheath attached to his belt. No cattle, no sheep. No animals of any kind. More lakes standing in the soggy field behind the farm. No birds chattered or wheeled in the clear blue sky. Then the back door opened. Seton-Charles came out to meet him. Anton hid his astonishment.

'Sandpiper,' he said.

'You have the weapons? Good. We'll get them to their hiding-place inside the house. Then drive your car and park it inside the first shed beyond the barn. There are doors at this end . . .'

Seton-Charles stood in the kitchen, watching Anton through his rimless glasses as the Greek ate ham sandwiches, drank mineral water. Seated at the table, Anton ignored the Professor. There was a distinct sense of unease between the two men. It had been different in Athens when Seton-Charles had lectured him at the university. Anton finished his meal, decided to establish his authority from the beginning.

'I'm in charge here. You know that?'

'So I was informed.' Seton-Charles' tone expressed no enthusiasm for the arrangement. He leaned against the dresser, folded his arms. 'What role are you playing here?'

'You leave this farm from time to time?' Anton asked cautiously.

'Not without your permission. I prepare the meals from now on. I give you any help you may need with your work. What work?'

'Communications,' Anton persisted. 'How do we keep in touch with Jupiter?'

'We don't. There is a phone in the hall. He calls us. We

432

make no calls, have no contact with the outside world. You buy fresh food supplies in Liphook when we need them.'

'And might anyone come poking around here?'

'No. Haven't you seen the state of the farm? The land is useless, waterlogged half the time. The next farm is miles away. Now, if you don't mind, I'd like some idea on what I'm supposed to help you with. The two furniture vans are hidden inside the huge barn, one behind the other.'

Satisfied with the security, Anton dabbed at his mouth with a silk handkerchief. He twisted round in his chair to stare hard at the Professor.

'You saw the short planks of wood still in the boot? I bought them at a timberyard on the way. You've seen the two boxes on the floor here?'

'Yes.' Seton-Charles stared down at the containers, made of heavy wood and like tool boxes. The lids were open. Inside one was a collection of wires, steel slides and other electrical-type equipment. The second box looked like a carpenter's and was crammed with planes, saws, screwdrivers and other tools. 'What are you up to?' he asked.

'A complex operation. Each of those furniture vans has to be fitted with a large sliding panel in the roof – electrically operated. The hydraulics will be difficult. And inside each van I'll be building a platform with steps – the platform top to be about three feet below the roof, fitted with a chair I'll clamp to the platform.' Anton grinned. 'Guess what all that is for?'

'I'm not in the guessing game,' Seton-Charles said coldly.

'We're in the business of building two mobile rocket launchers.'

PART THREE

The Greek Key

42

'We're coming in to land,' said Paula and gripped Tweed's arm. 'This is the bit I never like.'

'Look at the view over there out of the starboard windows,' he suggested and squeezed her hand.

They were aboard Swissair flight 801, approaching Zurich's airport, Kloten. The machine was banking and Paula saw framed in a window the magnificent sweep of the Bernese Oberland range, its peaks snow-capped. She sucked in her breath as she watched the mountain summits silhouetted against a backdrop of cloudless azure sky.

Tweed had taken one of his snap decisions. They had left London Airport at 9.30 a.m. and were due to arrive at 12.05 p.m. Before leaving Tweed had phoned Federal police chief Arthur Beck, an old friend. Beck was meeting them at Kloten. What worried Tweed was the closeness of their connection with the Swissair flight taking them on to Athens.

Flight 302, bound for Athens, departed from Kloten at 12.30 p.m. It gave them no time at all to check in on the fresh flight and Tweed needed time to consult with Beck. As the plane descended he laid his hand over Paula's and she turned and smiled.

'I'm OK now. Just a brief fit of nerves. Do you think Monica has got through to Newman, warning him we're coming?'

'It all depends on how early Newman makes *his* daily call to her. At least we know where to find him. The Grande Bretagne . . .'

Paula hardly realized the plane had landed as it skimmed along the runway. Beck was waiting for them at Passport Control. He wore civilian clothes and a Tyrolean hat with a little feather in the hat band, dressed like a man on holiday. The grey eyes under the thick brows gleamed as he spotted Paula. He took her arm.

'Welcome to Zurich, Paula.' He kissed her on the cheek. 'We bypass all the checks.' He looked over his shoulder as he led her to a side door which a guard unlocked. 'You'd better come too, Tweed. We have time to talk.'

Tweed smiled to himself. Beck had developed a soft spot for Paula when they'd met previously in Geneva. And he had organized their arrival so no one would notice them. He followed Paula along a corridor and into a starkly furnished room with maps on the walls.

'Thank you,' said Paula as Beck pulled out a chair for her from under a table. 'But what about our cases? Shouldn't I go to the carousel?'

'All taken care of, my dear. I phoned Jim Corcoran, security boss at London Airport. When you checked in a special small red label was attached to your luggage and Tweed's. Two of my men are at the carousel now, collecting your things.'

'Am I permitted to join you?' Tweed enquired mischievously.

'As a special favour, my friend. This is Kloten security chief's office I have borrowed. As you see, there is coffee and sandwiches. You would like some, Paula? Good.'

On the table was an electric warmer with a transparent flask of coffee perched on it. Sandwiches wrapped in cling-film. A telephone with a red button. Tweed sat down and stared at the instrument as Beck spoke while he poured coffee.

'Monica called you from London, spoke to the security chief and left a message. Can you call her urgently?'

Tweed looked at a clock attached to the wall with a red

second hand sweeping the dial. 'We're going to miss our flight we're booked on for Athens. It leaves at 12.30 as I told you.'

'So . . .' Beck waved a hand. 'It has been delayed. A bomb hoax. All passengers have to identify their luggage laid out on the tarmac before they board. That takes time.' He smiled. 'One of the advantages of being Chief of Police.' He sat next to Paula as he addressed Tweed. 'So, make your call, then we can talk.'

I should have guessed he'd tie it all up for us, Tweed thought. He reached for the phone, pressed the scrambler button, dialled Park Crescent. Beck and Paula talked in whispers while Tweed was calling London. She liked the Swiss: he had a wicked sense of humour. She put her hand over her mouth to suppress laughter and then noticed Tweed's expression as he replaced the receiver.

'Is something wrong?'

'Later,' he replied and looked at Beck. 'Greece. Have you heard anything unusual on the grapevine?'

'No. Unless this comes under the heading of un-usual . . .' For five minutes he recounted his two conver-sations with Kalos. He recalled how he had followed his quarry, kept an eye on him while he had spent a night at the Schweizerhof and then boarded a plane for Lisbon the following day.

'Lisbon?' Tweed's expression was grim. 'Are you sure, Arthur?'

'Of course I'm sure. I followed him myself to the airport. Later I checked with the pilot that he was on board. He was.'

'Sorry. That was a silly question. How long ago?'

'Ten days from today.'

'Hell's teeth.' Tweed stood up, began pacing the room. 'And I was congratulating myself that he was safely back in Athens. I'm getting this all wrong.' He looked at Paula. 'I said the solution lay in Greece, not Exmoor. Maybe it's the other way round.'

'Do we go on?' Paula asked.

'Yes. And we'd better hurry.'

'Might be as well,' Beck agreed. 'The baggage check should just about be over. You'll have to identify your own stuff. It will be all that's left on the tarmac . . .'

He hugged Paula, shook hands with Tweed. 'Anything more I can do to help – you give me a call.'

'You've helped a lot already,' Tweed assured him and they followed the Swiss to the aircraft.

They had eaten lunch. The plane was thirty thousand feet up and well south over the Adriatic Sea before Paula asked the question.

'You had bad news when you talked with Monica?'

'It's getting worse. Like the Klein problem we faced last year, the body count is rising. Butler called Monica. You remember that nice sharp old lady, Mrs Larcombe, we called on at Porlock Weir? This morning a neighbour noticed she hadn't taken her milk in. She started worrying, called the police. They found the front door unlocked and Mrs Larcombe battered to death.'

'Oh, that's awful. She was so bright for her age. Bright for any age. What do they think happened?'

'The *police* think some drunken youths called, pushed open the door when she reacted to the ringing of the bell, attacked her and walked off with fifty pounds she always kept in ready cash under her mattress. They found two empty beer cans in the front garden. No fingerprints.'

'I did catch your emphasis on "police". What do you think?'

'I'm convinced it was staged. Drunken youths don't remember to wipe beer cans clean of fingerprints. Something bothered me about what she said to us and I couldn't recall it afterwards. Now I can.'

'What was it?'

'When that four-wheel-drive vehicle stopped outside her house at midnight she opened the front window. She said that window *creaked*. My guess is the driver heard that creak. And no one believed her when she said she saw flashing lights out at sea and up the coast. She saw them all right.'

'I still don't follow,' Paula commented.

'That was the first run – bringing something, or someone – landed on the coast. There must have been a second run last night, an important one. They couldn't risk her seeing them – so they called on her, she opened the door, and that was it. The fact that she opened the door is significant.'

'Someone she knew?'

'I think so. She was a shrewd careful woman. And I noticed she had one of those spyglass things in her front door. She could see who was there before she opened it. Yes, someone she knew – or knew of. A respected citizen.'

'What a brutal thing to do.' Paula shivered. 'To kill an old lady like that just on the off-chance she looked out of her window at the wrong moment.'

'But we are dealing with a ruthless killer. Look at the score – Sam Partridge, Jill Kearns and now Mrs Larcombe. The stakes must be very high.'

He peered out of the window. The air was crystal clear, without a cloud. He looked down on the intense blue of the Adriatic. A tiny blur of white on the blue located the wake of a ship moving south: the ship was invisible.

'When we get to Athens,' he went on, 'someone must go to the Embassy to call Monica. I want her to contact Roberts of Lloyd's of London, get him to check the shipping register.'

'Why?'

'Remember what Beck told us about Anton. He took a flight from Zurich to Lisbon. Roberts can check the movements of any vessel sailing from Lisbon about ten days ago – a vessel bound for Watchet on the Somerset coast. The killing of Mrs Larcombe backs up a vague theory I'd developed – that the way Anton slipped in without any record was that he came ashore from some vessel during the night. Hence those flashing lights Mrs Larcombe really did see.' He grunted. 'And now he may be back on Exmoor again. I don't like that at all. Monica must warn Butler.'

'And you think Jill was killed because she knew too much?'

'I have another idea about that. She may have been run down simply to divert our attention away from Exmoor to London.'

'That would be too horrible,' Paula protested.

'I said we're up against a ruthless killer.' He looked round the interior of the aircraft. They were travelling first-class and the section was three-quarters empty, which enabled them to talk freely. He peered out of the window again, checked his watch, settled himself back in his seat. 'Less than one hour to Athens. I have the feeling we're going to stir up a hornet's nest.'

The heat hit Tweed like a hammer as he emerged from the aircraft on to the mobile staircase. He walked down the steps and, with Paula by his side, made for the main building.

'God!' said Paula. 'It's baking and you don't like the heat.'

'So it's a good job you reminded me to wear my safari jacket and tropical drill trousers. Now, let's get the show on the road . . .'

Newman was waiting for them in the reception hall. He grinned as he came forward, shook hands with Tweed, hugged Paula, took her case.

'I phoned Monica early and she told me your flight details. I have a car outside. Straight to the Grande Bretagne? Marler is there, looking after Christina.'

'Straight to the Grande Bretagne,' Tweed replied. 'Sarris must not know I'm in town. We have to organize an expedition into Devil's Valley. I must see Petros, cross-examine him.'

'That will have to be planned carefully,' Newman remarked as he sat behind the wheel and drove off after storing their cases in the boot. He sensed tension in Tweed, that he was in one hell of a hurry.

Forty minutes later they were sitting in the room Newman had booked for Tweed. Newman relayed to him all the details about Anton he'd extracted from Christina. As he listened, sipping mineral water in his shirt-sleeves, Tweed's expression became grimmer.

'A man of many talents,' he commented as Newman concluded his report. 'And now I'm sure he's returned to England.' He told Newman the news Beck and Monica had given him in Zurich. 'I don't like the sound of any of this. But when can we get down to Devil's Valley? Tomorrow?'

'That's pushing it. You'll need protection – and an interpreter. Petros doesn't speak English, you don't speak Greek. I think we have just the man. Nick the Greek, our driver. I've kept him on ice. He's holed up at the Astir Palace just across the square. He's even protested about the extra fee I pay him, saying he's doing nothing for it. Do you want to talk with Christina?'

'Yes.' He looked at Paula.

She shook her head, smiled impishly. 'Better you see her on your own. I'll cramp your style. I bet you have her eating out of your hand.'

'I doubt that.' Tweed finished off his second glass of mineral water. 'But one-to-one conversations normally get off the ground better.'

443

'Especially when you're with an attractive girl,' Paula went on.

'Oh, do shut up.' Tweed put on his jacket. 'Just going to the bathroom. Back in a minute . . .'

Paula waited until he reached the door, then called out. 'Don't forget to comb your hair!' Tweed gave her a glare and vanished.

'You do twist his tail,' Newman commented.

She became serious. 'I'm trying to relax him. I'm really worried about him. He's got the bit between his teeth over this business. He's become obsessed.'

'Can you explain that quickly? I'll be taking him along soon to Christina.'

'It started with Masterson's death. You can't kill one of Tweed's sector chiefs and expect him to shrug it off like Howard might. Then Jill Kearns – and he took a fancy to her – was murdered in London. Before that his old friend Sam Partridge was killed on Exmoor. And now an old lady in her seventies, a Mrs Larcombe, he interviewed has been battered to death at Porlock Weir. That was the last straw, I suspect. All the killings could be linked. If he decides Petros is in some way responsible I don't know what he'll do. Which is why I'm petrified about this Devil's Valley visit. Tweed has lost his sense of detachment.'

'Thanks for telling me. I'll bear it in mind. Now I must call someone.'

Newman went to the phone, dialled a number, perched on the edge of the bed. 'That you, Nick? Can you get over here for a talk? In about five minutes? Good. My room. See you . . .'

Tweed came out of the bathroom as he put down the phone. 'We'll be having a conference about the trip to Devil's Valley while you talk with Christina,' he told Tweed. 'Nick, Marler and myself.'

'The sooner the better. I'm ready for Christina. What about you, Paula? Going to peek at the shops?'

444

'She'll be joining us,' Newman said firmly. He seemed to have taken command of the situation, noted Paula. Noted it with relief.

Newman escorted Tweed to another room on the same floor. When he rapped on the door in a certain sequence it was opened by Marler. He gazed at Tweed, then at Newman.

'You might have told me he was coming. About time,' he continued, looking at Tweed. 'Glad to have you on board. We need to take some action.'

'You'll get all you can handle soon,' Newman promised him. 'Be a good chap, push off to my room. Here's the key. Tweed wants to talk with Christina.'

As Marler left he walked into the room, followed by Tweed, and introduced him to Christina. 'My Editor-in-Chief . . .'

Christina was sitting on a sofa, her back propped against one end, her long legs stretched out. She wore a low-cut emerald green dress, strapless, and backless to the lower part of her spine. She put down the book she was reading and stared at Tweed with her large eyes as Newman left the room, assessing him. Then she swung her legs off the sofa and sat with them crossed, one bare arm rested along the top of the sofa.

'Do sit down. Pull up a chair close to me. You look like a man who can take care of himself.'

'I've survived so far.' Tweed moved a chair, sat down so their knees were almost touching. She was a woman who liked close combat, who liked to touch a man if he passed inspection. Tweed had a feeling he'd done just that. And he wanted her to talk. She asked him if he'd like a drink. He said mineral water would be fine. She reached out to a table standing at the end of the sofa, poured him a glass from a collection of bottles, then she helped herself to a glass of white wine. She raised her glass.

'Here's to us.'

'To us . . .'

'And you're not an editor.' She peered at him over the rim and sipped some wine. 'You have the eyes of a policeman. They're nice eyes.'

'I was once a policeman.' He had decided frankness – up to a point – was his best tactic with this shrewd and glamorous creature. 'What can you tell me about the Greek Key? I need your help. Very badly. A lot of people have already died here and in England. I suspect more may die unless I find out what is going on.' He took off his glasses, laid them on the table. 'I need all the help I can get.'

'Will Newman or Marler be coming back?' She watched him through half-closed eyes.

'Not unless I summon them. I wasn't thinking of doing so.'

He had trouble keeping his eyes off her beautifully moulded shoulders. The dress fitted her snugly; her well-rounded breasts projected against the cloth. She leaned forward and kissed him full on the mouth.

'That was for starters, Tweed.'

'The Greek Key?'

'A group of the most dangerous men in Greece. Shadow men who operate in the dark. The police can't find them. They live secret lives. Does that sound melodramatic?'

'Yes. But it sounds just what I'm looking for. Tell me more.'

'So you don't really need your glasses to see?'

'Only long distance. When I'm driving. Times like that. Then I forget I'm wearing them. Tell me more,' he repeated.

'I've told you too much already. You want to get me killed?'

'No. I'd go a long way to prevent that. Is Anton a member?'

She blinked, lowered her eyes. He could have sworn the suggestion came to her as a great shock. That she was

446

thinking back over incidents she had observed – trying to link them up with his question.

'I never thought of that.' She opened her full red lips and ran the tip of her tongue along her lower lip. 'I can trust you?'

'You must decide that for yourself.'

'When my mother sent me to the university – she's dead, Petros killed her with overwork on the farm – there was an English professor, Guy Seton-Charles.'

'What about him?' Tweed asked in the same quiet tone.

'There were rumours. He came to lecture from England each year. Behind his back they called him The Recruiter.'

'Who were "they"?' His voice was very soft now, careful not to disturb her mood.

'You will protect me?' She leaned close again and her eyes were enormous. She slowly removed her earclips, placed them on the table.

'Yes,' he said. 'Providing you do exactly what I tell you when the time comes.'

'You're a nice man. Some of the students who attended the Seton-Charles lectures stopped going to them.'

'Who was he recruiting for?'

'The Greek Key.' Her smooth-skinned face was almost touching his and he caught a waft of perfume. He told himself to move back but he was frightened of breaking the spell. 'I asked what it was and they wouldn't tell me. You asked me if Anton was a member. He attended the lectures and finished the course. After that he was a changed man.'

'Changed in what way?'

'He used to lay women like rows of beans. He still kept his playboy image outwardly – but he seemed to have become colder, more purposeful – dedicated. That's it. *Dedicated*.'

'Dedicated to what?'

'I don't know. Really, I don't, Tweed. As though he'd found some mission in life. Almost like a religious conversion. But he's an agnostic. That's all I can say.'

Tweed eased his chair away. He stood up. Christina also stood up and walked towards him. He had a curious gleam in his eyes. He saw his glasses still on the table, picked them up. Before he could put them on she grasped him.

'Let's do it. Now.'

He sighed, shook his head. 'Christina, I said I would protect you. I will. But I can't if we get involved with each other. I must go. Pack your things ready for a quick departure. All except your night things.'

'I have to say thank you.'

She pressed herself against him, kissed him again.

'You'll be leaving tomorrow,' he told her.

'Unless Dimitrios or Constantine or Anton reach me tonight.'

'Which do you fear most?'

'Anton. Of course . . .'

'He is no longer in Greece. And you will continue to be with someone until you leave. It may be a woman.'

'What use will she be? In an emergency?'

'More deadly than a man. I must go. Lock the door and only open it for the special knock. You do have confidence in me?'

'Completely.' She ran her hands through her hair. 'We will meet again?'

'If possible. It depends on how things develop . . .'

He waited outside the closed door until he heard her lock it. His hands were wet with perspiration. And not from the heat.

Four people sat round a table in Newman's room. Newman himself, Nick the Greek, Paula and Marler. Two litre bottles of mineral water stood on the table with four

448

glasses. The bottles were almost empty. Tweed was introduced to Nick who clasped his hand in a firm grip and gazed straight at him. Tweed liked what he saw.

'Bob,' he said, 'take Paula along to Christina and introduce her. I want you to stay with her, Paula. Only open the door to the special knock Bob will demonstrate.'

Paula looked amused as she stood up and smoothed down her skirt. She stood close and whispered. 'Better go into the bathroom and comb your hair again. Clean up your mouth at the same time.'

Newman had reached the door with Paula when Tweed stopped them. 'Wait a moment.' He looked at Nick. 'I understand you can find weapons. We'll all be away when we go to Devil's Valley. Paula should have some protection. A small handgun. Can you obtain one for her?'

Nick, still seated, rolled up his left trouser leg and revealed the holster strapped to it. He pulled out a small gun, a .32 Browning automatic. He showed it to Paula.

'Do you know this gun?'

'Yes. It's a Browning. I've practised with it. That would do nicely.'

'And spare mags.' Nick handed her the gun and hauled the mags out of his pocket.

Paula dropped the mags into her handbag. She examined the Browning, released the magazine from the butt, made sure there was no bullet up the spout, all the time holding the weapon pointed at the wall. Nick watched with approval as she rammed the mag home again, dropped the weapon inside her handbag.

'You know the gun,' he said.

Tweed laid a hand on her shoulder. 'Only to be used in extreme emergency – if Christina's or your own life is in danger. You have no permit to use that in Greece. But if push comes to shove I'll square it with Peter Sarris. Take care.'

449

'And *you* take care,' she said vehemently. 'This whole secret expedition to Devil's Valley is madness . . .'

'Now go along with Bob and make friends with Christina.'

When they had gone he excused himself. Inside the bathroom he checked his appearance in the mirror. He should have done that before he'd left Christina. His hair was mussed up; traces of lipstick showed on his mouth. Christina had deliberately let him go like that – knowing there was another woman with him. Just to show Paula. Women! Thank God he'd kept control of himself.

He had a wash, used a tissue to clean off the lipstick. When he had combed his hair he went back into the bedroom.

'What's the plan?' he asked, sitting down at the table.

'She's quite a girl, Christina,' Marler remarked cynically.

'Don't you start.' Tweed jabbed his index finger at Marler. 'I said what's the plan?'

'Crack of dawn tomorrow we start out,' Marler began in a languid tone. 'We drive to the entrance near Cape Sounion. You go in on foot with Nick. He speaks Greek, he's the interpreter, and he knows the way. And we've devised back-up . . .'

Marler explained the details and Tweed listened in silence. He nodded when Marler had finished. 'You've been out here a while. You know what you're doing. At least, I hope so. I approve the plan.'

'It will be tricky – the timing,' Nick interjected. 'Dangerous, too.' He was looking at Tweed. 'What type of gun would you like? I can get most . . .'

'I never carry a gun.'

Tweed stood up. 'I have to attend to something now.' Newman came back into the room, using his key to unlock the door. 'I'm off to the Embassy,' Tweed told him. 'I have to talk to Monica, get her to contact Roberts at

450

Lloyd's. And warn Butler Anton is probably back on his patch.'

'I'll come with you,' said Nick. 'We pass the Astir Palace on the way to the Embassy. I can pick up another Browning from under my car in the garage.'

'I can go alone. I know the way. I studied a street plan of Athens before I left London. No one will recognize me.'

'I'm coming with you,' Nick persisted. 'Petros could have men watching this hotel. They would see you arrive with Newman and make the connection.'

'You're right. Thank you.'

Tweed cursed himself inwardly for not thinking of that. Maybe the heat was getting to him. They were crossing the road to the Astir Palace when Nick made the remark.

'It will be touch and go whether we survive in Devil's Valley.'

43

Dawn was breaking over the Temple of Poseidon when the two cars pulled off the coast road close to the skeletal hotel building site. Nick drove the Mercedes with Tweed beside him. Behind them Newman drove a hired Peugeot with Marler as his passenger.

'I'll drive,' he'd told Marler when they started from Athens in the dark. 'We want to get there in one piece.'

'I was a racing driver once,' Marler informed him.

'I know. You must have been a menace to the other contestants. I don't want to end up in the sea . . .'

Tweed stepped out of the Mercedes and stretched. He was wearing a pair of mountaineer boots purchased in

Kolonaki. He'd worn them for the rest of the previous day to break them in.

Nick lifted up the travelling rug on the rear seat, took hold of the twin-barrelled shotgun. He had a fresh Browning strapped to his leg, a .38 Smith & Wesson in a hip holster under his loose jacket.

'A walking armoury,' Tweed had joked.

'We'll need it,' Nick had replied without a smile.

While Nick was collecting the weapon, locking the car, Tweed gazed at the fantastic colours of sky and sea. A spectrum of rose pink, cobalt and sapphire sea. An incredible sight you wouldn't find anywhere else in the world.

'Ready?' asked Nick.

'On a job like this the thing is get moving. No palaver.'

Nick led the way behind the complex and they plunged into the wilderness of limestone bluffs looming above donkey trails which twisted and climbed. There was no sound once they'd left behind the screech of the gulls over the sea which soon vanished from view. Nick placed his feet carefully, treading wherever possible on tufts of grass to deaden the sound of his footfalls. Behind him Tweed followed suit, watching for any sign of human life.

He wore a wide-brimmed straw hat, his safari jacket, tropical drill trousers tucked into the tops of his boots. Despite Nick's long sloping strides, Tweed had no trouble keeping up with him. In London he'd taken to rising very early, walking two miles round the deserted streets every day. At the weekends he drove down to Surrey, parked his Cortina and climbed the North Downs. He was in better shape than for years.

They crossed the pass and began to descend into Devil's Valley. The tortuous path twisted as it dropped rapidly round boulders of limestone. Both Nick and Tweed carried water bottles slung over their shoulders. Nick carried the

452

shotgun in his left hand and paused as he came to each man-high boulder. He peered round it cautiously, waved to Tweed to proceed, and walked on.

The sun was climbing in a clear turquoise sky. Already it was becoming very hot: the heat from the previous day had never dissipated during the night. As they progressed deep inside the valley Tweed cast frequent glances up at the ridges enclosing them to east and west. No sign of movement. Only the occasional sheep came into view, head down as it searched for nourishment among the scrub grass.

Tweed saw a weird squat structure perched on the ridge against the eastern skyline. He guessed it was the abandoned silver mine where Newman had had his nightmare experience. They arrived at the base of the valley and the path ran to left and to right. Nick paused, drank from his water bottle, wiped sweat off his forehead. Tweed wrapped a large silk handkerchief round his own neck to mop up the sweat.

'What's that thing?' Tweed asked, pointing to a crumbling high building. A series of chutes ran at angles and all the metal was rusty. The derelict structure stood at the foot of a path climbing up the eastern slope.

'The old ore-crushing plant where they extracted the silver,' Nick explained. 'Hasn't been used for years. Donkey trains brought down the ore. Have you noticed how quiet it is? And no sign of anyone.'

It was the first conversation they had had since they started out. They had agreed in the car they wouldn't speak during the descent into the valley. Nick had explained that voices carried a long distance.

'Well, isn't that our good luck?' Tweed commented and drank from his own water bottle.

'It's too quiet. And I have not seen one single shepherd. That I do not like.'

'Why not?'

'It is almost as though they know we are coming. Fifteen more minutes' walk along this path to the left and we see Petros' farmhouse . . .'

It was creepy. Despite the glare of the sun burning down Tweed found the silence unnerving. Now they had to pick their way among a bed of stones and rocks and he realized they were walking along the path of a stream. In winter it would be a gushing flood.

Tweed paused to glance round. Dante's Inferno. That was what it reminded him of. The deep valley, the mountains closing in, the heat trapped in the wide gulch they were moving through. It was the sheer aridity of the slopes which appalled him. Scrub, nothing but scrub.

By now his boots and clothes were coated with fine limestone dust. It clung to his wet face. Nick turned and walked back to him. He scanned the slopes and shook his head.

'Maybe we should go back,' he suggested.

'Why?' asked Tweed.

'Look at that flock of sheep grazing high up on the mountain. No shepherd. There should be a shepherd. Something's wrong.'

'How many shepherds has Petros?'

'Between twelve and fifteen. It is a big farm. And all those men are armed.'

'I'm not turning back now. I have to see Petros. Let's keep moving.'

Nick shrugged. 'OK. Petros' farm is round the next bend. We approach very cautiously . . .'

The long tumbledown building with a veranda stretching its full frontage came into view. Nick stopped abruptly. The desert-like atmosphere was transformed. Tweed gazed at the olive groves climbing up behind the farmhouse, small stunted trees with tortured twisted trunks. On the empty

454

veranda stood a large wickerwork chair. Tweed noticed the cushions were depressed – as though someone had sat there recently. The silence was even more oppressive.

'I am responsible for your safety,' said Nick. 'I think that we should turn back at once. We are walking into a trap.'

When Newman had introduced Paula to Christina the previous day and left them alone the atmosphere had been frigid. Christina eyed Paula up and down, lit a cigarette and then asked her casually, 'You're Tweed's woman?'

Paula tensed, then relaxed. 'Not in the sense you mean.' She decided she'd start as she meant to go on. 'Let's get one thing straight between us. I'm here to protect you. Just like Newman and Marler were. We're going to be penned up inside this room. Even at night because I'll be sleeping in the other bed. We'll use room service for all meals, including breakfast. Two women cramped together like that is a recipe for an explosion. There won't be one. Now, shall we start all over again?'

By the following morning they were chatting like old friends. It was Christina who brought up the subject when the waiter had taken their breakfast things away.

'Have they gone into Devil's Valley?'

'I think they're somewhere in Athens. On some checking job.'

Christina sat close to Paula, laid a hand on her arm. 'I can tell you are fond of Tweed. I like him myself. If he's gone into Devil's Valley he'll be killed. Petros hates what he calls English. He thinks an Englishman killed both his sons during the war.'

'Tweed can look after himself . . .'

'Then that *is* where he has gone?'

Paula bit her lip. She'd been indiscreet: Christina was quick. And very worried. Which increased the anxiety

Paula was feeling. Christina gripped Paula more firmly, her tone emphatic.

'I know the area. Petros and his men know every inch of that Godforsaken wilderness. Even if they've all gone – Tweed, Newman and Marler – they won't survive. Your friends are committing suicide. Their bodies will never be found. They'll be dropped down the old silver mine shaft . . .'

'Don't.' Paula began to feel sick. Christina had conjured up such a vivid picture. 'I didn't say that's where they were going.'

'But it is, isn't it? You said Tweed can look after himself. Petros is crazy. He has no mercy, no feelings. He lives only for revenge. Don't you understand? He's obsessed.'

Obsessed. Paula was shaken. Tweed, also, she felt was obsessed. What would happen when the two men confronted each other? She got up out of her chair, began to pace round the room. I'm doing what Tweed does, she suddenly thought.

'You have to do something,' Christina insisted. 'Now.'

Paula stopped by the telephone and smiled. 'I think I'm going to do something which will lose me my job.'

'Do you mind? If it saves Tweed – and the others?'

Paula checked the phone book, picked up the receiver, dialled police headquarters, asked for Captain Peter Sarris.

Keeping well away from the farmhouse which was overshadowed by a limestone crag, Tweed walked slowly forward over the dusty ground. Nick walked alongside, gripping his shotgun in both hands, the muzzle parallel with the earth.

'You interpret for me,' Tweed said. 'I'll try to make it a quickfire conversation.'

'With who?'

'I sense there are people here – all around us . . .'

He stopped speaking as a large tall man emerged from

456

the farmhouse. He had a hooked nose and thick eyebrows, a lined face. For a man of eighty his movements were vigorous. He carried a double-barrelled shotgun similar to Nick's and was followed by two much younger men. From Newman's description they were Dimitrios and Constantine. Both carried rifles.

'I am Petros,' the old man announced as he descended the steps. 'Bring me a chair, Dimitrios,' he ordered.

Nick translated as Dimitrios carried the wicker chair into the sun. Petros sat in the chair, crossed his legs, laid the gun over his lap, the barrel aimed at Tweed's stomach. The safety catch was on. Seated in the open, Petros reminded Tweed of an Old Testament patriarch. His presence radiated authority and domination.

Dimitrios padded well to the right while Constantine also came into the open, taking up a position on the left – making it impossible for Nick to cover both men. He aimed his gun direct at the old man's chest.

'You were expected,' Petros said, and grinned.

'My name is Tweed. I hold a senior position in the British Special Branch. That is our version of a secret police force. I am investigating the deaths of Andreas and Stephen Gavalas, among others.'

'Listen to him!' Petros threw back his great head and roared with laughter. 'He expects me to believe his lies.' His manner changed, became menacing. 'The main thing is you are English. I hate all English. You made a big mistake coming here, a fatal mistake.'

'You are blind, old man? You can't see my friend has a gun aimed at you point-blank?'

'At the first sign of movement you are both dead. *You* must be blind. Have you overlooked Dimitrios and Constantine?'

Tweed had not overlooked them. They stood, feet slightly apart. Dimitrios had his rifle aimed at Tweed, Constantine aimed his weapon at Nick. Sweat was running down Tweed's neck into the already sodden handkerchief. More sweat trickled from his armpits. But inside he was as cold as ice as he held the old man's eyes.

'There have been more murders. One of my men, Harry Masterson, came here. He ended up at the foot of Cape Sounion. Don't say you've never heard of him. It was in the papers. You were responsible for his murder?'

Petros' eyes gleamed, locked on Tweed's. He patted his shotgun, as though to check it was there. There was pure hatred in the dark eyes.

'No,' he said eventually, 'I know nothing about that. He must have been the man who came into Devil's Valley by night weeks ago. We couldn't find him. You should have asked Florakis.' He waved his left hand towards the western ridge. 'He owns a scrap of land over there, two hundred hectares or so.'

'You call that a scrap of land?' Keep him talking, Tweed was thinking.

'I own two thousand hectares here.' Petros made a grand gesture. 'Another thousand in Macedonia. If I had killed your man I would tell you. Why not? You will not leave here alive . . .'

'You are a member of the Greek Key?'

Petros scowled, screwed up his thick eyebrows. 'You know too much, Mr Tweed. Yes, during the Civil War I was a member. But when I found they were controlled by Moscow I left them. You think I want some commissar telling me what to do?'

'So you won't like the idea that Anton is a member?'

'You lie!' Petros' face was distorted with fury. He uncrossed his legs and his shotgun barrel shifted, pointing into space. 'You dare to say that to me, English? Your time has come. I will listen to no more of your filthy accusations. You are at the end of your life . . .'

*   *   *

458

Tweed said the first thing that came into his head, something which would distract the old ruffian. 'You know about those diamonds which were taken from Andreas' dead body on Siros? A fortune.'

He reached up, removed his hat, scratched at his head, smoothed down his hair. 'Order your grandsons to freeze.' Nick translated rapidly.

The first shot hit the ground between Petros' splayed feet, kicked up a puff of dust. The second bullet struck within inches of Dimitros. The third a foot behind Constantine. Petros' gnarled hands gripped the sides of his chair. He sat motionless.

On the top of the eastern ridge Marler squinted through his telescopic sight, the crosshairs centred on Dimitrios' chest. At the summit of the western ridge Newman held his own rifle, aimed at Constantine. The telescopic sight brought up the Greek so close he felt he could reach out and touch him.

Tweed put his hat back on his head. There was a dry smile on his face. 'You really think I'd wander into this place without protection? My men are marksmen, as you may have realized. They could have killed both Dimitrios and Constantine – their bodies would be lying in the dust. Had you moved, Nick would have shot you dead. Who would have carried out your mission of vengeance? If anyone attempts to move they will be shot. Now, can we continue?'

'You are a brave man.' Petros spoke slowly, glancing up at the ridge crests. 'You are also a clever man. OK. Talk.'

'Let's talk about Anton. He went to England many weeks ago by a secret route. You sent him, I suspect. His mission? To locate three men. Colonel Barrymore, Captain Robson and CSM Kearns, the same three men who accompanied Andreas on the fatal raid on Siros. Am I right?'

Petros drew a hand across the grey stubble of his unshaven face and stared at Tweed. It was a long minute before he replied. Tweed could feel the furnace-like heat radiating up from the ground.

'You are right,' Petros told him. 'That was the first stage in my plan to kill the man responsible.'

'You know which one did it? Anton found these men?'

'We don't know which one. Yes, he found them. All living so close together. I thought that strange.'

'Then Anton returned, told you what he had discovered. But it took you only part of the way. Because you still didn't know who murdered Andreas on Siros, stole the diamonds, then returned to Cairo and killed Stephen, masquerading as Ionides? The killer must somehow have found out his real identity. That worried him sufficiently for him to decide Stephen also must die. Why was Stephen living in Cairo under an assumed name?'

Tweed waited while Nick translated. He was trying to keep his questions short, to encourage Petros to continue the conversation, but he had to extract the whole story.

'You are right,' Petros said again. 'About Anton's first trip to England. And the rest. The EDES mob sent Stephen to Cairo as a spy. They gave him false papers under the name Ionides.'

'Maybe it was the right-wing EDES which killed Andreas?' Tweed pressed on.

'No. They had their headquarters on Siros, under the nose of the German commanding general, Geiger. They wanted the diamonds. They would never have killed one of their own.'

'What about the Germans? Maybe one of them did the job, found the diamonds, took them?'

'I thought of that.' Petros paused. 'This will sound peculiar. I arranged a truce with General Geiger. He agreed. He did not want a bloodbath. A Greek killed in battle is one thing. But killed by a German soldier who steals from him, that is another. We met under a flag of truce. He was a reasonable man. He said he knew which patrols were near the area that night. He would question them himself. I knew I could trust him. Later he sent me a message. Only one patrol was near the place where we found Andreas. None of them had even discovered the body.'

'So that leaves the three commandos?'

'Yes. Now, I think we end this . . .'

'Wait! Anton is now in England again. Did you send him – or was it his idea? Did he persuade you it would be a good idea?'

For the first time Tweed saw doubt in Petros' expression. The old man stirred uncomfortably, looked away from Tweed towards the farmhouse and beyond.

'It was his idea,' he said slowly. 'He pressed hard for me to agree. Mr Tweed, do not remove your hat again. Do not make the signal a second time. Look behind the farmhouse . . .'

Tweed turned his head. Then he knew the reason for the absence of shepherds when they had made their tortuous way into Devil's Valley. A group of about a dozen men in shepherd's clothes stood scattered above the farmhouse, concealed beneath the overhang of the crag where neither Marler nor Newman could possibly see them. He had been out-manoeuvred.

'I have only told you all this because I knew you would never leave this place alive,' Petros told him. 'You see they are all armed.' He stabbed a finger at Nick. 'Now you are marked for the first shots. As you drop I shall move very quickly – which I can – inside the house. Away from your marksmen who will not react until you make the signal. Then it will be too late. So, Mr Tweed, you should never have come here . . .'

'Keep him talking for just a minute,' Nick whispered in English.

Tweed did not ask why. 'You haven't asked about

461

Christina. I know where she is. She is under my care. And not in Greece.'

The fury returned. The hands clutched at the chair. 'You hold her as a hostage? I do not believe it. I would do that, but you are not such a man . . .'

'A different subject,' said Tweed, seeking the maximum distraction, 'Why did you wait for so many years before trying to locate the three commandos? It doesn't make sense.'

Petros' eyes seemed to start out of his head. His right hand clenched the chair as he spat out the words. A streak of near-madness glittered in his expression. Obsessed, Tweed thought – I'm facing a man obsessed . . .

'First there was the Civil War . . . then the years of work to make money, to build up the farm . . . you need money to conduct a manhunt. I had my family to bring up. The years passed quickly, too quickly. And all that time the thought never left my head. I must track down the killer of my sons. I live with that each day. That is what keeps me going. *Revenge*. And now your time is up . . .'

Marler was a long way below the eastern crest where he had shot from. He knew he was taking a desperate gamble – that he was leaving one flank unguarded. But he had heard the tumble of rocks sliding, which meant someone was moving beneath the overhanging crag protecting the farm.

He knew he had assessed the geography correctly: Newman, perched high on the western ridge, couldn't possibly see beneath the great crag. As he made his rapid descent, his rifle looped across his back, he was helped by his small stature, by his slim build, by the fact that he was moving down the sandy bed of a dried-up stream – which enabled him to move silently.

He avoided shifting even the smallest pebble which might

give away his presence. His small feet skipped down the twisting bed. Then he slowed down, peered round the precipitous wall of the crag. The roof of the farm lay below. Under the shelter of the crag stood a group of shepherds, well spaced out, each holding a rifle or shotgun to his shoulder. Marler unlooped his own weapon.

Tweed could now hear the sounds which Nick's acute ears had picked up. The putt-putt beat of helicopter motors approaching fast. The machines appeared suddenly and at the same moment. One Alouette came over the western ridge, the second appeared over the eastern crest. Police choppers.

Petros stared upwards, exposing his thick neck. The chopper which flew in from the west was already dropping. Sarris was behind the swivel-mounted machine-gun, the glasses he had used looped round his neck. The window was open. A policeman beside him used an amplified loudhailer to shout the message in Greek.

'Drop your weapons or we open fire . . .'

A shepherd concealed behind a large boulder raised his rifle. He aimed for the pilot's cabin. There was a single report. The shepherd crumpled, shot in the back. Marler switched to another target. The shepherds panicked, hoisted their rifles to shoot at the chopper. Sarris' machine-gun began its deadly chatter, sweeping across those at the highest level. Shepherds threw up their hands, sagged to the ground.

'Run, Tweed . . .'

Nick darted forward, rammed the muzzle of his shotgun under Petros' jaw, shouted at him to get inside the house. The old man jumped out of his chair, fled for the veranda. Tweed was already running towards the house. On the western crest Newman saw one shepherd aiming his rifle over the rooftop at the running figure. He squeezed the

463

trigger. The shepherd dropped his weapon, took two paces forward, fell flat on his face.

Both Alouettes had landed. Uniformed police holding guns dropped to the ground, ducked under the whirling rotors, spread out, surrounded the farm. Sarris strode up the steps and into the farmhouse. Tweed held an axe he had snatched from the kitchen wall.

'Better late than never,' said Sarris.

44

They drove along Alexandras Avenue and pulled up outside police headquarters. Sarris had driven Tweed back from the helipad where the chopper landed after flying them from Devil's Valley. In the rear seats were Newman and Marler. Nick was driving his Mercedes back on his own; a uniformed policeman was bringing back Marler's hired Peugeot. Sarris switched off the engine, lit a cigarette.

'What was that business about the missing commando daggers at Petros' farmhouse?' Tweed asked.

'Six of them,' said Sarris, 'all collected from British commandos the Germans captured raiding the Cyclades islands. General Geiger apparently kept them as trophies. One night Petros and some *andartes* broke into his villa, walked off with them. Petros has kept them in a glass case at the farm.'

'I heard your conversation with him in Greek,' Newman commented. 'The old maniac used to gaze at them every evening before he went to bed – to remind himself of his mission of vengeance. I'd say there were five, not six, in Geiger's villa. The sixth could have been the knife which killed Andreas. It was Petros' lot who found the body and removed it – and remember the knife was still sticking in Andreas' back.'

'But how did you know Petros had this macabre collection?' Tweed asked.

'I had one of his shepherds in my pay. He's the man who dropped flat and survived when I opened fire. I had to twist Petros' arm to find out what happened when I noticed the case was empty.'

'And what did happen?' Tweed pressed. 'I have a reason for asking.'

'Petros eventually admitted they disappeared many weeks ago – about the time Anton left for his first trip to England.'

'Which *may* explain who killed Sam Partridge,' Tweed remarked.

'Why the doubt?' asked Marler.

'Because the three men on Exmoor would also have access to the weapon – when they were in the Army. We still don't know who the killer is. What will happen to Petros?' he asked Sarris.

'He'll end up behind bars. Maybe in a padded cell. Now, was your crazy expedition worthwhile?'

'Yes. I'm convinced Petros had nothing to do with the killing of Masterson. Which is why I came here. I also believe Petros was kept alive by his dream of vengeance, that he might never have taken any real action. The dream would have gone.'

Sarris opened the door. 'Let's go to my office, get a drink. I'm parched.' He looked at Tweed as he climbed out of the car. 'There's someone waiting to see you. And you'd better say thanks to her very nicely.'

Tweed asked the question suddenly, hoping to catch Sarris off balance. 'What precisely is the Greek Key?'

'It's an ancient symbol. You must know it. You see it used on embroideries, it appears in the friezes of temples.'

'Freeze is the word – what you all do when the phrase is mentioned.'

Tweed followed Sarris inside the building while Newman and Marler brought up the rear. They waited and then stepped inside an elevator. When they walked into the office Paula, who had been reading a magazine, dropped it and rushed to Tweed, hugging him.

'God! You're crazy,' she exploded. 'I warned you. Sarris sent a radio report from the chopper. You walked into an ambush.' She released him, stood back, spoke in a solemn voice. 'And I know I disobeyed your instructions. So I expect to be sacked.'

'Stuff and nonsense. I owe you my life.' Tweed sank into a chair while Sarris ordered coffee and mineral water over his intercom. 'But where is Christina? Is she on her own?'

'Of course not!' Sarris snapped. 'Paula phoned me. Before I drove to the helipad I left orders for a plain-clothes man to go to the Grande Bretagne to guard Christina – so Paula could come here.' He looked at Newman and Marler who had also sat down. 'Officially you were not involved. Which is why I've confiscated your rifles. They'll get lost. I won't ask how you obtained them.'

'That's big of you,' said Newman. 'Considering Marler shot down a shepherd who was aiming his rifle at the cabin of that chopper you were flying in. You could be cold meat on a slab now.'

Sarris grinned, looked at Tweed. 'Is he always so independent and aggressive?'

'Yes,' Marler interjected. 'A pain in the arse. But we did hold the situation until you arrived.'

'I think you all went mad,' Paula said and sipped at the cup of coffee served by a uniformed policeman. She was watching Tweed: there had been a major change in his mood and manner. The vehemence and tension seemed to have drained out of him.

A man came in and Tweed looked up. The Dormouse.

466

He stood up, smiled and shook hands. 'Good to see you again.'

'I would suggest,' Sarris began, 'that Kalos takes you for a ride away from here. That you ask him the question you put to me downstairs. I'd like the rest of you to stay while we cook up an official report, something that will make my superiors happy. The truth – but maybe not the whole truth . . .'

The Dormouse drove Tweed to the Plaka. He apologized for the transport, his battered old Saab. 'No one notices it,' he explained, 'which is why I favour it. Now the question.'

'What is the Greek Key?'

'I'll tell you when we reach my flat – that and a lot more. It's politically sensitive, which is why Sarris suggested we get out of police headquarters.' He manoeuvred the vehicle carefully inside the labyrinth, stopped outside a taverna, his engine still running. 'See that – Papadedes. Note the entrance to the staircase alongside – Papadedes hires out the room upstairs to men taking a woman up there. But other people have used that room. I will tell you in my flat.'

He parked the car inside a narrow alley climbing steeply up towards a hilltop. His flat was above a shop selling baskets and leather handbags to tourists. Tweed settled himself in an armchair after a good wash in a tiny bathroom. He felt more civilized after getting rid of the mixture of dried sweat and dust.

Kalos fussed about, making coffee. He placed the cup on a small round table next to the chair, produced a tin jug and two glasses. '*Retsina*,' he explained. 'If you do not like it leave it. And here is mineral water. Some bread with a little cheese – made from cow's milk. I do not think goat's milk cheese would appeal.'

'Very good of you, Kalos.' Tweed sipped at the

retsina. It tasted resinous. 'I like it. Now, can we talk?'

'The Greek Key,' Kalos began, settling himself in another armchair, 'is a highly secret underground organization of hardline Communists. It is run by a committee but the man who counts is Doganis, in his sixties . . .'

'Ah,' said Tweed, 'another man in his sixties. So he goes back also to the Second World War.'

'That is true.' Kalos leaned forward, tapped Tweed on the knee. 'And these are very hard men indeed. They are bitter because they just failed to take over Greece during the Civil War. We were saved by the American President, Truman. He sent a military mission, tons of arms. Now they have surfaced again. They are anti-Gorbachev.'

Tweed stiffened, put down his glass. 'Their activities are confined to Greece?'

'I don't think so. From the records, during the Second World War there were strong rumours the real controller of the Greek Key was an Englishman based in Cairo. Let me tell you what I have discovered.' He took a file from his briefcase. 'This is my secret report. You can read it later. Now, we start with the clandestine visit of General Lucharsky to Athens . . .'

Tweed ate the bread and cheese, listened grimly as The Dormouse described what he had found out. Lucharsky . . . Colonel Rykovsky. The arrival later of Lucharsky's aide, Colonel Volkov . . . the link with Doganis . . . Florakis, alias Oleg Savinkov, The Executioner . . . Pavelic, the Croat hardliner who had provided Kalos with secret information while drunk . . .

'This Pavelic,' Tweed said eventually, 'he is in touch with Moscow?'

'He boasted he had underground links with the hardliners inside Russia who hate and fear Gorbachev's reforms – that Gorbachev would not last much longer.'

Tweed recalled that Marler had seen Florakis carrying

a modern transceiver up a mountain on his land. The Dormouse listened with a gleam in his beady eyes.

'Who is he transmitting to?'

Tweed opened up, telling him about the three ex-commandos living on Exmoor; the long-ago murders in Cairo, on Siros; about the killing of Sam Partridge – who had been in Cairo as a very young man; the killing of Jill Kearns and Mrs Larcombe and the story the old lady had told Tweed.

Kalos nodded. 'We have uncovered a major conspiracy controlled by the hardline anti-Gorbachev faction in Moscow. I just cannot see where it leads.' He handed his file to Tweed. 'I would like you to read that – it includes times and photographs of the conspirators . . .'

Tweed read the file, automatically memorizing every detail. He studied the photos. Kalos sat with his hands clasped in his ample lap, waited patiently. When Tweed had finished he handed back the file.

'My God, it looks far worse than I ever dreamed. Could you get me copies of those prints?'

Kalos delved into his file, produced a large envelope which he passed to Tweed. 'I anticipated your request. I made copies myself in my own darkroom. All the dates are written on the back. I have signed my name and used a police headquarters rubber stamp. Sarris knows nothing of this. He destroyed the original file in my presence.'

'Sarris is involved?' Tweed asked.

A shake of the stubble-covered head. 'I'm sure he guessed I had already prepared a duplicate file. It was significant he did not ask for the negatives of those prints. Sarris would never forget a point like that. Except deliberately. We understand one another. Why do you think he suggested I took you away from HQ for a talk?'

'Of course.' Tweed smiled. 'It is just that I have a habit of trusting no one.'

'A very good habit. What are you going to do now? You

believe one of those three ex-commandos is the real head of the Greek Key?'

'I do now.'

'But which one? You have interviewed them all twice. Surely one of them let something slip? You are known for your flair for interrogation.'

'I think I know who it is.' Tweed paused. 'The devil of it is I have no proof.'

'And this Professor Seton-Charles you mentioned. The Recruiter, as Christina called him when talking with Newman. He too is involved?'

'Up to his ruddy neck would be my guess. Again, no proof. You asked me what I'm going to do. I'm very grateful to you, Kalos, for your cooperation. What you've dug up all on your own has filled in a lot of gaps. I am returning to England as rapidly as possible. The solution lies there.'

'Let me phone Sarris, see where they all are.' Kalos picked up the phone, dialled, spoke in Greek, waited, then spoke again at greater length. He put down the phone. 'Sarris tells me they are all at the Grande Bretagne, waiting for you. I hinted you may be leaving. He thinks that a good idea – after your experience in Devil's Valley. He looks forward to seeing you again.'

Tweed stood up. 'Thank you once more for everything. I am sure we will meet again.'

'There is always a next time in our work. I will drive you to the hotel.' The Dormouse smiled shyly. 'It has been a great pleasure to deal with you. I suppose you realize you may not have much time left to stop whatever is planned? They have been working on it for over a year.'

'That's what worries me. *I* don't think we have much time left. One more thing, could you leave Florakis alone? He sounds like the communications link. I don't want that disturbed.'

470

'I can persuade Sarris to agree to that. Now, as you say, you are short of time . . .'

They were all waiting for him in Newman's room: Newman himself, Marler and Nick. Newman told him Paula was still guarding Christina in her room.

'You see,' Nick intervened, 'I noticed at the farm that Dimitrios and Constantine were missing. I checked the bodies myself. I think they are in Athens, searching for Christina. It may be days before they hear Petros has been arrested. Sarris said he was keeping it out of the papers.'

'We are all leaving by a Swissair flight tomorrow,' Tweed told them. 'It leaves at 5 p.m., arrives at Zurich at 6.45 p.m. We stopped in the square on the way back and I bought tickets for everyone.' He dropped a folder on the table. 'Better collect your tickets now.'

'Why Zurich?' Newman asked. 'Why not a direct flight home?'

'Because we are taking Christina with us. I promised her protection. She will stay with our friend in Switzerland until this is all over.'

'May I make a suggestion?' said Nick.

'Go ahead.'

'You may well need strong protection until you have safely left Greece. If you take a taxi with Christina and Paula to the airport, Newman and Marler could follow close behind in the hired Peugeot the police returned.'

'That's good thinking,' agreed Tweed.

'But in case of emergency none of you is armed. Sarris took your rifles, as he took my shotgun. But I was not searched – I think that was deliberate.' He opened his jacket, took it off, exposing the hip holster carrying his .38 Smith & Wesson. Unfastening the holster, he laid it on the table. Pulling up his trouser leg, he unstrapped the holster containing a small Browning automatic, laid that on the

471

table. Then he emptied his jacket pockets of spare magazines and looked at Marler and Newman.

'Take your choice.'

'But we'll never get through airport security,' Newman pointed out.

'Yes you will. Because I will drive ahead to the airport to make sure it is safe. If I am standing leaning against my car when Tweed's taxi arrives, all is well. I then go to the men's room, followed by Newman and Marler. They hand the guns back to me.'

'Very bright,' Tweed agreed again.

Marler grabbed the Browning before Newman could object, saying he was smaller and wasn't going to lug the heavier Smith & Wesson about. Newman grimaced.

'Trust him to find the easy way.' He looked at Nick. 'You said you were running low on petrol.'

Nick jumped up. 'So I go and fill her up now. Do it at once is my maxim. I will be back later.'

Newman waited until they were alone. 'Tweed, shouldn't someone go to the Embassy, call Beck, warn him we're coming?'

'I was about to do that myself . . .'

'I feel like a walk. Give me his Berne number and I'll make the call.'

Tweed took out the pad he always carried with a sheet of plastic to stop the imprint of what he wrote being reproduced on the sheet underneath. He wrote down Beck's number from memory, gave it to Newman. After studying it for a few moments, Newman held the sheet over an ash tray, set light to it.

'I'm on my way . . .'

Tweed was left alone with Marler, who ran his hand through his fair hair before asking his question.

'What about Andreas' skeleton hanging inside that silver mine?'

'It *was* Andreas. Sarris told me he had questioned Petros

472

after I told him about its existence before we left the farm. Petros admitted he had kept the skeleton until he had administered justice – his phrase – to the murderer of his sons. Sarris sent a couple of men up to find the skeleton. I suppose it will be buried in due course. The whole episode shows Petros was crazy with his obsession.'

'And you're no further for'ard with who killed Masterson?'

'Yes, I am. After cross-examining Petros before the choppers arrived I'm convinced he told the truth. He had nothing to do with Masterson's death. So we're looking for someone else – which is what I came here to find out.'

'Any ideas?'

Despite their ordeal in Devil's Valley Marler looked fresh and ready for anything. He had cleaned himself up in the bathroom and emerged a new man.

'A lot,' said Tweed. 'I've been fed a whole load of new information. The trouble will be checking it out – and I'm not sure how much time we've got. You'll all be chasing your tails when we get back home. But Zurich comes first. Not that I expect it will be anything but a stopover . . .'

Beck met them at Zurich the following evening and they travelled from Kloten Airport to the Hotel Schweizerhof in two unmarked limousines. Inside the second car Christina was escorted by a plain-clothes policeman.

'She will be taken into the mountains,' Beck explained when they assembled in Tweed's corner room overlooking the Bahnhofstrasse and the main station. 'In a house near Santis,' he went on. 'Is there someone who needs smoke in their eyes? I didn't see anyone following us from the airport.'

'No. Just keep her out of harm's way,' Tweed replied. 'I'll give you a call when I'm sure the coast is clear. And we'll pay the expenses.'

473

'Oh, there will be a bill.' Beck smiled and sat down as Tweed gestured towards a chair. 'I have news. Is it for your ears only?'

'Everyone here knows what's going on.'

Tweed waved a hand, embracing Newman, Paula and Marler. When they arrived Christina had said she'd be taking a bath. She had been quite happy that Gustav, her guard, should stay in her room and drink coffee.

'I realized Anton Gavalas was important to you,' Beck began. He had chosen a chair next to Paula. 'I checked with Interpol in Paris, asked them whether anything unusual had happened in Lisbon. It has.' His voice became grave. 'And about just the time Anton was in the Portuguese capital. A murder.'

'God! Who was it this time?' Tweed asked.

'An unsavoury international arms dealer who went by the name of Gallagher. He ran a garage, apparently – as a cover for his real activities. He had been watched as he travelled all over Europe. No evidence. He was found stabbed in a service pit in his garage. Could there be a link with Anton?'

'Any idea what kind of knife was used?'

'Yes. It was left in the body. People don't realize it can be very difficult to withdraw the weapon if it is driven in deep. This one was. A British commando-type knife.'

'That sounds like Anton.'

'There is more. Some guesswork . . .' Beck waved a dismissive hand. 'But the dates are right. Anton stayed one night at The Ritz. The following day a Portuguese freighter carrying a consignment of cork for England sailed. The *Oporto*. After a few days it arrives at some port called Watchet in Somerset, unloads the cork, takes on board a cargo of wastepaper. Is this relevant?'

'More so than you might ever dream,' Tweed urged him on grimly.

'The *Oporto* had been shadowed by French aircraft.

French Intelligence, the *Direction de la Surveillance du Territoire*, had discovered the *Oporto* had visited Tripoli in Libya before arriving in Lisbon. Their aircraft lost it because of a storm and only picked it up again after it had left Britain and was sailing apparently back to Lisbon. Another storm drove it close to Brest. They sent out cutters and boarded it in French territorial waters. Anyone losing interest?'

'I'm fascinated,' said Paula. 'You're leading up to something.'

'I enjoy a little drama – as Tweed here sometimes does. They found in the hold an armoury of Sam missile launchers, missiles, hundreds of rifles and forty thousand rounds of ammunition. At the time there was an Irish fishing boat near Brest. Fodder for the IRA. Paris is certain of it.'

'I don't like the sound of this,' Tweed commented.

'Then you won't like the rest much. The DST interrogated Gomez, the *Oporto*'s captain. He wouldn't give any information. But a member of the crew he had rebuked did talk. He said before the ship reached Watchet it heaved to and someone carrying a large bundle was off-loaded into a waiting motorboat. The craft then headed for the British shore.'

'Did he recognize – I mean, see – anyone in the motorboat he could describe?'

'No. He was concealed behind the bridge and frightened of being found. End of story.'

'Or the beginning,' said Tweed. 'Sam missile launchers. That frightens me. What *was* landed on that remote stretch of Somerset coastline? And why? For what purpose? Those are the questions we must find answers to. And the solution lies back home in England.'

45

London. As soon as Tweed arrived back at Park Crescent he worried away like a beaver at the problem. He assembled all his helpers in his room, issued a whole series of instructions.

Newman, Marler, Paula and Monica were there. Everyone had to know what the others were doing. The Director, Howard, back from a long holiday, lounged in a chair, listening. He made a typical comment as he brushed imaginary specks of dust off his immaculate navy blue suit.

'This is costing us a fortune. Your trip to Athens alone . . .'

'Are you saying we are wasting our time?' Tweed enquired.

Paula sat behind her desk watching Tweed. He had lost his earlier manner of a man obsessed: seeing Petros had cured him of that. It was now the normal Tweed: calm, dogged, speaking in a controlled tone. Paula felt enormously relieved.

'No,' Howard replied. 'Not after hearing all the details. I don't like that business Kalos told you about General Lucharsky, Colonels Rykovsky and Volkov – above all the connection with Doganis. It does sound as though the hardline faction inside Russia – the anti-Gorbachev lot – has succeeded in establishing a power base outside Russia.'

'And that base is over here. All we have to do is to find it.'

'You make it sound so easy,' Howard observed.

'What gets me,' Paula persisted, 'is how they were able

476

to do that under our noses.' She frowned. 'Unless it was set up a long time ago and has recently been activated.'

'Monica,' said Tweed, 'double-check with Roberts, our man at Lloyd's. I want all details of the movements of that Portuguese vessel, the *Oporto*. Paula, drive down to Exmoor with Newman. Find out on the spot whether Butler and Nield have discovered anything more about movements in that area. Especially about Anton – and Seton-Charles, who seems to have vanished off the face of the earth. Marler, Interpol have persuaded Lisbon to send me that knife used to kill Gallagher. It's arriving at London Airport aboard this flight.' He gave him a sheet of paper. 'In the custody of the pilot of the plane. Bring it back here. I want to check if it really is a commando-type weapon.'

'We stay at The Anchor at Porlock Weir?' Paula suggested as she took from a cupboard the small case she kept packed for emergency trips.

'It's out of the way, a good place to stay under cover. And you can check on Mrs Larcombe's murder. Bob, you get out of the car short of the hotel, register as though you don't know Paula. It can come in useful to have a secret reserve.'

'And I'll have my Mercedes back, thank you very much.'

'Goody,' said Paula. 'I'll get to drive it. At ninety down the motorway,' she joked.

Tweed gave her a look as she left with Newman. Marler raised himself slowly from his chair. 'I'd better push off to the airport before you think of something else . . .'

'Just like old times,' Monica said when Marler had gone. 'It's all go – the way I like it.' She reached for the phone to call Lloyd's. 'Do you really think Anton is back in this country?'

'He's somewhere over here. What I'd like to know is what he's doing,' Tweed answered sombrely.

*   *   *

It was raining heavily at Cherry Farm in Hampshire. Anton could hear it beating down on the roof of the huge barn where he was working. Perfect weather: it kept potential snoopers indoors. Inside the second furniture van, parked behind the other vehicle, he turned round as Seton-Charles appeared and climbed up the lowered tailboard.

'How are you progressing?' the Professor asked.

'I will show you. We are far advanced.'

Anton moved a tool box on the floor among the straw, used his screwdriver to lever up the hinged floorboards. Beneath was the secret compartment he had constructed to store the Stinger launchers and the missiles.

Seton-Charles gazed round the interior of the huge vehicle. At the front, behind the driver's cab – shut off from the interior – Anton had erected a wooden platform, railed, and with steps leading up to it. A special wooden chair he had designed with an adjustable back was clamped to the platform floor.

Anton inserted a missile into the launcher, carried the weapon up to the platform, and sat in the chair. Reaching down, he depressed a switch. There was the faint sound of electrical machinery on the move. A large panel in the van's roof slid open, exposing the roof of the barn six feet above the top of the van.

He settled himself into the chair, raised the launcher, the stock pressed firmly into his shoulder. The Greek swivelled the weapon through an arc.

'Imagine open sky, a plane approaching three thousand feet up. I press the trigger, the heat-seaking device homes on the target. *Boom!* No plane. Satisfied?'

He didn't give a damn whether his companion was satisfied or not. The main thing was *he* knew it would work. He climbed back down the steps, detached the missile, wrapped it separately in a polythene sheet, did the same thing with the launcher, made sure they were safely tucked away and closed the floorboards. Then he rubbed dirt over the joins, moved straw over the compartment.

'Now I have to do the same job with the other van. It all takes time.'

'Maybe I could help by going in to Liphook and fetching the new food supplies?' Seton-Charles suggested.

He was getting housebound. Anton had not allowed him to leave the farm since he had arrived. The Greek shook his head. He had grown a thick moustache; he wore a greasy boiler suit and wore the type of cap affected by the average farm worker. His British boots were smeared with caked mud.

'I get the food,' Anton told him. 'You said Liphook. Do you not realize I buy each time from a different town? Where is your sense of security?'

'I am sorry. That was a foolish mistake . . .'

'Which could have been fatal. Let us go into the farm-house – I want to check the two rooms we have prepared for the prisoners. They will be brought here within the next few weeks . . .'

They entered the farm by the back door: Anton insisted that they never used the front entrance which was kept permanently locked. He led the way up the old staircase and along the corridor to the two rooms facing the back. They were separated by the bathroom.

Each door had two locks and a bolt Anton had fixed. In each door was a spyhole with a cap which closed down over it on the outside. They could look in but an occupant could not see out. He opened the first door, walked inside. The room was starkly furnished.

An iron bedstead screwed to the floor over which was spread a straw-filled palliasse and two blankets. An Elsan bucket in the corner for the performance of natural functions. Anton told Seton-Charles to operate the light switch which he had installed in the corridor. He walked over to the windows he had double glazed. No way of breaking out there – especially as the shutters were closed and padlocked on the outside.

'Who are these prisoners?' Seton-Charles asked.

'Just two men.' Anton continued as though talking to himself. 'I must remember no pork. Lamb and chicken is their diet – and somewhere I will find Turkish coffee. In a supermarket in Winchester, probably.' He looked round. 'Yes, all is ready for our visitors.'

'I would like to know what is going on,' Seton-Charles protested.

'Patience. In the meantime, when you are not helping me as labourer you can study your Greek books. Jupiter stressed in his last call you must remain here.' Anton grinned unpleasantly. 'And do you think you would sleep well at night if you upset Jupiter?'

Paula and Newman stayed for several weeks at The Anchor. When Newman phoned Tweed from a public call box one evening Tweed said he wanted them both to remain there until recalled. They were to explore the whole area, to listen to gossip in pubs, to try and find the route Anton used to *leave* the country.

'I don't think he boarded a ship the way he probably came in,' Tweed said. 'We've been very busy here, contacting every airport in the country. No passenger manifest shows that he left by a scheduled flight. And remember, Christina told you he was a pilot, experienced with flying light aircraft . . .'

When he put down the phone Monica queried his decision.

'You have a lot of people in one area. Paula, Newman, Butler and Nield. Isn't that overkill?'

'I'm deliberately saturating that district. I feel it in my bones the solution lies on Exmoor.'

'Anything interesting from Bob? I know it's on the tape I can listen to, but I find your comments more informative.'

'Everything seems normal. Dr Robson visits his patients

– riding his horse. He works long hours. Barrymore makes infrequent phone calls from the phone box in Minehead.'

'Isn't that peculiar? Surely you said he has a phone of his own at Quarme Manor?'

'Apparently it often goes on the blink, as Newman expressed it. Something to do with the overhead wires getting blown down. It's the stormy season down there. Gale Force Ten and heavy seas.'

'What about Kearns?'

'He leads a strange life. When there's a moon he rides up to Dunkery Beacon, stays there a while. Butler has watched him through night glasses. He sits on his horse, still as a statue. Then he disappears for a while before riding back to his house.'

'Makes sense to me,' said Monica. 'The poor man has lost his wife. He just wants to be on his own. And he's trying to keep his sanity by maintaining old habits.'

'Another funny development – Paula found this out from lunching in pubs on Exmoor. Kearns doesn't meet his chums Barrymore and Robson any more. No Saturday night dinners at The Luttrell Arms, no Wednesday lunches at The Royal Oak, Winsford. He has cut himself off from them completely.'

'You can't tell how grief will affect people.'

'It's a very major change in relationships,' Tweed pointed out. 'For years those three acted as though they were still members of an Army unit. Kearns walking away is bound to affect the other two, Barrymore and Robson. Psychologically, I mean. We are still seeing the thing develop.'

'You'll get there in the end,' Monica encouraged him.

Tweed took from a drawer the commando knife which had killed Gallagher in Lisbon. That had been a frustrating exercise. At the last moment the Portuguese police chief had refused to send the weapon direct to London: Marler had arrived at London Airport several weeks before, only to find the pilot had nothing for him.

The knife had been ultimately despatched to Interpol in Paris. Which was the correct procedure. Tweed's friend, Pierre Loriot, had immediately flown it to London, but it had all taken precious time. Then there was the report from Lloyd's of London on the *Oporto*.

The typed document had confirmed all Tweed had been previously told. The vessel's clandestine call at Tripoli in Libya. Its voyage from Tripoli back to Lisbon – the arrival at that port coinciding with Anton flying from Zurich to the Portuguese capital. The shadowing of the vessel by French aircraft, culminating in its seizure after leaving Somerset off the port of Brest. The discovery of the large armoury of weapons which, Paris was certain, was destined for the IRA. Another dead end, as Tweed termed it, leading them nowhere further.

It was now November. Rain fell in a slanting downpour outside as Tweed put the weapon back in the drawer.

'I'm missing something,' he said. 'I feel it is under my nose and I can't see it. Get out all those tapes of phone conversations. I want to listen to them again. With a fresh ear.'

The dacha was located in the hills north-east of Moscow. There was a colony of them nearby where the bigwigs relaxed in summer, but this one was isolated. It was used for high-security military conferences in the hot season.

General Lucharsky stopped the Chaika a few hundred yards away from the shuttered building, switched off the engine, walked the rest of the way. His gleaming fur-lined boots crunched in the crisp hard snow; there had been a light fall the previous night. The temperature was eight degrees below freezing and he pulled up his military great-coat collar, revelling in the invigorating air.

The building was made of timber. Steps led up to the veranda overhung by the projecting roof. The place was surrounded with birch woods flaked with white. Sunlight reflected off the snow crystals. Lucharsky climbed the steps, stood by the front door and looked around. He listened carefully and heard nothing in the heavy silence. He had not been followed. He rapped on the heavy door four times slowly.

When the door opened two men, also wearing the uniforms of generals, appeared. Lucharsky put a finger to his lips. With a swift gesture he indicated that they should follow him. He led the way back down the steps and into the woods. His arm brushed a branch and crusted snow fell on it.

'Why could we not stay in the dacha?' asked a short stocky general with stubby legs and thick eyebrows under his peaked cap. General Budienny.

'Because it may be wired for sound,' Lucharsky told him contemptuously. He towered over both his companions. 'Out here no one can hear us.'

He stopped inside a hollow encircled with trees. The Troika was assembled. Lucharsky kicked snow off his boots before continuing. The third man, an expert on armoured divisions, listened.

'The plan is proceeding,' Lucharsky informed them. 'I have now heard Gorbachev will land in Britain at the invitation of British Prime Minister Thatcher. We have him.'

'On the way to or back from the Washington summit?' asked Budienny.

'En route to Washington. Except his plane will never land. In one piece, that is. The missiles are in place.'

'How do you know where he will land? London Airport?' persisted Budienny.

'We don't know yet.' Lucharsky waved a gloved hand. 'It makes no difference. The missiles are located in a central

483

position close to many airfields – including RAF military bases. They are mobile. Can be moved to the correct area as soon as we get the precise data.'

'How do you know all this?'

Lucharsky sighed. 'We have direct communication with the man who will control the operation. By radio. A complex route. But coded signals are received by one of our men at the Black Sea naval base of Novorossiisk. He is an excellent radio operator and brings me the signals regularly to Moscow.'

'Routine is dangerous,' Budienny objected. 'And our necks are on the block.'

Lucharsky sighed again, his expression saturnine. 'Since that naval base is so important a courier flies frequently to Moscow to report on progress about enlarging it. Our man is that courier. And before you suggest he could be searched he carries the messages verbally in his head, then tells me.' His tone became mocking. 'If your fears are now allayed perhaps I can proceed? The plan has taken on new dimensions.'

'What are those?'

'As Number Two in the Politburo, Ligachev – who has openly disagreed with Gorbachev's so-called reforms – will automatically become General Secretary. He knows nothing, of course, of what we plan.'

'But what are these new dimensions?' Budienny repeated.

'Once Ligachev is in power the real hardline element inside the Politburo will take over. Those men Gorbachev has not yet got rid of. Then next year, in 1988, we launch the limited attack.'

'Attack?' Budienny's eyes gleamed.

'We manufacture a border incident – as Hitler did against Poland in 1939. Our armies, brought close to the western frontier at night when the American satellites are blind, invade West Germany. We outnumber NATO enormously with our tanks. With our artillery and our air force. We shall reach the Rhine in three days.'

'That means World War Three,' Budienny objected.

'No. We stop at the Rhine. We announce we are going no further. The Americans will be in the middle of their presidential election. Everything will be in confusion in Washington. You think they will want a conventional *limited* war – a three-day coup – to turn nuclear? To risk New York, Chicago and Los Angeles become incinerated ash-heaps? Then we have in our hands the Ruhr, the great German powerhouse of armament production. We become the greatest power on earth.'

'And who will bring down Gorbachev's plane over Britain?'

'I told you before.' Lucharsky clapped his gloves together without making a sound. 'Shi-ite Muslims. They will end Gorbachev's regime of anti-Leninist idiocy . . .'

46

At Cherry Farm Anton stood inside the second furniture van and surveyed his workmanship. He wore his boiler suit and his cap: he had developed the habit of wearing it all the time except when he went to bed. In the little spare time left over he had visited pubs some distance away, drinking beer while he listened to the locals' chatter. Anton could now talk with the accent of a working man. Holding a power tool in his right hand he turned to Seton-Charles.

'Well, you have seen the second demonstration. The sliding panel works, as it does in the other van.'

The two men stood close together; space was cramped.

Near the driver's cab Anton had erected another platform with steps leading up to it; a chair with an adjustable back was clamped to the floor below the sliding panel.

But the rear part of the van was crammed almost roof-high with old furniture – as was the van behind them. To leave the van they had to squeeze past the projecting legs of tables and a large wardrobe among other items. This was a precaution Jupiter had insisted on when he had given instructions to Anton after his landing on the coast.

'Then, if by chance you are stopped,' Balaclava had explained, 'the police will see a van stacked with furniture which will hide the launch platform . . .'

Before starting work on the rear van Anton had visited various furniture auctions, storing the junk he had purchased in the front van. Seton-Charles had studied the stack of local newspapers Anton had bought all over Hampshire, looking for furniture auctions. He had been surprised and pleased at how many there were.

'Let me see the panel open again,' Seton-Charles suggested. 'I want to be sure it works every time.'

Anton shook his head. 'The generator makes a noise. I tested it several times while you were inside the farm, keeping a lookout for snoopers. God, I've driven a long way, buying everything I needed from different shops. No one will have a clue about what we were constructing.'

'But why does each van need a small generator to operate the panel,' asked Seton-Charles, whose knowledge of mechanical problems was zero. 'Surely you could have used the power from the van's engine.'

'Which shows how much you know. For one thing the van will be stationary when we launch the missiles, the engine turned off. The driver will warn us over his walkie-talkie when the plane is in view. Only then do we open the panel.'

'It seems very well organized,' Seton-Charles agreed. 'That smell of fresh paint is turning my stomach. Was it really necessary to change the name on the outside?'

'Again, Jupiter's orders. We don't want any connection with Camelford Removals, the bankrupt outfit in Norwich you bought them from. Now we are Smith's Removals of Birmingham. There are two such firms in the city.'

Anton had spent hours with a paintbrush, first obliterating the old names, waiting for the paint to dry, then substituting the new names. But Seton-Charles had a point: the barn, with its doors closed at both ends, reeked of the stench.

'Tonight we'll open the rear doors of the barn after dark, let the smell out,' he decided. 'We'll take it in turns to stand guard while those doors are open. Later I'll rub dirt over the fresh paint . . .'

He stopped speaking as the phone extension he had rigged up from the farmhouse began ringing. He sent Seton-Charles back to the farmhouse, picked up the phone.

'Alfred Moss speaking.'

'Are both containers ready yet?'

The same supercilious, upper-crust voice Anton disliked. Like a commander giving orders to lowly subordinates. He took a deep breath.

'Yes. They are ready to move to the port.'

'Your two guests will be arriving today. Noon at the arranged meeting place. Foster and Saunders will be travelling with them. I must go. My garden is being ruined by magpies and goldcrests. I'd like to convert the place into a closed circuit. Don't be late . . .'

Anton put down the phone and swore in Greek. Arrogant bastard. But he was clever. In a few words – seemingly innocent if overheard – he'd conveyed a lot.

The two men who were bringing the prisoners to the lonely crossroads were called Foster and Saunders. They would give the password *magpies*. Anton would reply with *goldcrests*. He ran to the doors, opened one, closed it, snapped the padlock shut on the outside, ran into the farmhouse. Seton-Charles stood in the kitchen, waiting for the news.

'I have to leave at once. I'll come back with the prisoners. Be ready to open the shed doors . . .'

'Is it wise to keep on using the same Austin Metro you hired in Taunton? We've had it for weeks. And what about payment to Barton?'

'Jupiter arranges fresh payments in cash. It's risky changing cars, using that driving licence. I must be off . . .'

Driving at a modest pace along a winding country road, Anton reflected on the past. He kept a close eye on the dashboard clock, but he didn't want to arrive early. Hanging about – even in the middle of nowhere – was dangerous. A police patrol car might become interested.

He was thinking about Petros and his lust for revenge. Anton had never shared his father's one-track outlook on life. He had simply gone along with him for years; originally to make sure the money for his education was forthcoming. He had played up to the old man like mad. Later he had borrowed from him to help set up his chain of radio, television and video shops. Then he had met the man who had changed his life. Professor Guy Seton-Charles.

Anton had attended the first lecture at Athens University out of sheer curiosity. More intelligent – and cynical – than the other students, it had not taken him long to see through the professor. Under the guise of lecturing on Greek Studies, it had soon become apparent to Anton this was a course in political indoctrination. In the Communist creed.

In his turn, Seton-Charles had spotted Anton as the cleverest, most cold-blooded and ambitious of his students. Just the material he was looking for. They had formed an alliance rather than a friendship. Anton had decided the West was on its way out; the future belonged to Russia.

So convincingly did he appear to embrace Communism

he was in due course invited to join the Greek Key as a junior member. The fact that his father, Petros, had supported the Greek Key during the war helped. Anton simply saw it as the quickest route to power in Greece. That was until Gorbachev replaced Brezhnev. *Glasnost? Perestroika?* This was no route to a Communist takeover of Greece.

Recruited to the inner councils – after expressing his anti-Gorbachev sentiments – Anton had become a trusted member of the conspiracy. And then there was the detail of Petros' collection of British commando knives. It was Doganis who had suggested how these might come in useful when he learned of their existence.

'Steal them,' he advised Anton, before his first trip to England. 'You may have to kill someone. You could do that? Good. If it comes to that, use one of those daggers. It will confuse any investigation. The English are poking around still trying to find out who killed Andreas Gavalas. Use one of those daggers and they will go back over forty years, ignoring the present. An excellent smoke-screen . . .'

Anton glanced at the clock again, increased speed. When he arrived at the crossroads a Ford station wagon was pulled up inside the trees. A man dressed in a smart blue navy pinstripe suit appeared. He wore pigskin gloves. Anton noticed they were soiled, which did not go with the smartness of the rest of his appearance. He pulled up, switched off his engine, looked round and listened. The only sound was the crunch of the man's shoes on a gravel track where the Ford was standing.

'Excuse me,' the man said, standing by Anton's open window, 'I'm looking for the Magpie Inn.'

'I can tell you how to get to the Goldcrest Inn.'

'Thank God. Oh, my name's Foster. It's been a fraught business. We have them in the back of the station wagon. Hands bound behind their backs, ankles tied, their mouths

489

taped, eyes blindfolded. Saunders is over there and will help. How are you going to move the merchandise?'

'Under the travelling rugs in the back of *my* car. One on top of the other . . .'

Seton-Charles ran out as Anton arrived back at Cherry Farm. The Greek lifted the corner of a rug and exposed the two captive Shi-ite Muslims dressed in prison garb. They untied the rope round the ankles of one man, manoeuvred him out of the car. When he tried to struggle they frogmarched him inside the farmhouse, up the stairs and into the prepared room.

'Dump him on the bed,' Anton ordered. 'He'll be safe while we get the other one inside . . .'

Five minutes later they had both men in their separate rooms. Anton held a Luger pistol while Seton-Charles tore off the tape and removed the blindfold. The Shi-ite blinked in the unaccustomed daylight and glared. Anton gestured towards the canvas sack he had dragged up the stairs. From its open end protruded the head of a slaughtered pig taken from the chest freezer in one of the sheds.

'Any trouble with you and I kill you, then you'll be buried in a grave with this pig.'

'No! No! No . . .!'

Anton watched the man's terrified expression. It had worked. The only form of intimidation which would quell a Shi-ite. The Muslim religion regarded the pig as the most unclean and horrific of animals. Anton waited behind the pig lying on the landing floor while Seton-Charles released the prisoner's hands. The Shi-ite rubbed his wrists to get the circulation going and all the time he stared at the pig's head as though hypnotized.

Anton waited until Seton-Charles had left the room, then threw inside a bundle of clothes: three suits in different sizes, underwear, shirts, socks and shoes.

'You get out of that prison garb, choose the clothes which fit you best, wrap the others in a bundle. We'll collect them when we feed you. Put your prison stuff with the bundle.' He aimed the Luger at the trembling Shi-ite's head. 'If you try to get away I will shoot you dead. Then you will share eternity with a pig.'

Seton-Charles closed, double-locked, bolted the door. 'Let's hope one of those suits fits him.'

'One will fit well enough. A man escaped from prison doesn't always have the right clothes to wear. Now haul the pig sack along to the other room and we'll repeat the process . . .'

He watched as Seton-Charles heaved the heavy sack along the corridor, his rimless glasses perched on his nose. Anton had been careful not to comment on the fact, but he had been surprised at how useful the professor had been. He was stronger physically than the Greek had realized. He had proved a useful workmate during the conversion of the vans, handing up tools to Anton on the platform, finding the right screws, and a psychological change had taken place in the relationship of the two men.

Seton-Charles now accepted Anton was boss and he prepared good meals for them. Something I might have foreseen, Anton thought: the professor was a bachelor who lived alone, looked after himself and was fastidious in his habits. They paused in front of the second reinforced door.

'That latest phone call I had from Jupiter,' Anton told him. 'We've reached the stage of closed circuit.'

'What's that?'

'We stay under very close cover. We don't leave the farm for anything unless it's essential.'

'Then the operation must be close?'

'Soon,' Anton assured him, 'it has to be soon.'

491

47

Tweed had 'broken silence'.

He had sent out a general alert all over Europe to counter-espionage chiefs, to his personal underground network of informants. The message was always the same.

Any data on past and present movements of Anton Gavalas, citizen of Greece. Suspected member of hardline Communist group the Greek Key. Also identical data on Professor Guy Seton-Charles, British citizen, Professor of Greek Studies at Bristol University, England, and Athens University, Greece. Data required extreme urgency. Tweed.

Copies of a photograph of Anton – made from the print inside the file Kalos had provided for Tweed – accompanied the request. But only a word description of Seton-Charles was sent. Tweed realized they had made a bad mistake in not photographing the professor.

Howard wandered into Tweed's office a week after the messages had been sent. It was his blue pinstripe suit day. He perched his buttocks on the edge of Tweed's desk, adjusted his tie, smiled at Monica who was stunned by such amiability.

'Any progress from the boys abroad?' he enquired.

Tweed winced inwardly at the phraseology. 'Nothing that gives us any kind of lead. Later this afternoon I have a meeting with the Prime Minister. I thought it was time she knew about this business.'

He waited for the explosion of outrage. It didn't come. Instead, Howard ran his fingers over his plump pink face and nodded approval. 'I was just coming in to suggest maybe we ought to let her know. Frankly, I'm surprised you didn't seek an earlier conference.'

'No hard facts to go on. Ever since Masterson was killed it's been like seeing shadowy figures in the mists of Exmoor. You aren't sure whether you actually saw anything or not. It may be a tricky interview. She *does* like facts. Oh, Paula is on her way here, driving up from Somerset. I just hope she gets here before I leave for Downing Street.'

'And why is the delightful Paula driving back to London? She could have reported over the phone from that public call box in Minehead.'

'She said she had information she'd sooner give me face to face.'

'Sounds intriguing. I suppose you couldn't record her report so I could play it back later?'

'I'll do that.'

Howard glanced at the machine on Tweed's desk, the neat piles of cassettes. 'You've been listening to those things yet again? The tapes of Butler's phoned reports and that clandestine job Nield did during dinner at The Luttrell Arms? You still think you've spotted which one of the three is the killer?'

'Yes.' Tweed stood up, began pacing slowly. 'But no proof. In case anything happens to me I typed out a secret report which is inside a sealed envelope in the safe.'

Howard stood up, pulled down his jacket at the back. 'Damned if I could point the finger at any of them. And God knows I've listened to them often enough. Why be so cryptic?'

'Because I could be wrong. The main thing at the moment is two people have gone missing. Anton Gavalas. I checked with Sarris and there's no sign he has returned to Greece. Then Guy Seton-Charles has vanished off the face of the earth. He'd accumulated several months' leave, so Bristol University informed us. He said he was going abroad. No trace of him on any airline passenger manifest.

493

And he always flew everywhere – again according to Bristol.'

'So, we're up the proverbial gum tree. Good luck with the PM.'

On this encouraging note Howard left the office. Monica stopped studying her file. 'He's also worried. Like you are. And although I hate Howard's guts, his instinct is sometimes very sound. I wish you hadn't said that thing about in case anything happens to you. It's tempting fate.'

'Don't be so superstitious,' Tweed chided.

Monica slammed her pencil down on her desk. 'Have we got one damn thing to go on after all this effort?'

'Two things. When I was interviewing old Petros at his farm he mentioned there had been rumours during the Second World War that the Greek Key was controlled by an Englishman in Cairo.'

'Seton-Charles was in Cairo . . .'

'So were the three commandos. The second thing also came from Greece. Kalos told me a radio ham – a friend of Sarris' – had picked up a coded message. At the end there was an instruction in English. *From now on the call sign is changed to Colonel Winter.* History can be changed by such chance happenings.'

Paula arrived early when Tweed and Monica were standing by the window, drinking tea. She was behind the wheel of Newman's Mercedes. As she parked by the kerb further along the Crescent Tweed saw the automatic radio aerial retracting, sliding down inside the rear. He frowned, held his cup in mid-air.

'What is it?' asked Monica.

'Nothing. Just an idea.'

'She's made very good time. And she seems to be in a rush – she's almost running. And her clothes!'

Paula was wearing a pair of tight blue denims and a windcheater. An outfit neither of them had ever seen her adopt before. Paula was classic pleated skirts and blouse with a well-fitting jacket. She disappeared inside the entrance below them.

'I'll make her coffee,' Monica decided. 'She's had quite a long drive. Back in a minute. And I think something's wrong.'

Tweed had his back to the window when there was a knock on his door, he called, 'Come in,' and Paula appeared, carrying in one hand her briefcase, in the other her small travelling case.

'What's the matter?' he asked, coming forward.

'Does there have to be something?' she asked, went to her desk and dumped two cases. Her voice was cool, too cool. She turned, leaning against the desk, and smiled wanly as he gave her a hug, kissed her on the cheek. She was a shade too controlled.

She took off her gloves slowly, placed one neatly on top of the other. Then she folded her arms, tilted her chin in the defiant look he knew so well. She was white-faced and there were dark circles under her eyes.

'I drove like a bat out of hell to get here.' She smiled again at his expression. 'But within the speed limit all the way.'

'What's the matter?' he repeated.

'You really are the most perceptive man.' She paused. 'It's good to be back.' Another pause. 'I've just shot two men.'

Tweed concealed the jolt he'd felt. 'Why not sit down and tell me about it? Monica is coming with coffee. The Browning automatic I sent down by courier was for you then? Not for Newman or Marler, as I thought?'

'They've given me hell, those two.' She sat down, crossed

495

her legs. 'I gave them hell back. Am I – or am I not – a fully-fledged member of this outfit?'

'Very fledged.' He smiled and drew a chair close to her. 'I have always shown you that's the way I feel, surely?'

'Yes. *You* have. Want to hear about my target-shooting – with live targets?'

Her voice was steady but Tweed sensed tension under the surface. He fetched a bottle of cognac and a glass from a cupboard, poured a hefty snifter. 'Get that down inside yourself.'

'Thanks.' She held the balloon glass in both hands to drink – to stop the glass shaking, Tweed suspected. 'My, that's made a difference.' She relaxed against the chair-back, her normal colour started to return. 'I hardly know where to start. I suppose it was Marler who saved my life. He arrived soon after I did.'

'Because I decided we needed every possible person down there. Exmoor is a vast territory to cover. And why not start at the beginning? When you'd arrived with Newman at Porlock Weir . . .'

Monica had phoned ahead and there were two rooms reserved for them when Newman and Paula carried their cases into The Anchor. They reached Porlock Weir in the early evening – Newman had encountered heavy sea mist drifting across the road. The moor was blotted out.

They had a conference with Butler and Nield over dinner and divided up duties. Newman took charge, made the suggestion. The dining room was almost empty so they could talk easily.

'We have three people to watch – Robson, Barrymore and Kearns. Nield, you take Robson. I'll keep an eye on Barrymore. That leaves Butler for Kearns . . .'

'No go,' Butler informed him. 'Tweed has given me the

496

job of checking out the people who live on that bungalow estate near Kearns' place.'

'And I'd like to help Harry, if he doesn't mind,' Paula said. 'I was the one who thought there was something odd about the place.'

'Be my guest,' replied Butler with enthusiasm. 'I've been helping Nield watch the three commando types. The electoral register in Taunton is our first check,' he told Paula.

'Then I'll have to take on both Barrymore and Kearns,' Newman decided. He grinned at Paula. 'You're just about as bloody . . . independent as Marler.'

'You were going to say bloody-minded,' Paula told him. 'Maybe I am. Do I get the order of the boot?'

'I'll overlook it this time. Eat your dinner, it's getting cold . . .'

The problem solved itself the following day when Marler turned up at The Anchor, sent down by Tweed. Secretly Newman had been relieved the previous evening: Paula would have protection, working with Butler. He was careful not to point this out to Paula.

While Paula and Butler visited Taunton, Newman gave Marler the task of shadowing Kearns in his hired Peugeot. Apart from Newman, they all travelled in hired cars. It took a week for Butler and Paula to come up with a list of names of the owners of the bungalows on the estate. Once she had the names Paula took to visiting The Royal Oak at Winsford where she was soon firm friends with the heavily built barman. She always arrived before the crowd at lunchtime, always came alone.

Bit by bit she told Jack, the barman, about herself. 'I'm recovering from an illness – convalescent leave they call it, the insurance company I work for. And when I was a kid I used to come down to Taunton to visit relatives . . .'

Her psychology was shrewd: country folk liked to know who they were talking to. Gradually she extracted from

Jack information about the occupants of the bungalow estate. The one day she avoided was Wednesday: she had seen Barrymore and Robson lunching at their usual table. They were still keeping up the ritual meetings, but Kearns was not there with them. She checked his absence on two Wednesdays before avoiding that day.

'Thinkin' of buyin' one of those bungalows when it comes on the market?' Jack commented to her one day. 'You'll be lucky. A funny set-up that lot, you mark my words.'

'Funny in what way?' she asked.

'Ever 'eard of a bungalow estate put up fifteen years ago and not one of the original owners has moved? Six bungalows there are. Six men. You'd think at least one would have moved on. New job, somethin' like that. Not a bit of it. They're all still there. And keeps themselves to themselves.'

'You mean you've never met one of them?'

'Now I didn't say that, did I, miss? One of them came in here soon after they'd all moved in. Chap called Foster. Didn't take to 'im. Drank gin and tonics while he chatted. La-di-dah type.'

'What did he chat about? It sounds like a mystery. I love mysteries,' Paula glowed.

'Said he was an investment counsellor, whatever that might be. Works in Bristol. His wife has some big job overseas. Never seen 'er. Said his friend, Saunders, also had his wife abroad. Some job with the UN in New York. Funny sort of married life. Wouldn't suit me – visiting the missus once or twice a year.'

'You mean the wives never come here?'

'That's about the long and short of it. Then there's the crank. Professor Guy Seton-Charles. Bachelor. Something to do with Bristol University. In summer they mows their lawns at the weekends. That's about all you see of 'em. Stuffy lot, if you ask me.'

Paula swallowed a piece of her chicken and mushroom

pie, the day's speciality chalked up on a blackboard. She sipped at her glass of white wine. Jack was polishing yet another glass until it came up gleaming like silver crystal.

'I heard there was a Mr Simon Morle living in one of the bungalows,' she said casually.

'Maybe. I wouldn't know. They're there and yet they're not there.' People were beginning to fill up the tables. He turned to another customer. 'What can I get you, sir?'

That was the night they had the most almighty row back at The Anchor.

They were all assembled for dinner at their usual table. Paula sat between Newman and Marler. Butler and Nield faced them, and Nield, inadvertently, lit the fuse.

'Saw you today, Paula. I was tracking Robson when he tried to call on Kearns. Got no joy. I thought Kearns must be out. Robson pressed the gate bell several times, no one came out, so he pushed off. I had wondered whether Kearns was ill.'

'I think he is,' Paula replied. '*I* saw Robson call, then drive off. A few minutes later Dr Underwood – we met him in the bar if you remember – called. Kearns came out and let him in.'

'What did you mean, Pete?' Marler asked. 'You said you saw Paula. Driving along the road?'

'No. Parked in her hired Renault inside a gateway overlooking that bungalow colony – and Kearns' place.'

Marler turned to Paula. 'What the devil were you doing there?'

'Observing that bungalow estate. You can look down on it. It's odd – one woman seems to clean the lot. Furtively.'

'How do you mean?' Nield enquired.

'She always slips in by the back doors. She has a key to each of them. I've used night glasses to watch her after dark . . .'

499

'*After dark?*' Marler's tone expressed incredulity. 'How long have you been keeping up this vigil?'

'For about two weeks.'

'You do realize it's only a matter of time before you're spotted,' Marler persisted in a cold voice. 'It's madness.'

'I have already realized that.' She said the words deliberately, disliking his tone. 'I saw the solution today. There's a riding stable near Dunster which hires out horses. In future I'll ride – which means I can get on the moor, check the area from different angles.'

'You bloody well won't . . .'

'Partridge used a horse,' she snapped. 'For the same reason, I suspect. He could see more from a horse.'

'And look where it got him.' Marler leaned his long white face – his Grecian suntan had long since faded – close to hers. 'It got him a knife in the back. You should be armed. You shouldn't be doing it at all.'

'No one's going to stop me,' she said icily, staring hard at Marler. 'If you feel that way, get me a weapon . . .'

It was Newman who calmed the atmosphere. He knew Paula was seething at the unspoken suggestion that she couldn't take care of herself. He remembered times when Tweed had put her in the front line to toughen her up. Standing up, he said he was driving into Minehead to call Tweed, to ask him to send a Browning automatic with spare magazines by motorbike courier. While he was away the rest of the meal was eaten in silence.

The following morning after breakfast Newman tapped on Paula's door. Inside he handed her a Browning and spare mags.

'So, I've come of age,' she said and smiled drily.

'How are you going to carry it on a horse – so it's easy to get at in an emergency?'

She produced a makeshift but neat holster made of blue denim and took hold of the Browning where she had laid it on a table. Releasing the magazine inside the butt, she checked to make sure there wasn't a bullet up the spout, pushed the mag back inside the gun and slipped it inside the holster. Two straps of the same material were attached to it.

She was wearing tight denims thrust inside riding boots and a padded windcheater. All purchased the previous day. Then she strapped the holster to her right upper leg close to her crotch. Parading round the room, she made a gesture with her slim hand.

'I'm on a horse. You meet me. Would you notice it?'

'No. It blends in perfectly. How on earth did you make that holster?'

'By staying up half the night. I cut material from the bottom of my jeans – tucked inside my boots you can't see where I took it from. Then a lot of careful sewing.' She came close to him, kissed him on the cheek. 'I expected you to flare up like Marler last night. Thanks for your vote of confidence.'

Newman shrugged, grinned. 'You are one of the team. Marler's got a short fuse. What did that cleaning woman you saw down at the estate look like?'

'Middle-aged. Medium height. About a hundred and twenty pounds. Grey hair tied back in a bun. I've got several photographs of her. I was carrying my camera with the telephoto lens. Should we send the film to Tweed?'

'Let me have it. Maybe in a few days one of us will have to go up to London. You'd finished the film?'

She handed him the spool. 'Yes. And I've a fresh one in the camera. The one you're holding has pictures of all the men living there. Plus pictures of the bungalows. Including Seton-Charles' place with that weird complex of TV aerials attached to his chimney.'

She hid the Browning with its holster and the mags at the bottom of the wardrobe, then picked up neat rows of shoes and spread them over the gun. Straightening up, she looked at Newman.

'After that row at dinner last night I feel like a walk along the coast. I didn't get much sleep and I'm feeling restless.'

'Let's go . . .'

It was dark but the gale had slackened to a strong breeze as they strolled along the track westward. Paula glanced at the cottage where Mrs Larcombe had lived, then looked away. Newman was careful not to refer to it.

'What are the others doing?' she asked as they picked their way across the pebbles.

'We're keeping up the watch on the commandos. Kearns appears to have recovered, but he's limping a bit. Maybe he twisted his ankle. Butler followed one of the men who live in those bungalows to the Somerset and Cornwall Bank in Bristol. Watched him draw about a thousand pounds in fifties. He's reported it to Tweed who has now started a discreet check on where that money comes from.'

'Anything new on the commandos?'

'Not really, blast it. Robson still rides to see his patients at all hours. He has one old duck who delights in using her bedside phone and calling him out late at night. Lives in a creepy old mansion near Dulverton. Barrymore is still making calls from that public box in Minehead. Kearns has no help in his house – looks after the place himself, does his own cooking. Army type, I suppose . . .'

He stopped speaking as Paula grasped his arm. They were some distance west of Porlock Weir, walking close to towering cliffs. 'I heard something funny, a sinister noise,' Paula whispered.

Then Newman heard it. A crumbling sound, the noise of grinding rocks. He looked above them, grabbed Paula's hand, shouted at her to run. They headed for the sea. Behind them the sound increased, grew to a rumbling roar. At the water's edge Newman turned and Paula swung round with him. She gazed, appalled.

By the light of the rising moon they saw a gigantic slab

of cliff sliding down from the summit, a slab which broke into smaller pieces as it rolled towards the beach. Enormous boulders bounded downwards towards where they stood, their backs to the sea. The boulders lost momentum, came to rest two dozen yards away. A sudden silence descended. Paula shivered, huddled closer to Newman.

'It's OK,' he said. 'That's it.'

'My God, if we hadn't run we'd have been under that.'

She pointed towards a dark mass of rocks piled up the height of a two-storey house. They were making their way back, keeping to the edge of the sea, when Paula pointed again.

'Who can that be?'

In the distance, close to the track, a man on horseback was riding away from them. Hunched forward, close to the horse's head, it was impossible to make out his shape, guess his height. He reached the track and the horse broke into a gallop. When they arrived back at The Anchor there was no sign of any horseman and they hurried inside to report the landslip.

The violent incident took place next day.

48

Grey mist was curling over the high crests as Paula rode her horse over the high ground behind the bungalow estate. It lay about two hundred yards below her and from this angle she was able to observe features she had not seen before.

Behind the end of the cul-de-sac a path led down into a dip invisible from the road. An old barn-like structure huddled in the dip, a building with half-doors. Both upper halves were open and two horses' heads peered out. This was her first realization that someone living on the estate rode the moors.

She saw movement, the opening of a back door in Seton-Charles' bungalow. Lifting her glasses looped round her neck, she focused. It was the grey-haired cleaning woman, carrying a mop and a plastic bucket. Paula remained perfectly still: people rarely looked *upwards*.

The woman opened a gate in the back garden fence, walked into the next garden. She put down mop and bucket, fiddled with a bunch of keys, inserted one in the rear door of the bungalow and disappeared inside with her cleaning equipment.

Paula dropped her glasses, rode on, slowly circling the estate. As usual, no sign of cars. They had probably all driven off to their jobs. The cars she had seen earlier, arriving back in the evenings, were Jags and Fords. No Mercedes or Rolls-Royces, but the cars they drove still cost money. There seemed to be no shortage of that commodity.

She had watched them at weekends cutting their lawns with power mowers, big machines which did the job quickly. It was late November and she gave a little shiver: the cold clamminess of the approaching mist rolling down the slopes was making itself felt.

She kept moving slowly, like a rider out for a gentle morning bit of exercise. For the moment she was sheltered from the estate by a gorse-covered ridge. She guided her mount up the side and perched on a small rocky hilltop which gave a bird's-eye view. The two horsemen seemed to appear out of nowhere.

One moment she was alone on the hilltop, the next moment they rode out from behind a concealed ridge and confronted her. They stopped about two dozen feet away, staring at her. She noticed several things as she casually dropped her right hand over the holster.

They were experienced riders: neither had his feet inside the stirrups. Probably because they had mounted their horses in a hurry. She recognized their mounts as the horses which had peered over the half-doors. One man was tall, lean-faced and with jet-black hair. His cheekbones were prominent, almost Slavic. The other was short and heavily-built with an ugly round face and a mean mouth.

Both were in their forties, she estimated. Both wore windcheaters and slacks thrust into riding boots. The Slavic-faced man raised a hand, unzipped the front of his windcheater, left it open. The ugly man began guiding his horse, took up a position on her right side. She responded by turning her own horse.

'I like to face strangers,' she informed them and smiled.

'Why are you spying on us?' Slav-Face demanded.

'It's normal to introduce yourself in this part of the world,' she replied. 'I'm Paula . . .'

'And I'm Norton. Now, I'll ask you again – why are you spying on us?'

His right hand slipped inside his windcheater, emerged holding a gun. A 9mm Walther automatic as far as Paula could tell. She froze. The weapon was aimed point-blank between her breasts. Paula glanced to her left. A ridge higher than the hilltop masked the road. No help from that direction – even if Nield came driving along.

'This is moorland open to the public,' she snapped. 'You think you own Exmoor?'

'Gutsy, eh?' Norton commented. 'Now answer the question.'

'I ride all over the place. I don't know what you're talking about. And it's illegal to threaten someone with a weapon in this country.'

'She says it's illegal, Morle,' Norton said to his companion, still staring at Paula. 'She says she doesn't know what I'm talking about.'

His voice was cultured; high falutin' some would have called it. Almost a caricature of Marler's drawling way of speaking, but with an underlying sneer. Norton and Morle. Paula recalled the names she'd recorded while Butler examined the electoral register. These were two of them: she had all five names in her head.

'So if she doesn't know what I'm talking about,' Norton continued, 'how come she's been sitting in a parked car up the road day after day, watching the bungalows through field glasses?' He still held the gun levelled at her. 'I think maybe we will continue this discussion inside my bungalow, have a real cosy chat.'

Paula had been frightened when the two men first appeared. Now she remembered Newman putting her through her paces at a quiet spot on the North Downs. And he'd gone through the Special Air Services course before writing an article on the SAS. *Faced with a gunman there's always something you can do – say – to distract him, if you're armed* . . . And now, unsure of survival, she had gone as cold as ice.

'So you've confused me with someone else,' she said. 'Parked in a car, my foot. A horse is my form of transport here. You can tell the difference between a horse and a car? This is not very encouraging – when Foster asked me if I could take on the job of helping clean the bungalows.'

'He did what?' Norton's forehead crinkled with puzzlement. He turned to Morle. 'Do you know anything about this? He must be clean out of his . . .'

As he spoke the gun sagged, the muzzle aimed at the ground. It took seconds for Paula to haul the Browning from the holster, to grasp the butt in both hands, to aim it. Norton saw movement out of the corner of his eye. He began to lift his own gun. Paula fired twice. Norton slumped, was falling from his horse, when Morle ripped down his zipper, shoved his hand inside, began to haul out a gun. Paula had swivelled the Browning, her knees clamped to her horse to hold it steady. Twice more she fired.

Morle grabbed at his saddle with one hand, slowly toppled. A loud explosion echoed. Paula thought she was hit. Then she saw Norton had pulled the trigger in a reflex action as he hit the ground. The bullet winged across the moor.

The men's two horses galloped off in panicky freedom. Paula's mount threatened to rise up on its hindlegs. She pressed a firm hand on its neck, made soothing noises, dismounted, trailed the reins and approached Norton, still gripping her Browning. He lay unconscious, his fingers had dropped the gun. She bent down, felt his neck pulse. It beat steadily. Blood oozed from his right shoulder.

Standing up, she ran across to examine Morle. He also was unconscious. A red stain spread across his slacks close to his left hip. Again she checked the pulse. Again she felt its regular beat. Thank God, she thought and stood up, deciding what to do.

Two minutes later she was riding fast along the track which led to Exford, a four-mile trek. She left the horse at the riding stables she had hired it from. Nothing more to pay. Walking along the road, she entered the field where she had parked her Renault, got behind the wheel.

She drove across country, turned on to the A396 and arrived via Minehead at Porlock Weir half an hour later. To her infinite relief Newman and Marler had just returned to The Anchor.

Tweed drank three cups of coffee while he listened to Paula's story in his Park Crescent office. She spoke tersely, with not a wasted word. On his desk lay the sheet of handwritten names she had given him – the occupants of the six bungalows. He already knew them from the earlier report Butler had given him on the phone. He squeezed her hand as she concluded her account, stood up and went back behind his desk.

'So Newman and Marler cleaned up the mess,' he said.

'They were marvellous. I wondered if they'd say I'd made a mistake stopping at the first public phone box on my way back to Porlock Weir. That was when I phoned the police, refused to give a name and told them there'd been a shooting incident near the bungalow estate close to Simonsbath. That they'd better send an ambulance. I felt I couldn't just leave them there. Marler said he'd have done just that . . .'

'Marler would,' Tweed commented drily.

'But Bob said I'd done the right thing. He took the Browning, spare mags and my makeshift holster. They were going to end up in the sea. Bob also said it was lucky Norton's gun went off by chance. That would confuse the police investigation.'

'Eat your ham sandwiches,' said Monica. 'You need something inside you.'

'Now you mention it, I'm famished.' She devoured one sandwich and Tweed waited, glancing at his watch. 'Am I holding you up?' she asked.

'No. Our tame accountant is due soon. Butler reported that he had followed Foster twice to the Somerset and Cornwall Bank in Bristol. He saw him draw about a thousand pounds in cash each time. He heard the teller address him as Mr Foster. Perry has the details and is in the Engine Room phoning God knows who to trace where that money came from. It's so often the money which helps us find out who people really are.'

'Well, there is something wrong about that bungalow estate. I said it was funny when we first saw it,' Paula said defiantly.

Tweed nodded. He understood her attitude. She was bound to suffer a reaction from the experience sooner or later. And the sooner the better.

'It's the first time I've shot anyone,' Paula went on and sank her teeth into a fresh sandwich.

'They're only injured,' Tweed assured her. 'Newman drove over to the estate after you'd left in the Mercedes. He arrived as they were carting those two thugs into an ambulance. He showed his old press card and they recognized the name. He called the hospital later.'

Tweed omitted to tell her Norton was in a coma, that Morle was still unconscious. Police were waiting by their bedsides ready to take statements.

'More alarming,' he went on, switching her mind to another topic, 'Marler arrived at the estate and flourished his fake Special Branch card, so the police let him in. The bungalows are all empty. The cars have gone. Most sinister of all, they can find not a single fingerprint. Everything has been wiped clean. You were so right about that estate.'

'What does that mean – no fingerprints?' Paula asked.

'I think you discovered the secret base of sleepers established fifteen years ago by the Englishman who controls the Greek Key. A base which was recently activated – and has now been evacuated – thanks to your encounter with Norton and Morle. We have now made copies in the Engine Room of those photos you took – and circulated them to every police force in the country. We also have their names.' He glanced down at the list on his desk.

Foster, Saunders, Norton, Morle, Sully.

'Anything else?'

'Yes. Before I sent out the European alert I circulated the registration number of Seton-Charles' Volvo station wagon over here. And Newman visited Bristol University with a police artist. They used several students to build an Identikit picture of the professor. Copies of that have gone out.'

'Will anyone take much notice?'

'I think so,' Tweed said grimly. 'I named him suspected terrorist planner. Highly dangerous.'

509

'Talking of terrorists,' Monica chimed in, 'there's an interesting story I cut from a recent copy of *The Times*. Two Shi-ite Muslim killers were air-lifted by a chopper from Gartree Prison exercise yard. Most audacious. They killed an Iraqi diplomat.'

Tweed wasn't listening. Paula had remembered a further incident.

'There was a big landslip when Bob and I were walking from The Anchor one night along the coast . . .' She described the experience. 'They've put up a big notice. *Warning. Keep clear. Danger of cliff falls.*'

The phone rang. Monica answered, looked up at Tweed. 'Perry is ready to emerge from the basement with his report on the Foster bank account.'

'Tell him to come up.'

Perry was a small, precise, neatly dressed man who wore pince-nez. Monica thought he was a giggle but he had a shrewd financial brain. Clutching a blue file, he sat on the edge of a chair facing Tweed. He glanced at Monica and Paula.

'This is highly confidential.'

Tweed compressed his lips. 'You should realize by now Paula and Monica know more about what's going on than you ever will.'

'Then I will commence.'

He opened his fat file but Tweed glanced at his watch. He had to leave soon for his appointment with the PM. And now Paula had brought information – facts – which made his interview well worthwhile.

'Just tell me in a few words what you've found out.'

'Very well, but I think you should read the file later. The enquiry took longer than I expected. It is a devious trail – and I had to get Walton, head of Special Branch, to vouch for me before the bank manager in Bristol would talk. Then I had to use your name for Europe . . .'

'I know. Chief Inspector Kuhlmann of Wiesbaden in

510

Germany called me. So did Beck in Zurich. Do get on with it.'

'Foster originally had twenty thousand pounds in his Bristol account. He's closed it now. The money was telexed from the Deutsche Bank in Frankfurt. They received it from the Zürcher Kredit Bank in Zurich. That's the end of the road.'

'What does that mean?'

'Zürcher Kredit received the funds from Liechtenstein. That's an iron door no one can open. Not much help, is it?'

'On the contrary, it fits into the pattern which is appearing so rapidly at last. Thank you, Perry. Yes, I suppose you'd better leave the file.'

He waited until they were alone. 'A secret Soviet base is set up fifteen years ago – in hardline Brezhnev's time – at that bungalow estate. It's screaming at us now. Those five men in their early forties would be in their mid-twenties when they slipped into this country. They'd have identities cooked up at Moscow Centre's Documents Section. A Colonel Winterton – whom no one ever met – bought a piece of land with an old house on it. Marler found that out from pub gossip. He had the house knocked down, the six bungalows built in its place. All ready for the *Spetsnaz* unit to move in . . .'

'*Spetsnaz?*' Monica queried.

'You know – élite Soviet troops equivalent to our SAS. Trained to merge into the landscape of a foreign country. They were probably originally intended to assassinate specific key figures in the defence of this country. The leader of the Greek Key, an Englishman living on Exmoor, was their commander.'

'I know what they are,' Monica protested, 'but surely you're reaching, as the Americans would say. Guessing . . .'

'I'd sooner say I'm deducing the solution from clues now in our hands. They always kept to themselves. Foster visited The Royal Oak and chatted to the barman. Luckily barmen have good memories. Foster makes a point of telling him two wives have jobs abroad – which makes the place sound more natural, as opposed to six bachelors, including Seton-Charles. Having fed the barman that much – knowing it would be spread round the district – Foster never goes back there again. Paula finds one woman is cleaning all six bungalows . . .'

'In her forties, too, I'd say,' Paula interjected.

'That's very peculiar,' Tweed continued. 'Six men, all strangers apparently when they buy their bungalows, use the same woman. In England? Not likely. Now Perry tells us Foster draws large sums from a fund which originated in Liechtenstein. So we can't trace where the money came from. Now we hear they've all disappeared, leaving not one fingerprint behind. Everything those men did is shrouded in secrecy. Except the two in hospital. It stinks of *Spetsnaz*.'

'And it wasn't due to the shooting incident Paula was involved in,' Monica stated. 'How do I know that? Because I know how long it takes to clean my flat. To erase all fingerprints from six bungalows must have taken days of meticulous work by that woman. They were leaving anyway. Doesn't that mean an operation is imminent?'

'It means we have very little time left to trace them,' Tweed said grimly. 'And I have very little time to keep my appointment with the PM.'

'Anything more we can do?' asked Monica as he put on his Burberry. It was typical November weather outside, a heavy drizzle.

'Only wait. And hope. We've thrown out across the country all the information we hold. I'm off.'

'One other thing while I remember,' Paula said. 'Nield heard this in a pub. Kearns' dog kept on moping and whining for Jill. He shot it recently and buried it in the garden at the back of his house. Put up a wooden cross inscribed, *In loving memory of Jill*.'

512

'Damn!' Tweed hardly heard her as the phone began ringing and Monica picked it up. 'I can't talk to anyone . . .'

'It's Marler. Says it's very urgent.'

'Make it quick,' Tweed said after grabbing the receiver.

'Newman visited the hospital after hearing Morle was talking. Arrived, found Morle had a serious case of fever, high temperature. The policeman told Bob what Morle had mumbled. One word over and over. Then Newman heard it. Stinger. The police chap thought he was talking about the drink. *Stinger*. Do you get it?'

'Yes.' Tweed found he was gripping the receiver tightly. He said thank you and put down the phone.

'Bad news?' Paula asked.

'The worst. Now we know what Anton brought ashore. Stinger rocket launchers and missiles. God help us.'

He ran down the steps to the ground floor, forced himself to pause at the exit, glance round. Across the road stood the usual news seller. He stopped briefly to buy an *Evening Standard*. And this time he stared at the poster summarizing the main news.

Gorbachev To Meet Thatcher At Brize Norton En Route Washington.

49

Jupiter lay very still in bed inside his house on Exmoor. In the dark he ticked off in his mind the list of tasks dealt with. Everyone was now in place. It was 30 November: Gorbachev would land at Brize Norton on Monday 7 December.

Land? He would be blown to pieces in mid-air. The meeting with the British Prime Minister would never take place. Within days, Yigor Ligachev, Number Two in the Politburo, would take over as the new General Secretary. Ligachev had no time or sympathy with *glasnost*, with *perestroika*, and all the other nonsense. He had openly said so.

Jupiter had been trained as a youth in the hardline school. The world must be made safe for Lenin's Marxist principles. Only the Red Army could achieve the final victory. And I, he thought, will have contributed an essential role to that eventual victory I won't live to see. The Red Flag flying over Buckingham Palace, the White House in Washington. No, that would take more years than I have.

He smiled as he thought of the final signal he had transmitted to Greece. He had changed the scenario. The weak link was Florakis. It was ironic – that Florakis would pass on to Doganis the signal tomorrow, signing his own death warrant. *Closed circuit.*

Driving along the coast road to Cape Sounion just before dawn, Doganis hunched his huge, seemingly flabby bulk over the wheel. It suited him to be up early: he no longer slept well and woke with his brain churning with excitement. Everything had gone so well. Using Petros' insane lust for revenge as a smokescreen had completely foiled the opposition. He pulled up close to the hotel site, leaving his engine running.

'I have a fresh signal,' the lean-faced Florakis said as he got into the passenger seat. 'But why do I need the transceiver?'

'Put it in the boot,' Doganis ordered.

He waited until they were driving along the winding highway before he answered. Florakis glanced at Doganis who stared straight ahead: he disliked him intensely, this mountain of flesh, gone to seed. He should keep fit, an activity Florakis prided himself on.

'We are moving the location where you transmit from,' Doganis informed him. 'It is dangerous to transmit from the same area too frequently. You said it was a short message. Two words. What are they?'

'Closed circuit. That was all. Then he signed off.'

I guessed right, Doganis thought. And the timing is correct. Soon the operation will be accomplished. Unlike Florakis, he knew this would be the last signal. He went on talking as he drove closer and closer to Cape Sounion. And his own timing was correct – it was still half an hour before dawn.

'In future you will transmit from the summit of Cape Sounion. There is no one about at 2 a.m. I will show you the ideal place I have found – a dip in the ground beyond the temple.'

He stopped the car at the entrance to the track leading up from the highway. He told Florakis to fetch the transceiver. Inwardly Florakis sneered at this; the flabby bastard hadn't even the strength to lug the transceiver uphill.

They walked in silence past the restaurant and hotel which showed no lights. Then they climbed the twisting rocky path to the summit. Doganis wheezed, apparently with the effort. They reached the elegant Temple of Poseidon, its columns silhouetted in the dark.

Doganis led the way past it and down the slope towards the cliff edge. The ground was covered with scrubby grass and Doganis stopped at the edge of a bowl. He pointed one thick finger.

'That is the place. You make all future transmissions from here . . .'

'I see. But why bring the transceiver? I am not going to use it now.'

'Because you will not need it any more.'

Doganis raised his huge hands, clamped them round the throat of Florakis. The Greek was taken by surprise, but not frightened. Doganis had gone mad – even to imagine he could cope with a man of Florakis' strength. He tried to knee Doganis in the groin, but the attacker had turned sideways and the blow struck his thigh. Florakis felt a flash of fear. It had been like hitting the leg of an elephant. The pressure on his windpipe increased. Lights appeared before his eyes. Doganis' face seemed enormous as he began to bend Florakis whose back arched in a bow. If the process continued his back would be broken. Panic took hold. He kicked futilely with his right foot at Doganis' leg. It felt like striking ebony. Then he sagged, lost consciousness as Doganis went on strangling him.

Satisfied that he had done the job, Doganis let him slump to the ground. They were perched on top of the slope. Doganis used one foot to lever the prostrate corpse. It began to roll. The momentum increased. Like a broken rag doll Florakis vanished over the edge of the cliff. Doganis grunted with satisfaction, flexed his hands.

'I am arresting you for cold-blooded murder,' a quiet voice said behind him.

The Dormouse stood about two dozen feet away, further along the top of the ridge where it curved inland. He stood, a tiny figure, with his hands clasped behind his back, staring at Doganis, at the sea behind him which stretched away like a sheet of black steel. Stood as though about to make a speech.

'You came alone?'

Doganis could hardly believe it, looked round for reinforcements.

The plump tiny figure looked so absurd. There was no sign of anyone else.

'Yes,' said Kalos. 'I have been watching your apartment

516

in the Plaka for days – and nights. I followed you in my
Saab without lights. You were so intent on your murderous
plan you never dreamed you might be followed.'

'And you think *you* are going to arrest *me*?'

Doganis began to move slowly towards Kalos who remained quite still. Hands still clasped behind his back as
Doganis crept along the ridge, padding silently.

'Is this the way you killed the Englishman, Harry Masterson?' he asked.

'Yes. You might as well know it since you will end as food
for the fishes. Masterson was also deceived like Florakis –
by thinking I was a fat weak slob. I told him I could show
him where the leader of the Greek Key lived. He was
making too many enquiries about us. He was confident he
could handle me. And he was stronger than Florakis.'

'Stay where you are,' Kalos ordered. 'Do not take one
more step towards me. I have handcuffs behind my back.
I am taking you in.'

Doganis continued his ape-like progress. A sound came
from inside him, a rumbling noise which was his version of
a chuckle. He raised both hands, ready to grasp this doll
round the throat. He would be able to lift him off his feet,
throw him over . . .

Kalos brought both hands from behind his back. They
held the 9mm Walther automatic he had extracted from
the holster strapped to the middle of his back. He fired
once, aiming to disable. The bullet struck Doganis in the
left shoulder. He stopped. Then he came on again. Kalos
fired again. At the thigh. Still Doganis moved forward like
an enraged bull elephant. Kalos shifted his aim, shot him
through the heart.

Doganis slumped slowly to the ground on the seaward
side of the ridge, on to the slope. Like Florakis, his huge
bulk began to roll. He caught a medium-sized boulder a
glancing blow and the loosened boulder also started to roll.
Kalos stood watching as Doganis' body reached a steeper

517

section of slope, picking up speed. The gross corpse shot over the brink, dropped out of sight to fall three hundred feet, followed by the boulder.

He walked over to the transceiver Doganis had intended hurling off the cliff. He embraced its sides with both hands, his gun slid back inside his holster, and staggered back to his Saab, preserving Florakis' fingerprints on the handle.

50

Three men paced the snow-bound barracks square south-west of Moscow. In the centre of the group strode General Lucharsky, flanked by the other two members of the Troika. Their boots crunched the hard snow and they had the square to themselves: all officers and men were moving out aboard military transport for the annual manoeuvres in the Ukraine which would be watched by Lucharsky.

The timing suited Lucharsky admirably. He would be out of the way when the imminent crisis broke. His companions waited for him to speak. He kept them waiting. An assertion of his authority. A bitter wind whipped at his white bony face.

'Everything is prepared,' he said eventually. 'We are so far advanced radio communications are being cut. The weak links in the Greek Key are being eliminated. It all depends now on Jupiter in England.'

'Gorbachev has played into our hands,' commented General Budienny. 'Thank God he is landing in England. But British security is very good. Is Jupiter better?'

'The commander of the *Spetsnaz* unit which has been

518

activated is an ex-soldier in the British Army. A formidable man. He will find a way. Meantime, General Budienny, your armoured division will remain here ready to seal off Moscow should a crisis arise.' He stopped and stared hard at the stocky, wide-shouldered general. 'But on no account must you move unless you receive a direct order from Yigor Ligachev to preserve stability.'

'Of course not, Comrade General. My division has always had to stand by for that role – even under Brezhnev.'

Lucharsky resumed his walk in the square where they could not possibly be overheard. 'And the one general who might rebel because he is a *glasnost* enthusiast will be taking part in the Ukraine manoeuvres. At the slightest sign of resistance on his part I will have him arrested. So what can possibly go wrong?'

'You were worried at one time when your KGB associate warned you the British agent, Tweed, was in Greece.'

'Until I heard he was concentrating on that crazy old idiot, Petros. Then I knew he had taken the bait – incensed by the killing of his sector chief, Masterson, which is why I ordered Masterson's liquidation. You can forget Tweed. He is confused, like a ship without a rudder, sailing round in circles.'

Snow had begun to fall again, heavy flakes which drifted down out of the pewter sky. Lucharsky paused, bent down, scooped up some in his gloved hand and rubbed it on his face.

'That helps the brain to become alert, Comrades. The first snow of winter – the winter which will descend on *glasnost* and freeze it to death.'

1 December. Tweed had not returned to his office the previous day. He had to wait at Downing Street to see the PM. And when he did meet her the meeting had lasted far longer than he had anticipated.

Now he was walking in Regent's Park with Paula. The

wind was biting and he wore his British warm topcoat. Paula clutched her own coat collar at the neck as they made their way across the deserted open spaces.

'Let us go back to the beginning,' Tweed said. 'I still have the worrying feeling I have missed something.'

'You've done everything you can,' she assured him. 'It is a matter of waiting for a break.'

'But we have so little time left. Gorbachev lands at Brize Norton on Monday 7 December. That leaves only six days. So, recall how it all started for me.'

She summarized the early events and Tweed listened in silence. 'Then,' she went on, 'there was the murder of Sam Partridge on Exmoor. You had to identify him for that local policeman . . .'

She broke off as he stopped, gripped her arm. 'That's it. Why did I have to identify him?'

'Because his wallet was missing. And later discovered with plenty of money inside it – by a dog ferreting in the Doone Valley.'

'So robbery was certainly not involved.'

'They were new notes. The numbers ran in sequence,' Paula reminded him. 'No thief with half a brain would risk spending them.'

'Back to the office.' Tweed's tone was firm. 'I want to see the list Marler sent us of what was in that wallet. *Something* was missing.'

'Sam's driving licence.' Tweed's voice held a note of triumph as he sat behind his desk and studied the list. 'It wasn't in his wallet. That's what is missing. And he drove down to Somerset. He told me he parked his car in the street at Dunster.'

'Then why hasn't someone reported its presence – parked there all this time?' Monica objected.

'Because someone – maybe Winterton himself – drove

520

it away and parked it in some hidden place on Exmoor. Maybe an abandoned building. They didn't want the car – they're using the licence. Which means they probably hired a car on the strength of Partridge's driving licence.' He scribbled on his desk pad, tore off the sheet. 'Paula, here's his address. Call the Vehicle Registration people in Swansea immediately. Find out the licence number.'

'Which could take God knows how long. They don't move fast,' Paula warned.

'Tell them you're Special Branch.' He produced his card. 'And tell them I need a reply within one hour. That we are searching for an escaped terrorist. Dammit, they're using computers. Within one hour . . .'

It was one hour and ten minutes later when Vehicle Registration phoned back with the number. Tweed called the Commissioner of Police, identified himself, gave him the number. He had hardly put down the phone when it rang again. Newman reporting from Exmoor. No change in the situation.

Tweed explained what he wanted, gave him the licence number and urgent instructions. 'I want all four of you on this. Divide up the area into sectors. Then drive round to every place where you can hire a car. Show them the number. If someone used the licence to hire a car their records will show it. I need any information you can get within twenty-four hours.'

'We have as long as that?' Newman asked cynically.

'Quicker if you can.'

At Cherry Farm the balance of power had changed, much to Anton's chagrin. It had started with a phone call from Jupiter. He told Anton in his cryptic way that three more guests would be arriving. Foster, Saunders and Sully.

At the appointed time Anton drove the grey Austin Metro Seton-Charles had hired in Taunton weeks before to the crossroads where he had taken delivery of the Shi-ite prisoners. A Ford station wagon and a Vauxhall Cavalier stood parked alongside each other on the verge. The lean-faced smartly dressed Foster he had met before came towards him.

'Tawny Owl,' Foster greeted him.

'Night Heron,' Anton replied, wondering why Jupiter had thought it necessary for them to exchange agreed codewords when he knew Foster. There were two men in the Vauxhall who waited inside until Anton led the way, driving at the head of the convoy back to Cherry Farm. He didn't like the look of any of them. They had the smell of hardbitten professionals, almost as though they had undergone military training.

Foster introduced his companions after his two cars were hidden in the second shed. In the large kitchen at the back Seton-Charles examined the new arrivals through his rimless glasses. He also did not like what he saw. Foster, quick-moving and quick-talking, wasted no time.

'This is Saunders, my second-in-command. If I'm absent you take orders from him. This is Sully. We've brought our own food supplies. Sully will cook for the three of us . . .'

'Seton-Charles has been doing the cooking,' Anton interrupted. 'He can do the meals for all of us.'

'I said Sully will cook for us. You two look after yourselves. Now, where are the Stingers, the mobile launching platforms?'

Anton took them upstairs into the bedroom he occupied, opened a cupboard. Over his left arm was looped the handle of a walking stick with a hardened tip. He used both hands to push his clothes, suspended from a rod, to each side. Foster grunted.

'We'll need a better place than this in case a patrol car comes poking around.'

'Will we?' Anton snapped. 'Then find them yourself.'

522

Foster dropped to his knees, crawled inside, felt around the wooden planked floor. Anton looked at Seton-Charles, raised his eyebrows. *Bighead* his gesture conveyed. Sully, smaller, slimly built and also very fit-looking like the others, caught the expression.

'We can do without the sarcasm,' he growled.

Foster hammered hard at the back of the cupboard with his knuckles, expecting a hollow sound. He gritted his teeth – he had almost broken his knuckles on solid wood. He crawled out of the cupboard, stood up.

'All right, I can't find them,' he said and his tone was more polite.

Anton stepped inside, pressed hard with the tip of the stick on a knot of wood in a corner. There was a loud *click*. The rear panel opened inwards a few inches and Anton pushed it wide open, held it, revealing the compartment beyond with a long canvas bundle on the floor.

'You hold the panel open,' he warned. 'There is a spring-loaded hinge which closes it automatically. You haul that out . . .'

They stood inside the front furniture van after squeezing past the auction junk Anton had purchased. Seton-Charles had been told to stay in the farmhouse to keep watch. Holding a launcher with a missile inserted under one arm, Anton mounted the steps to the platform, followed by Foster and his two companions.

Anton settled himself in the chair, pressed the switch and the panel in the roof slid back. Foster stared, glanced at Sully and Saunders who also gazed up. 'Who created all this?' asked Foster.

'I did,' said Anton.

'Jesus, I'm impressed. The other van the same?'

'A replica of this one . . .'

There was an argument about who would drive each

523

van, who would use the launchers. Anton refused to give way. 'I've been trained in the weapon's use by the arms dealer. I'm firing one of the launchers. Who the hell drives is your problem.'

Foster compromised. He and Anton would fire the launchers; the vans would be driven by Saunders and Sully. He asked about communication and Anton produced a walkie-talkie from a leather sheath attached to the platform. 'The driver has his own, tells the launcher when the target is in sight. Anything else?'

Foster asked about the Shi-ite prisoners who would be left dead inside the vans, their hands pressed on the launchers to leave fingerprints. Anton told him about the dead pig he was using to keep them passive. Foster nodded. 'Except when it is on view,' Anton continued, 'I keep it in the chest freezer in the shed. I rigged up a generator to power the freezer.' Foster nodded again, then raised the delicate topic.

'You heard from Jupiter that before we leave nothing must be left to show we were here?'

'Yes. When the call was finished I asked Seton-Charles to dig a grave in the field at the back for the pig.'

'You know what will occupy this grave?' Foster asked quietly.

'Look, I've just told you.' Anton stared at Foster, who stared back with a poker-faced expression. Was he grasping what he'd been told, the Greek began to wonder. Maybe this cold-faced man wasn't too bright? 'It will be occupied by the pig,' Anton repeated.

'Together with Seton-Charles. He's expendable.'

2 December. An atmosphere of tension was building up inside Tweed's office at Park Crescent. There had been no further reaction to the long list of enquiries they had sent out. No one had called about Anton's photo or the

Identikit picture of Seton-Charles which had been widely circulated.

None of the four men scouring Exmoor had reported back on the phone. Tweed, Monica and Paula spent their time listening once more to the tapes of the conversations recorded. They reread the files, including the report Newman had dictated about their visit to Greece. They searched desperately for something they had overlooked. Late in the evening Monica brought more coffee and asked her question again.

'Can't you tell us anything about your interview with the PM?'

'At a certain stage – closer to 7 December when Gorbachev will land at Brize Norton – I shall recall Newman, Marler, Butler and Nield from Exmoor. They must stay there a day or so yet in the hope they find two things – if Sam Partridge's driving licence was used to hire a car in the area, and the route used by Anton to leave the country secretly. When they arrive back we hold a meeting. Then you will hear what has been decided.' He paused. 'I can tell you the PM was convinced I am right, that we have her full support to indent for any weapons we may need. And that two Westland helicopters have been put at our disposal. At my suggestion they are being equipped with swivel-mounted machine-guns and the words "Traffic Control" are being painted on the fuselages. They are at a private airfield called Fairoaks near Woking in Surrey.'

'What's the idea?' Paula asked.

'I should give the credit to Newman. He phoned me in the middle of the night and I outlined the situation. He knows what's coming. So does Marler. Newman made those suggestions.'

Paula glanced at the camp bed made up in the corner. 'So you didn't get an undisturbed night's rest.'

'I don't expect any of us will during the next five days . . .'

He stopped speaking as Howard strolled into the room and sat down in the armchair. He carried a sheaf of photo-prints.

'No developments yet, I assume? It's a tense time.'

'Nothing,' Tweed replied. 'And there's always tension at this stage.'

'As you know,' Howard remarked, 'I'm a bit of a car buff. It struck me that that *Spetsnaz* unit Paula uncovered must have moved to a new base prepared in advance.'

'I agree.' Tweed wondered what he was getting at.

'We know Foster has a Ford station wagon, Saunders a Vauxhall Cavalier, Seton-Charles a Volvo station wagon – from the information supplied by Vehicle Registration at Swansea. Sully left his Jag behind in the bungalow garage, so we can forget that. It occurred to me they won't dare hire fresh cars – they'd have to show their driving licences. With me so far?'

'So far, yes.'

'That means they'll have to use the same transport to move about. But they may respray their vehicles to disguise them.'

'Highly possible,' Tweed agreed.

'So I have used photographs of those three cars and traced them on a sheet of paper. But I filled the colours in with a solid black. Then I had these photocopies made. If we're looking for those cars from a chopper and use these photocopies we won't be fooled by any change of colour. They're all fairly common makes of car. We'll spot them by their shapes.'

He reached forward, dumped the photocopies on Tweed's desk and sat back again. Tweed studied the copies.

'I think this is a clever idea,' he decided. 'Everyone involved in the search will have a copy.'

'Then I need one,' said Howard and took back a copy.

'What for?' asked Tweed.

'Because I'll be in one of those choppers. You can ride in the other machine.' He raised a hand as Tweed started to protest. 'Don't argue. I'm good at spotting cars. And if you tell the PM I'll never speak to you again.' He stood up. 'So that's settled. I'm fed up with fighting the war from behind my desk with paper darts.' He glanced at Monica's stupefied expression as he left. 'And better give Monica a brandy. Looks like she needs it.'

'My God!' Monica burst out when Howard had gone. 'I'd never have believed it.'

'You always did underestimate Howard,' Tweed told her, and then the phone began ringing.

There was dead silence as Monica grabbed the receiver. She listened, looked at Tweed. 'It's for you. Peter Sarris. Athens.'

Tweed greeted the Greek police chief, then kept silent for five minutes. Gradually he hunched closer to the phone. When he put it down he stared bleakly into the distance for a long minute before speaking.

'It's very close,' he said gravely. 'Doganis strangled Florakis on Cape Sounion, sent his body over the cliff. He didn't know Kalos was following him. Doganis admitted he'd killed Harry Masterson. Apparently he's as strong as an ox. Kalos had to shoot him.'

'What does it mean?' Paula asked.

'It means the Soviet hardliners back in Russia – probably led by General Lucharsky – are wiping their tracks clean. Killing off anyone who could betray them. 7 December is definitely zero hour. Pray for a break soon.'

51

Friday, 4 December. At Cherry Farm the atmosphere was strained and becoming worse. Five men were living in close proximity inside the farmhouse. Anton had agreed with Foster's decision that no one must appear outside. The temperature was low and a biting wind swept across the waterlogged fields and rattled the closed shutters.

The Shi-ite Muslims, shivering with cold, had complained they were freezing. They were given extra underclothes and left to cope. Conditions were little better for their five captors. There was a tantalising pile of logs on one side of the large fireplace in the living room. No fire could be lit: smoke from the chimney would show a passer-by the place was inhabited.

There was no electricity, no gas, no water. All services had been cut off from the supposedly abandoned farm. Seton-Charles cooked a meal for himself at midday using Calor gas for the stove – an item he had bought on his way back from Norwich. He had very little left.

In the living room Anton and Foster pored over two ordnance survey maps, planning out the route to the general area of Brize Norton. Saunders and Sully stood behind them as they crouched over the table. They all wore extra clothes brought with them: woollen pullovers and two pairs of socks.

'Transport,' Anton said suddenly. 'We've talked about it but taken no decision. I'll drive the Austin Metro and park it so we can get away afterwards, then get inside the furniture van.'

'It's a risk, I agree,' said Foster. 'And I'll take the Ford station wagon – again a risk. But not so risky as trying to hire different vehicles. We'd have to show our driving licences. The Vauxhall can stay here.'

'What is the escape route?' Anton demanded. He stood with his arms folded. 'You fobbed me off before but I want to know now before we talk any more about routes.'

Foster compressed his thin lips. 'Very well. We're close to doing the job. Afterwards we abandon the vans, then drive back to Exmoor. We leave the way you came in – by motorboat from the beach at Porlock Weir. A ship will be waiting for us outside the three-mile limit. An East German freighter. The East Germans are not nearly so keen on *glasnost* as Gorbachev.'

'Another point – I'd like to discuss it with you alone.'

'Really?' Foster's cold grey eyes narrowed. 'Let's go take a breath of fresh air.'

The air outside the back of the farmhouse was more than fresh: it was bitter. Foster thrust his hands inside his jacket pockets. Until he was twenty-five years old he had been used to the razor-edged wind sweeping across the Russian Steppes. Fifteen years in England had made him more susceptible to the cold.

'What is it?' he demanded.

'I have decided I can't shoot Seton-Charles. Killing that arms dealer in Lisbon was child's play. He was a stranger. Seton-Charles introduced new opportunities into my life. I don't like him – but he's become a part of my life.'

Foster stood more erect, held himself stiffly as he stared hard at Anton, reassessing him. Anton forced himself to gaze back but inwardly he felt nervous. Suddenly he felt the force of the *Spetsnaz* leader's personality.

'That calls for a change of plan,' Foster informed him, his tone grating. 'I have been watching Seton-Charles. I thought he was no more than a theorist. He is dedicated – more dedicated than you will ever be. He will drive one of the furniture vans, Sully the other. That leaves Saunders and myself to operate the launchers.'

'But I can do that,' Anton protested. 'What would I do?'

'You drive the escape vehicle. When we met the second time at the crossroads and drove back here a Post Office van overtook us. He passes along the road at the end of the track every day, Sully tells me. First time early in the morning.'

'That's right. Seton-Charles told me. What's the idea?'

'On the morning of Monday 7 December, we stop the driver, seize his vehicle. No one notices a Royal Mail van.'

'What do we do with the driver?' Anton asked.

'Kill him, dump the body in that grave Seton-Charles dug. I'll do the job.' Foster's lip curled. 'I don't think you're up to it.'

'But I can fire one of the launchers . . .'

'But you won't. You've trained us. The Stinger is a weapon it is easy to use. Now, you can stay out here while your balls freeze – assuming you have any. I'm going inside to look at those maps again. Saunders and I are going to reconnoitre the route to Brize Norton.'

He walked inside the farmhouse, closing the door quietly. Anton shivered in the wind. The look in Foster's eyes, his manner, had frightened him. But he had to admit Foster was well-organized: they had brought with them three pairs of the type of overalls worn by furniture removal men. They had spent time rubbing dirt into them, crumpling them to take away the appearance of new garments.

Anton went back inside to find Foster and Saunders bent over the maps. Foster was tracing a route with a pencil, careful not to touch the maps. He looked up as Anton returned.

'And we'll be taking your Austin Metro for the reconnaissance – no one will know about that vehicle.'

*　　*　　*

530

Friday, 4 December. It was late afternoon when the call came through to Park Crescent from Newman. Monica told Tweed he was on the line and pressed the recording button.

'I've found out Sam Partridge's driving licence was used to hire a car. Weeks ago – and the car is still on hire. Someone with an upper-crust voice phones Barton's – the car hire outfit – and an envelope of money to extend the hire is pushed in the letter box at night. Barton's is in Taunton. The car is a blue Austin Metro, registration number . . . God, I called at enough places before I found the right one.'

'Good work, Bob. We'll circulate that car's details immediately. Now, can you contact the others within the hour? I want everyone back here tonight. It's an emergency.'

'I'm calling from the Minehead phone box. Couldn't find an empty one in Taunton – so I drove back here like a bat. Butler and Nield happen to be at The Anchor now. We'll be on our way within half an hour. Don't go, Marler has news for you. Here he is . . .'

'I know how Anton slipped out of the country,' Marler drawled. 'Got back here to find Newman monopolizing this box. Anton is an expert pilot of small aircraft. Remember – Christina told Newman. Dunkeswell Airport, a small private airfield south-east of Tiverton. He flew out in a Cessna.'

'You're sure? There's a manifest to prove it?'

'Like hell there is. I identified myself to a pilot, showed him Anton's photo, told him he was a leading terrorist. He went as white as a sheet. I had to exert a little pressure – you don't want to hear about that. Briefly, Anton paid this pilot a large sum in cash . . .'

'To fly him back to Lisbon?'

'Not quite. Anton insisted on flying the Cessna himself. Took the pilot along as passenger. The pilot flew the

531

machine back to Dunkeswell. The controller of the airfield was away, doesn't know what happened.'

'Another question answered. You're coming back to London. A disaster is imminent.'

'If weapons are in order,' Marler responded, 'I'd like a rifle with a telescopic sight. See you . . .'

On her other phone Monica was finishing giving details of the Austin Metro to the Commissioner of Police. She put down the phone, her eyes gleaming with excitement.

'It's all happening at once. Like it so often does.'

'And these things come in threes,' said Paula.

The call from Norwich came at 7 p.m.

Waiting for Newman and his three companions to arrive, Tweed had a meal of ham sandwiches, followed by fruit, with Paula and Monica. Extra camp beds had been erected in the office next door where the two women slept overnight. They were all beginning to feel housebound when the phone rang.

Monica frowned as she answered the call, listened, asked several questions, then put her hand over the mouthpiece.

'It's Norwich police headquarters. A Constable Fox. Calling in reply to our circulating Seton-Charles' Volvo description and registration number. Sounds tentative. He's called the General & Cumbria Assurance cover number we used.'

Tweed picked up his phone, asked how he could help.

'Constable Fox speaking, sir. In response to your enquiry re the Volvo station wagon.' The youthful voice hesitated. 'My inspector wasn't sure I should call. I keep a careful record in my notebook of even trivial incidents. You never can tell when the information may be needed.'

'Very sensible,' Tweed encouraged him. 'Do go on.'

'Back in October late one night. I can give you the date

in a minute. Left my notebook in my tunic pocket. As I was saying, I was on duty and I saw this Volvo park near a corner. A man got out and walked round to a furniture removal firm selling off bankrupt stock. It was eleven at night so I was curious. Especially as he could have parked in front of the warehouse. Am I wasting your time, sir?'

'Please go on.'

'There were lights in the warehouse so I thought I'd better check. This chap goes inside after Latimer answers the door.'

'Latimer?'

'The proprietor of the firm selling off the vans, Camelford Removals. When I saw it was Latimer I thought it must be OK, so I pushed off. Then the next morning I was walking near the same area when I saw the Volvo driver pass me behind the wheel of one of the furniture vans. Trouble is his description does not tally with your Identikit. He wore horn-rims and an old cap.'

'But the registration of the Volvo is the same as the one we sent out?'

'Quite definitely. I checked that in my notebook.'

'Could you contact this Latimer, persuade him to wait until I arrive? He'll be paid for his trouble. And can you wait for me at the station until I arrive? It will be after ten.'

'I'm on night duty again. And behind enquiries counter tonight. Latimer practically lives at the warehouse. I can phone him.'

'My name is Tweed. I'm coming. Your recording of trivial events could end up in promotion. I'm leaving London now . . .'

As Tweed had guessed, Constable Fox was in his early twenties. A thin, pale-faced man, he had an earnest manner

533

and blushed when he was introduced to Paula. Tweed was careful to show him his Special Branch card. Fox took the card, studied the photograph inside the plastic guard, stared carefully at Tweed and handed it back. He was carrying the Identikit picture of Seton-Charles in an envelope.

Outside police headquarters he opened the rear door of the Cortina for Paula, closed it, then joined Tweed in the front.

'Latimer is waiting for us, sir. I didn't give him any idea who was coming.'

'Very sensible,' said Tweed again, then concentrated on Fox's directions. They reached the furniture warehouse in a few minutes and a short middle-aged man opened the door as they pulled up. 'That's Latimer,' Fox whispered.

Tweed introduced himself and Paula, showed his card, and with only a cursory glance Latimer invited them inside. They sat round a rough-surfaced wooden table and Latimer drank tea from a tin mug. Tweed took the envelope from Fox, extracted the Identikit picture and pushed it in front of him. 'Is that the man who bought a furniture van from you?'

'Two vans. No, it doesn't look like him. He wore horn-rimmed glasses, not rimless, and a driver's cap.'

Tweed looked at Paula, pushed the Identikit towards her. 'You are the artist. Mr Latimer, please describe as best you can the type of glasses, the kind of cap. Miss Grey will convert the picture under your guidance . . .'

He changed places so Paula sat next to Latimer. She produced a small clipboard and a felt-tip pen from her capacious shoulder bag and worked on the picture, altering it from Latimer's instructions. Then she pushed the picture in front of him.

'That's the chap. Magic it is, the way you did that. I've a good memory for faces. No doubt about it.'

'You said he bought two vans. He had someone with him?' Tweed enquired.

'No. Collected them both himself, one by one. Both the same day. Was gone about eight hours before he came back for the second job. Twin vans, they was. Only one left now.'

'He spoke with an educated accent?' Paula enquired.

'No. Workingman's lingo.' Latimer scratched his head. 'Mind you, it didn't sound it came natural to him.'

'He paid by cheque?' Tweed probed.

'No. Cash. Fifties. I held them up to check them. You can't be too careful these days. Funny sort of bloke. And that cap didn't fit him too well.'

'You said you had only one van left,' Tweed reminded him. 'Is that the same as the two you sold to this man?'

'Came from exactly the same stable. Want to see it?'

'Yes, please.' Tweed looked at Paula. 'Did you bring your camera?'

'Always carry it. Plus flashbulbs . . .'

They were there another half hour. Paula took pictures of the van from different angles. Tweed then persuaded Latimer to drive the furniture van into the street, deserted at that hour. Paula peered out from a top-floor window in the warehouse, looking down on the van with her camera. In the street below Tweed saw three flashbulbs go off. Then Paula waved her hand.

Latimer backed the van further away, stopped it at the entrance to another street, presenting her with a sideways angle. Three more flashbulbs went off. Tweed told Latimer he could drive the vehicle back into the warehouse.

'What's this all about?' he asked as he climbed down from the cab.

'A gang of very dangerous terrorists. Now, I want to pay you for your time.'

'On the house, Guv. If it's bleedin' terrorists I'm 'appy

535

to oblige. Shoot the bastards when you catch up with 'em.'

'Thank you for your cooperation. I'll bear your advice in mind. Now,' he said to Paula who had reappeared with Fox, 'we have to get moving. And Constable Fox, I'll be recommending your work to your inspector when this is all over . . .'

It was 2 a.m. when Tweed and Paula arrived back at Park Crescent. All the lights were on in the building behind closed blinds. They went straight down into the Engine Room in the basement where the staff were waiting. Paula handed one of the technicians her film, Tweed told him to develop and print immediately, then to produce two dozen copies.

His office was full of people when he opened the door. A large table had been moved in and round it sat Howard, Newman, Marler, Butler and Nield. The remnants of a meal were on the table and Monica was pouring more coffee. Marler sat smoking one of his king-size cigarettes.

'Any joy?' he enquired.

Tweed explained what they had learned as Paula took a spare seat at the table. Most of his listeners looked weary except for Howard and Marler who appeared fresh and alert. Howard raised the query.

'What on earth would they need two furniture vans for?'

'Remember the Stingers,' Marler told him. 'That reference to them we got from Morle rambling in high fever. Those vans are mobile rocket launcher platforms. Who notices a furniture van? It stops, they drop the tailboard and fire the missiles from the rear opening.'

'Oh my God!' Howard was appalled. 'Hadn't we better contact the PM?'

'And alert the SAS?' Newman suggested.

'We're on our own,' Tweed said quietly. 'SAS teams are guarding the Brize Norton perimeter. The PM calls us her private insurance policy. And while I remember, each one of you must carry one of these cards. Force Z is what she's termed us – Z for zero hour.' He dropped a pile of fresh identity cards he'd collected from the Engine Room on the table. 'Sort them out. Each carries an individual photograph. Including one for you, Howard – if you still insist on coming.'

'I do.'

'All security personnel at Brize Norton have been informed about Force Z. If you run into one of them you'd better speak quickly, then show the card.'

'How the hell do we go about this?' Howard demanded.

In reply, Tweed walked across to a wall map he had pinned up. It covered Oxfordshire, Wiltshire, Berkshire, Hampshire and London Airport. A tiny village called Liphook came just within the large circle he drew with a felt-tip pen.

'We have to think ourselves into the mind of Winterton.' He glanced at Howard. 'That is the codeword for the Englishman directing this operation.'

'Who is Robson, Barrymore or Kearns, you still think?' Paula asked.

'Yes. Based on the fact that Petros heard during World War Two that the Greek Key was controlled by an Englishman located in Cairo. The fact that the *Oporto* seaman who talked saw Anton being taken ashore near Porlock Weir by a man disguised with a Balaclava. The facts which came out of the tape recording Nield made of their conversation at The Luttrell Arms. The fact that the secret *Spetsnaz* base was situated on Exmoor. The fact that the murders of Andreas and Stephen Gavalas took place when those three men were nearby. The fact that Partridge and Mrs Larcombe were murdered on Exmoor. The fact that when Jill Kearns was run down in London those

537

three men were staying at a hotel not a quarter of a mile away.'

'I get the point,' Paula agreed. 'But now you've withdrawn everyone from Exmoor. Shouldn't someone be keeping an eye on those men now we're so close to the climax?'

'Yes. And you're elected.'

There were protests at the idea. From Howard. From Paula. 'I want to be in at the finish,' she objected. 'I believe I have contributed to the investigation . . .'

'Agreed,' said Tweed. 'You were the first one who spotted – and persisted – something was wrong with that bungalow estate. To mention only one thing. But from what Newman told me on the phone all three men are still on Exmoor . . .'

'It's too dangerous,' Newman snapped. 'She's already had her taste of gunpowder confronting Norton and Morle. And Winterton may have left the area by now.'

'He hasn't.' Tweed was emphatic. 'I haven't had time to tell you – but the Chief Inspector at Taunton has set up roadblocks on every route east out of the area. Barrymore, Robson and our friend, Kearns, are well-known. If one of them – Winterton – tries to leave Exmoor I'll know within minutes.'

'So that explains why we were stopped by the police near to Glastonbury,' Newman commented.

'And Paula will again be armed.' Tweed took a Browning automatic and spare mags from a desk drawer, placed them in front of her. 'Now, are you happier?' he asked her. 'Your job is to see which of the three makes a move.'

'I'll settle for that.'

'Good. Now maybe we can get on. I've tried to think myself inside Winterton's mind. He would know in advance there was a good chance Gorbachev would land in Britain

538

to meet the PM – he would have found that out from Moscow, I'm sure. The hardline faction is there. He knows Gorbachev is coming, but where will he land? London Airport? Possible, but unlikely. Lyneham Air Force Base in Wiltshire? A good bet. Brize Norton in Oxfordshire? Another good bet – because security would be easier to set up rather than at London Airport. Makes sense?'

'Yes,' said Marler. 'How does he go on from there?'

'He sets up an advance base . . .' Tweed went to the wall map and waved his hand round the circle he had drawn. '. . . somewhere inside this area. This gives swift access to whichever landing point is chosen. The furniture vans will be hidden there. But I don't think we'll see them from the air until Gorbachev's aircraft is approaching Brize Norton on this coming Monday. Today is already early Saturday . . .'

'Surely as soon as daylight comes,' Howard intervened, 'we can fly over the area in the choppers. We might just see something.'

'No go,' Monica informed him. 'I called Fairoaks Airfield where the machines are being equipped and repainted. They said Sunday morning was the earliest they could be serviceable.'

'So we wait until Sunday,' Tweed announced. 'In any case, most of you look as though you could do with a good rest. I want you on top form when we fly in those choppers. Anything else?'

'Bob,' Paula suggested, 'could I use your Mercedes? I'll drive down there as soon as this meeting breaks up. Then I can grab a few hours' sleep at The Luttrell Arms and start searching. God knows, I'm familiar with Exmoor by now.'

'As a very special favour.' Newman stifled a yawn. 'Yes.'

'I don't think we should all be airborne.' Butler spoke for the first time. 'Nield and I were talking about that – after Monica explained what she knew of your plan. We'd both like motorcycles, equipped with radio so we can contact you in the chopper.'

'I'll think about that.' Tweed checked his watch. 'Now, if there's nothing else . . .'

'Weapons,' said Marler. 'What's available? We'll need a variety as I see it.'

'Everything you want. The PM gave me *carte blanche*. An armoured car is delivering an arsenal and standing by at Fairoaks. You'll get your rifle with telescopic sights. Handguns. Grenades. Take your pick when the time comes.'

'One final point,' said Paula. 'You still think you know the identity of Winterton?'

'Yes. But no evidence. And I expect him to stay in the background during the operation. On Exmoor. Maybe you'll spot who he is.'

Paula said nothing. She opened her hand and a stick of French chalk rolled on the table.

52

Saturday, 5 December. It was after midnight when Foster took Anton into his bedroom at Cherry Farm, closed the door. Fatigue was registered on the faces of both men and tempers were getting short.

'Those Shi-ite prisoners are getting restless,' Foster opened with. 'What did you tell them they were here for?'

'That they were hostages for an exchange of two men kidnapped in Beirut. That negotiations were proceeding but they took time. They think we're British Government agents. You'd best leave them to me.'

'With pleasure. I have enough on my hands. Practising

weapon drill for one thing. It's Saturday and everyone is feeling the strain. Today we keep under cover. Get some rest. We have to be on top form tomorrow and Monday.'

'Tomorrow is Sunday. What happens then?'

'We do a trial run. Saunders and I found two perfect places to hide the furniture vans as close to Brize Norton as we need to be. Your turn to empty the Elsan buckets. Do it before you go to bed . . . .'

He stopped as he heard the phone ring downstairs. Automatically Anton turned towards the door. Foster pushed him out of the way. 'I'm taking all calls now.'

He hurried down the creaking wooden staircase into the hall where the phone was perched on a table. He lifted the receiver and gave the agreed false number. The familiar cold distant voice spoke.

'Is everything ready for the Monday conference? All delegates fully briefed?'

'Yes. We've checked the conference site. I'm double-checking it tomorrow, Sunday, to make sure nothing has been overlooked.'

'I should hope not at this stage. You'll give me a report when we meet? That's all.'

Foster put down the phone, knowing that would be the last call he would receive from Jupiter. The reference to 'when we meet' was a hint they would meet aboard the East German freighter, *Stralsund*, which would be waiting for them at the mouth of the Bristol Channel. Only then, after all these years, Foster thought, will I know who has been controlling us on Exmoor.

'Any crisis?' asked Anton, who stood at the foot of the stairs.

The question confirmed to Foster he had been right to stop Anton operating one of the two precious launchers. He was growing more nervous by the hour. Foster glanced at the phone.

'How is the bill for the calls made on this phone paid

for? You said earlier you had a phone booth you called at certain times.'

'All taken care of by Jupiter. A local solicitor in Taunton receives the bills, pays for them from a large sum Jupiter sent him in cash after instructing him over the phone.'

Foster was satisfied: it was tiny details like this which could upset all their plans. Jupiter never seemed to miss a trick. Anton was still standing by the staircase.

'What is it?' Foster snapped. 'Time we all got some sleep.'

'That Post Office van . . .'

'Don't shit yourself. I'll kill the driver. You can just bury him. And dump the Elsan closets we've been using for lavatories on top of the body. We leave this place neat and tidy. Don't forget to keep your gloves on – no fingerprints.'

'The Post Office van,' Anton began again. 'If you'd listened I was going to say it's a long drive to Porlock Weir. We'll need to top up the tank with petrol . . .'

'And we still have plenty of the stuff left in spare cans in the boots of the two cars we came here in. And also dump all our sleeping bags in that grave. Now, push off . . .'

He called after Anton as he was mounting the stairs. 'How much mineral water left?'

'A dozen litre bottles. I have kept a watch on supplies,' Anton rapped back.

'Good for you.' Foster's mind was checking other details. They would take the oil stoves and lamps which had provided heat and illumination with them. They could be thrown into ditches one by one on their way to Brize Norton. He went upstairs, nodded to Saunders who sat in a wicker armchair in the corridor where the Shi-ites were imprisoned. Saunders had a Luger lying in his lap. Any trouble in that direction and he'd crack their skulls with the Luger barrel, which was their ultimate fate anyway.

It was Foster's turn on the duty detail to watch the approach to the farm from the front window. Later in the night Seton-Charles and Sully would take over. Rest for everyone. Sunday would be a busy day – making the trial run to Brize Norton.

In Tweed's office at 3 a.m. everyone had left to get sleep except for Monica, Tweed and Butler. Newman had remarked that Butler had had more sleep than any of them, so he could make the report on Exmoor. With a cup of black coffee in front of him, Butler spoke tersely.

'You'd almost think they were setting out to look normal. Dr Robson still rides the moor at all hours to see patients. One old semi-invalid lady at Dulverton is always calling him in the middle of the night to her decrepit mansion. He goes . . .'

'How does she call him? Do you know?'

'By phone. She has an extension by her bedside upstairs. Barrymore drives into Minehead after dark to call someone from that public box we use. Pub gossip has it his housekeeper, Mrs Atyeo, is threatening to walk out on him. No one knows why – she's been there for years. Kearns still goes riding during the night. Nield was driving along that lane which leads to the Doone Valley after dark. He noticed Kearns' horse tethered beneath some trees at a lonely spot midway between Quarme Manor and Endpoint.'

'So Kearns could have been calling on Robson or Barrymore?'

'That's what Pete said. He didn't hang around – he'd have been seen. Barrymore and Robson still have lunch together at The Royal Oak each Wednesday. Dinner together every Saturday at The Luttrell Arms. Oh, and one night Marler was trying to follow Kearns on his horse riding up to Dunkery Beacon. Near the summit Marler heard a single loud explosion – a cracking sound like a grenade detonating. He couldn't find out what had been going on.'

'Unless Kearns was destroying something,' Tweed

543

suggested. 'I think you'd better get some shut-eye, Harry. There's a camp bed for you. Second door on the right when you leave here . . .'

For the next half hour Tweed was on the phone. He called Frankfurt, where Marler's deputy was standing in while his sector chief was away. He called Vienna and spoke with Masterson's deputy to check the Balkan sector. He called Berne and spoke with Guy Dalby about the situation in the Mediterranean. Finally, he called Erich Lindemann in Copenhagen, the sector chief for Scandinavia.

'All quiet,' he commented as he put down the phone. 'Except in Vienna where they report extensive military manoeuvres in the Ukraine. Under the command of General Lucharsky. Which they always carry out at this time of the year.'

He stretched his arms, got up and walked round to ease the stiffness out of his limbs. Monica marvelled at his stamina, his encyclopaedic memory which forgot nothing.

The staff running the European sectors were based in a building further along the Crescent – together with the complex technical communications, including satellite reception from the weird seeing eyes orbiting in space. Tweed suddenly returned to his swivel chair.

'I've overlooked something vital. Imagine the position of that *Spetsnaz* group. They've lost their Exmoor base, they're blown. After they accomplish their mission – as they hope – they need an *escape route*. Contact Roberts at Lloyd's. Ask about any Iron Curtain vessel sailing off our shores.'

'Sorry. Roberts is taking a weekend holiday. Don't know where. I could try to ask someone else . . .'

'Don't. Roberts knows the need for secrecy. Monday will have to do.' He took off his tie, loosened his collar. 'I'm going to get some sleep.'

Monica was already folding back the blankets from the

camp bed in the corner for him. She plumped up the pillow. He was taking off his shoes when he stopped.

'I wonder what happened to that cleaning woman Paula saw at the bungalow estate . . .'

'Bed,' said Monica firmly. Then she swore. The phone was ringing. She listened for a moment, then looked at Tweed. 'It's Paula. Calling from Somerset. I can tell her you're asleep . . .'

'I'll take it.' Tweed grasped the receiver, standing in his socks. 'Something wrong? You should be in bed.'

'So should you, but I took a chance. I'm talking from the public box in Minehead. I got lost in the dark. Don't worry – I called The Anchor and the night porter will let me in. Lucky I've stayed there before. The main thing is I wasn't stopped by any police checkpoint. That worried me.'

'That was because you were *entering* Somerset. The checkpoints are concealed. They're checking everyone *leaving*. I'm glad you called. In the morning contact Inspector Farthing in Minehead. He's reliable – the chap who turned up when Partridge's body was brought down from Exmoor into Winsford. Tell him frankly about the three men you're watching. You'll need help.'

'OK. Will do. Now, get some rest . . .'

'Bed,' Monica repeated. 'Stop thinking. Sunday is going to be hell.'

He put his head on the pillow, his mind churning. Then he fell fast asleep.

Sunday, 6 December. Foster was up early at Cherry Farm despite his night duty. They ate a hurried breakfast while he outlined the plan. 'I will be going over the route with Seton-Charles and Saunders. We'll use Anton's Austin Metro. That's the safest vehicle. I want several places where the furniture vans can be hidden *east* of Brize Norton

– the direction Gorbachev will be flying in from. The hiding-places have to be well away from the airfield perimeter. Security there is already ferocious.'

'What will I do?' Anton asked truculently.

'You will help Sully clean up this place. Ready for instant departure tomorrow. As soon as we've grabbed that Post Office van and dealt with the driver. Stack all the Elsan closets except one by the back door. What's that?'

He stood up, ran to the back of the house. Round the table they could now all hear what Foster's acute ears had caught. A steady chug-chug of a helicopter's motor. They froze as Foster peered out of the back door he had opened a few inches.

'Only a Traffic Control chopper,' he said when he returned. 'We get moving in the Metro now.'

Inside the Wessex helicopter – roomy enough to take ten men – Tweed peered out of the window from his seat. Newman sat in front of him by the door where the swivel-mounted machine-gun was positioned. A member of an airborne division sat beside him, his beret slanted at a slight angle. He was satisfied Newman could handle the weapon. They'd had a practice shoot while the machine hovered above Fairoaks Airport. The target, a pile of wooden crates, had been shattered by Newman's first burst. The airfield had a notice at the entrance. *Closed for Repairs*.

Marler was travelling with Nield in the second machine which was not visible. The radio op was keeping in close touch with its twin helicopter. Tweed was impressed with the swift conversion job. Both machines carried the legend *Traffic Control* in large letters. Only Butler was somewhere on the ground, riding one of the two waiting BMW motor-cycles. Nield had said, 'Thanks, but no thanks. I'm not riding one of those death-traps.' Butler had made a rude reply and wheeled his bike aboard the other Wessex.

The second machine had landed on a deserted main road, waited briefly while Butler disembarked with his BMW near Brize Norton, and had immediately taken off.

Tweed stared down at Cherry Farm from two hundred feet. Raising the glasses looped round his neck, he scanned the buildings carefully. No sign of life. He dropped the glasses and spoke into the microphone, part of the headset he had attached to himself.

'Nothing down there, Bob. That place has been derelict for a decade at least.'

They flew on as the airborne soldier, Harper, shifted to the seat on the starboard side and raised his own glasses. Very little traffic on the roads at this hour. The wind was strong and Tweed was thankful he'd had the foresight to take Dramamine as the chopper rocked like a boat in a storm.

At the last minute Howard had been forbidden to join them, much to his chagrin. The PM had phoned. 'Someone must be there to mind the shop . . .'

But every member of the search party had copies of the car outlines Howard had produced – together with Paula's photographs of the furniture van seen from different angles. Everyone – including Butler riding his motorcycle round the country lanes – was concentrating on detecting a furniture van. Except Tweed who kept studying the car silhouettes, with an Austin Metro added.

They had been cruising round the edge of the forbidden flying zone over Brize Norton for an hour without seeing anything. Marler came on the radio from his machine at regular intervals. 'Nothing to report.'

Then Tweed saw the Austin Metro.

Behind the wheel of the Metro Foster was driving along a winding country lane east of Brize Norton, close to the village of Ducklington. He saw the chopper appear over a ridge straight ahead about half a mile away. Beside him Saunders leaned forward. In the rear seat Seton-Charles peered out of the window.

'Yes, it's that bloody Traffic Control machine,' Foster snapped. 'Something funny about it – there's no traffic round here.'

He slowed down as a large copse of trees masked them from the helicopter. The copse was beyond a bend in the road. Glancing to his left, Foster saw a crumbling barn, the roof still intact, open at both ends. He looked in his wing mirror. Road deserted, behind as well as ahead. He jammed on the brakes in an emergency stop. Saunders was thrown forward; only his safety belt saved him diving through the windscreen.

'What the hell,' he rasped.

Foster made no reply. He swung the Metro through ninety degrees, drove off the road straight at the ancient farm gate. As the car hit it the gate fainted, collapsed inwards. Foster drove over it and continued across the field, pulling up inside the barn.

'Let the bloody thing find us in here.' He switched off the engine. 'At least we've found four possible places to site the vans tomorrow.'

'The chopper's coming,' warned Seton-Charles.

'You must have imagined it,' Newman commented. 'I didn't see a car.'

'Please keep flying along the country road below us,' Tweed instructed the pilot. He raised his glasses again as he replied to Newman. 'I tell you, I saw an Austin Metro. It matched the outline. And it was darkish – could have been blue.'

'We'll find it . . .'

'Which is exactly what we're trying to do.'

They were flying at eight hundred feet – the minimum altitude permitted because they were close to the forbidden flying zone round Brize Norton. The pilot followed the winding course of the empty road below. Tweed had the glasses screwed tightly against his eyes. He scanned every likely hiding-place.

A dense copse of evergreens came up in his lenses, a copse which straddled the road where it turned a bend. He ordered the pilot to circle it so he could study it from every angle. Where the devil had the Metro gone to? The pilot completed one circuit, commenced another.

Tweed saw an isolated barn standing in the fields a short distance from the road. From that height he looked down on the sagging roof. Nothing. Anywhere.

'Fly a mile or two, behind that ridge we came over. Then turn and come back,' he ordered.

Inside the Metro the chopper sounded like a giant bee circling. Saunders was sweating. He mopped his forehead. Foster sat patiently, gloved hand tapping the wheel. Saunders stiffened, lowered his window. A blast of icy air came inside.

'We might as well keep warm,' Foster told him.

'That chopper's going away. I can hear the engine sound receding. We've done the job. We might as well get back.'

'Not yet. It could be a trick. Go away and then come back – find us in the open.'

'You're assuming it's looking for us.'

'I always assume the worst. We wait . . .'

Five minutes later they heard the helicopter returning. Foster stared ahead in silence. It wasn't his way to say, 'I told you.' He waited half an hour until the machine had flown off a second time, then started the motor, backed on to the road, drove back the way they had come.

The Wessex cruised round the approaches to the

perimeter of Brize Norton air base for another three hours. They frequently crossed the Vale of White Horse, maintaining the permitted altitude of eight hundred feet. Tweed's eyes were aching from staring through his field glasses. As they returned to Fairoaks, coming in to land, Newman made his comment.

'Well, you were wrong about the Metro. And we've found damn-all. Marler reports the same result from his machine.'

Tweed had a map of the Brize Norton area spread out on his lap. He had marked with a cross the place where he was sure he had spotted the Metro. Using a ruler, he measured three miles in each direction from the cross, then drew a circle with a diameter of six miles. He handed the map over the seat to Newman.

'That's the area we concentrate on tomorrow.'

'Why? We never found your Metro.'

'For that very reason. I could have been wrong – the car could have belonged to anyone. But it did a vanishing trick. And we scoured the ground without finding it. I think it went into hiding. That's highly suspicious. I scanned every road after it disappeared. No sign of it.'

'If you say so.'

'And,' Tweed added as they were landing, 'I'm changing the dispositions of Force Z tomorrow. We need more men on the ground.'

They drove back to London to spend the night at Park Crescent, to see if any further information had come through. Butler left his motorcycle at Fairoaks. 'Didn't see a thing,' he reported as they drove back. 'But I have a few more roads to check – to the east of the air base.'

'Which I'd guess is where Winterton's men would place their missile launchers,' Tweed remarked. '*East*. Because that's the direction Gorbachev's plane will fly in from. And

I have to call the PM when I get back. She was insistent on that for some reason I can't fathom . . .'

They had just arrived back at Park Crescent when Paula called from Somerset. 'I'm speaking from Minehead again,' she opened. 'I've had quite a day. The police brought back a woman's body found in the Somerset Levels – that sinister area we crossed on our first trip here.'

'I remember. Sounds a bit grisly.'

'A peat digger found a hand sticking out of the place where he was digging. When Inspector Farthing told me I had an idea. I asked to visit the mortuary. It was the cleaning woman from the bungalow estate. I showed Farthing the photo I'd taken. She'd been shot once in the back of the neck.'

'They were cleaning up before they left. No macabre pun intended.'

'And Farthing has been very helpful. He's put two men in plain clothes to help me watch the commando trio. They're all still here. That's it.'

'Take care. I have an important call to make.'

The four men sitting in his office and Monica watched him as he called the PM on scrambler. He listened, said he understood and put down the phone. He looked around at Newman, Marler, Butler and Nield.

'She's just heard from Moscow Gorbachev will be flying here in *four* Ilyushin 62s.'

'Four?' Newman enquired. 'I know he's unusual but how can he do that?'

'It's a clever Soviet precaution – security. No one will know which of the four machines Gorbachev and his wife will be aboard. Maybe the PM gave him a hint of possible trouble. I don't know. Now, we've eaten, so everyone get some sleep. Tomorrow is the day.'

53

Monday, 7 December. 7 a.m. Sully lay in the road covered with blood near the entrance to Cherry Farm. It was real blood: Foster, against Anton's protests, had used a knife to cut his forearm lightly. He had then smeared blood all over Sully's face and neck. Inside the farmhouse Seton-Charles was using sticking plaster to cover the flesh wound.

Nearby Sully the Austin Metro had its bonnet pushed against a tree trunk, positioned at an angle across the road. The driver's door was wide open. George Hobart, driving his Post Office van, slowed, then stopped as he saw the body sprawled in the road. He jumped out. Only twenty-two years old, he wore his Post Office cap, unlike the more veteran postmen who went bareheaded.

'Nasty accident,' said Foster, appearing from behind a tree. 'It just happened. Could you take him to hospital? We've no transport.'

'Of course I'll help.' Hobart approached the 'body' and swallowed. 'He looks in a bad way.'

'Something for your help . . .'

Foster reached into his breast pocket, hauled out his wallet, dropped it on the road at Hobart's feet. He was slow retrieving it and Hobart bent forward to pick up the wallet. Foster pressed the muzzle of his Luger against the back of Hobart's neck, pulled the trigger. The old method of execution used in the motherland when he'd been young. Hobart slumped to the ground.

Saunders appeared with a large wheelbarrow. Foster picked up the dead youngster and his cap, askew, dropped off. When he'd dumped the body inside the wheelbarrow and Saunders was taking it towards the farmhouse Foster picked up the cap. Climbing into the cab of the large van, he drove it off the road along a track into the woods opposite the farm entrance.

Then he checked his watch. They'd all better give Anton a hand to fill in the grave. He got behind the wheel of the Metro, closed the door, backed it on to the road and drove it back to the shed. They'd be on their way in fifteen minutes.

Tweed wore a thick woollen pullover, a heavy sports jacket, a woollen scarf round his neck, and corduroy trousers tucked inside knee-length boots with rubber-grip soles.

The Wessex chopper was again flying at eight hundred feet and Tweed sat in the same seat, map in his lap, binoculars looped round his neck. In front of him Newman sat holding the handle of the swivel-mounted machine-gun by the closed door. On the starboard side the airborne soldier, beret slanted at exactly the same angle, sat peering out of the window through his field glasses.

There had been very little conversation since the machine took off from Fairoaks. There was an atmosphere of rising tension inside the helicopter. Then the pilot passed on the message to Tweed through his earphones.

'Marler and Butler have landed. They are on the ground.'

'Thank you,' said Tweed.

Marler would now be driving the Land Rover waiting for him at the appointed rendezvous, a crossroads in the middle of nowhere near Ducklington village. Butler would be riding the BMW motorcycle which had been transported to the crossroads by truck during the night. All arranged by Tweed over the phone in the early hours. Nield was at Fairoaks, running the radio control room set up inside an administrative office.

Tweed studied the area he had circled on the map the

previous day. He was gambling everything that the attack would be launched from somewhere in that area. It was logical. And Winterton had shown himself to be logical in everything he organized.

The second chopper would return to Fairoaks. At the last moment Security Control at Brize Norton had sanctioned one machine, not two. Tweed gathered they did not take Force Z too seriously. He raised his glasses as they crossed the Vale of White Horse. They were moving into the danger zone.

The furniture van driven by Foster, with Saunders alongside him, turned off the road into the worked-out chalk quarry. It had been carved out in a semi-circle. A chalk cliff enclosed it on the west, south and north sides. To the east it looked out across open country and the sky. Foster backed the vehicle until it was facing due east with the rear of the van a few feet away from the cliff. Then he stopped the engine.

They jumped out, went to the back, lowered the tailboard and went inside. Foster led the way, squeezing past the piles of old furniture. He climbed the steps to the platform, sat in the chair and pressed the switch. The panel in the roof slid back. He settled himself in the chair, picked up the Stinger launcher, inserted a missile.

He picked up the walkie-talkie Anton had specially amplified to increase its range. Holding it close to his mouth with his left hand, he spoke.

'Coastguard Number One in position.'

There was a crackle. Then he clearly heard Sully's voice.

'Coastguard Number Two in position . . .'

Marler drove the Land Rover along the narrow country lane at speed. He was moving through open country so he couldn't miss anything. He was following routes which

Butler had not covered the previous day but which were inside Tweed's circle. Half a mile behind him Butler followed on his motorcycle.

He reached a crossroads and drove straight on. Round a bend he was confronted with a tarring machine taking up the whole road. A workman came up to him.

'Didn't you see the bloody diversion sign, mate?'

'No, because there wasn't one.'

'Must be blind as a bat. You can't pass.'

Marler swore, turned the Land Rover and went back to the crossroads. He turned right just as Butler appeared over a rise. He drove on, more slowly: there were clumps of trees on either side, clumps which became woodland. He turned a corner and saw a sign in the distance. *Diversion*. The sign pointed right at a point where the road forked. Marler frowned, then drove his vehicle straight at the sign, sending it into the ditch as he took the left fork.

On the floor lay his rifle, telescopic sight attached. They had installed a small transceiver, complete with microphone. He had tested it earlier and it was tuned to the waveband Nield was operating on at Fairoaks. He turned the wheel as the winding road curved round another bend. Then he slowed to a stop.

At the base of the chalk cliff Foster saw four Ilyushin 62s flying one behind another coming in from the east. He grabbed the microphone. 'Coastguard One reporting. Four blackbirds in view. Repeat, *four* blackbirds. I'll arrest three and four. You take one and two. Over.'

'Four blackbirds sighted,' Sully confirmed. 'Will take one and two. Over and out . . .'

Marler had stopped where the rear of a large furniture van was parked half inside a wood. Beyond, the trees had been felled by storms, leaving the sky open. On the tailboard sat Seton-Charles, eating a sandwich. A rug covered his lap. He threw back the rug and pointed an Uzi machine-pistol point blank at Marler. Somewhere beyond the pile of furniture Marler detected signs of further movement. Behind him he heard the sound of an approaching motorcycle.

'Stay very still. Hands in sight,' rasped Seton-Charles, dressed in overalls. 'Wait like that till the biker has gone.'

Marler raised both hands in the air. 'Drop them!' screamed the professor. 'In your lap.' Marler let his hands drop. The BMW was very close. He hoped Butler had seen his gesture. The BMW slowed down, turned out to pass Marler's stationary Land Rover.

As he cruised slowly past Butler tossed the grenade he'd extracted from his saddlebag into Seton-Charles' lap. Marler ducked, fell crouched on the floor. There was an ear-splitting *crack!* Marler's windscreen shattered.

He looked up, grabbing his rifle. Seton-Charles was plastered all over the furniture. Blood and flesh strips everywhere. Marler saw movement high up at the front of the van. The mass of ancient furniture had saved Sully. His head peered over the top. Marler shot him through the forehead.

He leapt out and ran to the right side as Butler ran to the left. They met on opposite sides of the cab. Empty. Somewhere beyond the trees a vehicle's engine started up, moved off. Marler ran to the rear, pushed his way inside, leapt up the steps. Sully, flopped over the back of the chair, was dying but not dead. He looked into Marler's eyes as the Englishman bent over him. His eyes were glazed. The bullet had missed the brain and his expression showed a glimmer of hatred.

'Anton,' he whispered. 'Bastard ran for it. In Post Office van. Ex . . .' Then he died.

*　　*　　*

556

Foster aimed his launcher to take out Ilyushin Number Three, the plane carrying Gorbachev. He waited for the first two machines to disintegrate. Then decided he could wait no longer. In his concentration he failed to hear the sound of the chopper.

Aboard the Wessex Tweed was scanning the countryside below. He swept over a chalk quarry, then swung his glasses back again. The van came up clearly in his high-powered glasses. So clearly he could see the open panel in the roof, the man seated inside holding something rammed into his shoulder.

'The chalk quarry!' he shouted into his mike. 'It's there . . .'

The airborne soldier swung open his door. Icy air blasted into the chopper. Newman aimed his gunsight, pressed the trigger, swept the opening in the roof with bullets. Inside Foster was training the Stinger's sophisticated gunsight on the third Ilyushin. The chopper pilot – at Tweed's urgent request – had earlier ignored regulations, descending to one hundred feet, and now he hovered. In response to Newman's shouted request. He held the trigger back in the firing position. A stream of bullets laced Foster's back and chest. Blood splotches burst out of his overalls. He sagged in the chair. His last reflex action was to fire the launcher's missile.

But as he'd slumped the barrel had dropped, was now aimed inside the vehicle. The heat-seeking missile *whooshed* from the launcher, sped the few feet towards the vehicle's engine, which was still warm.

'Climb!' Newman shouted.

The pilot reacted instantly, began to ascend vertically. Tweed was staring at the quarry. As the missile detonated there was a blinding flash, a low rumble like thunder. The climbing chopper rocked from side to side as the

557

blast hit it, then steadied. Tweed and Newman gazed down.

The furniture van had disappeared, blown into a million fragments. A cloud of white chalk dust rose from the quarry. Tweed searched in vain for any debris which might be a relic of the van. His hands were sweating and he wiped them on his handkerchief as the airborne soldier hauled the door shut. The interior of the machine was like an ice box from the raw wind which had penetrated inside.

'Fairoaks reporting,' the pilot said, his tone calm. 'Marler has intercepted Vehicle One.'

'Thank God! Tell Fairoaks Vehicle Two also intercepted. Pass the message to Marler,' Tweed told him.

Overhead the four Ilyushin 62s were continuing their descent to Brize Norton. Tweed finished wiping his hands, put on a pair of gloves. He spoke again to the pilot.

'Please return to Fairoaks. We have unfinished business to attend to.'

54

Monday, 7 December. 'I will be driving down to interrogate Colonel Winterton,' Tweed told Monica, Newman, Butler and Nield in his Park Crescent office. 'Before he leaves the country.'

'On Exmoor?' Butler queried. 'You know who he is?'

'Yes. Monica has heard from Roberts at Lloyd's. The Shipping Index shows the only Iron Curtain vessel off our shores is an East German freighter, the *Stralsund*. At this moment it is unloading timber at Swansea. It sails for Rostock in the Baltic before the end of the day. That means it could heave to after dark at the mouth of the Bristol Channel. Ready to take aboard Winterton.'

'You really know who he is?' Monica asked. 'And he is one of the three ex-commandos?'

'Yes to both questions.' He turned to Butler. 'We left Fairoaks in a hurry. You talked with Marler. Why did he wait instead of coming with us?'

'Apparently just before Sully died he told Marler Anton had fled in a Post Office van. Heard the grenade I threw, then the shot Marler fired, I suppose. Ran for it. Headed for Exmoor, according to Marler. He's going after him. Trouble was the chopper we didn't use had a mechanical defect. And the pilot of our machine insisted on a thorough check-up before he'd fly Marler anywhere. That blast from the quarry really hit us.'

'Up to Marler, then. You heard me call Paula. She'll wait to meet us in the Mercedes by the call box in Minehead. Newman, you can come with me. Butler and Nield, you stay here. We're desperately understaffed if something else breaks.'

The phone rang. Monica said it was the call Tweed had booked to Arthur Beck at Federal Police headquarters in Berne. Tweed took the phone.

'Arthur. Check with Sarris, I suggest. But I think it's safe to send Christina back to Athens. Send me the bill.'

'No bill.' Beck chuckled. 'But now you owe me one. And don't think I won't call in the debt when it suits me. 'Bye.'

Newman stood up. 'I'm ready to leave when you are. As it is, we won't reach Exmoor before dark. Winterton could be aboard the *Stralsund* if we don't move. I'll drive the Cortina.'

'We need to be armed.' Tweed opened a drawer, took out from it a Smith & Wesson short-barrelled .38. Plus a shoulder holster. 'The armourer recommended this for me. You agree?'

'You never normally carry a gun. I'll give you some practice at a quiet spot on the way. Yes, that's OK. A hip holster would have been better. But it's short-barrelled, shouldn't snag if you have to snatch it out. I'm keeping the Magnum .45.'

'That blows a hole as big as a cave through your target.'

'Which means it does the job.'

Newman had become harder since he first knew him, Tweed reflected. His experience behind the lines in East Germany. Newman seemed to read his mind.

'Why is Winterton boarding an East German vessel?'

'Because the East Germans are not sympathetic to *glasnost*. And I doubt he'll report precisely what he was involved in. We'd better go.'

'Do give us a clue,' Monica begged. 'About the identity of this Winterton.'

'He must have needed to keep contact with the *Spetsnaz* group when it moved to a new base close to Brize Norton, wherever that was. So, he needed a phone he could use which wasn't his own – in case we'd put a phone tap on it. Which I wouldn't risk. A phone, Monica . . .'

It was early evening, just before dark, when the Wessex carrying Marler approached Dunkeswell Airfield south of Exmoor. On his lap Marler nursed his rifle with the telescopic sight as he peered out of the window. 'Can you land somewhere close to Dunkeswell, but not on the airfield?' he asked the pilot.

'Might manage it. You spoke in time. Not yet dark. How long a walk do you fancy?'

'No more than five minutes. It's an emergency.'

'When isn't it? There's Dunkeswell.'

Marler looked out of the window, frowned. Two main runways crossed each other almost at right angles. One had lights on at either side. Ready for a plane to take off?

The chopper was descending towards a deserted country road. Marler grabbed his rifle, headed for the door after one last word.

'Land me on that road. Then you'd better take off, head back for Fairoaks . . .'

He tore off his headset, splaying his feet as he made for the door. The machine was rocking gently. He felt it touch down, opened the door, dropped to the ground. Ducking to keep clear of the rotors, he ran towards the main airport building. He reached the open gate at the main entrance as an old Rover driven by a middle-aged man appeared from the opposite direction. The car stopped, half-turned to drive through the entrance. The driver lowered his window, leaned out.

'Who are you?' he enquired, staring at the rifle Marler held in his right hand.

'Don't go in there,' Marler warned. He used his left hand to extract his Special Branch card, shoved it in the driver's face. 'And who are you?'

'I'm the controller of this airfield. Those damned gates should be kept closed. I've told Abbott before . . .'

'Who is Abbott? Quick. There's probably an armed terrorist inside.'

'Maintenance mechanic. Odd-job man. Really runs the place . . .'

'Where do I find this Abbott?'

'Should be inside that office with the lights on . . .'

'Drive off. Up the road. Unless you want to risk getting shot.'

Marler darted inside the entrance, crouched low as he ran, rifle gripped in both hands. He avoided the office door, which was closed. Very carefully he raised his head, peered in through the window. Then he ran back to the door, turned the handle, threw it open. He had found Abbott.

The mechanic was sprawled forward over a desk. Blood

was congealing from a hole in the side of his skull. Marler felt the neck pulse. Nothing. In the distance he heard the sound of a light aircraft starting up. He ran outside, keeping close to the side of the building, peered round the corner.

A Cessna was taxiing slowly along a runway. As he watched, it turned. The engine revolutions increased in speed. He raised his rifle, peered through the sight. Inside the cockpit a face wearing a pilot's helmet jumped at him. Anton Gavalas. The machine began to move forward along a course parallel to the building. Moving target. Marler held the crosshairs fixed on the Greek's head. He took the first pressure on the trigger, waited until the small plane was opposite him, pulled the trigger rapidly three times.

He saw the perspex craze. The aircraft proceeded on down the runway. Marler thought he'd missed. The machine began leaving the ground. It was gaining height when the nose dipped and plunged swiftly down on to the runway. The tail was poised in mid-air. Then the fuel tanks exploded. Fire enveloped the Cessna, a fierce blaze which was smothered with a cloud of the blackest smoke. Silence suddenly descended on Dunkeswell.

'Lord, I'm glad to see you.'

Paula jumped out of the Mercedes parked by the call box in Minehead as the Cortina driven by Newman pulled up. It was dark as Tweed stepped out and she hugged him. 'They go to bed early here,' Tweed commented, glancing along the deserted street. He squeezed her, let her go as Newman approached.

'Look what Inspector Farthing gave me.' She took them both by the arm, guided them to the Mercedes and pointed at the dashboard. A mobile phone unit had been attached. Tweed got in behind the wheel, pressed the switch which operated the aerial and watched it slide down out of sight in the wing mirror.

'No, elevate that,' Paula protested as she got in beside him and dropped her shoulder bag in her lap. 'It helps contact. Farthing has a policeman with a walkie-talkie watching each of the houses. Barrymore, Robson and Kearns. They report back to a radio car and I hear their observations over that phone. In a kind of code I can understand. They're all at home. Farthing has been marvellous.'

'I have to get moving,' Tweed said as he elevated the aerial. 'Bob, take Paula with you. Drive to The Anchor and keep your eyes open.'

'For what?' Newman asked.

'In case he gets away from me. I'd say a four-wheel drive – heading past The Anchor and west over that pebble beach. And cover him with that Magnum. He's lethal. Out you get, Paula.'

'I'm coming with you.' She spoke calmly and produced from her bag the Browning. 'I can protect myself. I did with Norton and Morle.'

It was the controlled way she spoke which stopped Tweed arguing. He shrugged, glanced at the call box. 'Has Barrymore used that this evening?'

'Not so far.'

'Then we'd better move off.' He waved to Newman, drove through Minehead and climbed Porlock Hill. The Mercedes purred up the steep ascent. At the top he passed Culbone Inn, continued along the coast road, took the first turning to the left.

'It's the Doone Valley,' Paula said quietly as they descended the steep winding lane, crossed the ford at the bottom, turned right. Towards the Doone Valley.

'We located the two furniture vans they were using as mobile missile launcher platforms,' Tweed remarked. 'Just in time. One was blown to bits. Marler found a dead Middle Easterner in his. Maybe a Shi-ite. They were going to be left behind as the scapegoats. Monica read out a news story about two Arabs being airlifted from Gartree Prison. Shi-ites.' He stopped and backed the car through a gap in the hedge into a field, switched off the lights. 'No one will see you here. Keep the Browning in your lap until I get back.'

'You've stopped midway between Quarme Manor and Endpoint.'

'Lock all the doors,' Tweed said, then he was gone.

He pressed the bell. The man who opened the door was dressed in a leather windcheater unzipped down the front, cavalry twill trousers tucked into riding boots, a woollen scarf round his neck. The hall beyond was as cold as the biting wind moaning across the moor.

'May I have a word with you, Dr Robson?' Tweed asked.

'Come in, my dear fellow. Can't give you long. I'm expecting a call from a patient. They phone me at all hours. Goes with the territory as the Americans say.'

All this as Robson closed the door, led the way into the sitting room. The curtains were almost drawn with a gap where they should have met. Tweed sat down at a polished wooden table as Robson gestured and then sat opposite him. His host moved an old-fashioned doctor's bag on to the floor by his side without bothering to close it.

'I've come to arrest you for murder,' Tweed said. 'Quite a few murders. You've probably heard on the news your plan failed. Gorbachev is now in Washington.'

Robson's face crinkled into a smile. His pale blue eyes watched Tweed as he pulled at his straggly moustache.

'I don't follow any of this. You look sane enough.'

'One thing which pinpointed you was your conversation at The Luttrell Arms over dinner. Barrymore referred to the Greek Key. You pooh-poohed the idea. Out of character. When you all had houses like fortresses. Especially this place. I asked my man Nield, who was recording secretly, who was *facing* him. Barrymore was. So were you. The tape sounded like someone had spotted the tie pin microphone Nield kept fiddling with to get the right angle. And you made the mistake of asking Barrymore if Nield was wearing an earpiece when he met him on the moor. Only a professional would spot that. You spotted it. Hence your strange remark – considering you were all supposed to be scared stiff someone was coming from Greece to avenge the murder of Ionides . . .'

'Gavalas . . .' Robson stopped. His expression changed. The eyes were blank and cold.

'I never told you Ionides was a Gavalas,' Tweed remarked.

Robson sat very still. The only illumination was a plastic-shaded bulb which hung low above the table. Robson reached down into his bag. He pointed the Luger as Tweed reached inside his jacket.

'Don't bring your hand out with anything in it but your fingers. I still find your reasoning feeble.'

'Winterton – as we codenamed the killer – needed access to a safe phone. You wouldn't like using the one here. Your sister, May, could have overheard you. Where is she?'

'I sent her off for a holiday to my brother's place in Norfolk . . .'

'You needed access to a safe phone,' Tweed continued, 'to keep in touch with the *Spetsnaz* group you'd set up on that bungalow estate, to give orders when they'd moved to their new base. You kept visiting the bedridden old lady down in Dulverton at night. She has an extension upstairs by her bedside. That means the main phone is downstairs – the one you used.'

'Pure guesswork. You're crazy . . .'

'The first thing which drew my attention to *you* was when I heard you'd found homes for Barrymore and Kearns on Exmoor. Two reasons would be my guess, as you call it. Camouflage, in case suspicion centred on this area. Three suspects – and you made Barrymore look the most suspicious. I heard in Greece the voice changing the call sign in English over Florakis' transceiver. Very upper-crust. Very Barrymore. You mimicked him. The second reason for bringing your two commando friends here was a genuine fear of the vindictive Petros.'

'Why should I fear him?' Robson moved his left hand and then held it still: he had felt the need of his pipe, his prop.

'Because you murdered Andreas Gavalas on Siros. Another guess. You took a spare knife on the raid to do the job.'

'You'll be accusing me of stealing the diamonds next.'

'Of course you did. Which is why Andreas was killed. He was going to hand them to the right-wing EDES people. Probably you were told by your controller in Cairo to keep the diamonds for future use . . .'

'And I live in such luxury,' Robson sneered.

'Not for you. But it must have cost Colonel Winterton – again a pointer towards Barrymore – a packet to build that bungalow estate ready for the *Spetsnaz* group you'd been told to establish. Plus financing them in little businesses to give authentic backgrounds for them when they arrived from Russia. Plus buying the Stinger launchers and missiles from Gallagher, the Lisbon arms dealer. By then those diamonds were worth far more than the original hundred thousand pounds.'

'And what other murders am I supposed to have committed?' Robson enquired sarcastically.

'Stephen Ionides in the Antikhana Building for one. There was a lot of blood. My guess – again – is you wore an Army waterproof buttoned to the neck to save your uniform.'

'Oh, really? Entering the realms of fantasy now, are we? I suppose you worked out how I escaped when there wasn't even a convenient fire escape?'

'Poor Sam Partridge worked that out. There was a strong iron rail elevated above the wall on the roof. You took inside a briefcase – or something – a length of knotted rope. When you had cleaned up the blood from your hands in the bathroom you went back on the roof. You dropped the rope over the rail on the native quarter side – an equal length on either side. You shinned down the wall, holding both pieces of rope with the knots. Reaching the empty street, you simply hauled one length of rope down and coiled the lot in a loop. Very easy to lose that inside the available native quarter.'

'Any reason for all these acrobatics? And my killing Ionides?'

'Commandos *are* acrobatic. And Ionides – who was really Stephen Gavalas – had become suspicious of the killing of his brother, Andreas. You tied up a loose end.'

'Two murders so far. Any more?'

'It's not amusing. Mrs Larcombe's death was a fresh pointer – clue, if you like. She was a careful woman. Who would she let in to her house at night without fear? The local doctor. You said you needed to use her phone for an emergency?'

Robson ran his tongue briefly over his lips. In the dim light there was moisture on his brow, but the muzzle of the Luger aimed at Tweed's chest was steady.

'One thing which put me off the track,' Tweed went on. He had to keep Robson talking. 'Barrymore kept making clandestine phone calls from a public box in Minehead. What was wrong with using the phone at Quarme Manor?'

An unpleasant smile. 'A touch of romance, Tweed. Barrymore has fallen in love with a woman in London, hopes she will agree to marry him. But not sure of his chances. If it doesn't come off he'll still need Mrs Atyeo to run Quarme Manor. So he goes to extreme lengths to make sure she doesn't know anything. She might up and leave.'

'Extraordinary.' Tweed was momentarily non-plussed. 'A small domestic detail I never dreamed of.'

'Like your theories. All bits and pieces . . .'

'Which complete the jigsaw. And expose the face of Dr Robson. The killing of Sam Partridge on Exmoor was another pointer. The knife was driven in at exactly the right angle, the pathologist told me. A doctor would know how to do that. Much better than ex-commandos who had grown rusty with the passage of time. And Harry Masterson, who visited you, sent me a clue. *Endstation*. A clever clue. Pointing in two directions – here to your bungalow, Endpoint, and describing the atmosphere down at Porlock Weir, the end of the world. Harry was clever – I think he guessed it was you. He hoped to get confirmation by telling all three of you he was flying to Greece – to see which one of you turned up when he arrived.'

'I didn't.' Robson gripped the trigger of the Luger more firmly under the lampshade. 'I'm holding this gun on you because I appear to face a lunatic with a gun under his own arm.' He glanced at his watch.

'No. You sent a message to Doganis to do the job for you.' Tweed noted the glance at the time – which must be running out. But like a real professional, Robson was curious as to how he had tripped up. 'And,' Tweed went on, 'you fired at my Mercedes, aiming to miss – you couldn't afford the furore which would follow my murder at that stage. But you aimed – literally – to throw suspicion on Kearns. I'd just left his house.'

'You simply have no proof of these mad assertions.'

'Then take me up into the conning tower where you spend so much time at night. That curious structure which is supposed to be a watch-tower. Then I can satisfy myself there is no transceiver up there. Plus an aerial which automatically elevated while you were transmitting to Florakis in Greece, receiving messages from him. The retracting aerial on a Mercedes gave me that idea.'

The Luger wavered, then steadied. Robson's eyes became colder still. No smile. The bedside manner had vanished. His face became a frozen image, reminded Tweed of pictures of the statues on Easter Island.

'You're clever, I'll grant you that. But it was all in a great cause. Lenin's cause which I embraced when I was a young man. The cause Gorbachev is trying to pervert with his mad *glasnost*.'

'You killed Partridge because he was getting too close to the truth,' Tweed went on. 'You killed Mrs Larcombe because her window creaked and you heard it that first night you collected Anton Gavalas off the *Oporto*. You couldn't afford to risk her seeing you the second time when you brought the Stinger launchers ashore.'

'Dear me.' Robson's lips curled cruelly. 'You have worked it all out.'

'And you killed Jill Kearns in London. Why?'

'Simply to divert attention to London from Exmoor. She was a foolish sort of woman . . .'

Tweed saw movement by the gap in the curtains out of the corner of his eye. There was a tremendous smashing sound, glass breaking under a hammerblow. He thought he saw a rifle butt. Robson glanced at the window, swung the Luger round. Tweed reached up, grasped the plastic shade, pulled it down over the bulb. There was a brief flash, the room was plunged into darkness. Tweed threw himself sideways on to the floor as the Luger roared. Confusion. Bodies moving, feet running. A door shut. A vehicle's engine started up, moving at speed down the slope, skidded as though turning along the lane.

Tweed felt his way into the hall, along the wall, opened the front door. The sound of a second vehicle starting up, driving along the lane towards Quarme Manor. He ran down the slope, ran all the way back to where the Mercedes was parked, jumped in behind the wheel. Paula had released the locks as she saw him coming.

'Two vehicles driving at speed along the lane,' she said tersely. 'First a four-wheel-drive job, like we saw parked by the side of Robson's house. Then a car. Couldn't see the make.'

'We must hurry.' Tweed was driving through the gateway, turning along the lane, lights full on, driving away from the Doone Valley. In his wing mirror he saw a police patrol car coming up behind him. He passed Quarme Manor, reached the ford gushing with deep water, drove through it. Behind him the patrol car stopped half-way through the ford. He drove up the hill, kept going when he turned right on the coast road, heading back towards Minehead.

'The Toll Road!' Paula shouted.

He was almost past it, swung the wheel, began the descent and slowed as he nearly took them over the brink. They arrived in front of The Anchor and Newman was just climbing into the Cortina. He left it as Tweed approached, dived into the back.

'Two vehicles heading for the pebble beach,' he reported.

'I know. It was Robson . . .'

'Robson?' Paula gasped. 'I thought it was Kearns.'

They had driven along the track, began bouncing across the pebble-strewn beach. Something jumped up under the Mercedes, there was a loud clang. The car stopped. Tweed jumped out, began running over the pebbles, careful not to lose his footing. In the distance both vehicles had also been stopped by the terrain. He glimpsed two running figures, a hundred yards between them. Behind him Newman ran with Paula, ready to catch her arm if she slipped. Then the searchlight beam came on, aimed at the foot of the looming cliffs. The light shone from the edge of the sea.

570

It took Newman a moment to grasp the searchlight was mounted at the bow of a motorboat which had been driven up on to the edge of the beach. Tweed ran on past the sign reading, *Warning. Keep clear. Danger of cliff falls.* He passed an empty Renault, then the four-wheel drive vehicle.

Robson was caught in the searchlight beam as he kept to the lee of the cliffs. A shot rang out. The bullet sang past Newman's head. Paula was fumbling for her Browning when Newman saw inside the beached boat a bulky figure, clad like a seaman, aiming a gun. He swung up the Magnum, gripped in both hands, fired two shots. The seaman was hurled back, tried to recover his balance, toppled, fell over the stern of the boat. His body drifted with the outgoing tide.

Robson, hair awry, flung up a hand to shield his eyes against the glare of the light supposed to lead him to the boat. Tweed saw the tall figure a hundred yards from Robson reach inside a satchel slung from his shoulder. He hoisted his right arm like a cricket bowler, threw an object high up the cliff.

His hand delved again inside the satchel, came out and his arm hoisted a second time. There was a deafening crack on the cliff top above Robson. Tweed stopped, grabbed Paula by the forearm to halt her. She was gasping for breath as the second grenade detonated.

From high up on the cliff they heard a muttering rumble, prelude to a cataclysm. A vast slab of cliff broke free, slowly slid downwards, then faster. Robson looked up, opened his mouth. A cascade of rocks roared towards him. He turned to flee. The cascade engulfed him, like a rising tide, swallowing him up to the waist. In the searchlight beam he was a man half buried alive. He opened his mouth again and screamed and screamed, waving his arms. Then a Niagara of boulders stormed down, bounding against each other. One struck his head and seemed to telescope it deep into his body. Paula gulped.

A fresh fall of massive rocks poured down, tumbling over each other like some mad race. The head vanished. The boulders piled over the invisible corpse, building a grisly funeral pyre. Slowly the noise receded, the cliff settled, returned to stability as a great cloud of dust, a dense fog, spread over the whole ghastly scene.

Kearns, still carrying the satchel, walked back to Tweed, his wrists held out, as though waiting for handcuffs.

'He killed Jill,' he said in a choked voice. 'It had to be one of them. I've lived with the conviction Robson or Barrymore killed those Greeks during the war. But we were afraid of Petros, so we stuck together. I followed you the previous walk you took along here, saw the landslip. I kept several Mills hand grenades when I left the Army. I tested one up at Dunkery Beacon the other night – to make sure they were still working. I'm ready to go.'

'Two questions,' Tweed replied. He opened his hand, exposing the stick of French chalk he'd taken from his pocket. 'Paula picked that up in your house – you used it to simulate grief, to chalk your face. Why?'

Kearns walked a few slow paces until they were on their own. 'When Barrymore phoned, asked me to come and meet you at his house, I'd been sobbing like a child – because of Jill. So I had to clean up my face somehow. I used that stick of French chalk – the one Jill used when she occasionally did a bit of dressmaking.'

'I see.' Tweed changed the subject. 'During the raid on Siros, why land below a German lookout post?'

'Bravado. Barrymore's. And because of the lookout there were few German patrols at that point. Made tactical sense – we relied on a sea mist to cover us, which it did most of the way. Now, I'm ready to go.'

'Then go,' said Tweed. 'I don't recall ever seeing you here. Leave Exmoor. Petros is in prison. Go,' he repeated, 'build yourself a new life.'

'Thank you . . .'

'I said go!'

As Kearns walked slowly away Tweed stared towards Porlock Weir. No sign of activity: they were too far west for the thunder of the falling cliff to have been heard. 'Poor devil,' he commented. He glanced at the pile of rocks where the dust was settling. 'It will be months before they find out what is under that lot, if ever. Now, let's get rid of that boat.'

Standing on either side of the motorboat, Tweed and Newman exerted all their strength. They heaved it upside down, pushed it over the pebbles, which made a grinding noise. The craft slid over the edge, floated for some distance half-submerged, drifted out to sea.

Kearns had managed to start up his Renault while they were occupied and it disappeared into the distance. Between them they tackled the Land Rover which still had the key in the ignition. Within ten minutes Newman had driven it to the water's brink. One final shove propelled it off the pebbles and it sank from view.

'Back to The Anchor,' Tweed ordered. He put an arm round Paula who was shivering with reaction. 'You need a good stiff drink. It's all over. Détente is intact – for better or worse. And I'll report to the PM on the quiet about Lucharsky and his allies. It's up to her what she does after that.'

Epilogue

It is reported that Deputy Chief of General Staff, Andrei Lucharsky, General Budienny, and a third unnamed general, together with their aides, Colonels Rykovsky and Volkov, perished while flying in a helicopter over the Caspian Sea. The pilot saved himself by parachuting from the machine. No further details are available of this tragic accident.

Extract from December issue of PRAVDA.

'Odd that so much top brass should be committed to one chopper,' Tweed commented after reading the report. He handed it back to Monica. 'File it.'